LAURIE BRETON

FINAL EXIT

The danger is real—the passion undeniable

MIRA
$6.50 U.S.
$7.99 CAN.

ISBN 1-55166-660-X

"Remember those Sunday nights?" he said. "Remember what we used to do?"

While her heart thudded erratically, she said with forced lightness, "You mean the hot jungle sex in your friend's apartment while he worked the graveyard shift? What was his name?"

Humor flickered in Conor's eyes, but his mouth remained serious. "O'Halloran," he said. "Dennis O'Halloran. And I wasn't thinking so much about the hot jungle sex as I was about what came before it."

It came back to her then, in a riot of color and sound and scents. "The dance hall in Revere. I haven't thought of that place in years."

He lowered his head, pressed his cheek against hers and said softly, "We'd spend three or four hours every Sunday night slow dancing, getting all hot and horny and primed, waiting for O'Halloran to leave for work so we could go to his apartment and screw our brains out."

She squeezed her eyes shut at the intensity of the emotions that crushed her chest so tight, she could barely breathe. "It was the only place we could be alone."

"Caro," he said softly.

"What?" she whispered.

"We're alone right now."

LAURIE BRETON

FINAL EXIT

MIRA®

MIRA

ISBN 1-55166-660-X

FINAL EXIT

Visit us at www.mirabooks.com

Printed in U.S.A.

In memory of my mother
Carolyn Smith Gage Runnells
who shares a name with my heroine
and who taught me what it means
to be a strong woman.

ACKNOWLEDGMENTS

Thanks, as always, to Judy, for laughter, pithy advice, flying pigs and a good swift kick whenever I need it.

Thanks to the girls at RWU, especially for helping me kick my dialogue-tag addiction.

Thanks to my agent, Ethan Ellenberg, for waving his magic wand and helping me make my dreams come true.

And last, but most assuredly not least, thanks to Paul, Jay and Jen, for all the years of living with a crazy lady who habitually chains herself to the computer and snarls at anyone who dares to come near. I love you guys.

Prologue

Katie'd come a long way in the ancient Datsun that was being held together with duct tape and prayer. All the way from Finley, North Dakota. This was her first time away from home, and it had been scary, crossing the country by herself. But the freedom was exhilarating. Her mother had cried when she left. *So far away,* she'd said. *So very far away.* But distance was what Katie wanted. She wanted to put seventeen hundred miles between herself and her doting, overprotective parents. Wanted to spread her wings and fly, needed to prove to them, and to herself, that she could do it.

Just outside of Providence, her temperature gauge started climbing. Katie glanced at it in dismay, then resolutely hunched over the steering wheel. *Just one more hour,* she told herself as darkness swallowed the lights of Providence in her rearview mirror. One more hour and she'd be in Boston. There was no sense in checking into a motel for the night when she had a perfectly good dorm room waiting for her just an hour down the road. The old car wouldn't let her down this close to her destination. Not after they'd traveled so far together.

She'd been on the road for three days, but the last fifty miles, dark and spooky and lonely, were the longest of the entire trip. There wasn't much between Providence

and Boston except for trees, and her gaze kept darting to
the steadily climbing temperature gauge. When she finally
saw the city lights glimmering in the distance, Katie let
out a sigh of relief. She'd made it. She'd proven her parents
wrong. She'd traveled halfway across the country
alone, and nothing terrible had happened.

In downtown Boston, she flicked on her directional signal
and slowed for the Storrow Drive exit ramp. Halfway
down the ramp, her engine stalled, and the idiot lights on
her control panel flashed red and amber warnings. Katie
rolled the car to a stop and turned the ignition key. Nothing
happened. The ignition clicked a couple of times, but
the engine didn't even turn over.

Now what?

It was eleven o'clock on a Tuesday night, and she
didn't know a soul in Boston. But she was determined to
see the glass as half-full instead of half-empty. It could
have been worse. She could have broken down somewhere
on that desolate stretch of highway between Providence
and Boston. At least she'd reached civilization before
her car blew its cookies.

Above her head, downtown Boston's towering office
buildings glittered like so many shimmering stars, their
brilliance luring her like an exotic fairyland. She flicked
on her four-way flashers, got out of the car, and popped
the hood. At this time of night, even here on the expressway,
traffic was sparse. Taking out the flashlight her dad
always insisted she carry, Katie played its beam around
under the hood, not really sure what she was looking for.
She'd never understood anything mechanical. Katie Ann
Perry knew light and form and color, the lush green of
viridian, the rich bloody crimson of alizarin. She knew
how to manipulate them into something that pleased the
eye, something unique, something that touched people's

emotions. That was what had gotten her into the prestigious Commonwealth Art Academy, not any knowledge of what lay under the hood of her Datsun.

A car pulled up behind her, some kind of dark, late model sedan, and the driver dimmed the lights. Youngish, dressed in jeans and a black turtleneck pullover, he climbed out, his face shadowed as he crossed the pavement to where she stood. "Having car trouble?" he said.

Her dad had always warned her not to talk to strangers, but it was eleven o'clock at night and she was stranded. Besides, he seemed nice enough. "It died on me," she said, "and I can't seem to get it started again."

In the glow of the flashlight beam, he smiled. A friendly, clean-cut, all-American smile. "Let's have a look."

The stranger bent and fiddled with wires, checked the hoses and belts. "Why don't you get in," he suggested, "and we'll try it again?"

Katie scooted in behind the wheel and slid the key back into the ignition. "Okay," he shouted, his voice muffled by the hood. "Give it a shot."

She turned the key, but nothing happened. Not even the hollow clicking she'd heard earlier. "Again," he instructed.

Again, she turned the key. Again, nothing. He came around to her open window, wiping his hands on his jeans. "Doesn't look like it's going anywhere," he said. "Not tonight. Battery's dead."

This was not good news. Even though she'd be living in a dormitory, she needed to be frugal with her money, save it for expenses. He crouched beside the car until they were at eye level. "I can give you a lift if you're not going far."

Again, she remembered her father's warnings. How

many times had he told her never to get in a car with a stranger? "I don't know," she said.

He gave her that smile again, reassuring her that he understood her reluctance. "My folks always warned me about strangers, too. And they were right. It's not safe out there on the streets for a young girl like you." He paused suggestively, and in spite of her bravado, she shuddered at the picture his words painted in her mind. "I can't just go away and leave you here. If anything happened to you, I'd feel responsible."

Katie hesitated a moment longer, looked around at the deserted street, and gave in. "All right," she said, grabbing her purse and locking the Datsun carefully. Everything she owned was in it. Her clothes, her art supplies, all her Madonna and Jewel and Shania Twain CDs.

"We'll call a tow truck," he said as she settled into plush navy upholstery. "If we leave it here, the cops will tow it, and it'll cost you a fortune to get it back."

The intimacy of being alone in the car with him made her uncomfortable. Katie cleared her throat. Running a hand along the rich leather of the dash, she said, "You have a nice car."

"Thanks. I'm a clean freak. Wash and wax it twice a week, vacuum it every Saturday."

She smiled politely and looked out the window, away from him. "So," he said heartily, "where are you headed?"

"Commonwealth Art Academy." Gnawing on her lower lip, Katie turned to look at him, but in the darkness, his profile was shadowy and indistinct. "Do you know where it is?"

He glanced in his rearview mirror and signaled for a turn. "Sure," he said. "I've been by there a few times. So, you're an art student?"

It made her feel so adult, hearing herself described that way. "I will be, as soon as classes start up in September."

"I saw your North Dakota plates. Ever been to Boston before?"

"No," she said, a little embarrassed at having to admit to him just how much of a hick she was. "I've never been out of North Dakota before."

"I bet your folks are proud of you. Going to college, and everything."

"They didn't want me going so far from home," she confided. "Especially since I don't know anybody here. But I think it's great. I'm old enough to be on my own."

"I should think so. You must be…what? In your mid-twenties?"

Her mouth fell open. "Do I really look that old?"

"Sure. You've got a real sophisticated air about you. If anybody asked, I'd peg you for twenty-five, twenty-six."

"I'm eighteen," she said.

His eyes widened. "No way."

She giggled. "Yes. Really."

Flattered that he'd thought her older, she sat a little straighter in the seat and glanced out the window. They passed a brick building with its windows boarded up and graffiti spray-painted all over it, and uneasiness tickled her stomach. "Are you sure we're going the right way?" she said. "This doesn't look like a very good part of town."

"Don't worry. This is just a shortcut."

They passed a deserted warehouse encircled by a chain-link fence. Behind the fence, garbage spilled out of a rusting Dumpster. From the corner of her eye, she saw something small and furry dart out of the shadows. Katie shivered. "Maybe," she said tentatively, "you'd better let me out now."

"In this neighborhood?" He laughed. "If I put you out here, they'd be fishing you out of Boston Harbor by tomorrow morning."

Her hands tightened on her purse. All her money was in it and, in spite of his smile, something about him creeped her out. She hoped he wasn't going to rob her. Next time, she'd heed her dad's warning.

He wheeled the car around the corner of the warehouse and pulled to a stop by the waterfront. In the distance, beyond the chain-link fence and the tall weeds, she could see the lights of downtown Boston. "What are you doing?" she said.

Instead of answering, he reached past her, opened the glove compartment and took out a bloodred scarf.

She leaned against the door, away from him. "I think I'll get out now."

In the shadows, his smile had a diabolical cast. "I don't think so," he said.

She reached for the door handle, discovered there was none, and then he looped the scarf around her neck and pulled it tight. A surge of adrenaline shot through her veins. Propelled by terror, her hands sought her neck and she fought him, her nails digging into the soft material of his shirtsleeves as she struggled for air, her lungs screaming for oxygen and her vision gone a hazy red. But he was incredibly strong, strong as ten men, and her meager strength was nothing compared to his.

"Don't fight it, angel," he said, his breath coming in short, shallow gasps. "I've waited a long time for you."

She flung out a fist, connected with his temple. He cussed, dropped the scarf, and tightened his hands on her throat. Choking, gasping, she fought the blackness swirling around her, clung tenaciously to consciousness. She thought about her mother, a stalwart rancher's wife who'd sacrificed for years to send her only daughter to art school seventeen hundred miles from home. Thought about her father, who'd worked so hard to provide for his family. About her older brother, Kenny, her favorite person in the whole world. She thought about Misty, the roan mare, the first horse she'd ever ridden, and about her dog, Rory, that she'd had to leave behind.

Oh, Mama. I'm so sorry.

She opened her eyes and looked into the face of madness. Beyond his shoulder, in the distance, the lights of Boston flickered and twinkled, growing smaller and more blurred as oxygen deprivation began to take its toll. No longer in her body, Katie hovered, too weak to fight anymore, drifting on a soft, silver cloud, until the silver, too, turned to black.

And eighteen-year-old Katie Ann Perry, who had come to Boston to knock 'em dead, floated gentle into that good night.

1

This was absolutely her last case.

It would have been quicker to fly to Boston from Quantico, but Carolyn Monahan loved to drive, and the snazzy red Mitsubishi Eclipse ate up the miles like cotton candy. Besides, the hours behind the wheel gave her time to mull over the mess she'd made of her life. At the top of the list was her impending resignation from the Bureau, followed closely by the breakup with Richard.

Getting involved with her boss had been idiotic. She was old enough to know better than to fall for the sweet talk of a philandering worm like Richard Armitage. Yet she'd fallen into his trap anyway. She'd been mesmerized by a set of perfect white teeth and a pair of riveting blue eyes. She'd believed his lies about the wife he was going to leave as soon as the kids were old enough, had believed him until the moment she saw him walk into that Alexandria cocktail lounge with nineteen-year-old Brandy Warner on his arm.

At thirty-two, she was a cliché. Somebody to be talked about and pitied, a woman who, instead of finding someone of her own to love, had squandered her most intimate emotions on another woman's husband.

Richard had begged her not to leave the agency. He'd reminded her about how much she had accomplished in seven years, had pointed out that people in positions of authority, right up to and including the director, were saying very good things about Carolyn Monahan. Had warned her that leaving the Bureau now was a career move equivalent to slitting her own throat.

But not once had he asked her to reconsider ending their relationship.

So she was free, free to start a new life, just as soon as this case was settled. Carolyn rolled down the window and let the wind tangle in the blond hair that she wore long because Richard had told her it looked sexy that way. On the radio, the Stones were reminding her that they had no intention of being anybody's beast of burden. She cranked up the volume, punched the accelerator, and sang along with Mick and the boys as she shot up the home stretch of I-93 toward Boston at a steady eighty-two miles per hour.

The city skyline rose in the distance. She hadn't been home in four years, but Boston was still here, just as she'd left it, with all its hassles and headaches. Richard had hand-picked her for this assignment because she knew the city, and she'd accepted it because it meant a quick escape from Quantico, where she still had to look at his face every day. But going home was difficult. She hadn't been at the top of her mother's list of favored people before her sister died and, since Meg's death, their relationship had deteriorated into an uneasy state of armistice. When she'd finally left Boston, it had been with the intention of escaping her blue-collar roots once and for all. Yet here she was, back again, just like a damn homing pigeon.

She took the downtown Boston exit off the expressway. Traffic was a nightmare, courtesy of the multibillion-dollar Big Dig, which had rerouted traffic patterns causing endless snafus. The Mitsubishi crept from traffic light to traffic light, squeezing down narrow streets flanked by concrete guards and chain-link fencing. The detour took her in a maddening circle that ate up a good twenty minutes of time. It was nearly three-thirty when she finally pulled into a parking spot on the fifth floor of a garage near City Hall, where the task force had been given the use of an office suite for the duration of the investigation. She'd been driving since dawn, and she was a little stiff, but her mind was alert, ready to jump into the case and get right to work. Carolyn stretched her cramped muscles, smoothed her gray suit, and picked up her briefcase.

At City Hall, she used the first rest room she came to, then followed the directions she'd been given to task force headquarters, located on an upper floor in what was arguably Boston's ugliest building.

The fourth-floor office was a beehive of activity, phones ringing, computer keys clacking, every available inch of wall or desktop space taken up by files and papers and charts. Tossing her blond hair over her shoulder, Carolyn marched up to the receptionist and flashed her ID.

"Special Agent Monahan," she said. "I'm here to see Captain Shaughnessey. He's expecting me."

The young woman's eyes flickered. "Not any more, he isn't," she said in that flat Boston accent that Carolyn hadn't heard in four years, one that shot an unwelcome stab of nostalgia right through her. "He's in Mass General, in the CCU. Had a heart attack last night. Gave his wife one hell of a scare."

This was not an auspicious start. "I'm sorry to hear that," she said. "Who's in charge of the investigation?"

"That would be Lieutenant Rafferty."

Carolyn's heart skittered in her chest. It couldn't be. Boston was a big city. There must be two dozen Raffertys on the police force. It couldn't possibly be him. God wouldn't be that cruel to her. Not even after the screwup with Richard would God be that cruel to her.

She cleared her throat. "And what would the lieutenant's first name be?"

The receptionist eyed her knowingly. "Conor," she said, not quite successful at hiding a smirk. "You know him?"

Carolyn winced and closed her eyes. Luck of the draw. It was nothing more than luck of the draw. Damn Richard Armitage, and damn the entire Federal Bureau of Investigation for placing her in this position. "Yes," she said grimly. "I know him."

"Good. That means I don't have to introduce you. Down the hall, first office on the left."

She approached his door with trepidation, pausing at the threshold. He was on the phone, his back to her, and she couldn't see his face. But she knew it, knew every line of it intimately. Conor Rafferty, damn his Black Irish hide. Jet-black hair, the greenest eyes this side of Dublin, and a body that had driven her to distraction the summer she was twenty-two. She hadn't seen him in ten years, but she could still remember, in elaborate detail, the scent of him, the taste of him, the feel of his fingers on her flesh. When she'd left Boston for good, Conor Rafferty had been one of the things she'd been running away from.

Carolyn set down her briefcase and skirted his desk, moving toward the bulletin board, where he'd pinned photos of the victims. She studied each of them in turn, matching faces with the names she'd already memorized. Anna Magnusson. Becky Shields. Lindsay Helms. Katie Ann Perry. Four victims, four beautiful young women whose lives had come to a sudden, cruel and needless end. Each victim bore a striking resemblance to all the others. The UNSUB—unknown subject—had typecast his victims in minute detail. Each of them young, blond, blue-eyed and beautiful. Slight in stature, no more than five-four. Each one strangled and sexually assaulted, each found wearing only panties, a single earring, and a silk scarf tied jauntily about the neck.

She'd gotten into this line of work because of Meg, because her need to make sense of her sister's death burned in her with white-hot intensity. But she'd stayed because the faces of the victims were burned indelibly into her brain. She could recite the intimate details of each of their deaths, all the way back to her first. They were with her always, haunting her sleep and driving her on.

"He's a sick bastard," Rafferty said quietly from behind her.

She hadn't even heard him hang up the phone. Carolyn took a quick breath, wiped all expression from her face, and turned. In the ten years since she'd last seen him, his face had matured. Tiny laugh lines flanked those green eyes now, but the eyes themselves were still warm, still intimate, set beneath brows dark as a raven's wings. The rakish South Boston bad boy was gone, replaced by a man who, at thirty-four, was still the handsomest son of a bitch she'd ever seen.

"Congratulations," she said. "I hear you're a lieutenant now."

"It was Shaughnessey's idea," he said, "calling in the Feds for help. Personally, I don't believe in all this psychological hocus-pocus you people practice. But I was outranked. Overruled. So you're free to practice your witchcraft. Just stay out of my way while you're doing it, because I'll be busy finding my killer."

Her smile was strained. "You don't seem to be having much luck so far."

Stonily, he said, "I have orders to cooperate fully with

you, Monahan, so I'd suggest you make up your mind where you want to start.''

So there would be no small talk, no tender reminiscences. That was fine with her. She was here to do a job, not to take a sentimental stroll down memory lane. Briskly, she said, "First, I'd like you to call your key people together so I can talk to them. It won't take long. Then—" She glanced at the slender gold watch on her wrist. "Then," she continued, "I'd like to see the dump sites."

Within minutes, he'd gathered a group of about a dozen people in a small conference room. Carolyn took her place behind the podium, her stomach roiling with the familiar queasiness that always struck her when she had to speak in public. As she looked out over the assemblage, mistrust and hostility shimmered in the air like heat waves off hot asphalt. It was something she'd long since grown accustomed to. Local law enforcement professionals tended to resent what they considered the intrusion of the Feds into their ongoing investigations, in spite of the fact that she was there by invitation. It didn't help that she was female, blond, and a perfect size six. As a woman who operated daily on traditional male turf, she'd struggled to overcome those handicaps right from her first day at the academy by building, brick by brick, a hard-earned reputation for having brass balls and the best shooting record in her graduating class.

Don't let them see how scared you are. It was something she'd learned in her first public speaking class in college. If your audience saw that you were terrified, they'd eat you alive. But nobody was going to chew up Carolyn Monahan and spit her out, not if she had anything to say about it. Willing the nausea to go away, she grasped the edges of the podium, pressed her knees together to stop them from quaking, and adjusted her posture to the ruler straightness that the sisters had demanded back in parochial school.

"Good afternoon," she said. "I'm Special Agent Carolyn Monahan from the Federal Bureau of Investigation. But I prefer to be called just plain Monahan."

The expressions on the faces scattered around the room ranged from bored to hostile to condescending. "I'm going to make this short and sweet," she said. "I'm not here to hotdog, I'm not here to steal your glory, I'm not here to run the show. Lieutenant Rafferty—" she nodded curtly in his direction "—is in charge of this investigation, and I'm here strictly as a consultant. It's not my job to catch your killer. My job is to create a profile of the personality type most likely to commit this particular crime, so that you can narrow your list of suspects and find your perpetrator. Identifying those suspects is up to you. That's the bottom line, ladies and gentlemen. We're all here for the same reason—to see that what happened to these four young women doesn't happen again. Now that we have our roles straight, let's work together to do our jobs and get this animal off the streets. Thank you."

She was briefly introduced to key members of Rafferty's staff, and she quickly filed names, faces and first impressions in her mental data bank. Lorna Abrams had watchful eyes and chestnut-brown hair that was clipped short in a style as no-nonsense as her handshake. Greg Lassiter was long and lean, skin the color of café au lait offset by a snowy-white shirt and a mauve necktie. Ted Rizzoli's smile didn't reach his eyes. Recognizing the attractive young detective as one of the more hostile faces in her audience, Carolyn made a mental note to watch her back around him.

Rafferty whisked her down a honeycomb of artificially

lighted corridors that reminded her a little of the underground labyrinth at Quantico. Now that she'd stepped out from behind the podium, the wrenching fear had stopped gnawing at her stomach, and her pulse rate had returned to normal.

"That was a stellar performance," Rafferty said dryly. "Hard as nails, aren't you, Just Plain Monahan?"

"I believe in laying my cards right out on the table," she said. "I've learned from hard experience that it's best to clarify expectations at the beginning of any operation. That way, misunderstandings don't rise up later to bite me on the ass."

"Good," he said. "Then I'll lay my cards out, too. Shaughnessey called you in because we're running out of time. The first two homicides were approximately three months apart. We kept it under wraps as long as we could, because we didn't want to throw the whole city into a panic. But after the second one, our killer started to escalate. The last two victims were only two weeks apart and, now that word's leaked out that these homicides are related, you can imagine the pressure that's coming at us from every direction. So far, we haven't made any headway. So we turned to you as a last resort."

"Very flattering," she said. "Tell me about the dump sites."

"So far," Rafferty said, "our boy has dumped all his victims in highly public locations. We found the first one in City Hall Plaza. The mayor was particularly impressed by that one."

"I can imagine. It must have done wonders for his image."

"The second victim was left at Copp's Hill Burying Ground. The third was in Charlestown, at the base of Bunker Hill monument. The most recent was found in the fountain behind the Park Street T station on the Common.''

They reached the end of the corridor and paused before a bank of elevators. ''This guy has a warped sense of humor,'' he continued, pressing the button for the elevator. ''Wants to give the tourists a little extra bang for their buck.''

''Witnesses?''

His mouth thinned, giving that handsome face a grim expression. ''You tell me,'' he said.

With a sigh of resignation, she said, ''Nobody saw anything.''

''Give the lady a gold star.''

The elevator dinged, and the doors slid open. They stepped inside, and Rafferty pushed the button for the lobby. The elevator began to move. ''These are all locations,'' she mused, ''that get a tremendous amount of tourist traffic. But he seems to be hitting them at random.''

''Exactly. No discernible pattern, no rhyme or reason. Our boy dumps his victims wherever and whenever it strikes his fancy.''

''I assume you're running round-the-clock surveillance?''

''Yes. Just in case our friend gets a sudden urge to come back and gloat over his handiwork.''

They started at the fountain on Boston Common, near the corner of Park and Tremont. Pigeons fluttered and squirrels scampered from tree to tree as college students and tourists milled about, enjoying the late-summer afternoon, most of them blissfully unaware of the body that had been found here just thirty-six hours ago.

The fountain itself was roped off with yellow crime

scene tape and guarded by a uniformed officer with a military haircut and the merest suggestion of peach fuzz on his upper lip. When he recognized Rafferty, he swallowed hard, his Adam's apple bobbing up and down, and stood rigidly at attention. "Lieutenant," he said.

Rafferty glanced at his name tag. "Officer Stern," he said. "This is Special Agent Monahan of the FBI. She's consulting on the case."

A faint flush colored the young man's cheeks. "Ma'am."

"Officer. Why don't you give me a rundown of the crime scene?"

"Yes, ma'am." He turned toward the fountain, raised the crime scene tape, and the three of them stepped under it. "The victim was found here," he said, indicating the fountain's basin, now dry and empty. "She was clothed only in panties and a silk scarf. The body was floating faceup, the legs spread wide and dangling over the edge. The fountain was operating at the time."

She'd seen the crime scene photos, but hearing his description of the scene helped her to visualize it. "He poses his victims," she said, more to herself than to anyone else. "Stages his scene for maximum effect."

"Our perp wants to make a statement," Rafferty said.

Carolyn straightened and made a sweeping study of her surroundings. In order to understand her killer, she needed to see what he'd seen, hear what he'd heard, smell what he'd smelled. She needed to think like him, to feel like him, to step inside his skin. That was how she worked. If she wanted to catch a monster, she first had to become one.

Atop Beacon Hill, the late-afternoon sun glinted off the gold dome of the Massachusetts State House. A stone's throw away in either direction, Park Street Church and

Saint Paul's Cathedral stood sentinel, both of them vigilant, neither of them powerful enough to have prevented the evil that had taken place directly in front of their watchful eyes.

She took a deep breath, drawing in the mingled odors of carbon monoxide, roasted peanuts, and the rich, earthy smell of summer. Closing her eyes, she heard the rumble of traffic, the babble of conversation in several different languages. She recognized Japanese, Hindustani, French. A smattering of Lebanese. She'd lived upstairs over a Lebanese couple in Alexandria for a couple of years. Their fights had been vocal and legendary, and had lent several colorful new phrases to her vocabulary.

"He picked her up on the exit ramp," she mused. "Took her someplace dark, someplace private, where he could perform his little ritual. When he was done with her, he looked for a place to dump her. Or maybe he already had it picked out. Boston Common, middle of the night, very little traffic, no witnesses. It would have been after 1:00 a.m., after the T shut down for the night. He knew it would start back up at five-thirty in the morning, and there'd be people passing by. Commuters. That's part of the high he gets from this—he can manipulate people's emotions, their actions. It makes him feel powerful, in control. And that's what it's really all about. Control."

Carolyn opened her eyes and blinked at the sudden brightness. "The victim was found by whom?" she said.

"A college student," Stern said, "out for his morning jog."

"Lovely way to start the day. I'll want to read through the transcript of his interview. Postmortem results?"

"No report yet," Rafferty said, "but all indications are that this one is identical to the others. Death by strangulation, victim transported and disposed of postmortem. Possibly up to three hours after death.''

She wondered what he'd done with them during that three-hour time period. The answer to that question could be the key to identifying the perpetrator. ''Thank you, Officer,'' she said to Stern. ''You've been very helpful.''

It took them two hours to examine all four crime scenes, two hours of fighting hellish traffic during the busiest time of day, two hours of assimilating data, of absorbing sensations, of sifting and sorting them until she'd created a road map of sorts in her mind. When they'd finished, she wasn't sure she knew anything more than she'd known before she started. But if she wanted to understand Mr. X, she needed to explore every possible angle, no matter how obscure it might seem. Some seemingly insignificant detail could break the case.

City Hall hadn't grown any prettier in the past two hours, and now she had a killer headache. Carolyn flopped down on a hard wooden chair in Rafferty's office and rubbed her temples.

He walked around the desk and opened a drawer. ''Here,'' he said, and tossed her a bottle of aspirin.

She caught them in mid-air. ''A regular Boy Scout, aren't you?'' she said dryly. ''Always prepared.''

''It comes with the territory.''

''Being prepared?'' She uncapped the bottle and sprinkled four tablets into the palm of her hand.

''Headaches. There's a drinking fountain just down the hall to your right.''

When she returned, he was reading through the autopsy report that had just arrived on his desk. Carolyn sat in the wooden chair and began working her way through the crime scene photos. Now that she'd visited the dump sites, it was easier to fit together the scattered pieces. Each victim had been posed in a disturbingly suggestive position, robbed of any dignity that might have been left to her after death. The brightly colored scarf tied around the neck of each victim was a clear message. Flashy, almost festive in appearance, the scarf was a flagrant display of the lack of respect Mr. X felt for his victims. The perp was acting as though this were some kind of a game. For him, it probably was.

Across from her, Rafferty set down the autopsy report with a sigh. "No surprises here," he said.

"Were you expecting any?"

"Not really."

Carolyn glanced back at the stack of photos in her hand, then dropped it on the corner of Rafferty's desk. Rubbing the back of her neck, she said, "No strong suspects?"

"No. Just the usual nutcases, the ones who confess to every murder that comes down. This kind of thing brings them out of the woodwork in droves."

She studied Rafferty's face. The faintly drawn lines around his eyes were more pronounced than they'd been earlier, and she wondered when he'd last gotten a decent night's sleep. If he was half the cop she suspected he was, the answer to that question was "not lately." Not since he'd been involved in this case, anyway.

Out of the blue, he said, "Are you staying with your folks while you're here?"

It was the first personal comment he'd made, and it irritated her that he'd violated their unspoken agreement to restrict their conversation to business, irritated her further that he'd even asked such a question. He knew as well as she did that her mother blamed her for Meg's death, knew that she and Roberta Monahan couldn't spend more than two hours in the same room without fighting.

Against her will, her attention was drawn to his hands,

those damn elegant hands that she could have identified blindfolded, just by the memory of the way they'd felt against her skin. She steered her attention back to where it belonged, on her work. "I'm staying at the Boylston House," she said briskly, lifting the stack of photos. "It's easier."

"I'm sure it is."

Her head snapped up and she studied him suspiciously, but he'd returned to the autopsy report, and there was no way to judge the intent behind his words. Unsettled, she unlocked her briefcase and took out her case file. "I suppose you realize," she said, "that he's thumbing his nose at us. He wants us to know that he's ever so much more clever than we are. He's gloating right now."

Rafferty leaned back in his chair. "He's also a meticulous son of a bitch. The victims were sexually assaulted, probably after death. He took the time to remove their clothes. And then, when he was done, he took the time to put their panties back on. Neatly."

"It's so comforting to know that he's tidy."

"As if that weren't enough—" he picked up a folded newspaper from the desk blotter and tossed it across the desk to her "—take a gander at what else we have to deal with."

She caught it with both hands, unfolded it to the front page. It was this morning's *Tribune,* a local tabloid whose proclivity for lurid headlines and yellow journalism made the *Herald* look tame. The headline splashed across the top of the page read *Police Say Serial Killer at Large in Hub.*

"Oy," Carolyn said, and began reading.

Boston—A source close to the investigation into the murders of four local women, speaking on condition of anonymity, has confirmed that Boston police are treating the homicides as a related series of crimes. "We are convinced," the source said today, "that these crimes were committed by the same perpetrator." According to our source, police have kept this information from the public in order to prevent mass hysteria.

Carolyn checked the byline. "Who's this Tommy Malone?"

Rafferty leaned back in his chair again. "He's been working the crime beat for a couple of years now, and we've been butting heads since day one. He's a one-man literary swat team. And I'm using the term 'literary' very loosely."

Carolyn tapped a fingernail against the newspaper. "Maybe," she said, "we could use him to our advantage. Do you think if you fed him something he'd spit it back out in the morning paper?"

"I think Malone would write up his own grandmother for shoplifting."

"This could be a good thing. You want to catch Mr. X? Challenge him. The guy has an ego as big as all outdoors. Toss it right back in his face. Via Malone, and the *Trib*."

Rafferty raised a cup of coffee from his desk, studied its contents, and set it back down with a grimace of distaste. For a full ten seconds, he considered her words. "Give me a for instance," he said.

"Plant a story. Just a brief one. Bury it somewhere in the Metro section. 'Lieutenant Rafferty, who's in charge of the case, announces that the Department is working on a number of leads and may be close to an arrest.' Keep it low-key. Let him know we think he's nothing more than a flea, a pesky little nuisance, easily extinguished." She studied one of the crime scene photos. "Make him mad. Make him so mad that he starts getting careless. When he starts to unravel—" she dropped the photo, leaned back in her chair, and met Rafferty's eyes "—that's when he'll make that one fatal error. And then we nail him."

For a long moment Rafferty sat silently, his eyes intent on hers. Then he nodded and reached for the phone. Pushed a button. "Isabel," he said brusquely, "get me Tommy Malone over at the *Tribune*."

2

Rafferty had received a frosty reception when he'd shown up forty-five minutes late at the door to Gwen's brick town house in the tony suburb of Newton. Now he had compounded his sin by becoming hopelessly lost somewhere on the North Shore. They passed under a streetlamp, and Gwen squinted as she attempted to read the name posted on a corner street sign.

"I'm sure you took a wrong turn back at that last intersection," she said.

Rafferty wasn't sure of any such thing, but since he already had two strikes against him, he clenched his jaw and kept his mouth shut. Gwen Sloane might look soft and feminine in the sleek black cocktail dress, with her dark hair combed into a fashionable upsweep, but anybody who'd seen her in action in the courtroom could testify that the outer package was merely a soft-focus camouflage for what was hidden inside: a razor-sharp intellect and a steamroller ambition that didn't care how many casualties it left flattened behind.

"Wait!" she said. "This is it. Hopewell Road. Take a right here."

Hopewell Road ran for half a mile along a trim white fence before the home of District Attorney Cameron Matthias hove into view. It was a massive white Colonial, set back from the road behind acres of green pasture. To one side was a long, low barn, painted the same immaculate white as the house and the fence. At the sound of their approach, a half-dozen Arabian horses stopped grazing and raised their heads. Cameron Matthias was a gentleman farmer. Translated, that meant he paid an overseer a great deal of money to manage and care for his horses, thus safeguarding his expensive Italian loafers from having to step in anything offensive.

The entrance to the private drive was flanked by a matching pair of wrought-iron black jockeys holding carriage lanterns. Apparently, political correctness hadn't yet reached this particular rural enclave. Rafferty followed the paved drive to the house and pulled up beneath the porte cochere, where a uniformed valet hired for the occasion waited to park his car.

Parked in a neat row beside the barn were a Mercedes, a couple of Volvos, a Lexus or two, an entire fleet of BMWs, and one shiny new Range Rover. Rafferty handed over the keys to his car, and the young man took them with the same deference he would have shown had the lieutenant been driving a luxury sedan instead of a dented six-year-old Ford Taurus. The kid was good, but that didn't do anything to quash the feeling, deep in Rafferty's gut, that he was out of his element here.

This wasn't his turf, and these weren't his people. He suffered through these little soirees because they were important to Gwen, and because Gwen was the first woman he'd ever dated for six months straight. She was the ideal companion: beautiful, intelligent, sexy, and as gun-shy as he was. He knew she occasionally saw other men; she knew he occasionally saw other women. The relationship worked because they enjoyed each other's company, and because they were both up-front about their disdain for commitment.

"I know you don't care for this kind of thing," she said as he rang the bell and they waited at the impressive front entrance, "but I promise we'll stay for just one hour, and then we can leave." As the door swung inward, she added, "We can have a quiet dinner later at my place."

She was making an effort at compromising. Rafferty supposed the least he could do was try to make a similar effort.

He knew the ritual by heart. First, they'd greet the host and hostess, then make a quick sweep around the room as a couple. After that, they'd split up so Gwen could circulate and do her politicking. Generally it wasn't a problem. He'd grab a bottle of Sam Adams and nurse it, wandering aimlessly until she decided she'd done enough ass-kissing for one night.

But tonight he was restless, antsy, all revved up with no place to go, and the last place he wanted to be was here, listening to these people yammer endlessly about the latest mayoral campaign or the exclusive private school where they sent their kids. He wanted to be out on the street, tracking down the worthless scumbag who was strangling young women. Instead, he was stuck here in Danvers, making nice with the D.A., his loyal staff, and half the judges in the Commonwealth of Massachusetts.

Cameron Matthias was big-boned and hearty. Somewhere in his sixties, the Suffolk County District Attorney had a full head of thick, white hair, incisive blue eyes that missed nothing, and a handshake like a grizzly bear. In his heyday, he'd been a brilliant strategist and a thundering orator. Nowadays it was his underlings, Gwen among them, who did most of the dirty work, while he sat behind an oak desk, polishing his image and maintaining his political connections. The buzz on the street was that Matthias was a shoo-in for the next governor of Massachusetts, and he was expected to officially announce his candidacy within the next couple of months.

"Gwen!" he boomed. "Glad you could make it." He kissed her cheek, then shot Rafferty a wink. "This little girl," he said, pulling her hard against his side, "is the best damn attorney in the Commonwealth."

Rafferty could practically see the steam coming out of Gwen's ears. Matthias was probably the only man on the planet who could call her a little girl and get away with it. Had he been anybody else, she would have slapped a sexual harassment suit on him faster than you could say Jack Sprat. But Matthias was her boss, and Gwen intended to leave her current position when she was good and ready, accompanied by a glowing recommendation from her former employer.

Smiling stiffly, Gwen managed to escape, and as she smoothed wrinkles out of black silk, Matthias crushed Rafferty's hand in his huge paw. "Lieutenant," he said. Leaning closer, he lowered his voice and added somberly, "Any progress on the stranglings?"

Matching the D.A.'s solemn expression, Rafferty said, "We're following every possible lead. We have the FBI working with us now. We *will* catch him."

"I wasn't aware that the FBI had been called in," Gwen said petulantly.

"It was Shaughnessey's idea."

The D.A.'s eyebrows drew together into a shaggy knot. Gravely, he said, "Any word on Shaughnessey's condition?"

"I talked to his wife this afternoon. Seems the captain's already complaining about the hospital food."

Matthias threw back his head and brayed like a donkey. "The old goat's too ornery to die," he said. "Shaughnessey and I went to school together, you know. Saint

Dom's in Chelsea. Back when we were both still full of piss and vinegar.''

Rafferty tightened his hold on Gwen's arm. She took the hint, beamed brightly at Eloise Matthias, and they began circulating, greeting people, shaking hands and exchanging pleasantries. Gwen hovered on the fringes of this world—a world she so badly wanted to be a part of. He had to give her credit: she was a pro at the schmoozing. But to him all the nicey-nice was at best tedious, at worst asinine.

It took them nearly a half hour to make their rounds, and when Gwen ditched him in favor of discussing urgent business with Senator Hynes, Rafferty took his Sam Adams with him and stepped through the French doors onto the backyard patio. The summer night was sticky, with just the hint of a breeze rustling the leaves of the giant ash tree that overhung the house. Somewhere in that vast backyard, a cricket chirped. He sat in an Adirondack chair that smelled of fresh paint. Setting his bottle of beer on the chair arm, he stretched out his legs, leaned his head back, and closed his eyes.

And drifted.

A sunny day. A warm beach, soft grasses nodding in the summer breeze. A man and a woman, walking barefoot on the sand. Hot, needle-sharp pricks of sand against his bare feet. Smell of salt air. The woman turned to him in slow motion, like the leisurely pan of a movie camera. Silky blond hair, blue eyes, and a smile that encompassed the whole world.

Caro.

The longing hit him hard in the midsection. He reached out for her, but his arms weren't long enough, and he clawed at empty space. She backed away from him and then, in the way of dreams, the sunny summer day evap-

orated, and the evil was upon him, its hot breath scorching the back of his neck. He couldn't see it, couldn't identify it, but it permeated his pores, choking him, strangling him. He called out her name, tried to warn her, but she refused to listen. Hands pressed flat against her ears, she continued backing away, heedless of his words of warning. He tried to run, tried to save her, but his legs were paralyzed, his feet buried deep in heavy, wet sand. Helpless, his insides roiling like the sea that had turned dark and ominous, he stood before the evil thing that reared up behind him, and waited for it to swallow her alive.

"Conor?"

He awoke abruptly, disoriented, his heart hammering, his body damp with sweat. He blinked his eyes, and Gwen's face swam into view. It was not a happy face. "I've spent the last ten minutes looking for you," she said, crossing slender arms and tapping an impatient toe. "And all this time you've been out here on the patio, sound asleep!"

A trickle of sweat ran down his spine. He sat up, still muddled, and ran a hand through his hair. Jesus Christ. He couldn't remember the last time he'd had a dream like this. This damn case had him wound so tight he was about to detonate. And Caro. Why had he dreamed about Carolyn Monahan? Whatever they'd had between them, it was over. Had been over for years. She was nothing more to him than a professional colleague. If a Federal agent could actually be considered a colleague. Professional nuisance would be more accurate.

He mumbled some kind of apology and lurched to his feet, and Gwen looked at him queerly. "You're working too many hours," she said. Then added, more charitably, "What you need is a back rub and a good night's sleep."

They made their goodbyes, and he retrieved the Taurus

from the valet and set the air-conditioning to frigid. "Thank the merciful gods," Gwen said, settling back into the seat and kicking off her stiletto heels. "I wasn't sure how much more I could take of standing on these twentieth-century torture devices." She pushed the button for the window, letting in the heavy night air, and he cranked the air-conditioning up a notch. "Can you believe that old bag of wind?" she said in mild outrage. "Cozying up to me like that, and then calling me a *little girl*. I hope he doesn't think he'll get my vote. Having that Neanderthal in the governor's office will set back women's rights by half a century."

"Maybe," he said. "Maybe not. Knowing you're one step behind him, snapping at his heels and waiting to take over his job, might just keep him in line."

Gwen grimaced and rubbed a bruised toe. "He knows how badly I want to prosecute this strangler case. But he's already told me he wants to take this one himself. The old goat figures he can ride a guilty verdict all the way to the State House. Which reminds me. Why didn't you tell me you were working with the FBI?"

"It never came up. And Agent Monahan just got here today."

"Hmph. Some aging bureaucrat in an ill-fitting Brooks Brothers suit, I suppose."

"Actually," he said, "I think it was a Donna Karan."

Her head swiveled around, and she appraised him carefully. "The gentleman is a lady?"

He pictured Carolyn Monahan's shapely legs beneath the hem of that expensive gray suit. "Definitely," he said.

"I see." She was uncommonly silent as they pulled onto the highway. The dashboard rattled as he brought the car up to speed. "You really should get a new car," she said.

Rafferty grunted noncommittally. He liked the car. He liked the goddamn rattling dashboard. The Taurus had gotten him through six brutal New England winters, starting without fail on every subzero morning, while his neighbor, the one who owned the expensive new Japanese hatchback, had been dependent on AAA for a boost at least half a dozen times.

"Conor?"

A muscle twitched in his cheek. For some reason, Gwen was pushing all his buttons tonight. But it wasn't her fault that he was in a foul mood. Slowing for a red light, he shoved aside his resentment and determined to remain civil. "What?" he said.

"I think we should get married."

He nearly rear-ended the Mazda Miata that was stopped ahead of him at the light. It was one of the things he'd always admired about Gwen. Whatever she wanted to say, she just came right out with it, no matter who she skewered in the process. "Why?" he said. "I thought we agreed that we weren't ready for something permanent."

"Christ, Con, I'm thirty-five years old. My biological clock is ticking. I want a baby before I'm too old to have one. Just think what a great team we'd make. The cop and the prosecutor. You catch the bad guys, I put them away. There's plenty of room for both of us in my condo, and it's just a short commute into the city."

"You've really given this some thought."

"We'd be good together, Conor. We want the same things out of life. We get along well, and we're compatible sexually. We've been together long enough to know what we want. Marriage is the next logical step."

He tried to imagine spending the rest of his life with Gwen, sleeping beside her every night, waking up beside her every morning. Having children with her. Growing

old together. And wondered why he didn't find the idea
more appealing. "You've really thrown me for a loop,"
he said.

"You don't have to give me an answer tonight. Think
about it. You'll see that I'm right."

He pulled into the parking lot behind her town house
and left the engine running. Gwen bent to collect her
shoes, then popped her head back up. "You are coming
in, aren't you?" she said.

"Not tonight. I'm beat."

"But it's been two weeks!"

He wondered if she kept track of how often they made
love on that electronic date book of hers. How long it
took each time, and what positions they used. Which
words were spoken in the heat of passion. A database for
future reference. "It's been a long day," he said. "I'm
taking a hot shower and then I'm hitting the sack."

She pouted. On another woman, it might have looked
sexy. On Gwen, it looked infantile. "I do own a shower,"
she pointed out sulkily. "And a bed."

"I'll call you in a few days."

"Oh, God, I've frightened you, haven't I? That wasn't
my intention. Not at all."

"I'm tired tonight. This damn case is getting to me. It
has nothing to do with you."

She opened the car door. "Fine," she said tersely. "I'll
be in court tomorrow on the Heffernan case. I'm not sure
when I'll be available after that. You'll just have to take
a chance on catching me. Or you can leave a message on
my voice mail."

She shut the door with a little more force than was
necessary, and he watched her stride barefoot up the brick
walkway, her shoes tucked beneath one arm. She took a
key from her purse and unlocked the security door. With-

out looking back, she entered the building and let the door close behind her.

When she was out of sight, he exhaled the breath he'd been holding. Every one of her arguments made sense. The two of them had been more or less monogamous for the past six months. He already spent a good deal of time at Gwen's town house. Living together wouldn't be that big an adjustment. So why was he so reluctant to commit to marriage?

It might have something to do with the resentment he was feeling at the prospect of being used as a sperm donor. Whenever he'd thought about marriage, he'd expected that kids would be part of the picture. But Gwen made it sound so clinical and impersonal. She wanted a baby, and had decided that he should be the father. Period. She hadn't once asked if he was ready for parenthood. What Gwen wanted, Gwen got. And right now, Gwen wanted him. Or, more precisely, his DNA.

But that wasn't enough to account for his hesitation. It was something else that held him back. For all her logical, well-thought-out arguments, there'd been one crucial element missing, one that Gwen probably hadn't even considered. Or if she had, she'd dismissed it as antiquated and trivial.

Not once during her sales pitch had she uttered the word *love*.

The night was steamy and thick as molasses as Caro stretched out in the bathtub in her hotel room on the fifth floor of the Boylston House, rolling a cold bottle of Molson over her heated skin while Stevie Ray's hot guitar licks washed over her and worked the kinks out of her neck and shoulders. It was a funny thing about the blues, the way they worked on your body. They could heat you up like a blast furnace, or they could turn you limp and loose and allow you to forget.

That was one of the things she and Richard had never seen eye to eye on, what he'd called her *working-class penchant* for hot blues and cold brew. He'd been much more civilized, preferring Mozart and a good Montrachet. "You can take the girl out of South Boston," he'd said more than once, "but you can't take South Boston out of the girl." He'd said it because he knew it hurt her, because it was the most effective put-down he could use to keep her in her place.

Her place. She took a hefty swig of Molson and gazed balefully at one pink knee, peeking from the bubbles, as she pondered just where her place really was. Not at Quantico, not anymore, not with her co-workers whispering furtively around the water cooler about her aborted affair with Richard. Not in Boston, where she couldn't seem to reconcile the Carolyn she'd created, the one who wore designer suits and attended the symphony twice a month, with the Carolyn who'd eaten corned beef and boiled cabbage every Saturday night of her life, growing up on the third floor of a triple-decker on K Street in Southie.

As Stevie Ray's guitar wept and wailed and wove its magic, her thoughts turned, inevitably, to Conor Rafferty. She closed her eyes, sank deeper into the suds, and let her head loll back against the tub. At twenty-two, fresh from U Mass with a degree in psychology, she'd fallen in love with a blinding intensity that had nearly been her undoing. But she didn't want to be a cop's wife like her mother, tied to a blue-collar existence and terrified each time her husband stepped out the door that this would be the time he didn't come back. Then Meg had died, and everything had gone to pieces, including her relationship with Conor

Rafferty. When Carolyn walked away from him, she had never looked back.

Ten years had passed since then, ten years that should have erased his inexplicable hold over her. Ten years when her body should have forgotten that the very sight of him possessed the power to suck every molecule of oxygen from her lungs. *Hellfire and damnation.* If she'd known he would be involved in this case, she would have turned it down. Let one of the other agents take it. Sully, or maybe Michaelson. She would have stayed in Quantico and found a way to avoid Richard.

But she hadn't stayed in Quantico. She'd taken on the case. Now she needed to figure out a way to survive it without losing her mind.

Work. That was always the best solution. She could always lose herself in work. It was the force that drove her. Every time she avenged the death of an innocent young girl, it was really Meg's death she was avenging. Every time she helped to put away some monster who preyed on defenseless women, she was really putting away the monster who'd killed her sister. She was smart enough to recognize it. Just not smart enough to figure out a way to keep from taking her work home with her at night.

She drained the Molson, set the bottle on the floor. Reaching for a towel, she rose from the water with a minimum of splashing. She dried off with the thick hotel towel, wrapped it around her head, and slipped into a Japanese silk robe that had been a Christmas gift from Richard.

The table by the window was cluttered with the tools of her trade: cell phone, briefcase, laptop, file folders, pages of her scribblings dotted here and there with sticky notes. Her beeper sat atop the rubble, beside a thick pile of glossy crime scene photos.

She'd read the autopsy report while Rafferty was on the phone with the reporter, but she skimmed it again, just to be sure she hadn't missed anything the first time. *Eighteen-year-old female Caucasian…five foot three, 118 pounds…fractured hyoid bone, petechial hemorrhages, consistent with manual strangulation. Evidence of postmortem sexual assault.* Just like the other three girls. Carolyn's mind registered the details while filtering out the horror. She'd learned a long time ago that it was her only chance for maintaining sanity. It was only at the end of the day, after the job was done, that the horror came back to haunt her. But tonight, she didn't have time to dwell on it. Tonight, there was work to do. Briskly, she flipped open her laptop, turned it on, and pulled up her word processing program.

When the telephone rang, she was so engrossed in her own thoughts that it rang a second time before it registered. Rereading the last sentence she'd written, she fumbled for the receiver.

"Monahan," she said distractedly.

"Welcome home, Carolyn."

The words were spoken in a harsh whisper. She hit the command to save and watched her file disappear into cyberspace. "Who is this?"

"I've been waiting for you," he whispered. "Hoping."

She had no patience for game playing. "That's flattering," she said, "but you still haven't told me who you are."

"I know all about you. And I know all about Meg. I know what happened to Meg."

Her heart took a sudden leap. Hearing her sister's name

coming from the lips of a stranger seemed somehow vile and invasive. "What is it that you know?" she demanded.

He chuckled. "I'll talk to you again soon. Have a nice night, Carolyn."

And he was gone. She stared dumbly at the telephone receiver, then broke the connection and dialed the front desk. "This is Special Agent Monahan in Room 513," she said when the desk clerk answered. "Did you just put a call through to my room?"

"Sorry, Agent Monahan. There haven't been any calls for you all evening."

"Somebody must have put it through. I didn't imagine the conversation I just had."

"It didn't go through our switchboard," the clerk said. "Your caller must have dialed direct."

"Direct," she said. "They can do that? Bypass the switchboard completely?"

"Yes, ma'am."

"But how would somebody get my number?"

It was a stupid question. She knew it was a stupid question the moment it left her mouth. She was a Federal agent. She of all people should know that anybody could find out anything if they knew the right place to look. "Never mind," she said. "Thanks anyway."

It was going to eat at her all night. He could have been anybody. Somebody with a grudge against her. Somebody with a grudge against the FBI in general. Meg's death was a matter of public record. There was no evidence to indicate that the caller had known anything he couldn't have read in a ten-year-old copy of the *Boston Globe*. But it was creepy. A little too personal. A little too unsettling.

For a fleeting instant, she thought about calling Rafferty, then wondered where on earth that thought had come from. Conor Rafferty was a homicide cop, not a private hand-holding service. And she was a Federal agent, not some trembling innocent in need of rescuing. Whatever problems she encountered, she would handle them herself. It was the way she'd always done it. It was the way she'd continue to do it.

But it was still going to eat at her all night.

3

Rafferty backstepped, swung the racquet, and made contact with the ball. It slammed against the wall with a dull whump, bounced back, and he sprinted to catch it. Clancy beat him to it, caught the ball, and smashed it with brute force. It struck the wall and returned on a high arc. Rafferty leaped high, swung and missed. The ball hit the wall in back of him and bounced, and as Clancy ran after it, Rafferty bent forward, hands on knees, chest heaving. "Goddamn it," he said.

Clancy returned with the ball, eyes twinkling in a gaunt Irish face that was just this side of handsome. "A little out of shape, are we, Rafferty? Desk job getting to you?"

"Up yours, Donovan. At least I don't have a candy-ass job like yours."

Clancy studied the ball, bounced it in the air a couple of times, tossed it and smacked it smartly with his racquet. "Seems to me," he said, "that we're in the same business."

The ball bounced back. Breathing hard, Rafferty hit it into the wall. "Yeah?" he said. "How do you figure that?"

"We're both in the business of—" Clancy leaped, grunting as he made contact with the ball "—rehabilitating sinners. You offer 'em incarceration. I offer 'em salvation."

The ball shot back into his corner of the court, and
Rafferty backstepped to catch it, but it was too high, and
it slammed into the wall behind him. "Game," Clancy
said cheerfully. "That's five bucks you owe me."

Rafferty pulled off his sweatband and swiped his arm
across his forehead. "Does the Church condone your
gambling?" he said irritably.

Clancy bounced the ball into the air and caught it
smartly in his hand. "If Granny O'Herlihy has the
Church's blessing to play bingo every Saturday night, I
can certainly sucker a few bucks out of you twice a week.
And all my winnings go directly into the Donovan House
fund. A few more matches with you, Rafferty, and our
funding woes will be history."

"I don't remember you being this competitive when
we were kids," he grumbled.

"I don't remember you being a sore loser when we
were kids." Clancy picked up a snowy white towel and
dried his face, then slung it over his shoulder. "So," he
said, "how's Gwen?"

Rafferty retrieved his own towel and mopped his sop-
ping-wet hair. "She wants to get married."

Clancy turned to look at him. "Say what?"

"You heard me. She wants a baby. Her biological clock
is ticking."

"And your stand on this issue is…?"

He gave Clancy a cool stare, and his friend nodded
slowly. "That's about what I thought."

They left the racquetball court, threaded their way
through the maze of corridors toward the locker room.
"Caro's in town," Rafferty said with elaborate casualness. "She's consulting on the strangler case."

"Ah. That explains the lousy game."

Against his will, he pictured Carolyn Monahan, heard

in his mind that sultry, smoky voice, part Marlene Dietrich, part Kathleen Turner, that never failed to turn him inside out. "That was ten years ago," he said. "Ancient history."

Clancy shrugged agreeably. "Whatever you say."

They showered and dressed, stuffing their sweaty clothes into gym bags. Rafferty pulled out his wallet, extracted a five-dollar bill, and held it out to Clancy. "Here," he said. "You earned it."

Clancy was sitting on the dented wooden bench, tying the laces to his shoes. He adjusted the cuff of his pant leg and straightened. Took the bill and tucked it into his pocket. "The parishioners of Saint Bart's thank you."

After all these years, it still surprised him, seeing Clancy wearing that clerical collar. He'd been such a hellion as a boy, in and out of trouble all the time, giving his mother constant grief. Truancy. Smoking. Shoplifting. Stealing the principal's car right out of the high school parking lot and dumping it in Fort Point Channel.

That little stunt had led to a suspension, but Clancy had told him afterward that it was worth it, for it had brought him legend status. Twenty years later, high schoolers still talked about the kid who'd dropped old Morrison's Chevy Nova into the drink. Most of them would have been shocked to know that the "kid" was now their parish priest. For at the age of twenty-four, fresh from a mysterious three years spent in the Far East, Clancy Donovan had found, of all things, religion.

Rafferty slid his wallet back into his pocket. "You should call Caro," he told the priest. "Give her a tour of Donovan House. She'd be impressed with what you're doing."

"I will if you'll tell me where she's staying." Some of

the light left Clancy's eyes. "Somehow, I suspect it's not with her folks."

"You suspect right. Try the Boylston House."

"This strangler thing," Clancy said, suddenly serious. "Are you making any headway?"

"Just between you and me?" He set his mouth in a grim line. "No. No witnesses, no evidence, no nothing. This guy is slick as shit, Clance. If we don't catch him, he'll keep on killing."

"Do you think Caro will be able to help?"

He pictured Carolyn Monahan's face as he'd given her the deluxe tour of all the crime scenes. The way she'd relentlessly made him go through the details, over and over, until she had them firmly in mind. "If not," he said grudgingly, "it won't be for lack of trying."

Clancy nodded somberly. "Is there anything at all that I can do?"

He swung his gym bag over his shoulder. "There is one thing you can do for us."

"Name it."

He clenched his jaw. "Pray for us, Father. Pray that we get this miserable son of a bitch off the streets before he kills someone else."

When Rafferty came into the office, dark hair slicked back and smelling of shampoo, she was sitting at his desk, nursing a cup of black coffee and reading Tommy Malone's front-page article in the *Tribune*. She'd been up half the night, working on her profile, and the coffee was the strongest legal stimulant she could get her hands on. "This Tommy Malone," she said by way of greeting. "He's good."

Rafferty perched on the corner of the desk. "Malone's a real go-getter," he admitted, picking up a crystal paperweight and running his fingers over its glassy surface. "But he's a pain in the ass, sniffing around the Homicide Division like a bloodhound tracking a scent."

"He certainly did a hell of a job with this story. Now we just have to see if it reels anybody in." She folded the *Tribune* and set it aside, nudged a manila folder across the desk to him. "Here's your preliminary profile, Lieutenant."

He raised a single dark eyebrow. "Fast work."

"You have to understand," she said, "that this is just a rough sketch, based on the facts available to me now. New evidence could change the profile."

He set down the paperweight and picked up the folder, opened it and began reading. "The coffee at Starbucks is a lot better than that stuff you're drinking," he said.

Eyeing him through narrowed lids, she said, "I happen to like this stuff I'm drinking."

"Maybe so," he said, turning a page, "but I don't."

"Is that your way of asking me to play the little woman and fetch coffee for you, Rafferty?"

A smile played at the corner of his mouth, broadened and took hold, softening the expression in his eyes. "Just across the courtyard, Monahan. At the Steaming Kettle. Black, two sugars. You fetch—" he tapped the folder with his knuckles "—while I read."

When she came back, he was hunched over the desk, one hand buried in the thick black hair, a frown of concentration on his face as he read. "Here's your coffee, Lieutenant," she said, setting it on the desk. "You owe me a buck fifty."

"Thanks," he said absently.

She hated to admit that he was right, that the coffee was better than the ghastly stuff she'd been drinking. But it was. Not as effective, but one hell of a lot easier on the taste buds. While he read, she paced his office, sipping her coffee, pausing at the window to stare out at the never-ending traffic on Congress Street.

When he finished, he closed the folder and cleared his throat. She turned, waiting for his appraisal. He lined up the folder at a precise angle with the edge of his desk. "All right," he said, leaning back and folding his arms. "I've read your profile. Now explain it to me."

She sat on the hard wooden chair facing him and crossed one leg over the other. "Since the victims were white," she said, "and this kind of killer rarely crosses racial boundaries, we're looking for a white male. Twenty-five to thirty-five years old, probably on the upper end of that range. There's a level of sophistication to these crimes that suggests a certain maturity and experience—"

"Wait a minute. Back up. Are you saying you think he's killed before?"

"It's highly likely. At the very least, he's escalated to killing from lesser crimes—rape, burglary, assault. Every one of his victims was abducted from a public place. Every one of them was dumped in a public place. This is the work of a man who's confident, probably more than a little cocky, a risk taker. He's clever to have eluded capture, and he knows it."

"We've gone over the records of every sexual assault case in Boston for the last five years. We've questioned dozens of suspects. We've found zip."

"Keep looking. This guy could very well have priors, although it's possible that he's gotten away with any earlier crimes. For all you know, he could be sitting right under your nose, trying to interject himself into your investigation. Be wary of anyone who shows an inordinate interest in the case."

"That narrows it down to about five thousand people. Now all we have to do is use the *eeny-meeny-miney-mo* method of identification."

She raised her coffee cup to her mouth, took a sip. Over the rim, she said, "At this point, it's as good as any other."

"That's comforting," he said. "Keep going."

"He either lives or works locally. He's very comfortable and familiar with the area. Average in appearance, not the kind of man who'd stand out in a crowd. As far as we can determine, four women got into his car of their own free will. This tells me that there's nothing odd or frightening about his appearance. He's probably quite personable. Chances are good that he works in a job where he comes into contact with the public on a regular basis. Possibly sales. Maybe he works the counter at McDonald's, or sells tickets at the Museum of Fine Arts. He may be working in a job that's beneath his skill level because he doesn't want to distinguish himself. He's cordial with his co-workers, but not overtly friendly—it's too risky."

She took another sip of coffee and leaned forward in the chair, warming to her subject. "We know he has a car, because the victims were abducted from one place and dumped in another. Find the car, and you'll find indisputable forensic evidence."

"Great. In a city of half a million people and seventeen million cars, that should be easy enough."

"Narrow your search. He's probably driving a late-model sedan in an unobtrusive color, something anonymous that potential witnesses won't remember. A Ford Taurus, maybe, or a midrange Oldsmobile. Dark-blue, maroon. It'll have high mileage because of the time he spends cruising for victims, but it will be immaculate inside and out, because he doesn't want to leave evidence behind. By the same token, he'll keep it in perfect running order, because he can't take the chance that it will break down with one of his victims inside.''

"I suppose that next, you're going to tell me what color undershorts he wears. And what brand."

She squared her jaw. "Do you want to hear this or not, Rafferty? Because if you don't—"

He ran the fingers of both hands through his hair, massaged his scalp. "I'm sorry," he said. "Go on."

She stood and began pacing his office. "He's probably not involved in a relationship with a woman, but if he is, it's a given that the relationship has serious problems." She perched on the corner of his desk and crossed her arms. "The postmortem sexual assaults indicate that he has trouble maintaining a normal sexual relationship with a woman. It's possible that the only way he can relate to a woman is if he has total control over her. He may have a history of assault or domestic violence. Look closely at his family history. Chances are good that the father was absent from the home, and that discipline—what there was of it—was inconsistent. There may be a family history of alcoholism or petty crime. Drugs, B and E, drunken driving, that kind of thing. Mother may have exhibited inappropriate sexual behavior in front of him. A long string of live-in boyfriends, Saturday night pickups, possibly even prostitution."

Rafferty glanced at the folder on his desk. "Presuming that you know what you're talking about—and I'm not saying I think you are—how is this supposed to help us? You haven't given me a damn thing to go on."

"No profile is going to point out your killer for you. It's a tool, not a crystal ball. You have to identify your suspects the hard way. Lots of feet pounding lots of pavement, lots of interviews with lots of people. It wouldn't hurt to have a healthy dose of luck thrown into the mix. What the profile can do is help you eliminate the wrong suspects and know when you've found the right one.''

A voice at the door startled them both. "Excuse me, Lieutenant," Isabel said in a soft Hispanic accent. "Somebody here to see you."

They both turned toward the door. Isabel smiled apologetically and retreated. The woman who stood in the doorway was trim and middle-aged, her light-brown hair worn in a casual cut. She wore tidy navy-blue polyester pants and a matching print top, and her eyes were red-rimmed and swollen. Behind her stood a young man in his twenties, grim of face, one oversize hand resting on the woman's shoulder in a protective gesture that Carolyn found touching.

Conor stood up. "I'm Lieutenant Rafferty," he said. "What can I do for you?"

The woman looked from him to Carolyn and back. "I'm Ada Perry," she said. "Katie's mother. This is my son, Kenny. We came to take Katie home. But nobody will tell us when they're going to release her—her body." A single tear welled up and flowed down her cheek, and Carolyn exchanged a glance with Rafferty.

"Mrs. Perry," she said, "please, come in. Sit down. I'm Special Agent Monahan from the FBI." While she eased the weeping woman into a chair, Rafferty walked to the door and quietly shut it.

Carolyn hated this part of the job. There was nothing she could do for the victims; it was too late for them. But she had to deal with the survivors. They were the ones who suffered the most, the ones who had to try to piece back together the remains of their ravaged lives. She should know. She'd been there. And every time she spoke with one of them, every time she listened to somebody's newly minted grief, it reopened the wound in her own life that she couldn't seem to keep closed.

Kneeling on the floor, she took the woman's work-worn hand in hers. Ada Perry could have been her own mother. They were of a similar height, similar coloring. They even had the same taste in clothes. "I'm so sorry," she said. "I know this is terribly difficult for you."

The older woman opened her handbag and removed a floral-patterned handkerchief. Dabbing at her eyes, she said, "Katie was such a good girl. She never gave us any trouble. I just can't imagine—" She trailed off, shook her head as new tears filled her eyes. After a moment, she continued. "My husband stayed at home. There's nobody else to feed and milk forty cows. The neighbors took up a collection so Kenny and I could come here. But we can't even make funeral arrangements until—" She paused, shook her head, and turned away.

"We just want to know what happened to my sister," her son blurted out. "That's all."

Rafferty perched on the corner of his desk and folded his arms. Quietly, he said, "It looks as though her car broke down on the expressway ramp. The perpetrator—" He cleared his throat. "We believe this man offered her a ride."

Mrs. Perry raised disbelieving eyes. "But her father always told her, over and over again, never to get in a car with a stranger! Katie would never do something like that!"

"It was late at night," Rafferty said. "She was alone, in a strange city. If he came along, offered her a ride, she probably believed she was making the right choice. We didn't find any signs of struggle, Mrs. Perry. We're almost certain that she got into his car of her own accord."

"But why? Why her? Why my baby?"

The agony behind the woman's question brought a hard lump to Carolyn's throat. It was a question that had no answer. Or at least none that was acceptable to a grieving parent. Rafferty cleared his throat and said, "She fit the profile."

Mrs. Perry looked bewildered. "I don't understand," she said.

"Your daughter was not his only victim. This man has killed before, and he'll kill again unless we stop him. Katie was his fourth victim in six months. All the victims had similar physical characteristics."

"Dear God," Mrs. Perry said.

"A serial killer?" Kenny said. "That's what you're talking about?"

Rafferty and Carolyn exchanged a steady glance. "Yes," he said.

"In other words, if you people hadn't been so god-damned incompetent, my sister would still be alive!"

"Kenneth!"

"It's the truth, Ma!" He paced swiftly across the room, kicked at the wastebasket, spun around and glared at Rafferty. "It's your fault my sister is dead!" He drove a brawny fist into the door, creating a six-inch hole in the veneer. "Damn it! Damn it all to hell!" He leaned his face against the battered door and began to cry, great wrenching sobs, each of them driving the knife-sharp pain deeper into Carolyn's heart.

It wasn't the first time she'd seen this kind of reaction to the death of a loved one. Kenny Perry needed someone to blame, and in the absence of the killer himself, his next best choice was to shoot the messenger. Rafferty let him run down, get it out of his system, before he continued.

"We've assembled a task force to work on the case,

and now the FBI is working with us. That's why Agent Monahan is here. She's something of an expert on serial killers.''

All eyes turned to Carolyn, and she squeezed the woman's hand. ''We're doing everything that's humanly possible,'' she said. ''I promise you that we'll catch him.''

''I'll call the medical examiner's office,'' Rafferty offered, ''and see what I can find out.''

While he made his phone call, Ada Perry continued to sniffle into her handkerchief, Kenny paced the corridor outside the office, and Carolyn rubbed the back of her neck as the familiar headache took hold and began to throb. Rafferty hung up the phone and said, ''They're going to release your daughter's body this afternoon, Mrs. Perry. You can go ahead and make arrangements to take her home.''

Kenny, standing at the open doorway, said, ''I'm not going back to North Dakota. I'm staying here until you find the monster that killed my sister. I want to see him, face-to-face.''

Revenge. Justice. How many times had Carolyn fantasized about Meg's killer and what she would do to him if she ever met him face-to-face? She rubbed her temple absently as Rafferty said, ''That's up to you, of course, Mr. Perry. We can't stop you from staying in Boston. But you might want to rethink your plans. Your mother needs your help right now.''

Kenny scowled, but he didn't argue. Ada Perry stood. ''Come on, Kenneth,'' she said. ''We've taken up enough of the lieutenant's time.'' Now that she had something concrete to deal with, she seemed to have regained her backbone. While Rafferty escorted the Perrys back through the labyrinth to the elevators, Carolyn sat on the wooden chair in his office, head in her hands, thumbs massaging her aching temples. His footsteps returned and stopped in the doorway.

"You okay?" he said.

"Peachy."

"You get these headaches often?"

"I'm fine," she said raggedly. "Just give me a minute."

He knelt on the floor in front of her, caught her chin in his hand, and gently but forcefully raised her face until her eyes met his. Slowly, enunciating each word with knife-sharp precision, he said, "You were not responsible for Meg's death."

As the pain intensified, she stared at him, wondering how he'd managed to hit the jugular with his first swipe of the blade. "Don't touch me," she whispered.

"What happened to Meg was a random act. Nobody could have prevented it. She was in the wrong place at the wrong time—"

"Because of me!" She swiped his hand away from her face. "Because I wasn't where I was supposed to be that night!"

"Damn it, Carolyn, you can't second-guess the past. Stop torturing yourself over something that happened ten years ago, something you couldn't prevent."

"I could have prevented it! My sister would be alive now if I'd come by for her after work that night, like I was supposed to."

For an instant, she thought she saw, somewhere in those green eyes of his, a tiny spark of the same guilt she felt. Then it was gone, leaving her to wonder if she'd imagined it. "But I was too busy rolling between the sheets with you," she said bitterly, "to care if my sister had to walk home alone."

His face went still. "Caro," he said quietly. "Don't."

"I have to live with that, Rafferty." Furious, she brushed a strand of hair away from her cheek as she stumbled to her feet. "I have to live with that for the rest of my life."

And she left him there, still kneeling on the carpet.

4

When the Mitsubishi crossed the Congress Street bridge over Fort Point Channel, Carolyn abruptly entered a different universe. The young turks with their power ties and cell phones were left behind, replaced by old men with lined faces and baggy pants who lingered in doorways because there was nothing else for them to do. Instead of the shoe stores and the salad emporiums that characterized the banking district, Southie boasted of empty storefronts plastered with bumper stickers that read Joe Morrissey For President, Local Number 462. Behind a chain-link fence, a weed-choked lot advertised parking for five dollars a day. The attendant, a brawny young man in a black T-shirt with the sleeves cut out, leaned against a section of fence, a lit cigarette dangling from the corner of his mouth, and watched as she drove past.

After a couple of blocks, she turned and began to climb the hill. She'd grown up on these narrow South Boston streets, and she navigated them with the familiarity of a native. Even if she hadn't recognized the lay of the land, the clenching of her stomach would have told her she was home. As she climbed higher, the warehouses and factories and trucking companies gave way to pizza shops and beer joints, then to the apartment buildings, the schools and the churches that had dominated her childhood.

K Street was lined with cars. Most of the houses in

Southie were three-family, wooden triple-deckers, set close to the sidewalk and built close together, with only a narrow walking space in between. Because there were no driveways, turf wars were continually fought over prime parking space. Today, she got lucky and found a spot directly across from her parents' house. Carolyn squeezed the Mitsubishi into the empty space, closed the sun roof and locked the doors behind her.

She stood on the sidewalk, momentarily lost in the memory of three kids who had roller-skated and squabbled and played hopscotch on this street. Caught in the past, she yearned for the childhood innocence that had been theirs. But it was gone, gone as irrevocably as those three kids were gone. Meg was dead. Mike was still living in Southie, working on a construction crew, with a wife and three kids of his own. And Carolyn had escaped to Quantico and the arms of Richard Armitage.

Shaking off the past, she squared her shoulders and briskly crossed the street. Tall and narrow, the house where she'd grown up stood shoulder to shoulder with its neighbors on either side, and wore an air of perpetual fatigue. Caro climbed the steps and swung open the front door. The hallway still smelled of boiled cabbage and overripe garbage, and the clusters of gaudy purple grapes in the stained wallpaper were still as ugly as she remembered. Old Mrs. O'Hannon, who'd lived for forty years in the second-floor apartment, had passed away in February, and a young married couple had moved into her apartment. As Carolyn climbed the crooked stairs past the second-floor landing, she could hear the wailing of an infant behind the closed door.

She reached the third floor, ran a hand along the spindly railing, and paused before the door of the apartment where she'd grown up. The drone of the television penetrated the thin wooden door. Her father would be sitting in his recliner, watching the nightly news, nursing a beer and brooding over the state of the world. Her mother would be bustling about the kitchen, a faded apron tied around her gaunt frame, her mouth pursed in disapproval at the vices she was certain would land her husband in hell one of these days.

Despite its familiarity, this house had long ago ceased to be home. Squaring her shoulders, Carolyn knocked on the door. Footsteps approached, the door swung open, and her mother stood on the other side.

Roberta Monahan still wore her graying hair in the same pageboy style she'd worn in high school. Her apron was threadbare, and the polyester pantsuit hung limply from her bony frame. In the faded blue eyes was a kind of resignation, as though Roberta had seen life for what it was and had long since given up hope.

"Hi, Mom," Carolyn said.

Her mother's eyes took her in, head to toe, and Carolyn stood rigidly erect beneath her scrutiny. She'd left behind the Donna Karan suit, the Manolo Blahnik shoes, dressing instead in a simple cotton T-shirt, new jeans, and Nikes. *Please, Mom,* an inner voice said, *just this once, be happy to see me.*

"About time you got here," her mother said. "You can help me with the vegetables." And without so much as a smile, she turned away from the door.

Carolyn's hopes shriveled and died. Shoulders braced, she stepped into the apartment. The instant the door shut behind her, it came rushing at her, the insistent feeling of suffocation that always came over her in this place. The dark walls began to close in on her, and the faded pink cabbage roses in the ancient carpet took on a sinister appearance. Her father sat in his usual spot, eyes focused on the television, barely nodding when she greeted him. On the wall over the couch, right next to the picture of Jesus bleeding on the cross, her sister's high school graduation portrait was prominently displayed. Meg Monahan, permanently frozen at the age of eighteen. Had the family been this dysfunctional before Meg died? She honestly couldn't remember.

Roberta was in the kitchen, poking the boiled potatoes with a sharp fork. "You can drain the carrots and the peas," she said. "Put them on the table in serving bowls."

Her mother somehow always managed to reduce her to the age of twelve. Carolyn obediently drained the vegetables, added a pat of butter to each, and placed them on the table. It was set for four, and she wondered who the extra plate was for. Before she could open her mouth to ask, there was a knock on the door. "That'll be Father Donovan," Roberta said. "I saw him at the market this afternoon, and when he heard you were coming here tonight, there was nothing would suit him except that he have dinner with us."

"Clancy's coming for dinner?" Carolyn tossed down the dish towel she'd been wiping her hands on and sprinted from the kitchen, past her father's droning television and the makeshift shrine to Jesus Christ and Saint Meg. She flung open the apartment door and said gleefully, "Clancy Donovan! I'm so glad to see you!"

His eyes, the color of good Irish whiskey, held a devilish twinkle. His unruly hair was a dark, rich mahogany, and considerably longer than what she imagined the Church would approve of.

"Hello, Caro," he said, and they embraced warmly.

Behind her, Roberta said darkly, "For the love of God,

girl, let go of the Father before God strikes you dead for cozying up to a priest!''

She stepped back, and Clancy rewarded her with a quick wink. He couldn't possibly have missed seeing the desperation in her eyes. "We rode our tricycles together, Mrs. Monahan,'' he said evenly. "I doubt that the Church would have a problem with me hugging your daughter.''

Carolyn shot him a look of gratitude, wondering whether he'd finagled this dinner invitation because he wanted to see her or because he knew she'd need a buffer to survive dinner with her parents. Either way, it didn't really matter. He was an old and dear friend, and she was delighted to see him.

The table was set with Grandma Sullivan's good dishes, the gold-filigreed bone china plates of palest pink sprinkled with yellow tea roses that Carolyn had spent half her childhood begging her mother to use. But except for special occasions like Christmas or Easter, weddings or wakes, Roberta had always found excuses to keep it tucked away in the china cabinet. How many times had Carolyn heard the words "It'll get broken,'' or "What, the everyday china's not good enough for you?'' Never once had her mother given in to her wheedling. Tonight's showing had to be for Clancy's benefit.

Her parents sat in the same spots they'd always occupied, at opposite ends of the table. Roberta had situated the priest at her right, in Mike's old chair, and Carolyn at the other end of the table, near her father's elbow. To Caro's right, abandoned and deafening in its silence, was her sister's chair, empty now these past ten years. Peeved, Carolyn wondered if a single living soul had mustered the audacity to sit in that holiest of holy places.

It must have been some perversity that took hold of her. She shoved her place setting down the table, pulled out Meg's chair, and plunked her derriere into it. Directly across the table, Clancy Donovan smiled at her, either unaware of the heresy she'd just committed, or determined to ignore it. Roberta's face paled, and her nostrils flared, proof that she was displeased. But she wasn't about to air her dirty linen in front of the priest. Carolyn knew she would receive a nasty dressing-down once he'd gone but for now, at least, she was safe from her mother's wrath.

At Roberta's urging, Clancy said grace, and they all dug in. Her mother's pork roast was heavenly, but Carolyn took just a sliver. Ditto for the buttered vegetables and the mashed potato with its full complement of milk and butter. At home in Alexandria, she rarely ate meat, and she shuddered inwardly at the thought of all that animal fat clogging up her arteries.

"You're not eating," her mother accused. "Just pushing food around on your plate. Look at the girl, Gerry. Is it any wonder she's so skinny? She doesn't eat enough to feed a bird."

Her father paused in his chewing. Raising his eyes from his plate, he said, "She looks fine to me," and returned to chewing.

"Mrs. Monahan," Clancy said, "I'd like to compliment you on the meal. This roast is the best thing I've eaten in months. I don't suppose I could sweet-talk you into taking pity on a poor priest who can't even boil water, and wrapping up some leftovers for me to take home?"

Twin splotches of color appeared on Roberta's otherwise pale face. "Why, of course, Father. I'll be glad to make up a plate to go home with you."

Not on Grandma's china, I'll wager, Carolyn thought, then chided herself for her pettiness.

Her father smeared butter on a homemade yeast roll.

"These murders," he said gruffly. "That's why you're here, isn't it?"

Roberta's eyes narrowed. "Gerry!" she said. "You know I hate that kind of talk at the table."

Roberta Monahan had always frowned on her husband discussing police work at the dinner table. In the beginning, it had been to prevent small ears from hearing things they didn't need to know about. But as the years went on and the children grew, so did Roberta's resentment of her husband's career, until eventually that resentment colored everything she did and said. When Roberta had turned a deaf ear on her husband, it had been his eldest daughter who'd listened to his stories of life as a beat cop on the streets of Boston.

Then Meg had died, and that same year a back injury had forced Gerald Monahan into early retirement, and everything had changed. For Gerald, who'd been born a cop and who would die a cop, the transition from flatfoot to couch potato had been extremely difficult.

Carolyn nodded. "That's right, Dad," she said. "The task force called me in to help them get this monster off the street."

Roberta's jaw clamped tight in disapproval as Gerald said, "Who's running the investigation?"

Carolyn set down her fork and picked up her napkin. "Conor Rafferty," she said, and dabbed at the corner of her mouth.

Her father nodded gravely and said, "He's a good cop." In Gerald Monahan's book, there was no higher praise.

Roberta's eyebrows drew together. "That boy," she said darkly, "has broken the hearts of half the women in Eastern Massachusetts. But so far, nobody's caught him. Not permanently anyway, although I hear plenty have tried.'' She pursed her mouth in displeasure. ''I was talking to his mother just the other day at the butcher shop. She's beginning to despair of him ever giving her grandchildren.''

''What's the rush?'' Carolyn said with forced pleasantness. ''Josie and Frank both have kids. She already has grandchildren.''

''The point,'' her mother said, ''is that you should have snatched him up while you had the chance. According to Fiona, ever since you practically left him at the altar, all he's done is flit around from woman to woman.''

Carolyn's muscles began to tense, one by one. ''Roberta,'' Gerald said gruffly, ''leave it alone.''

''I worry about her, Gerry. She needs a man to take care of her, and the older she gets, the less chance there is of finding someone who'll bring home his paycheck every week instead of drinking it.''

Anger and pity warred inside Carolyn. Was this the sum total of her mother's expectation of life? Three meals a day, a roof over her head, and a man who brought home his paycheck instead of drinking it? She wanted to shake her mother, wanted to rail at her that there was so much more than that. But her protests would be useless. Roberta Monahan believed what she chose to believe, and nothing Carolyn said would make one iota of difference. ''So far, Mother,'' she said coolly, ''I've managed to take care of myself just fine.''

Clancy picked up the gravy boat and poured a healthy dollop onto his mashed potato. Brightly, he said, ''So, how are Mike and Mandy these days? I haven't seen them in months.''

He might as well not have spoken, for all the response he got. ''If that's your idea of taking care of yourself,'' Roberta said. ''Thirty-two years old, and no intention of ever settling down. When a woman's still single at thirty-two, people start to talk. They start to wonder if she's one of those man-haters who prefer their own kind.''

Across the table, Clancy let out a choked sound that was half laugh, half cough. "Excuse me," he said, hiding his mouth behind his napkin.

"For the love of God, Roberta," Gerald said, "will you give it a rest? The girl will settle down when she's good and ready. There's nothing wrong with her."

But Roberta was on a roll. "Your cousin Maureen," she told her daughter, "has three babies now, and a fourth on the way. And she's only twenty-six. That's the way the good Lord intended it to be. Isn't that right, Father? Home and family. Those are the things that matter, home and family and church, and Maureen understands that. Her mother doesn't have to hide her face when she goes out in public because her daughter spends her life consorting with perverts and criminals."

"Roberta!" Gerald thundered. "Put a lid on it!"

His wife's mouth fell open as Clancy leaned over the table and said, "I don't suppose I might have another helping of those potatoes?"

The rain that had started while they'd been eating had done nothing for the ambiance of the neighborhood. A dismal, sodden evening had painted the triple-decker houses the same tired color as her mother. Carolyn pulled out her car keys and turned to the priest. "I think," she said dryly, "that you might just have a bit of the blarney in you, Father Donovan."

Clancy patted the bulging Tupperware container in his pocket. "You're welcome," he said.

"Thank you. My stab wounds are relatively few. Are you parked nearby?"

Clancy poked his hands into his pockets and hunched his shoulders against the drizzle. "I walked," he said.

"I'm right across the street. I'll give you a lift."

"Nice car," he said, eyeing the Mitsubishi with open admiration.

"It gets me where I want to go."

"And ahead of everyone else, I'll bet."

She blipped the door locks and they both climbed in. The car was a welcome refuge from the rain. Carolyn settled into soft leather, leaned her head back and closed her eyes. Took a couple of deep breaths and said, "I did it deliberately."

Clancy, fiddling with his seat belt, said, "Did what deliberately?"

"Sat in Meg's place at the table." She opened her eyes. "I did it deliberately to provoke her. I'm going to hell, aren't I?"

He snapped the seat belt into place. Benevolently, he said, "I don't recall seeing 'Thou shalt not provoke' anywhere in the Ten Commandments."

Her smile was brittle. "What about 'Honor thy father and thy mother'?"

"That's sometimes more difficult than we'd like it to be."

She rested her hands on the steering wheel and stared blindly out into the drizzle. "We can't ever connect," she said. "Meg's ghost is always there between us. Ten years she's been dead, but still she's the only one who matters. The only one my mother ever loved." She stopped abruptly, remembering too late that before Clancy Donovan had become a priest, he'd been an ordinary man, and that he, too, had loved her sister. For a time, he'd been the prime suspect in Meg's murder, until the police had come to the conclusion that there wasn't a single scrap of evidence to connect him to the crime. "I'm sorry," she said.

"No offense taken. You have to understand that your parents are dealing with Meg's death the only way they know how."

"Oh," she said bitterly, "I understand. I understand that my mother declared war on the entire free world, and my father simply retreated into his own reality. Mike hasn't spoken to me in ten years, and as for me—" She paused, rubbed the back of her neck slowly, wearily. "As for me," she continued, "I just ended an affair with my married boss. There's a broken commandment for you, Father. Hell, if you looked up the word *dysfunctional* in your *Funk and Wagnalls,* you'd probably find a family portrait of the Monahans."

"I think you're courageous," he said.

Carolyn snorted. "Right. It takes a lot of courage to sleep with another woman's husband."

"You're courageous in the way you dealt with Meg's murder. You've dedicated your life to putting killers behind bars so that what happened to her won't happen to other women. You want to know how I dealt with it? By running away."

His words, and the sadness behind them, surprised her. "You're a priest," she said. "You minister to people. You save souls. I'd hardly call that running away."

"You might be surprised to know that there are people who believe the priesthood is overrun with cowards who've chosen to retreat from reality because they can't cope with it." The rain pattered softly on the roof. "There are times," he added, "when I wouldn't disagree with them."

Because there was nothing else to say, she pulled the car away from the curb, and for a time there was only the swish of the windshield wipers. After a couple of blocks, he said, "I play racquetball with Conor twice a week."

Her fingers tightened on the steering wheel. "Oh?" she said.

"His game's been off since you came back to town."

She told herself that her stumbling heartbeat had nothing to do with Conor Rafferty. Caustically, she said, "And you're telling me this because…?"

"Because he's my friend." Clancy turned and studied her profile. "And because you are. You can let me out here."

"Here?" she said, peering into the rain at the dark street corner.

"The rectory's just around the corner. You know—" he unlatched the door, held it open just enough for the dome light to illuminate the car's interior "—when I see a friend about to make a mistake, I can't help wanting to shout out a warning."

"I don't know what you're talking about."

Clancy climbed out of the car and stood there holding the door open. "He's still on M Street," he said, "living upstairs over his parents."

The door began to swing shut. "Wait!" she said. "Wait a minute! Rafferty's still living in Southie?"

"Second-floor apartment. G'night." Before she could protest, he shut the door and disappeared into the swirling wet darkness.

She found M Street easily, crept past the cars that lined the curb, stopping in front of the old wooden triple-decker house with its concrete steps and open porches. Unlike her parents' home, the Rafferty house was freshly painted, its facade brightened by window boxes teeming with geraniums. Engine idling, wipers slapping, Carolyn lingered in the darkness, her eyes drawn to the single light burning in the second-floor window.

A shadow passed behind the closed shade. Her heart leaped, and she cussed violently under her breath. What in bloody hell did she think she was doing, skulking outside Rafferty's window like a teenage girl with her first crush, waiting for a glimpse of her paramour? Mortified, Carolyn crammed the Mitsubishi into first gear and shot off down the street.

She was still struggling with the thorny matter of her motives when the portion of her brain that always remained cool and analytical registered the car that pulled away from the curb a hundred yards behind her. The placement of the headlights told her it was a midsize late-model sedan. Its high beams reflected off rain-washed pavement, and she adjusted her rearview mirror to cut the glare. Strictly as an experiment, she turned right at the next intersection.

Behind her, the other car did the same.

It was reflex to check for the snub-nosed .38 she carried in her purse. Older and bulkier than the government-issue Glock 9mm she wore when she was on duty, the police special had been a gift from her father. The day she'd graduated from the academy, Gerald Monahan had presented her with the gun he'd worn at his hip for two decades. She took pride in carrying it, took pride in carrying on the family law enforcement tradition her father had begun. Caro ran her fingers over cool, smooth steel, comforted by its familiarity. Calmly, in no particular hurry, she took her next left and waited to see what the other driver would do.

A moment later, headlights turned the corner behind her.

She felt the first prick of annoyance. Who the hell

would be tailing her? More to the point, why? Deciding
that two could play at this game, she began zigging and
zagging her way around South Boston, back and forth on
the cross streets at a steady, unhurried pace. In her rearview mirror, the headlights maintained an even distance,
close enough so their reflection bouncing off wet pavement blurred visibility, yet far enough away to remain
anonymous.

She ran her fingers over the .38 again, remembering
what she'd been taught at the academy. *Shoot only to kill.*
From the first day of firearms training, it had been drilled
into her head. *Never draw your weapon unless you've
already made the decision to take a human life.* What that
boiled down to, in most cases, was self-defense. If an FBI
agent fired his or her weapon, you could almost guarantee
that it was to save either his own life or that of someone
else.

Whoever her tail was, Carolyn's instincts told her that
somebody was trying to annoy her, to draw her into some
psychological game of cat and mouse. If he'd meant her
any harm, it would have been easy enough to find a way
to corner her, run her off the road, force her into an in-
escapable situation. But this game playing was like Chinese water torture, designed to drive her crazy.

And she was getting royally pissed.

In a split second decision, she slammed on the brakes,
and the Mitsubishi came to a skidding halt. The son of a
bitch wanted to play? Fine. She'd give him what he was
asking for. Heart thundering, adrenaline whooshing
through her veins, Caro snatched up her gun, flung open
the door, and stepped out of the car to face her pursuer.

If Richard ever found out about this, she'd be busted
to a desk jockey assignment in Des Moines. For a full ten
seconds she stood in the rain in the blinding glare of high-

beam headlights, legs braced apart, hands gripping the .38 like Dirty Harry, the barrel pointed straight at the windshield of the car behind her. The other driver shifted into reverse and began backing away, transmission whining as it gained speed. When the car reached the intersection, the driver spun it around, crammed the shifter into gear, and sped off into the rainy darkness, tires screaming on the slick pavement.

Carolyn lowered the .38 and slumped against the side of her car to wait for her thundering heart to slow. First the phone call, now this. She supposed that she was going to have to spill it all to Rafferty.

He wasn't going to be pleased.

Her breathing restored to normal, Caro climbed back into the Mitsubishi and locked the doors. In the distance, she could see the fuzzy blue glow of the sign outside Hugh Rafferty's bar, its lettering obscured by the fog and the drizzle. After the summer when Meg had died, she'd stayed away from Rafferty's. Meg's death, her own doomed love affair with Conor, had been too closely tied to the place, the memories too painful to face. But working this case had opened a number of old wounds. It was time to face her demons and put them to rest.

Carolyn pulled up to the curb in front of the bar and parked, unsnapped her seat belt, and took a quick look around. The street was empty, the streetlights haloed by fog. The tail had apparently given up. But she was more spooked than she'd realized; when she reached for the door latch, her hand trembled. Glancing around one last time, she locked the Mitsubishi and kept her hand on her weapon as she approached the entrance to the bar.

The instant she opened the door, it rushed her senses, the chatter of a dozen raucous voices interspersed with boozy laughter. Overlaid with a gauzy haze of tobacco smoke, the yeasty scent of beer mingled with the odor of stale grease. Nobody would ever mistake Rafferty's for a yuppie bar. There wasn't a fern in sight. No piano player tinkled the ivories with bland and tasteful tunes. The walls were old brick, rough and crooked, the tables marred by rings left by thousands of beer mugs and adorned with the scratched initials of several generations of young lovers. From a corner jukebox, George Thoroughgood rasped about one bourbon, one scotch, and one beer.

At a table in the center of the room, beneath a ceiling fan that was making a desultory attempt to recycle the stuffy air, four members of Boston's finest were playing poker. Cigar smoke rose from their table, hovering before it was captured by the ceiling fan and redistributed to spread lung cancer to the rest of the room. As the daughter of a beat patrolman, Carolyn had spent a good part of her life around cops, and she had a knack for spotting them, in or out of uniform. Even without uniforms, these four guys, paunchy, middle-aged, and balding, screamed "cop." It was something about their demeanor, their attitude, the way they carried themselves. And Rafferty's was a cop hangout, had been one for as long as she could remember.

Carolyn felt her muscles begin to loosen, one by one. She crossed the room to the long wooden bar and settled herself on a stool. On the color television suspended above one end of the bar, the Sox were playing a night game at Toronto. Garciaparra hit a line drive, and two burly guys in white overalls and painter's caps roared and hammered their beer mugs against the wooden bar.

Home. For the first time since she'd arrived in Boston, she felt truly at home.

The man behind the bar glanced up at her, and a grin spread across his face. He set down the beer he was drawing and strode around to her side of the bar. "Caro," he said warmly. "Our little Caro, all grown up."

She grinned. "Hello, Hugh."

He folded her into massive arms like twin oak trees. At sixty, Hugh Rafferty was still vital, still handsome, and she had no doubt that he could hold his own against any younger man who possessed either the audacity or the poor judgment to cross him. He held her at arm's length. "I still remember the days when your dad used to bring you in here," he said. "You were no bigger than a peanut."

She grinned. "I was so short, he had to lift me onto the bar stool."

"We miss you around here, sweetheart."

Warmth flooded her heart. "I've missed you, too. How's Fiona?"

"Still as bossy as ever. I get no respect at all." His face sobered. "So," he said, "you're here because of the killings."

"Yes."

His eyes saddened. "It's a disgrace," he said bitterly, "and a tragedy, when a young girl isn't safe walking the streets of her own neighborhood."

She knew they were both thinking about Meg, both shouldering a portion of the blame for what had happened to her. "He's not getting away with it," she said firmly. "We're going to put this one away."

"You'll get him," Hugh said. "You and Conor. He's been so wrapped up in this case that Fiona and I hardly see him. And when we do, he's not really there with us. I think it's eating him up."

"He doesn't really want me here," she admitted. "Not that I blame him, after what happened between us."

He took both her hands in his huge, warm paws. "My

son is professional enough to bury his personal feelings if he believes you can help him with this case. I want you to know that Fiona and I don't feel any differently toward you because of what happened with you and Conor. We were disappointed when things didn't work out. But we still love you like a daughter. We always have.''

To her mortification, tears stung her eyelids. ''Thanks, Hugh,'' she said. ''I feel the same way about both of you.''

He patted her shoulder. ''So what can I get you, darling? Fiona made a wonderful roast beef this morning. Pink and juicy, so tender it melts in your mouth. How about a nice, thick sandwich? You could stand to put some meat on those bones.''

She closed her eyes and groaned. ''Fiona's roast beef,'' she said with longing. ''Sometimes I wake up in the middle of the night, dreaming about it.'' She opened her eyes, smiled at him. ''I just had dinner with my folks. Otherwise, I'd take you up on it. But I'd love a cold Molson if you've got one.''

''A Molson it is.''

While he bustled around behind the bar, she turned her attention to the ball game. It wasn't looking good. In the bottom of the ninth, the Sox were trailing the Jays, nine to three. Carolyn nursed her beer and tried not to remember the summer that Meg had died. But the floodgates had opened, and there was no holding back the memories.

She'd been waiting tables at Rafferty's that summer when Hugh and Fiona's youngest son returned from the police academy. She'd known Conor Rafferty all her life, but for most of those years, he'd been nothing more than Josie's older brother. He'd left for college while she was still in high school, and their paths had crossed only a few times in the ensuing five years.

But all that had changed one Wednesday night in June when he'd walked into the bar alone, an off-duty rookie cop in a starched blue uniform, looking handsomer than any man had a right to look. She'd brought him a beer and a turkey sandwich. Because it was a slow night and neither of them had anything better to do, she sat down with him to shoot the bull.

The chemistry between them was instantaneous and scorching. Four hours later, at closing time, he walked her home and kissed her good-night in the entry hall outside her apartment, and she'd instantly fallen off a steep cliff and into the most intense relationship of her life. From that moment on, they'd been inseparable.

Until Meg died. Sweet Meg who, at eighteen, already had her future planned out. Beautiful and brimming with life, Meg was planning to become a lawyer and practice family law right here in South Boston. Like Caro, she was waiting tables at Rafferty's to pay her way through college, and she and Clancy Donovan had been a hot item since his return from the Orient in January. Earlier that summer, she'd accepted his marriage proposal. Meg wanted lots of babies, and she wasn't at all intimidated by the idea of juggling a career with motherhood. Meg Monahan had the energy and the temperament to accomplish the impossible with style and panache.

Then, the unthinkable had happened. Meg had left work one hot August night and never arrived home. Her body had been found the next morning in an alley a few blocks from Rafferty's. She'd been raped and strangled, and the monster who killed her had never been caught.

After that night, none of their lives had ever been the same. The knowledge of the part she'd played in Meg's death had sullied Carolyn's relationship with Conor, had erected a wall Caro wasn't sure she could scale. Her romance with Rafferty had been inextricably tangled with her guilt. Their carelessness had led to Meg's death, and a future with him had seemed somehow wrong.

She became a woman with a mission. When September rolled around, she left him behind to pursue a graduate degree in criminology at the University of Denver, two thousand miles away. Conor had stayed in Boston to work his way up through the ranks of the Boston P.D. And Clancy had hidden himself away in the priesthood.

In one way or another, Meg's death had influenced all their lives. In one way or another, they'd each tried to run away. But none of them had been able to escape the specter of Meg Monahan.

Carolyn stared dolefully into the depths of her beer bottle. *Here's to you, Meggie,* she thought, raising the bottle to her mouth and upending it.

"Carolyn Monahan."

She was so engrossed in the past that it took her a moment to return to the present. She set down the beer bottle and glanced over her shoulder at the man who had spoken her name. He had a ruddy Irish face, longish hair, and blue eyes that were sharp with intelligence. He was wearing a tweed jacket over a white dress shirt open at the throat, and there was something vaguely familiar about him, although she didn't think she'd met him before. Names and faces had a way of sticking with her, and in spite of the sense of familiarity she was experiencing, Carolyn was drawing a total blank.

"Now that we've clarified who I am," she said, "who might you be?"

He shifted his beer bottle from right hand to left. "Tommy Malone," he said, and stuck out his hand. *"Boston Tribune."*

She swiveled around on the bar stool and took his hand.

His grasp was firm and confident. "Ah," she said. "Rafferty's ambulance chaser."

He flashed a boyish grin. "I see that my reputation has preceded me."

"With a vengeance. And how, precisely, do you know who I am? Are you psychic?" Thinking about the tail she'd chased off, she narrowed her eyes and looked at him a little more closely. Had he been in the bar when she arrived? "Or have you been following me?"

Something flickered in those blue eyes, and the boyish manner dissolved. Sharply, he said, "Has somebody been following you?"

Mistake number one, she thought. *Never let the circling piranhas smell the blood.* "It doesn't matter," she said.

"Why don't you tell me about it and we'll see if I agree?"

"Thanks for your concern, but I can take care of myself. You still haven't answered my question. How did you know who I am?"

"Nothing mystical or sinister," he said amiably. "South Boston High School."

"Really." She studied him more closely. If he were telling the truth, it could account for the familiarity. "We went to high school together?"

"I was two years behind you, and I had a major crush on you for a while. But you were an older woman, one of the untouchables. I, on the other hand—" he shrugged with good-natured insouciance "—I was an overweight geek with glasses and a bad acne problem."

She tried to picture the attractive, confident man before her as a plump, pimply-faced adolescent, but it was difficult. "Congratulations," she said, and saluted him with her bottle of Molson. "It looks as though you've overcome those early stumbling blocks and managed to turn into a regular person."

"It's amazing, isn't it, how life has a way of evening out the odds after high school? Listen, I have a table over there in the corner. I was hoping you might join me."

"So that you can pump me for information on the case?"

He gave her that "aw, shucks, ma'am" grin and said, "It's my job."

"And keeping my mouth shut is mine. If you're looking for information, you should really be talking to Rafferty. It's his case. I'm nothing more than a hired gun."

"Lieutenant Rafferty and I," he said, "are a volatile mix. Maybe it's because he thinks I'm a bottom feeder and I think he's an uptight jackass."

"Yet here you stand," she said, "kicking back with a cold brew in the bar that, by some amazing coincidence, happens to belong to his father. How do you explain that?"

"Easy. I was waiting for you."

"For me?" she said, trying not to show her surprise. "How did you know I'd be here, considering that I didn't know it myself until a few minutes ago?"

He propped an elbow on the bar. "I know that you put yourself through college waiting tables here. I figured you'd show up sooner or later. I got lucky. You showed up sooner."

"A regular pit bull, aren't you, Malone? Just how is it that you know so much about me?"

"I make it my business," he said, "to know everything about this case." He reached into a dish on the bar and took a fistful of peanuts. "Including the fact that the police don't have a single solid lead."

"Oh? And just what makes you think that?"

"I told you, Rafferty thinks I'm a bottom feeder. He never would have called me for help unless his back was flat against the wall." Malone popped the peanuts into his mouth.

"I see. And what, precisely, do you want from me?"

His grin was back. "Easy again. An exclusive."

"You're barking up the wrong tree, Malone. I'm not discussing the case with you."

"Fine. We can talk about your work. What you do, how you help the cops catch bad guys. You're quite a celebrity, you know. I've been following your career with interest."

Amused, she said, "Have you, now?"

"Maybe we could do some kind of profile. Local girl makes good, that kind of thing."

"Thanks for the offer," she said, "but this local girl's had enough for one night." She tucked a five-dollar bill beneath her half-empty beer bottle and shouldered her purse. "Good night, Mr. Malone," she said, slipping down off the stool. "It's been enlightening."

Traffic was light, and the trip downtown in the foggy drizzle took only ten minutes. Carolyn kept watching her rearview mirror, but nobody was tailing her. Nobody was paying her the least bit of attention. At the Boylston House, she tipped the valet, walked on plush carpeting through the elegant lobby, and took the elevator to the fifth floor. The strain was finally getting to her, and she couldn't wait to sink into a hot bubble bath.

The instant she opened the door to her hotel room, she saw it lying on the carpet just inside the door, a plain white business envelope with her name written on it in block letters. Caro drew her gun, flicked the light switch, and made a quick search of the room. Nobody was here, and nothing had been moved. She checked the lock, found no evidence that it had been tampered with. The envelope must have been slipped beneath the door.

She locked the door, put her gun away, and unsnapped her briefcase. In a side pocket, she kept a miniature evidence kit: rubber gloves, tweezers, pocket knife. With the tweezers, she carefully lifted the envelope by a corner. Holding it up to the light, she saw what appeared to be a single photograph inside. She pulled out the pocket knife, slipped the tip of the blade beneath the flap, and slit the envelope open.

Inside was a Polaroid photo of a woman she'd never seen before. Young, slender, blond, and very naked. Her eyes wore a permanent expression of surprise. Across the bottom of the photo, in lurid purple ink, were the words, "Tell Rafferty he can't stop me."

"Shit," Carolyn said. "Shit, shit, shit."

5

He'd just gotten to sleep when the phone rang, and it took him a few seconds to switch from heavy slumber to full cop mode. He rolled over, fumbled for the phone, dragged the receiver across tangled sheets and propped it between his ear and his shoulder. Clearing his throat, he mumbled, "Rafferty."

"Wake up, Lieutenant. I have something here that I think you'd better see."

He glanced at the clock, blinking at the brightness of the LCD display. It was past eleven. "Carolyn," he said, still not fully awake. "What is it?"

"I'd rather not discuss it over the phone. Do you think you could come to the Boylston House?"

There was an edge to her voice, one he hadn't heard before. He rolled to his feet and fumbled, naked, in the darkness for his clothes. Pulling a T-shirt over his head, he said, "Are you all right?"

"I've had better days, but I expect I'll survive this one."

He stepped into cotton briefs and Levi's, zipped and snapped, buckled his belt. Gauging the cross-town traffic at this time on a week night, he slipped his watch onto his wrist and said, "Give me twenty minutes."

He was there in ten. He parked the Taurus out front with the blue light rotating on his dash and, ignoring the contemptuous frown from the valet, left it there. Carolyn was waiting at the door to her hotel room, looking tired and pale. She nodded in the direction of a Polaroid photo that lay on the table. Rafferty walked over, looked at the photo, and did a double take. With the edges propped between his fingertips, he picked it up and studied it. "Jesus H. Christ," he said.

"Somebody slipped it under the door. He's proud of his handiwork, wouldn't you say?"

"Did you call hotel security?"

"They're on standby. I thought you'd probably want your own people to do the questioning."

"Shit," he said. "What the hell am I supposed to tell them? That there's been another murder, but we don't know who or where or when, and we don't even have a corpse? Shit."

"There's more," she said.

"Of course there is," he said with resignation. "Do I want to hear it?"

She crossed her arms over her chest. "Probably not."

He listened in growing disbelief as she told him about the phone call, the tail, the goddamn Clint Eastwood performance she'd put on right in the middle of Dorchester Street. When she was finished, he just stared at her. "And precisely when were you going to share this information with me? Forgive me if I sound confused, but I thought I was still the one running this investigation."

She squared her jaw. "I'm telling you now, Lieutenant."

"Goddamn it, Monahan, this is why I don't want you people screwing around in my investigations. You always make it worse. Why the hell don't you go back to D.C. and let me deal with this mess on my own?"

"Because it's too late," she said. "For some crazy reason, he's fixated on me. I have to see it through to the end. If I leave now, you'll lose him."

Rafferty opened his mouth to argue and realized she was right. "That's great," he said, slowly rubbing the back of his neck. "Just great."

He pulled out his cell phone and called Lorna Abrams at task force headquarters. "I need you and Rizzoli at the Boylston House ASAP," he told her.

He knew that Lorna had already put in a twelve-hour day and was nearing the end of her shift, but she didn't question his orders. She never did. If he was ever in a sticky situation, Lorna was the one he'd want covering his back. "I'm on it," she said, "but Rizzoli went home a couple of hours ago. You want me to wake him up and drag him back in here?"

"I got hauled out of bed. Why should he sleep when I can't? While you're at it, give Forensics a call and tell them I need somebody over here. And tell them to keep it as low-key as possible." He glanced at Carolyn. "I'd really hate to see Agent Monahan ousted from this place because her colleagues got too rowdy."

He left Carolyn waiting for Forensics and went downstairs to talk to the security people. While he was there, Ed Bragg from Forensics arrived, followed closely by Lorna Abrams. He sent Bragg to the fifth floor and filled Abrams in on what had happened. "Where's Rizzoli?" he said.

"I don't know."

He raised an eyebrow. "Care to explain that one, Detective?"

"I couldn't find him. I called his apartment, but there was no answer, so I tried his beeper. He never called back. So I called Greg instead. He's on his way over right now."

Sometimes he had to remind himself that this was what he'd spent ten years working for. Right from his first day on the force, he'd been bucking for an assignment to Homicide. He'd landed here by a combination of hard work and meticulous attention to detail, had been promoted to lieutenant at a relatively young age through more of the same. Now, he was in charge of a case that could make or break his career. With the job came the headaches, and once in a while, he couldn't help wondering if it was worth all the bullshit he had to wade through.

He introduced Abrams to Ephraim Cleaver, who was head of night security, then he phoned upstairs. "What time did you leave tonight?" he asked Carolyn.

"About quarter to seven. I got back just before eleven."

Over his shoulder, he told Cleaver, "I need the security camera videotape. Everything from six-thirty to eleven." Into the phone, he said, "Meet me downstairs in ten minutes. I want you to go over the tape with me."

While Lorna Abrams and Greg Lassiter interviewed every employee who'd been on duty that evening, he and Carolyn sat in the cramped security office, watching hours of grainy black-and-white VHS tape on a nineteen-inch Sony. The Boylston House was one of downtown Boston's elegant older hotels, built around the turn of the century, and their security system was woefully inadequate and hopelessly outdated. They had a single closed-circuit television camera mounted on the ceiling behind the front desk, and it monitored the comings and goings of hotel guests, employees and the public.

After close to five hours of nonstop viewing, his eyes were burning out of his head and he'd gone past tired to that bizarre place where everything was slightly out of focus and he knew his sudden burst of energy would drop him flat on his face in another hour or so. And they'd found nothing. Zilch. They'd studied face after face after face, the faces of tourists and businessmen, doing what tourists and businessmen do. Nothing suspicious, nobody who looked out of place, nobody who looked even vaguely familiar to either of them.

He switched off the VCR and turned to Carolyn. In the wrinkled T-shirt and jeans, she looked more like a teenager than a veteran FBI agent. Her hair was a mess, and she could have packed for a trip to Europe with the bags under her eyes. She yawned, leaned back in the swivel chair and stretched. "I wouldn't want to say you're a dull date," she said, "but I could have spent the last five hours sleeping."

He felt a smile tug at the corner of his mouth. "You up for breakfast?"

"It depends." She studied him speculatively through heavy-lidded eyes. "Am I off your shit list?"

"For the time being," he said. "But watch your step."

They ordered breakfast in the hotel coffee shop, and while they waited for his bacon and eggs and her cantaloupe with a side of whole wheat toast, he toyed with the handle to his coffee cup and said, "I don't suppose you'd consider moving to a different hotel?"

"Are you crazy?" she said. "Our perp knows who and where I am. If we play our cards right, we can reel him in like a big fat fish on a line."

He took a sip of strong black coffee. "This guy likes to wring necks. If he wrings yours on my watch, I'm not going to like it."

Her nostrils flared and she drew back her shoulders in a combative stance. "Are you suggesting, Lieutenant, that I can't handle myself?"

"Cut the shit, Caro. You're a woman. The guy kills

women. Young, pretty, blond women. Women who look a lot like you. That's the bottom line.''

Her cheeks flushed scarlet. She rested both hands on the edge of the table and leaned forward. ''The bottom line,'' she said heatedly, ''is that I'm a seasoned FBI agent. I've worked over two dozen serial murder cases in the last three years. I was the best marksman in my graduating class at the academy, and I have a black belt in karate. How dare you belittle what I've accomplished?''

''I don't give a damn about your credentials,'' he said, too weary to battle. ''It's your neck I'm worried about.''

''Your concern is touching, Rafferty, but it's misplaced. My neck isn't in any danger. Nor is it your responsibility, even if it were. Besides, if I did go into hiding, how do you think it would affect the case?''

He knew damn well it could derail what little of a case they had, and he wasn't any too happy knowing that he'd blow the goddamn case sky-high in an instant if he discovered that she was in jeopardy because of it. He'd always been a cop first, a man second. It was the way he was wired, and he'd never before allowed a conflict of interest to taint his handling of a case. But there was no denying that the involvement of Special Agent Carolyn Monahan in this particular case had distracted him, distorted his focus, weakened his concentration.

The food arrived and, for a time, they were silent as he concentrated on filling his hollow belly and she pushed pieces of cantaloupe around on her plate with a shiny silver teaspoon. ''The damning thing,'' she said finally, ''the thing that really gets to me, is that every one of these girls is somebody's daughter.'' She looked at him, her face ashen in the unforgiving morning light. ''Somebody's sister.'' She halted abruptly, dropped her spoon, and rubbed her eyes with the heels of her hands. "Jesus," she said, "I think I'm losing it."

Compassion stirred inside him. "You've been on your feet for too long," he said. "You need to sleep. You'll feel better afterward."

"He's out there somewhere, Rafferty. Goddamn it, he's out there somewhere and there's not a damn thing I can do about it!"

Because he understood, he said nothing. She picked up her napkin, dabbed at her mouth. "I'm going to bed," she said, pushing back her chair and fumbling in her purse. "You'll call me if—" She pulled out a crumpled five-dollar bill, shoved the long hair back over her shoulder with her free hand, and corrected herself. "When—"

"I'll call you. And put your money away. I'll take care of breakfast."

"Fair enough." She tucked the five back into her purse. "You still owe me for the Starbucks."

In spite of everything, he grinned as he watched her walk across the coffee shop, a petite blonde in jeans and Nikes and a wrinkled T-shirt, slender but with curves in all the right places. At the entrance, she paused with the plate glass door half-open and turned to see him watching her. "Get some sleep," she told him, and disappeared through the door.

There was a message waiting for her at the front desk. "Call Richard Armitage at 703-555-3812. Urgent."

"Shit," she muttered, staring at the handwriting until the letters blurred. She crumpled the note and tossed it into an ornate gold-trimmed wastebasket on her way to the elevator. She'd get back to him when she was damn good and ready. He no longer had any power over her, personally or professionally. For seven years, she'd played by the rules, never made a misstep, maintained her composure under the most trying of circumstances.

But this case was different. There was something eerily personal about it, something she couldn't fully explain to Richard Armitage, or even to herself. Maybe it was being here in Boston, on home turf, where she had to face the wearisome familiarity of her mother's criticism. Perhaps it was the parallels between this case and Meg's. Or maybe it was simply working so closely with Conor Rafferty that had her ready to unravel. Whatever the reason, like the Lone Ranger, she'd ridden into town on her trusty steed, and she wasn't leaving until, one way or another, this case was settled.

In her room, she double-locked the door and fell across the bed with her clothes still on. Sleep overtook her within seconds, a murky sleep filled with the images of women's faces, all of them begging for her help. When the telephone rang, she had to claw her way through a molasses-thick fog to reach consciousness.

At the other end of the line, with amazing good cheer, Rafferty said, "Rise and shine, Sleeping Beauty."

Sitting on the edge of the bed, she braced her elbows on her thighs and swept the long hair back from her face. "God," she said thickly. "What time is it?"

"Seven-thirty, give or take. We have ourselves a body, Agent Monahan."

She let out a hard exhalation of breath. Tersely, she said, "Where?"

"Behind a Dumpster in an alley off LaGrange Street. I'm on my way. Do you need a ride?"

LaGrange Street ran for a single block between Washington and Tremont, near Chinatown, in the heart of the Combat Zone. "No," she said, and ran a hand through her hair. "No, I'll meet you there. Ten minutes. Fifteen, tops."

"No need to rush, Monahan. She's already dead." He broke the connection and left her holding a silent receiver. She replaced it in its cradle and stumbled to the shower, stripping off her clothes and letting them lay where they fell.

Ten minutes later, with her Glock in its shoulder holster and her wet hair wrapped in a loose bun, she was back on the street. She ignored the row of cabs lined up outside the hotel's front entrance. She was only going a few blocks, and in downtown Boston traffic, on a weekday, it would be quicker to walk.

She hadn't been to the Zone in years, and she was surprised by the changes. On the corner of Washington and Avery, where the old Hotel Avery used to stand, there was a new high-rise complex. The notorious Naked I had been razed, and most of the XXX-rated establishments had given way to legitimate Chinese and Vietnamese businesses. The Combat Zone was losing its turf battle with Chinatown.

LaGrange Street was blocked off by a bored-looking uniform standing next to an orange sawhorse. She showed him her ID and he lifted the tape and let her through. The narrow street was crowded with vehicles. A rescue unit sat, radio squawking, beside a panel truck with the M.E.'s insignia on the side. There were a couple of black-and-whites and a dented Ford Taurus with a blue flashing light on the dash. Rafferty's? she wondered. If it was, they weren't paying lieutenants as much these days as they should. Carolyn squeezed past the black-and-whites and nodded to the Forensics guy—Ed somebody-or-other—who'd carted off the Polaroid in a plastic evidence bag last night.

The girl lay behind a rusted Dumpster, discarded like the paper cups and fast food wrappers that surrounded her. A police photographer was shooting flash pictures while a young assistant M.E. stood nearby, hands in pockets, rehashing last night's ball game with one of the paramedics. Rafferty was on his cell phone, head lowered, his hand cupped over his ear so he could hear. He was unshaven, still wearing the Levi's and the loafers without socks that he'd thrown on when she dragged him out of bed last night. If he'd managed to catch any sleep, he hadn't done it at home.

Carolyn stepped closer to the body and knelt to take a look. The victim lay on her hip, her arm flung out and one knee drawn up as though she'd been tossed there like a sack of garbage. Her hair was tangled with dried leaves and debris. Judging from the condition of the body, Caro estimated that she'd been dead for about ten or eleven hours. That was consistent with the time frame they'd established, based on the time she'd received the Polaroid.

Carolyn got up, skirted the photographer and walked to the end of the alley. Unlike most of Boston's numerous alleys, this one didn't go straight through to the next block. Instead, it ended in a solid brick wall, and appeared to serve mainly as a parking space and rear entrance for the businesses that flanked it on either side.

She turned and walked back past the body to the street. To her right was a boarded-up storefront, to her left an anonymous-looking brick building with a heavy steel door and a neon sign overhead proclaiming it the Golden Pussycat. On the door, stenciled in black lettering, were the words Under 21 Strictly Prohibited. From where she stood, she could see both ends of the block-long street. Traffic on Tremont passed by at a rapid clip, pausing only when the light at the intersection with Stuart turned red.

On Washington, traffic moved in the opposite direction, traveling more slowly but paying little heed to LaGrange Street or its frenzy of unusual activity.

When she turned back to the alley, Rafferty was making his way toward her. He eyed her up and down, pausing when he reached the five-hundred-dollar shoes, before raising his eyes back to hers. Crisply, he said, "You're looking good on two hours of sleep."

"And you're looking lousy on none." It was a lie. Even unshaven and wrinkled and starting on his second twenty-four-hour round without sleep, he still looked good enough to make her insides clench into a tight ball. She drew in a deep breath, exhaled it. "Something feels different about this one."

"You weren't at the other crime scenes."

"No, but I saw the pictures. I read the reports. I've crawled inside this guy's head, Rafferty. This doesn't feel like the others."

His weariness was evident as he ran a hand through the whisker stubble on his cheek. "If you tell me that our perp didn't do this one, Monahan, I may strangle you myself."

"He did it. There's no doubt in my mind. But it's highly unusual for a sexual predator to change his signature in the middle of a series of crimes."

"Meaning?"

"All the other victims were left in heavy traffic locations. As you put it yourself, the guy was looking to give the tourists more bang for their buck. He's a show-off. He wanted his victims found quickly. And publicly. That's his reward for all his hard work. It's what gets him off. But this one—" She looked around her, at a seedy neighborhood that was gradually evolving from bad to worse. "LaGrange Street isn't exactly City Hall Plaza.

Most of the action around here takes place after dark. He wasn't in any hurry for this one to be found. And she wasn't posed like the others. No scarf, no panties, no earring. This one was just unceremoniously dumped, like yesterday's garbage."

"What do you think it means?"

She considered it at length. "I think it means that this one wasn't random."

His eyes narrowed, focused on her face. "You think he knew her."

"It's possible. It's possible that he knew her and was angry with her, and that's why he killed her like he did the others. I wish I knew what he did with her clothes. Have your people searched the Dumpster?"

"Not yet, but we plan to as soon as the body's gone."

"Good. I'd recommend that you also search everything within a radius of four or five blocks. Trash cans, Dumpsters, alleys. Talk to the street people, see if any of them have found any bundles of women's clothing. We haven't found clothes yet from any of the other victims. He's probably keeping them somewhere as trophies. But if he ditched her clothes, it would tell us that this one was personal, that he killed her not for sexual satisfaction, but because for some reason he was royally pissed off at her."

"So why bother to send you the picture, if this one was personal?"

"He's playing a cat-and-mouse game. It's an intellectual exercise, like playing chess. Sometimes I'm the cat, sometimes I'm the mouse, depending on whose move it is. He wants to prove to the world that he can outsmart his opponent."

"And he's chosen you as his primary opponent."

She turned around, taking a final look at the crime scene. "Your turn for a gold star, Lieutenant."

* * *

When he got back to City Hall, he found a half-dozen print media people camped out in the lobby. They descended on him, shouting his name, clamoring for information. "No comment," he growled as he shoved past them.

"The public has a right to know!" The voice echoed above all the others, bouncing off the hard surfaces in the cavernous lobby and seeming to come at him from all directions at once. "If women are in danger, they have a right to protect themselves!"

Jessica Ames of the *Herald* had a reputation for toughness and tenacity, and her point was valid. Thinking of his own sister, his own mother, he wheeled around and spoke directly to Ames, ignoring the others.

"Tell your readers to use common sense. Keep their doors locked. Don't walk alone at night. Never get in a car with a stranger. Never take anything, or anyone, at face value. Be a little extra cautious."

"What about last night's murder?" asked a young Asian-American reporter. "Can you confirm that this is connected to the others? Who was the victim? What are you doing to catch the killer?"

"It's too early at this point in time to make any kind of public comment. When we have something, you'll hear." Without another word, he turned and strode toward the elevators.

Twenty minutes later, he was standing at the water fountain, filling a paper cup with water, when Ted Rizzoli came into the office looking like he'd either gotten drunk last night or should have. Rizzoli passed him without speaking, slammed his car keys and a stack of file folders on his desk, and went to the coffeemaker to pour himself a cup. Lorna Abrams looked up from her computer keyboard and met Conor's eyes. He raised an eyebrow, and she shrugged.

"Hey, Ted," she said, swiveling around in her chair. "Where were you last night?"

Rizzoli stirred sugar into his coffee and took a sip. His back to both of them, he said stiffly, "I was out. You got a problem with that?"

Lorna clamped her mouth shut, and Conor stepped away from the fountain. "Rizzoli," he said.

Still not looking at him, Rizzoli said, "Yeah?"

"My office. Right now."

This was the part of the job he hated most, having to reprimand one of his people when he knew how much heart, how much soul, they poured into what was essentially a thankless job. In Rizzoli's case, he would need to approach the situation with some delicacy. His promotion to lieutenant didn't sit well with Ted, who'd been with the Department five years longer and, since Ted's transfer from Vice to Homicide six months ago, their working relationship had been sticky. But he couldn't let the situation continue indefinitely without addressing it. For weeks now, Rizzoli's attitude had been insufferable, and he'd already let it go on for far too long.

"Sit down," he said, shutting the door behind them and walking around the desk. While Rizzoli slouched in the wooden chair across from him, Conor picked up a sheet of paper and began fashioning it into a paper airplane. Folding it meticulously into two halves, he said, "Care to share what's got your ass in a pucker?"

"Not particularly," Rizzoli said.

He glanced up. Rizzoli's body language clearly said *back off*. Smoothing a crease with the tip of his finger, he said, "Is it the case?"

"Look—" Rizzoli stood and began walking around the

office "—I just have a lot going on in my life right now. That's all."

"I understand that. Just like you understand that you're not supposed to bring it to work with you. You're a cop, Rizzoli. You're supposed to check all that baggage at the door when you walk through it. People's lives depend on you functioning at one hundred percent capacity."

Rizzoli maintained a stony silence.

Rafferty sighed and abandoned his marvel of engineering. "Look, Ted, when Shaughnessey asked me to head up this task force, he gave me free rein to pick my own people. I chose you and Abrams because you both do good, solid police work. But lately, you don't seem to give a damn. Maybe you're burned-out. Maybe you're just overtired. Christ knows, we all are. But Abrams is your partner, and it's not fair to her. If you want out, just say so. You can go back to your regular duties, and I'll assign somebody else to work with Lorna. I'm an easy guy to get along with. I'm flexible. But if you won't talk to me, won't tell me what's wrong, I have no way of knowing how to fix it."

Rizzoli stood before the bulletin board, coffee cup in hand, shoulders squared stubbornly. Without inflection, he said, "Jeannie left me. For good this time. She took the kids with her and left for her sister's place in California three weeks ago."

All the pieces fell into place. The lousy attitude, the late nights, the hungover mornings. Ted and Jeannie Rizzoli had been having marital problems for months, and they'd already been through several trial separations. This had to be killing him. Losing Jeannie was bad enough, but his two daughters were Ted Rizzoli's life.

"Shit, Ted," he said, "I'm sorry."

Still not looking at him, Rizzoli shrugged.

Conor picked up a pen from the desk and turned it, end over end, between his fingers. "Maybe you should take some time off. Get yourself straightened out."

Rizzoli finally looked at him. "I need to be working, Conor. Otherwise, I'll go crazy."

He set down the pen. "All right," he said. "But try to go a little easier on people. And you might want to talk to Lorna."

"Yeah. Okay." Rizzoli paused, hand on the doorknob. "Lieutenant?" he said.

"Yes?"

"Thanks."

When Rizzoli was gone, he let out a hard breath and leaned back in the chair to stare at the ceiling. The past twenty-four hours had left him drained. As if it weren't bad enough that the hotel's security tape had revealed nothing, Abrams's and Lassiter's interviews had been a dead end, too. Nobody on duty at the Boylston had seen anything suspicious. There was an unlocked employee entrance at the back of the building that the perp could have used without being noticed. If he'd even delivered the envelope himself, which wasn't by any means a certainty. Forensics hadn't found any prints on the envelope, and now he had another Jane Doe on his hands and a pack of bloodthirsty reporters screaming for some kind of official statement.

This morning, he'd spoken on the phone with Police Commissioner Randall Bradford. To say that Bradford wasn't happy about the latest developments would be a vast understatement. Although the brass was scrambling to put some kind of spin on this mess before it got any worse, Bradford had made it plain that responsibility for clearing the case lay squarely on the shoulders of Lieutenant Conor Rafferty.

While he had the commissioner on the phone, he'd raised the question of whether it would be advantageous to put a tracer on Carolyn Monahan's phone line at the Boylston. He hadn't gotten a straight answer. The Boylston House was owned by a group of wealthy investors led by one Francis Valeriani, a Revere businessman reputed to have mob connections, and Bradford's desire to close the case was inversely proportionate to his desire to make enemies in high places.

Politics. Always politics getting in the way. In Boston, those politics had a history of smelling worse than Boston Harbor on a bad day. Growing up in Southie, hanging around his father's bar, he'd listened by the hour to Hugh Rafferty and his cronies lamenting the sad state of local politics. Like it or not, the police commissioner was a political appointee. It didn't take an Einstein to figure out that no political appointee who wanted to keep his job was eager to step on the toes of anybody with the kind of power Valeriani possessed.

Not that he'd ever heard the merest suggestion that Bradford was dirty. Not even so much as a whisper. The commissioner had always conducted himself with dignity. But the reality of Boston politics was that everywhere Rafferty turned in this investigation, he ran up against one brick wall or another. It was maddening, and just one of the reasons he'd begun to question his own future as a member of Boston's finest.

There was a knock on his door. "Yes?" he said, and sat straighter in the chair.

The door opened, and Lorna came in and closed it behind her. "You know," she said, leaning against the door, "in spite of what you may believe, you're not single-handedly responsible for this investigation. That's why you have us. We're called support staff."

Relaxing, he leaned on his elbows over the desk. He and Lorna went back a long way, all the way to the police academy. "Right," he said. "Why don't you go tell that to Bradford?"

"Conor, you're dead on your feet. Go home and get some sleep."

He eyed her speculatively. "And how much sleep have you had?"

"More than you," she said. "Go home."

"I can't." He leaned back on his tailbone. "We still don't have an ID on this morning's victim, and the commissioner's planning a news conference as soon as the spin doctors decide what to tell the media. Meanwhile, I have this nutcase running around town, leaving a trail of bodies behind him and thumbing his nose at me while he does it. If I jump ship now, Bradford will cut out my heart."

She crossed her arms over her chest and gave him a wry grin. "Just think. Only thirty more years to retirement."

"Thanks so much. You really know how to hurt a guy."

"There is one thing," she said. "You might want to consider changing your clothes. If you show up for a press conference in jeans and a T-shirt, it probably won't do much to boost our confidence rating with the citizenry."

He glanced down at himself, surprised to discover he was still wearing last night's clothes, and uttered a weary expletive.

"Go home, Conor," Lorna said. "Get a shower, shave that gorgeous face, and change your clothes. You'll feel better afterward. Rizzoli and I will hold down the fort."

Her name was Tonia Lavoie, and she worked as an exotic dancer at the Golden Pussycat. They'd made the

ID easily from her prints; Lavoie had been hauled in three or four times for prostitution and a couple of times for possession of a controlled substance. The only next of kin listed on her rap sheet was a boyfriend named Eric Dudley, with whom she shared an apartment on Columbus Avenue, in the South End.

Freshly showered and shaven and fortified with a thirty-minute power nap and a cup of Starbucks, Rafferty found Caro sitting at his desk, hunched over a pile of paperwork.

"We just got an ID on the victim," he said. "I'm headed over to talk to the boyfriend. You want to come along?"

She dropped her pen and scooped a stack of manila file folders into her briefcase. "I wouldn't miss it for the world."

The South End, formerly a crumbling inner-city neighborhood, was undergoing the painful process of gentrification, a process that had not yet reached the Dudley-Lavoie residence. The house was an old redbrick brownstone like a thousand others in Boston, the copper trim on its bay windows turned green by time and oxidation. The front door was missing, and a couple of the windows on the ground floor were boarded up.

"Home, sweet home," Carolyn said as they climbed the steps from the sidewalk.

Patches of stained wallpaper hung loose from the wall near the stairs, and a bag of garbage had been ripped open, its contents strewn in an aromatic trail along the shadowy corridor. Judging by the odor, it had been here for a while. They paused in the entry to read the names on the mailboxes. Dudley and Lavoie were on the third floor. Peering up the gloomy stairwell, he said darkly, "Cover my back. I'm going in."

"Your humor is underwhelming, Rafferty," she said. "And *you* can cover *my* back."

He followed her up the stairs into the stale darkness. On the landing above them, something scurried away at their approach. She stumbled over a loose tread and he caught her by the elbow to steady her. "Watch your step," he said.

"I can manage on my own, Lieutenant."

He eyed the flimsy contraptions masquerading as shoes that she wore on her feet. It was a wonder she didn't fall and break her neck in the damn things. They were ridiculously inappropriate. Where were the stodgy, thick-soled brogans she should have been wearing? What kind of self-respecting civil servant wore bright-red fuck-me shoes on the job?

"Sorry," he said, tearing his attention away from her feet. "I have this nasty habit I can't seem to break. It's called courtesy."

He could hear the music as they climbed the stairs, savage, angry rap music, its thudding beat assaulting his senses like a series of hard slaps. The higher they climbed, the hotter and staler the air, the louder the music. On the third floor, light trickled weakly through a dirty window that faced out onto a back alley. Two anonymous doors opened onto the narrow hallway. He and Caro exchanged glances and by unspoken agreement moved simultaneously toward the source of the music.

He rapped on the door. The noise pollution continued unabated. He looked at Carolyn, and she shrugged. With his fist, he banged hard enough to buckle the wooden door. The music stopped abruptly, and a moment later, the door opened.

The man who stood in the doorway was built like a bull moose. Veins bulged in his thick neck. The front of his sleeveless gray muscle shirt was ringed with sweat. His hair was clipped short and bleached white-blond, and a gold ring adorned his nostril. Another pierced his eyebrow. One massive bicep was tattooed with a bright-blue swastika. His hands were enormous, strong enough, Rafferty noted, to choke the life out of a hundred-pound woman with virtually no effort.

"Eric Dudley?"

"Yeah," he said. "What do you want?" The bull moose stood his ground and waited.

"Lieutenant Rafferty, Boston P.D." He held up his badge. "This is Special Agent Monahan of the FBI. We'd like to talk to you."

"FBI? Shit, man, I haven't done anything."

"May we come in?" Carolyn said.

He turned without speaking. They followed him inside the apartment. Dirty clothes had been tossed around haphazardly, and the place could stand a good vacuuming, but it didn't look as bad as Rafferty had expected, given the condition of the building. The apartment was full of expensive toys: a sophisticated stereo system, a wide-screen TV, a state-of-the-art computer. Dudley walked over to an elaborate weight bench and picked up a towel, mopped his head and shoulders with it. Apparently they'd caught him in the middle of a workout.

"You lift," Rafferty observed.

"I bench-press two-fifty." Dudley lowered the towel. "So what do you want?"

"I understand that you share this apartment with Tonia Lavoie."

"Shit," Dudley said. "What'd she go and do now? She got herself arrested again, didn't she? I told her the last time that I wasn't bailing her out again. Stupid bitch."

"Mr. Dudley," Carolyn said, "maybe you'd better sit down."

He sat on the padded weight bench, his face expressionless, while Rafferty performed the duty that every cop dreaded the most.

"Dead," Dudley said blankly. "Tonia's dead?"

Watching the young man's face closely, he said, "I'm sorry."

Dudley ran a massive hand through his hair. "Shit," he said. "Oh, shit." He blinked two or three times in quick succession, and said gruffly, "Give me a minute." He stood and walked to the kitchen, braced both hands against the counter and leaned forward over it. Rafferty met Carolyn's eyes in a long, steady glance. Dudley's broad back shuddered once, twice, and then he straightened, squared his shoulders, and came back into the living room. "Dead," he repeated, as though comprehension were impossible.

Rafferty waited for him to ask what had happened to her. When the question didn't come, he leaned forward, elbows braced against his knees. "Mr. Dudley," he said, "I understand that this is difficult for you, but we need to ask you some questions."

"Questions?" Dudley's eyes narrowed. "What kind of questions?"

"Where were you last night between 6:30 and 11:00 p.m.?"

"Me?" he said. "Oh, no. You got the wrong guy. I didn't give her that shit. I don't know where she got it, but it wasn't me. I'm a bodybuilder. You couldn't pay me enough to put that poison into my body. I'm the one that kept telling her it was gonna kill her one of these days, but she wouldn't listen. She had it bad."

Rafferty cleared his throat, and Carolyn leaned forward.

"Mr. Dudley," she said with that same soothing, earnest tone she'd used with Katie Ann Perry's mother. "Tonia didn't die of a drug overdose." She turned the full force of those blue eyes on him, those eyes that were so good at sucking a man in and snaring him in her trap before he realized what was happening to him. "She was murdered. Strangled and left in the alley next to the Golden Pussycat."

Dudley gaped at her, his mouth open. "Christ," he said.

"So you can see, Eric, why we need your help. May I call you Eric?"

"I—uh, yeah. Sure."

"Eric." Her expression conveyed empathy. Understanding. "What time does Tonia usually get home from work?"

"Two, two-thirty," Dudley said. "Why?"

Rafferty glanced at the kitchen clock, prominently displayed above the sink. "It's eleven-thirty in the morning, Mr. Dudley. Almost noon. Your girlfriend never came home last night. Are you telling me you weren't at least curious about her whereabouts?"

Dudley scowled. "I'm used to it," he said. "Sometimes she disappears for days. Usually, she ends up in the drunk tank. She'll call me and I'll go bail her out."

Changing tack, he said, "Where do you work, Dudley?"

"A little health club over on Huntington. Out by Northeastern. Why?"

"Mind telling me what you do there?"

"I'm the manager. Look, I don't see what any of this has to do with Tonia."

He glanced around the apartment. "You have a lot of nice things here. The job must pay pretty well."

Dudley reddened. The color was not becoming on him. "Just what the hell are you trying to get at?"

Carolyn leaned forward again, said gently, "What kind of car do you drive, Eric?"

He looked from her to Rafferty, then back at her. "What is this, the Spanish Inquisition?"

"The lady asked you a question, Dudley. Answer it."

Dudley looked at Carolyn and his mouth worked, but no sound came out. "A fucking Hyundai," he finally said. "What difference does it make?"

"We're just trying to piece things together," she said soothingly. "So we can figure out what happened."

Dudley opened his mouth, closed it as comprehension dawned. "Christ," he said, "you think I did it. You think I killed her."

"We just want to ask some questions," Rafferty said. "It's standard procedure in a homicide investigation to question the people who were close to the victim. Husbands, boyfriends...lovers." He deliberately left the suggestion hanging there in the air.

Dudley curled his massive hands into fists, opened and then closed them again. "You think I don't know how this shit works? You think I don't know the way you people twist a man's words around until he ends up saying something he doesn't mean? Well, you're not hanging this on me, you hear? I know my rights, and I'm not saying one more goddamn word until I have my lawyer with me!" Muscles bulging, he stood, towering over both of them. "There's the door," he said, pointing. "Take it."

He didn't have to say it twice. When they reached the sidewalk, Rafferty took in a deep breath of fresh air. The apartment had been stifling. He unlocked the car and they got in. "That was productive," Carolyn said, fumbling for her seat belt.

''Maybe more than you think.'' Rafferty turned the key, and the engine came to life. ''Any impressions you'd like to share?''

''Let's say I wouldn't want to meet him in a dark alley some night. Not unless he was on my side.'' She fell silent, thinking, he supposed, of Tonia Lavoie, who had most certainly met up with someone in a dark alley and had not lived to tell about it. Instead, she had been tossed like so much rubbish behind a filthy, rusting Dumpster.

''He does have a temper,'' Rafferty said, maneuvering around construction on Columbus Ave. Driving in Boston these days was a nightmare. The whole damn city was torn up. ''He went for the bait like a rat to a trap.''

''It can be a lethal combination,'' she said. ''Muscles and a hot temper.''

''Big muscles,'' he said.

''He's certainly physically capable of the crime.''

Ahead of him, traffic was backed up at a red light. He signaled for a turn and took a sharp right down a narrow street. ''But?'' he said.

She rubbed absently at the back of her neck. ''For starters,'' she said, ''he doesn't drive the right kind of car.''

''Did you get a look at those hands of his, Monahan? He's carrying a side of beef at the end of each arm.''

''I noticed.''

''Do you mean to say you think he was telling the truth?''

''It's hard to say for sure. He seemed genuinely surprised to hear she was dead.''

Rafferty squeezed past a car that was double-parked at the curb. ''Or,'' he said dryly, ''he could be a really good actor.''

''Or he could be a really good actor.''

''Speaking of which, for a Fed, you weren't half-bad

at that good-cop-bad-cop routine. Where'd you learn that?''

"What?" she said. "You thought I slept through my classes at the Academy?"

"You're a profiler, Monahan. I thought you only shrunk heads."

"I was a field agent in Detroit for three years before I got into profiling. And in the past four years, I've interviewed more than my share of guys who make Eric Dudley look like Little Bo Peep." She leaned her head back against the seat. "You weren't so bad yourself," she said. "For a flatfoot."

"Hey, watch it." His cell phone rang, and he clutched the wheel with his left hand and flipped it open with his right. "Yeah," he said.

"Conor?" Lorna Abrams said. "Where the hell are you? We have a press conference scheduled to start in a half hour, the place is crawling with media people, and the commissioner and his cronies have been cooling their heels in your office for the past twenty minutes. He wants to meet with you for a briefing before the conference."

"Shit," he said.

"That's precisely what's about to hit the fan if you don't show your face in the next five minutes. Where's our illustrious profiler? He's been asking for her, too."

"She's with me," he said. "I'm just turning onto Charles. I'll take a shortcut over the Hill. Five minutes, tops. I don't suppose you know any tap dance routines?"

"Are you kidding? I've already been dancing for twenty minutes."

"While you're on your toes, get somebody to run me a sheet on one Eric Dudley. That's D-U-D-L-E-Y. He lives on Columbus and works in a health club on

Huntington. Anything you can find. This guy smells like he has priors.''

He made it in four minutes, some kind of a record for downtown Boston. City Hall was surrounded by media vehicles, SUVs and vans and panel trucks with TV and radio station call letters on the side. Near the main entrance, a young black woman holding a microphone was talking earnestly into the lens of a television camera. Sidestepping the electrical cables that were snaked all over the lobby, he and Carolyn ignored the reporters, bypassed the elevators, and took the stairs.

Lorna was waiting on the fourth-floor landing. ''Thank God you're here,'' she said, falling into step with them. ''Lassiter's in there right now, briefing him on last night's fiasco at the Boylston House.''

''Wonderful. We'll look even more incompetent. Anything on Dudley?''

''Isabel's working on it. Your tie's crooked.'' Lorna paused outside the closed door to his office, and her quick and capable hands untied and reknotted his tie, smoothing it into place. ''There,'' she said. ''Kick some ass, Lieutenant.''

He reached for the door knob and made a sweeping gesture to Carolyn. ''After you, Agent Monahan,'' he said, and followed her into the room.

Commissioner Bradford was seated behind Rafferty's desk, looking down his aristocratic nose at the cup of sludge somebody had brought him from the coffee machine. A tall, rawboned man with sandy hair that was running to gray, Bradford was flanked on either side by the politicos he'd brought along to witness the carnage. At his right elbow was Captain James Brooks, without whom Bradford was rumored to never make a move. To his left, leaning against the wall, wearing a pale-yellow power tie and an expensive navy three-piece suit, was Jeff Cranston, the mayor's chief spin doctor.

Rafferty made quick introductions, and Bradford got right down to business. "Mayor Reardon and I," he said, "have decided that our wisest course of action at this point in time is to appeal to the public to help us catch this madman."

"Excuse me?" Rafferty said, gaping at Bradford, not believing what his brain was telling him he'd just heard. "You want to do *what?*"

Bradford leaned forward in his chair. "The mayor and I discussed it at length this morning. Even with the FBI's help—" he nodded in Carolyn's direction to acknowledge her presence "—we're making no headway with this case."

"With all due respect, sir," Rafferty said, "I think we'd be making a mistake. A mistake of epic proportions. And you have to give Agent Monahan a little time. She's only been on the case for a couple of days."

Cranston stepped away from the wall. "We have to do something, Lieutenant," he said waspishly. "Women are being murdered out there. It makes us all look like incompetent idiots."

And does nothing for the mayor's reelection campaign, he thought, but didn't say it out loud. Instead, he said, "Might I remind you gentlemen of what happened in a similar case, right here in Boston, almost forty years ago? The media riled up the public, and there was mass hysteria. Women were calling to turn in their husbands as punishment for running around on them. Little old ladies with nothing better to do were spying on their neighbors and keeping records of their comings and goings. Everybody suspected somebody, and every one of them had the Department's number and a busy dialing finger."

"Your point, Lieutenant?" Bradford said.

"My point is this—every one of those leads had to be checked out. The department wasted countless man-hours, and it got them absolutely nowhere. The Boston Strangler was never convicted, and to this day, we don't know for sure that the man who confessed actually did the killings. If we ask the public for help, this case will turn into the same kind of fiasco that one did."

"On the other hand," Carolyn said, "Ted Bundy was caught after the police distributed a composite drawing to the media."

Rafferty glared at her, and she folded her arms and held her ground. "Look," he said, speaking directly to her, "there are six daily newspapers sitting out there. A handful of weeklies. Half a dozen radio stations, and every goddamn TV network except ESPN. If we hand them something like this, it'll turn into a freaking media circus. We can't handle the workload we have now. How are we supposed to handle it when it quadruples overnight?"

Bradford studied him thoughtfully, fingers tapping the edge of the table. "Agent Monahan?" he said. "You've been through this kind of thing before. Would you care to address Lieutenant Rafferty's concerns?"

"I share the lieutenant's concerns," she said. "If you're going to invite the public to help solve this case, you're going to have to make available the manpower to handle the substantial influx of leads you're going to generate."

Bradford continued to tap his fingers. "How many people do you have working the task force, Lieutenant?"

Rafferty let out a hard breath. "Six detectives, three clerical people, and myself." He glanced over at Carolyn and she held his gaze. He cleared his throat. "And, of course," he said, "Agent Monahan."

"Fine. We'll pull a half-dozen detectives from other divisions to assist you."

"We need Homicide detectives," Rafferty said. "They're the only ones properly trained to do the job."

"Then we'll pull them from Homicide."

"I'm not sure the division can function fully if we pull any more officers. We had a stabbing this morning in the Fens, a guy in East Boston last night who decided to chop his wife into pieces with a kitchen knife and bury her in the backyard, and two separate drive-by shootings yesterday in Dorchester. People aren't going to conveniently stop killing each other so that we can concentrate our efforts on this case."

"It's already been decided," Bradford said flatly. "This is the Department's official position. Find a way to work with it, Lieutenant, or we'll find somebody else who can."

6

There were men who had temper tantrums when they were angry, men who struck out at anyone and everyone within arm's reach, men who ensured that everybody within hearing distance knew they were royally pissed. Conor Rafferty, on the other hand, was the kind of man whose silence grew in direct proportion to his escalating temper. But his body language was eloquent. He stalked from the lobby to his office, his jaw squared and his shoulders thrown back, and anybody who got a good look at his face as he passed was suddenly very busy doing something that required their full attention elsewhere.

Carolyn was following so closely on his heels that when he flung his office door shut behind him, he nearly hit her in the face. She closed the door quietly behind her and watched as he walked around the desk and began rummaging through the papers piled neatly on the desk blotter. When he didn't find what he was looking for, he picked up the phone and pushed a button.

"Isabel," he said brusquely. "What do we have on Dudley?" With the phone cradled between his ear and his shoulder, he leaned forward and went through the stack a second time. "I don't see it," he said. "It's not here."

Carolyn walked across the room, leaned over the desk, and pulled a sheaf of paperwork from the stack. Rafferty looked at it, and his eyes narrowed. "Never mind," he said into the phone, and replaced the receiver firmly in its cradle.

He reached for the paperwork, but she held it out of his reach. "I'm back on your shit list," she said, "aren't I?"

"Give it to me, Monahan."

"Damn it, Rafferty, he already had his mind made up. No matter what I said, it wouldn't have made a difference."

Those green eyes went hard and flat. "Carolyn," he said coldly, "give me the goddamn rap sheet."

"I did you a favor," she said. "I got you six more people."

"To do four times the work. I'm afraid your mathematical computations are a little screwy."

"If I'd kept my mouth shut, you'd be doing four times the work *without* the six goddamn people!"

"They'll be worthless anyway. We can't afford to lose six people from Homicide. They'll have to come from somewhere else. How the hell can I run a serial homicide investigation without trained Homicide cops?"

"It's not my fault! What I said was true. There's a slim chance that it could actually work."

"*Slim* being the operative word."

"Look," she said, "somebody out there has to know this guy. Somebody out there has to know something. Maybe it's something they don't even realize they know. But if we can get it out of them, we could wrap up this case, and I could go home to Virginia."

"Any time you want to go back to Virginia," he said, "be my guest. I don't want you here anyway."

She leaned over the desk. "Listen, Rafferty," she said, "if you think you're going to scare me off this case, you're having pipe dreams, because it's not going to happen. I'm sticking, and I don't give a damn how mad you are at me."

"I'm not mad at you."

"Then why the hell are you being such a jackass?"

He took off his suit coat and hung it on the coat rack behind his desk. Beneath his shoulder holster, his white cotton dress shirt was wrinkled. He sat in his chair and rolled it close to the desk. Wearily, he said, "I just got a public dressing-down from the police commissioner. Then I had to sit through that farce of a press conference and pretend that I meant every single word the spin doctors had put into my mouth. I have bodies stacking up like cordwood, an investigation that's about to spiral out of control, and in the past—" he glanced at his watch "—thirty or so hours, I've had approximately forty-five minutes of sleep. You want to know why I'm acting like a jackass? That's why. It has nothing to do with you."

His words had the intended effect. She felt herself redden. "I'm sorry," she said, sheepishly handing over the sheaf of papers. "We're all tired. And of course, it's hardest on you, because you're the one with all the responsibility."

"Thank you." He took the sheet from her and began reading it, while she stood there, uncertain of what to do next. He glanced up from his reading. "What?" he said irritably. "You're still here?"

"I don't have any place to go. I'm living out of a briefcase, in case you've forgotten."

He dropped the papers and sighed. "I'll see if Isabel can dig up some office space for you."

Stiffly, she said, "Thank you."

There was a soft rap on the door. "Yes?" Rafferty said.

The door opened, and a familiar head poked into the office. Father Clancy Donovan looked from Rafferty to

Carolyn and back to Rafferty again. "Hi," he said. "Am I interrupting something?"

"No," Rafferty said flatly. "Agent Monahan was just leaving."

"Good," the priest said. "She's the one I was looking for, anyway."

"Go," Rafferty told her. "Vamoose. I'll talk to you later."

She lifted her briefcase and turned to Clancy. "What can I do for you, Father Donovan?"

"If you can spare an hour," he said, "I thought you might take a ride with me. I have something I want to show you."

"Hey, Monahan, before you go—"

She swung around to face Rafferty. "What now?" she said.

His green eyes softened as his bad humor began to dissipate. "I lied."

She brushed a stray wisp of hair back from her face and tucked it into the bun at the back of her neck. "About what?" she said.

"When I said I didn't want you here anyway. I was lying."

The heat began somewhere deep in her belly, spread like warm honey through her body, tickled her fingers and her toes. She escaped before he could see the hot flush on her cheeks, and fell into step with the priest.

"It looks like I stepped in it again," she said.

They stopped at the elevator, and Clancy pushed the button. "How's that?"

"With Rafferty. He's so damn touchy. He runs hot and cold, sometimes both at the same time. Is he always like this?"

The elevator doors opened, and they stepped inside. "I

think the case is getting to him,'' Clancy said. ''And then, of course, there's you.''

The elevator began to descend. ''Me?'' she said. ''What about me?''

''The attraction's still there between you. I suspect it's driving him crazy.''

She felt the flush climbing her cheeks again. ''Don't be ridiculous.''

''Now, Caro,'' he said, ''it's not nice to lie to a priest.''

''You and my mother. Both of you are determined to keep my soul from burning in hell. Okay, Father, you want the truth? Fine. Every time I look at him, I feel like I just got kicked hard in the gut. Is that the kind of truth you're looking for?''

The elevator reached the lobby. The doors opened, and they stepped out. ''I don't suppose it's occurred to you,'' he said as they crossed the lobby, ''that Conor's probably going through the same thing every time he looks at you?''

''No.''

''Then maybe you're not looking closely enough.'' They reached the door, and he held it open for her. ''My car or yours?''

''Where are we going?''

''Braintree. But it'll have to be a quick trip. I have a marriage counseling session with a couple of my parishioners at two.''

''In that case,'' she said, ''why don't I meet you at the church and we can ride together from there? That way, you won't have to bring me back downtown.''

At midday, traffic between downtown and South Boston was horrific. She spent ten tedious minutes that felt more like an hour following a gravel truck that was traveling at the speed of a slug. When she finally reached

Saint Bart's, she found Clancy waiting next to a conservative blue Saturn sedan, wistfully eyeing her Mitsubishi sports car.

"Why don't we take my car?" she said. "Would you like to drive?"

"No," he said. "I couldn't. Really." But he continued to gaze at the little red sports car with the same longing another man might have shown for a particularly attractive but unattainable woman.

"Of course you can." Carolyn opened the driver's door and climbed out. "She's all yours, Father. Open her up and see what she'll do. Just try to keep it under a hundred."

Clancy folded his lanky frame behind the wheel and adjusted his seat belt, his mirrors. He rested a hand on the gearshift, ran through the gears a couple of times. "It's been a long time," he said, "since I drove anything like this."

"It'll come back to you," she said. "It's like sex. You never forget how." She realized what she'd said, and who she'd said it to, and she closed her eyes in mortification. "I'm sorry, Father. It's just that I have trouble sometimes remembering that you're a priest."

"It's all right, Caro. I've heard the word a time or two before. And although I may be living a celibate existence these days, there are certain things I remember with considerable fondness."

"And you're not afraid God will strike you dead for having such impure thoughts?"

He backed the Mitsubishi slowly and cautiously into the street, shifted it into first gear. "I prefer to think that He has a sense of humor. Hold on." He popped the clutch and shot down the street, laying a good fifty feet of rubber behind him.

Once she regained her equilibrium, Carolyn held on. There was little else she could do. When they reached the Southeast Expressway, he stepped down hard on the accelerator, driving fast and aggressively, darting in and out between cars with the classic insouciance of a born Boston driver. Carolyn gripped the armrest and kept her mouth shut, hoping there was some truth to the bumper sticker philosophy that God was his co-pilot.

They arrived alive, and Carolyn was certain she would never again look at solid ground in quite the same way. He pulled up to the curb in front of a small bungalow on a quiet residential street. A discreet sign tacked up next to the front door identified it as the Erin J. Donovan House. "My pet project," he said. "Come on in. I'll show you around."

They were greeted at the door by a small furry dog who yapped ferociously but remained at a safe distance, just in case they really were intruders. "Hey, Pepper," Clancy said, bending to scratch the dog's head. The dog stopped yapping and began to wag all over. In the living room, a slender teenage girl was sprawled on the couch, paying more attention to the toenails she was painting than to the television program droning in the background. She saw them, and her face lit up.

"Father Donovan!" she said. "You did come!"

"I told you I'd be stopping by today. How's summer school going?"

The girl rolled her eyes. "It's the pits. But I don't have a choice if I want to graduate next year."

"I'd like you to meet a friend of mine," he said. "This is Carolyn Monahan. She's an FBI agent. Caro, this is Melody."

Melody's eyes widened. "You're an FBI agent? For real?"

"For real," Carolyn said.

"Cool. Maybe you could come to my school sometime and give a talk."

"Maybe."

"Where's everybody else?" Clancy said.

"LaVonna's in the kitchen," she said. "Terry's at work. Freddie and Helen are upstairs somewhere."

"Love the nails," he said. "Great color."

Carolyn followed him to the kitchen, where a tall black woman wearing a tank top and shorts was bent over the sink, plunger in hand. She looked up at their approach. "Finally!" she said in exasperation. "About time a man walked through that door. This sink's been stopped up since breakfast." She eyed Carolyn coolly. "I hope you can do a better job of it than I have, Father."

"I'll be glad to try." Clancy unbuttoned his cuffs and rolled up his sleeves. "LaVonna, this is a friend of mine. Carolyn Monahan. We've known each other since we were kids."

The woman thawed a little. Nodding, she said, "Hey."

"Nice to meet you," Carolyn said.

"Those are some shoes, girl," LaVonna said. "You buy those around here?"

"No. They're Manolo Blahniks." At the woman's blank look, she said, "They're designer shoes. I bought these the last time I was in New York."

"Hunh. I used to have a pair looked like that. But mine came from Payless, down on Washington Street."

Clancy wrestled with the plunger. He gave it a mighty heave, and the sink began gurgling. "I think that did it," he said, and turned on the faucet to test his work. "It seems to be draining now."

"This house," LaVonna said darkly, "is going to hell in a handbasket."

Clancy tucked the plunger into the cabinet beneath the sink, rinsed his hands, and dried them with a towel. "Is something else giving you problems?"

"Besides Terry?" she said. "No more than usual."

He finished drying his hands, hung the towel on a cabinet handle. "Don't tell me she's using again."

"I got no way to prove it, Father. But I've seen enough of it to know."

Clancy sighed. "I made sure she was crystal clear on the rules last time. One more infraction, and she's out."

"I'm just telling you what I see with my own two eyes, and it ain't good."

"I'll talk to her. Come on, Caro, I want you to meet the rest of the girls."

She followed him up a steep flight of stairs. Upstairs, all the bedroom doors were open. She glimpsed neat, well-kept rooms, the beds made, no clutter anywhere. In one room, a poster of Ricky Martin hung above the headboard of the bed. In another, a plush white stuffed bear rested against a pillow. They paused before the door to the room at the end of the hall. On one of the twin beds, a blond girl was folding laundry. A plump redhead lay on the second bed, reading a paperback book. "Hi, girls," Clancy said.

"Hey, Father," said the red-haired girl, closing her book. "How goes the battle?"

"Oh," he said with a shrug, "you know how it goes. Some days you're the windshield, some days you're the bug."

"Ain't it the truth. Who's your friend?"

"This is Carolyn Monahan. Caro, this is Freddie."

"Frederika," the girl said. "But everybody calls me Freddie."

"And this shy young lady—" He reached out to ruffle the hair of the young girl folding laundry, "is Helen."

"It's nice to meet both of you," Carolyn said.

"I got my GED," Helen announced timidly. "It came in the mail yesterday."

"Way to go! I told you, didn't I? I told her she could do it, didn't I, Freddie?"

They chatted for another fifteen minutes, until Clancy glanced at his watch and said, "I'd love to stay longer, girls, but we have to run, or I'll be late for my afternoon appointment."

Melody followed them to the door and stood there holding Pepper, watching them as they walked to the car. Clancy tossed Caro the keys. "You can drive now," he said. "I got my little taste of the secular life. It should hold me for the next little while."

For the first time in years, Carolyn drove sedately. "So," Clancy said, leaning his seat back at an angle. "What did you think?"

"I think, Father Donovan, that you have a number of ardent admirers. Do you intend to tell me their story, or leave me guessing?"

"I intend to tell you. What did you think of Melody?"

"She's adorable. A real doll."

"She's HIV-positive."

"Dear God. How old is she?"

"Fifteen. She picked it up from some john on the street. She's a prostitute, Caro. They're all prostitutes. Or they were, before I pulled them off the streets and gave them a second chance at life."

"The Erin J. Donovan House," she said slowly. "Of course."

"They were all ready to leave the life behind. I just gave them the opportunity."

"And the Church is financing the program?"

"Fifty percent of it. The girls are expected to be either in an educational program or gainfully employed. The ones who are working contribute half their weekly earnings. The rest comes out of my pocket."

"What's the recidivism rate?"

"Surprisingly low. The program seems to be working. I just wish we could do more. At any given time, we have between five and ten residents. We don't have room for any more. They come, they go. Most of them stay until they're on their feet financially and ready to become self-supporting. Some of them are with us on a long-term basis. But there are so many of them out there on the street under the age of eighteen. It's heartbreaking."

"Don't these girls have parents?"

"Parents who are too busy to care. Or parents who've tried and failed so many times, they've given up. Some of our girls are of legal age, and their parents no longer have any say in their lives. Some, like Melody, are second-generation prostitutes. Their mothers worked the streets before they did. Every girl has her own unique story."

She saw in her mind a vivid picture of Erin Donovan, Clancy's mother, who had turned tricks on the docks of South Boston to put clothes on his back and food in his mouth during hard times. Erin had died five years ago from AIDS. "Jesus," she said, and blinked back tears.

"Yes," he said. "Exactly."

"Father Donovan," she said, "you are truly one of the good guys. I just wish there were more like you out there."

Eric Dudley had a rap sheet as long as the Tobin Bridge and twice as ugly, and Rafferty was diligently combing through it when the phone rang. "Lieutenant Rafferty," he said distractedly.

"Hey, bro, what's happening?"

He set down the sheet and rubbed the back of his neck. "Frankie," he said, trying to hold back his irritation. The last voice he wanted to hear right now was that of his older brother. "What's up?"

"I just wanted to remind you about Josie's birthday party tomorrow afternoon. Mom's afraid you'll forget."

"Tomorrow?" he said. "I don't remember hearing anything about a party tomorrow."

"Jesus, Con, Mom said she told you three weeks ago so you'd have plenty of advance planning time. Where the hell is your head at these days?"

"I'm running a murder investigation, Frankie. I'm busy. I don't remember everything. And I haven't talked to Mom in—"

"Weeks. I know. She's been bitching about it to anybody who'll listen."

The day had started out lousy and was going steadily downhill from there. "Look," he said, "I don't know if I can make it. I'm in the middle of a disaster here. I don't think I can take the time off."

"Tomorrow's Sunday," Frank said. "You do remember Sunday, don't you? The day of rest?"

He let out a small snort of laughter. "I'll keep that in mind."

"Hey," his brother said, "you want to let Josie down, it's no skin off my teeth. Just remember that Mom has her ways of making people pay for their transgressions. And right now, you're pretty high on her list of sinners."

He sighed, knowing he was defeated. "Where and what time?" he said.

"Noon at Josie's. Bring your appetite. We'll supply the food."

He hung up the phone, wondering when his life had gone spinning completely out of control. When he looked up, Carolyn Monahan was standing in his doorway, looking cool and imperturbable, her briefcase in one hand, a white paper take-out bag in the other. At the sight of her, the muscles in his thighs clenched involuntarily. Rafferty opened his mouth to say something pithy and intelligent. What came out instead was, "I like your hair better down."

She raised a single elegant blond eyebrow. "Excuse me, Lieutenant?"

He was losing his mind. There was no other explanation for the fact that his mouth had become disengaged from his brain. Pushing his chair back from the desk, he said, "Never mind. What's in the bag?"

"Peace offering. I realized it was midafternoon and I hadn't eaten since breakfast. I figured you were probably in the same boat, so I bought a couple of pita wraps. If you're really, really nice to me, I'll share with you."

He'd been too engrossed in work to notice that his stomach was scraping against his backbone, but now the hunger hit him with ferocity. "You," he said, "are a goddess. Let's take it to the conference room. There's a table in there, and I have some things I want to go over with you."

The conference room was dark. He flipped on the overhead fluorescents and they settled side by side at the gleaming wooden table. She opened the bag and took out a foil-wrapped pita.

"Here you go," she said.

"Thanks." His stomach began growling as he opened

the foil. "So," he said, "what did you think of the Erin J. Donovan House?" He took a huge bite of his pita.

Carolyn unwrapped hers and brushed crumbs from her hands. "How did you know that was where we were going?"

He chewed and swallowed. "It was my idea. I told him he should take you to see it."

"I think," she said, "that he is a most amazing man. And extremely liberal-minded, for a Roman Catholic priest."

Rafferty bit off another piece of his pita. "He's done battle with the Church," he said, and swallowed the mouthful of food, "on more than one occasion. His practices are pretty controversial, especially with the older parishioners who still remember what it was like living under the tyranny of Father O'Rourke."

"Father O'Rourke," she said. "I haven't thought of him in years. He used to terrify me."

"He was a strong believer in one of the tenets that the Catholic religion was founded upon—that winning by intimidation is infinitely preferable to losing."

"It certainly worked with me." She picked at her pita bread, pulled out a sliver of chicken and ate it. "Clancy told me that part of the financing for the Donovan House is coming out of his own pocket. That seems rather extreme."

"He's dedicated."

"Or trying to rewrite history."

He grunted noncommittally and finished off his pita. Carolyn had taken only a couple bites of hers. He eyed it, decided to go for broke. "If you're not going to eat that…"

"Here," she said, and tore it in two, sliding the larger portion down the table to him.

"You're sure?"

"Eat, Rafferty. Then you can tell me what you have on Dudley."

He inhaled the rest of the thing, and his stomach finally stopped screaming at him. Brushing the last of the crumbs from his hands, he crumpled the foil wrapping and tossed it into the bag. "While you were out gallivanting with our favorite priest, I was busy. I made a few phone calls and found out some interesting things about our friend Dudley."

She wet the tip of her finger and picked up a crumb. "Such as?"

"Such as he's been arrested no less than nine times in the last four years, primarily for domestic assault and threatening criminal behavior. I have witnesses who've heard him threaten to kill Tonia Lavoie more than once, and he sent her to the E.R. on three separate occasions in the past six months. Once with a dislocated shoulder, once with a broken finger—she claimed she shut it in a car door—and once with a split lip."

"Arrested every time?"

"Arrested, held for a few hours, and released. You know what a domestic's like. Hard to make it stick, especially when the injured party refuses to press charges."

"And that's what Lavoie did?"

"Over and over. I also talked to one of the girls she worked with at the Golden Pussycat. It seems that Dudley wasn't overly enthusiastic about her choice of a career."

"One could hardly blame him for that."

"No, but it gives him a motive for killing her."

"Okay, just for the sake of argument, let's say Dudley killed Lavoie. What about the others? What's the motive?"

"I thought serial homicide was a motiveless crime. You're the expert here. You tell me."

"That's not quite accurate. Murder is never motiveless. It may not be a motive that makes sense to you or me— greed, jealousy, hatred, rage, or any of the other standard reasons we humans have for doing away with each other. But there's always a motive, even in a sexual homicide. It may seem obscure to us, but to the killer, it's a valid motive."

"Such as," Rafferty said dryly, "the only way he can get his rocks off is with his hands wrapped tight around the throat of some gorgeous young blonde."

She smiled. "There you have it, Lieutenant. I couldn't have said it better myself."

"So why don't you like Dudley for this thing?"

"Tell me this—if you were an eighteen-year-old girl from East Bumfuck, North Dakota, who'd never spent a night away from Mommy and Daddy, and your car broke down on an expressway ramp in downtown Boston, would you get in a vehicle with a guy who looked like Eric Dudley?"

He opened his mouth to speak, exhaled a hard breath. "Shit," he said, and thought about it some more. "Shit," he said again.

"I'm not saying we should discount him as a possible suspect. I just don't think we should concentrate all our efforts on him to the point where we miss something we should have seen, simply because we weren't looking for it."

The investigative team met in the conference room late that afternoon, a short-tempered, grim-faced group of cops who were short on both sleep and patience. In spite of the air-conditioning, the room possessed the close, humid feel that came from too many bodies crowded into too small a space. There was an overlying scent of antiperspirant that disguised the subtle but acrid odor of sweat.

Caro studied some of the weary faces that lined the rectangular table. The purplish half-moon circles under Lorna's eyes could have qualified her for work as an extra in a "Thriller" remake. Rizzoli's cheeks were dark with five o'clock shadow. Aubrey Hailstock nursed fragrant, hot coffee in a plastic travel mug from 7-Eleven, tucking it closer against his chest when he saw the covetous glances of his co-workers. Even the perennially dapper Greg Lassiter wore a wrinkled shirt, and his tie had long since disappeared.

Rafferty came in and quietly shut the door behind him. His hair was mussed, as though he'd been running his fingers through it. "One of our uniforms," he said, "just found what we believe to be Tonia Lavoie's clothing in a trash can about three blocks from the scene. We've sent it to the lab for testing, but we're pretty sure it's hers. Skirt, blouse, underwear and shoes, rolled into a ball and tossed in a city trash receptacle." He glanced at Caro, and their eyes locked. She could see the fatigue in his. "Good call on that one, Monahan."

"So where does this leave us?" Lassiter asked.

"For those of you who missed this morning's little media circus, here's the word, directly from the top. As of Monday morning, we'll be working with six new detectives. They're coming in to man phone lines that will also be installed on Monday. The phone company is working on giving us a new 800 hotline number so concerned citizens can call in tips—"

"Oh, for Christ's sake," Mendez muttered.

Rafferty's mouth thinned. "My sentiments exactly. But my opinion doesn't seem to count for much around here these days. The mayor and the commissioner are both adamant that we have more warm bodies in place, and they're putting a massive amount of heat on the person in charge, namely, me. So for my sake, I'd appreciate it if you'd all just put on your smiley faces and pretend you're thrilled with the arrangement.''

Detective Kayla Smith swatted at a fly that had somehow made its way indoors and was now indolently circling the table. ''How about an update on the status of the Lavoie homicide?''

''Tonia Lavoie, twenty-eight years old, killed last night by an unknown assailant and left behind a Dumpster in the alley next to her place of employment. Nothing to indicate who her assailant might be, but Agent Monahan has an interesting theory I'd like her to share with the rest of you. Monahan?''

Carolyn cleared her throat. ''The Lavoie homicide was different from the others. The victim was not posed, there was no scarf, no panties, no earrings. She was left naked in a low-traffic location, probably in the hopes that her body wouldn't be found for a while. My theory is twofold. First, because there's no evidence that the UNSUB took any trophies, I suspect this killing wasn't motivated by a need for sexual gratification, but by anger. Instead of taking her clothes with him, he discarded them in a municipal trash can. Second, because Lavoie's body was left right outside the Golden Pussycat, where she worked, my guess would be that a) she was killed at the location where the body was found, and b) she knew her attacker.''

Detective Smith looked up from the notes she was taking. Eyebrows raised, the young woman said, ''You think she knew her attacker?''

''Think about it. Lavoie runs into somebody she knows, either inside the club or outside. She gets into his car, fully trusting, never questioning her safety because she's been in his car before. It's dark, it's late, the place isn't exactly hopping. He attacks and strangles her right there outside the club, strips her body, and tosses it into the alley. Then he drives away calmly, goes a couple of blocks and drops her clothing into a trash receptacle.''

''What leads you to believe he killed her there?'' Lassiter said.

''We know she was working last night. It makes no sense that he would have taken her somewhere else to kill her and then run the risk of being caught by bringing her body back to the club to dump it. Mr. X may take some risks, but he's not a fool. And if he'd been willing to take that kind of risk, he would have wanted to advertise it. He would have left her in plain sight, as some kind of statement.''

Smith nodded her head in agreement. ''That makes sense.''

''I also see a change in signature, which is unusual. Up until now, he's been a classic organized type. But with this killing, he's starting to exhibit some disorganized traits. This tells me he's probably starting to disintegrate.''

''If you could cut the psychobabble,'' Rizzoli said, ''and speak English, maybe we could follow what you're saying.''

A hot flush crept up her cheeks. ''Sorry,'' she said. ''I'm accustomed to dealing with people familiar with the terminology. The signature is what the UNSUB brings to the crime scene that's uniquely his. It's his raison d'etre, the thing that gets him off. No two offenders have the exact same signature, which helps us to know whether a series of crimes was committed by a single perpetrator or several.''

"Isn't that the same thing as modus operandi?" Lorna asked.

"There's a difference. Modus operandi is how. Signature is why."

Lorna nodded slowly. "So what's our boy's signature? What gets him off?"

"He wants to shock us. But, as I pointed out, this killing was different in that he didn't pose the body, didn't add his special little touches. He just killed her and got the hell out, which is why I suspect this killing wasn't planned. It was a spur-of-the-moment thing. Something Lavoie did or said upset him badly, so he killed her."

They were all looking at her now, waiting, some of them nodding agreement, others appearing more skeptical. "We've categorized serial sex offenders into two distinct types," she continued. "The organized offender is usually fairly intelligent, tends to be average or above average in looks. He's suave, a smooth talker, uses charm to ensnare his victim. He plans ahead, often carries a rape kit in his vehicle. Takes the time to clean up afterward, to stage the scene for maximum effect."

She leaned back in her chair and crossed her legs. "The disorganized offender, on the other hand, may dress or act strangely. He probably has difficulty talking to people. He's more likely to be unattractive, has a lower I.Q. than the organized offender. He's the kind of man that most women would overlook, or possibly even find frightening in appearance. Since he lacks the social skills or the intellectual capacity of the organized offender, the disorganized killer tends to approach his victims suddenly and without warning. Because his only chance is to disable his victim from the start, there's a kind of savage frenzy to his actions. His crime scenes can be messy, and he doesn't take the time to clean up afterward. Neatness isn't a necessary part of his ritual.''

In the chair beside hers, Rizzoli yawned. ''So what's the point?'' he asked.

''The point is that Mr. X is showing signs of mixed behavior. This last killing appeared unplanned, rushed. He dumped her in a place where she wasn't likely to be found for a while. He wasn't trying to prove anything to anybody, wasn't trying to shock anybody. He just wanted to be rid of her. When a killer begins to exhibit mixed traits, it's often a sign that he's starting to break down, starting to get careless. That's usually when he gets caught.''

''Jazzy little psychological theory,'' Rizzoli said. ''But I'd like to know what we're doing, besides formulating theories, to get this creep off the street.''

Caro felt as though he'd slapped her in the face. She glanced at Rafferty, sitting across the table, and saw barely concealed anger in his eyes.

''Christ Almighty, Ted,'' Lorna said, ''could you possibly be any more charming?''

''I'm tired.'' Rizzoli slouched in his chair and narrowed his eyes. ''If it doesn't interfere with your plans too much, Abrams, I'd like to go home sometime tonight.''

''We're all tired,'' Lorna said. ''That's no excuse for being rude. There's such a thing as professional courtesy, and you just stepped over the line. Agent Monahan's just doing her job.''

''What is this, some kind of sisterhood thing? I am woman, hear me roar?''

''That's enough.'' Rafferty's voice was silken and deadly. ''You can squabble when you're off duty. I'd like to move along now and hear updates from each of you. Mendez, you've been following up with friends and relatives of Lindsay Helms. You can start.''

The meeting dragged on as each detective gave a brief update on his or her progress with the investigation. Caro listened, tried to concentrate, but exhaustion was winning the battle. When the meeting finally ended, she packed her briefcase, shared a quick, searching glance with Rafferty, and headed for the elevators.

Lorna Abrams caught up with her as she was waiting for the car to reach the fourth floor. "You okay, Monahan?"

"I have a tough skin. It comes with the territory."

"Rizzoli is a shithead." The elevator arrived, the doors opened, and they stepped inside.

"I've met cops like him before," Caro said. "Loaded with self-importance and running on sexist, macho bullshit. I can handle him."

"You should try partnering with him." The elevator reached lobby level, and the doors opened. "It's a real picnic."

They stepped outside together into a late afternoon that was hot enough to make her go instantly limp. "Christ, I thought Virginia was bad," she said. "I'd forgotten how hot Boston could get in August."

"Dog days of summer," Lorna said. "The time of year when people kill each other just because they can."

"I'm too tired to care. I'm going to get in a bathtub filled to the brim with cool water and lubricate myself with a couple of Molsons. How about you?"

"Unfortunately," Lorna said as they crossed City Hall Plaza, "I have a Little League game I can't miss. But while I'm sitting there, sweating and yelling, I'll be thinking of you and your cool, comfy tub."

"Little League," Caro said wistfully. She'd never been particularly domestic, had never lamented her childless state. Yet something about Lorna's words resonated within her. "Your son plays?"

"Daughter. A lot's changed since we were kids." They reached the subway entrance, and Lorna paused. "Look," she said, "don't let Ted get to you. Believe it or not, he's a pretty good cop. He just has a rotten attitude that colors people's perceptions of him."

Caro raised an eyebrow. "You're not telling me that underneath that prickly exterior, Rizzoli's really a warm and fuzzy teddy bear?"

Lorna grinned. "I said he was a good cop. I didn't say I was crazy." She checked her watch. "Gotta run, or I'll miss the game. Ciao."

Caro stood watching as Lorna disappeared into the crush of people squeezing through the subway entrance. Then she picked up her briefcase and headed for her hotel to spend another solitary Saturday night.

7

His sister Josie lived with her son in a modest three-bedroom ranch on a postage-stamp-size lot in Revere. Rafferty turned into the driveway and parked behind his brother Frank's SUV, and beneath the sycamore tree that needed pruning. The lawn could stand a good mowing, and the paint on the eaves was peeling off in big chunks. If he ever got any time off, he intended to come over with a ladder and a saw and do some work around the place. Josie's husband, Ed Porter, had always kept the yard tidy and the house maintained. But two years ago, Josie and Ed had split. Now, Josie was left to deal with the house by herself.

He'd liked Ed Porter, had been sorry to see his sister's marriage come to an end. Ed was big and blustery, and he seemed to dote on Josie and the boy. Rafferty had never asked Josie what went wrong. If his sister had thought it was any of his business, she would have volunteered the information. It appeared to be an amicable divorce. Ed saw his son twice a month, and he gave Josie money whenever he could scrape it together. Still, Rafferty knew it was hard for her, even with Ed's help, to pay the mortgage and keep the place up.

He followed the sound of music and voices around the corner of the house, where Frank, wearing a red apron that said Kiss the Cook, was flipping steaks on Josie's backyard grill. Frank speared a huge T-bone and turned it while Sheila, his pert blond wife, busied herself setting the picnic table. Somebody had propped a set of stereo speakers in the kitchen window and was blasting Springsteen for the neighbors. In the backyard pool, five-year-old Jake and his eight-year-old cousin Brandy splashed and giggled. The twins, Teddie Jo and Belinda, watched with cool teenage disdain from a safe distance.

Normal life. Family. It had been so long since he'd seen it, he'd forgotten there was another world out there, one where death wasn't waiting around the next corner, one where he didn't have the grisly task of dealing with the dead or the overwhelming duty of avenging their deaths. He hadn't realized until now just how wrapped up in this case he really was.

His mother saw him first. "Conor!" she exclaimed, rising from her lawn chair and crossing the grass with the queenly bearing that had earned her the admiration and the hearts of men from eighteen to eighty. Fiona Rafferty, the woman against whom he'd spent his entire life measuring other women and finding them lacking.

He bent and kissed her cool cheek. "Hi, Mom," he said.

"We haven't seen you in weeks," she scolded. "Doesn't the city ever give you a day off?"

He'd never been able to make her understand that his job wasn't like everybody else's, that he couldn't manipulate his schedule to suit her plans. She'd never had to deal with the dark side of life, and, God willing, she never would.

"I'm here, aren't I?" he said, and waved a greeting to his father, stretched out on a lounge chair in the sun. "Where's Josie?"

"Inside. You look wan. Sheila, what do you think? Doesn't he look wan?"

Behind his mother's back, his sister-in-law shot him a lascivious wink. "He looks pretty good to me," she said.

"Oh, you!" his mother said good-naturedly.

He found Josie at the kitchen sink, preparing a salad. Lines bracketed her mouth, and she looked tired. His sister was a slender, dark-haired beauty who incidentally happened to have brains and one hell of a big heart to complete the package. By now, some guy should have snatched her up, some white knight with big bucks who would swoop down on her and carry her off to the life of luxury she deserved. But it hadn't happened yet, and it bothered him to think of her sleeping alone in this house, night after night. Taking out her own garbage, unclogging her own gutters, paying her own bills.

"Happy birthday, Jose," he said, bending and kissing her. "How's life treating you?"

His sister neatly cored a head of iceberg lettuce, tossed the core into the trash, and began ripping the lettuce apart. "Oh," she said, "you know how it goes. Another year older, and deeper in debt."

As he leaned against the counter to watch her work, a picture flashed through his mind, a picture of Josie and Carolyn Monahan, both of them eight years old, kneeling side by side on his mother's living room rug, their heads close together, Josie's as dark as ink, Caro's platinum blond. Back in those days, he had loved to torment them, just because that was what big brothers were supposed to do. He wondered if either of them remembered.

Josie finished with the lettuce and finally looked at him. "Jesus Christ, Conor," she said, "you look like something that crawled out of the sewer. You're working too damn hard. Mom must have had a fit when she saw you."

His grin was rueful. "She said I looked wan."

"Wan, my ass. You look like shit." Josie chose a ripe tomato, placed it on a wooden cutting board, and began slicing it with a lethal-looking knife. "I don't suppose I should even bother to ask how things are going in your life, since you don't seem to have one."

"What's that supposed to mean?"

"Look at yourself, Con. How many guys do you know who'd show up at a family barbecue wearing a dress shirt, a tie, and a loaded gun?"

His shoulder holster was so much a part of him that he'd forgotten to take it off. "I have to go back to work in a couple of hours," he said. "If you'd feel more comfortable, I could lock the gun in my trunk."

"You know," she said, "there's a psychological theory about men who feel the need to carry a loaded weapon." She sliced the tomato with rapid motions of the knife, then glanced at him innocently through lowered eyelashes. "It has something to do with feelings of inadequacy. The gun's a phallic symbol. Sort of a substitute penis."

He blinked twice in rapid succession. Then the back door swung open and his mother breezed through. *Saved by the cavalry,* he thought with immense relief. "The steaks are ready," she trilled. "How's the salad coming along?"

"Fine, Mom," Josie said. "Why don't you take the watermelon outside? Conor, toss me that green pepper over there, would you?"

He tossed it to her, hoping she'd drop the subject. But he should have known better. His mother went back outside, toting the watermelon, and Josie sliced the pepper neatly into two pieces. "Speaking of your sex life," she said, scraping out the seeds, "why didn't you bring Gwen along?"

She'd been pestering him for months to bring Gwen to a family gathering, but for some reason he'd been avoiding it. He wasn't sure which idea he found more intimidating: Gwen meeting his crazy family, or his crazy family meeting Gwen. "I never thought about it," he said. "I can only stay a couple of hours, anyway. This case has me running day and night."

"So I've heard." She deftly swiped the mess from the cutting board into the trash and began chopping the pepper into small pieces. "I hear she's a barracuda."

"Who told you that?"

"Lester. They sort of run in the same circles."

"Lester Moskowitz?" he said. "That ambulance chaser?"

She shrugged. Josie knew her divorce lawyer and friend had a less than stellar professional reputation, but it didn't seem to faze her. "In legal circles," she said, "everybody knows everybody. People talk."

He would have liked to rush to the defense of his fair lady, but truth was truth. Gwen's reputation in the courtroom was legendary. And out of the courtroom, she was a woman accustomed to getting what she wanted. "She wants to get married," he said, not sure why he'd chosen to confide in Josie.

His sister stopped chopping to stare at him in dismay. "You're not going to marry that woman?"

"Come on, Jose, don't judge her before you've even met her. You might like her. And I didn't say I was going to marry her. I said she wanted to get married."

"Are you in love with her?"

It wasn't an unreasonable question. As a matter of fact, it was the same one he'd been asking himself ever since the night Gwen had broached the topic of marriage. He respected Gwen tremendously. She was probably the most intelligent woman he knew. She was ruthless in the court-room, fully committed to her career. Driven by ambition, but that was only part of her commitment. She possessed a powerful belief in justice, a powerful vision of what was right and what was wrong. She had a tendency to carry over those beliefs, that drive, into her personal life, and as a result, she sometimes came on a bit too strong. But he understood her, understood what drove her, and he liked her in spite of it.

"Never mind," his sister said in disgust. "If you have to think about it, I guess that gives me my answer." With her knife, she scraped the chopped pepper into a huge salad bowl, and shoved the bowl into his hands. "Here. Make yourself useful."

He sat around the picnic table with them, these people who shared his blood, enjoying their interaction. His father, the grand storyteller, was always good for an after-noon's entertainment. In his line of work, Hugh Rafferty heard it all. More people dumped their problems on their local barkeep than on all the Harvard-educated shrinks in Christendom. Hugh always changed the names, of course, to protect the innocent—and the guilty—but the stories were true, enhanced with just a trace of blarney if he deemed them worthy of spicing up.

Josie blew out her birthday candles, and everybody had a slice of cake. The kids wandered off to do whatever kids do on a hot summer afternoon, leaving the adults alone at the table. He wasn't prepared for them to pounce on him *en masse,* like a pack of wolves. But that was precisely what they did. "Conor," his mother said, "we're worried about you."

He stopped chewing. Swallowing the bite of chocolate cake in his mouth, he glanced around the table at all the concerned faces. "Worried?" he said. "About what?"

"You're working too hard on this case," his father said. "It's starting to take a toll on you."

"You look like death," Josie chimed in helpfully.

"We never see you," his mother said. "You live upstairs, but your father and I never even hear you come in and out. If I didn't see your car parked in the yard, I'd think you weren't even living there anymore."

He set down his fork and wiped his mouth with his napkin. "Don't be ridiculous," he said. "I work crazy hours. You know that. I try to keep quiet so I won't bother you." He looked to his brother for support, but Frank just shrugged his shoulders. Rafferty turned back to his mother. With grim humor, he said, "What is this? An intervention?"

Ignoring him, his father said, "When was the last time you took a day off? And I don't mean a couple of hours. I mean a whole day."

"I can't take a day off. I'm carrying full responsibility for the investigation. I have to be there."

"You don't have to be there 24/7," Josie said. "Damn it, Conor, it's just a job. The world would not stop revolving if you failed to show up for work."

He looked around the table at their earnest faces, touched by their caring, wondering how he could ever make them understand that it was more than just a job. Maybe they would never understand. Maybe it was something that only another cop could understand. "I'm fine," he said. "Really."

"What you are," his mother said, "is pigheaded. You get it from me. And I'm not letting you leave here today until you promise to take some time off."

Frank spoke for the first time. "We were thinking you might want to go down to the Cape for a day or two.

Spend some time on the water. The *Lady*'s looking pretty lonely these days.''

He opened his mouth to argue, but damned if the idea didn't sound appealing. It was mid-August, and he'd only had her out twice this summer, before Shaughnessey had put him at the helm of the task force and he'd become too busy to even think about being at the helm of a sailboat. But how could he possibly take time off right now? There was nobody to turn the investigation over to, and there was a madman running around who could strike again at any minute. There were leads to check, suspects to interview—

''I'll think about it,'' he said.

His mother got that look on her face, the one they all knew meant it was time to run for cover. ''That's not acceptable,'' she said. ''I want you to promise.''

He'd learned thirty-four years ago that Fiona Rafferty was not the kind of woman a man argued with. When she put her foot down, that was it. No arguments, no questions. ''Fine,'' he conceded. ''Christ only knows how I'll pull it off, but I'll take a day off and run down to the Cape.''

He thought about it all the way back into the city. The more he thought, the more the idea appealed to him. He'd bought the *Painted Lady* three years ago, and that first summer he'd spent every spare moment on the water. The *Lady* wasn't much of a sailboat, just a single-masted fiberglass twenty-footer that he'd picked up for a couple grand from a kid in Truro whose father, a state senator, had bought him a shiny new cabin cruiser as a high school graduation gift. The kid had given him a deal on the *Lady*, and Frank and Sheila had been more than happy to let him keep her at the place on the Cape that they'd inherited from Sheila's father. In return, he let Frank take the *Lady*

out whenever he and Sheila needed to get away from the
kids for a few hours.

Task force headquarters was quiet, with a skeleton staff
minding the phones. People who had lives didn't work on
Sundays. He nodded to Detective Aubrey Hailstock as he
passed through on the way to his office. Feeling more
hopeful than he had in weeks, he leaned back in his chair,
put his feet up on the desk, and called Gwen. ''What's
your schedule look like for the next couple of weeks?''
he said.

''Dreadful.'' He heard paper rattling, and then a muffled curse.

''Problems?''

More rattling paper. ''It's this damn Heffernan case,''
she said. ''I thought it would be wrapped up in two days,
three at the most, but it looks as though it's going to drag
on for weeks. If you can believe it, I'm spending my
Sunday afternoon reading through a two-hundred-page
deposition.'' She exhaled a hard breath. ''Why do you
ask?''

''If I can work it in, I'm taking a day off to go to the
Cape, take the *Lady* out on the water. I thought maybe
you could sneak away and go with me.''

''Absolutely impossible. Any other time, I'd jump at
the chance. But I have to be in court until this case is
over, and God only knows how long that will be.'' She
sighed. ''Can I get a rain check?''

''Sure. I'll give you a call.''

He hung up the phone, feeling a little deflated. Suddenly, the last place he wanted to be on a beautiful Sunday
afternoon was here, in this stuffy room, four floors above
the city. He got up and sauntered down the corridor, stopping at the door of the cramped office space that Isabel,
his crackerjack administrative assistant, had managed to

find for Carolyn. The walls were an ugly beige, high-lighted by the single overhead fluorescent that sputtered and winked. Designed for use as a storage closet, the room was almost big enough to fit two people into, as long as neither of them tried to close the door.

Caro was bent over the desk, a frown of concentration on her face as she made notations on a computer printout. He leaned against the door frame, hands in his pockets, and studied the way all that blond hair fell around her shoulders. He wondered if it still felt as soft as he remembered.

She sensed his presence and glanced up. "Lieutenant," she said.

He jingled a fistful of coins in his pocket. "Afternoon," he said.

Her pen poised over the printout, she said, "Something I can do for you, Rafferty?"

"All work and no play," he said, "makes Caro a dull girl."

"Right," she said crisply. "I see that you're here working on a Sunday, too. What's your excuse?"

"According to my sister, I have no life." He jingled the coins again. "Buy you an ice-cream cone?"

"Make it chocolate, and you have yourself a deal."

They settled on an Italian ice from a Quincy Market vendor, chocolate for her, strawberry for him. They wandered for a while, ducking in and out among the tourists and the suburban housewives and the teenagers let loose for the summer. Past the Godiva chocolates, past Crate and Barrel, past Victoria's Secret, settling at last on a wooden bench near Faneuil Hall, cradle of liberty and purveyor of expensive and useless trinkets. "So," she said, "Josie's been giving you a hard time, has she?"

"Josie's only the tip of the iceberg. This afternoon I

went to a family barbecue. It was supposed to be a birthday party for Jose. But in reality, it was an excuse for the whole family to gang up on yours truly. I've been given an ultimatum.'' He licked at a drip of strawberry that was about to fall from his cone. ''Take some time off, or endure the wrath of Fiona Rafferty.''

''That's a no-brainer,'' she said, and nibbled delicately at her cone. ''I'd rather face a serial killer than Fiona when she's on a tear.''

''They don't understand. None of them.'' He leaned back on his tailbone, stretched out his legs. ''They don't understand how you get so wrapped up in the job that it becomes your life. It's not just what you do, it's who you are. It's your whole damn identity, and you can't stop doing it, because if you quit, you won't know who the hell you are anymore.''

''That's pretty heavy philosophy for a Sunday afternoon, Rafferty. Are you all right?''

He stared at her for a minute. ''Do you have any idea what I'm talking about?''

She studied her Italian ice. On a bench directly across from them, a small Chinese boy was trying to figure out how to eat a slice of pizza without pulling off the cheese in a single gooey thread. ''Oh, yes,'' she said softly. ''I understand.''

''So how do you deal with it?''

''The same way you do. I have no life.''

''Do they give you grief over it? Your family?'' She glanced at him, eyebrows raised, and he said, ''Never mind. Stupid question. For a minute there, I forgot that your mother's the drama queen of South Boston.''

''Actually,'' she said, eyes trained on her Italian ice, ''I did something really stupid. I had an affair with my boss. I ended it right before I came here.''

He waited for her to elaborate. When she didn't, he said steadily, "What happened?"

She looked at him over the remains of her cone. "His wife," she said, "didn't seem to appreciate it much."

Rafferty waited, and she shrugged. "And," she continued, "he made lots of pretty promises, and I was stupid enough to fall for every one of them. Hook, line and sinker. Until I found out about the nineteen-year-old bimbo he'd started squiring around town. That was when I finally came to my senses and broke it off."

He was silent, not sure how to respond. If she'd intended to shock him, it hadn't worked.

"Sometimes," she added, "when you don't have anything, you'll settle for whatever you can get."

"Christ, Carolyn, you don't have to settle."

She leaned back against the bench and studied his face. "We've finally gotten past it, haven't we?"

"Past what?"

"You. Me. Ten years ago. You've stopped being mad at me."

"I was never mad at you."

"You didn't want me here when I first arrived."

He got up from the bench, tossed his napkin and what was left of his cone into a trash can. "That was as much professional as it was personal," he said. "I resented your intrusion into my investigation."

"And now?"

"I'm grasping at straws. At this point, if you were reading tea leaves or chicken gizzards, I'd at least consider what you had to say."

Her smile was wry. "You're so flattering, Rafferty." She swallowed the last morsel of cone and dabbed at her lips with her napkin. "Just in case you're wondering," she said, tossing the napkin into the trash, "I'm not exactly proud of what I did. My mother raised me with the full complement of Catholic guilt. 'Thou shalt not commit adultery' was high on her list of favored attributes in a daughter.''

He tucked his hands into his pockets and they started walking back toward City Hall. ''I'm not sure life is all that black-and-white. I think there are dozens of shades of gray in between.''

''And you a Homicide cop. I thought that 'all or nothing' went along with the badge.''

''It just could be possible,'' he said with a lightness he was far from feeling, ''that I'm in the wrong line of work.''

She was silent for a moment before she said softly, ''Maybe they're right, Conor.''

He glanced over at her in surprise. It was the first time she'd used his given name. ''Who's right?'' he said.

''Your family.'' She laid a hand on his sleeve, and deep in his belly, he felt the shock of her touch. ''Maybe you really do need to take some time off.''

They walked back to City Hall in silence. Still thinking about what she'd said, about his reaction to her touch, he left her at the door to her cubicle and continued down the hallway to his office.

The phone was ringing. He plopped heavily into his chair and reached across the desk to answer it.

''Lieutenant Rafferty,'' said a chirpy voice, ''this is Melanie Burke from Channel 5 News. Can you give us an update on your progress with the strangler case? Do you have any suspects in the murder of Tonia Lavoie?''

He bit back the retort he was tempted to make. Instead, he forced himself to remain polite and even-tempered. ''You know I can't make specific comments regarding an ongoing investigation, Ms. Burke.''

"I understand that Lavoie's boyfriend, Eric Dudley, has a history of domestic abuse. Would you care to comment on that?"

"We're investigating all avenues. Mr. Dudley is not, at this point in time, considered a suspect."

"Might that change in the future?"

"Anything could change at any given moment. We're continually receiving new information. Sooner or later, that information will lead us to the right person. But I repeat, Mr. Dudley is not currently considered a suspect."

"How many interviews have you—"

"Goodbye, Ms. Burke." He pressed the button to disconnect and quietly replaced the phone in its cradle.

When she came into task force headquarters on Monday morning, everything was chaotic. Six more desks had been crammed into the already crowded central area where the detectives were housed. Six new faces sat behind those desks, manning six shiny new telephones that were ringing incessantly. The noise level was roughly comparable to that of the Concorde preparing for takeoff. Somewhere in the midst of this circus, Rafferty had to be bouncing off the ceiling. Deciding it would be better to avoid him until he'd had at least half a dozen cups of coffee, Carolyn skirted the last row of desks and took the long way to her cubby.

Inside the door of her office, she nearly tripped over a pair of muscular male legs clad in skintight jeans. The legs were attached to a man lying on the floor beneath her desk. Holding her coffee cup aloft, she followed their considerable length with her eyes until she reached the tool belt slung around narrow hips. "Excuse me," she said.

The man poked his head around the corner of her desk,

looked up at her, and a grin spread across his handsome face. "Hey, there," he said.

"Can I help you?"

"I don't think so, *chica,* but I can help you. Ray Ortiz. Telephone company. I'm connecting you to the rest of the world."

"Lucky me," she said.

"Even more lucky for me, to meet such a lovely lady this early on a Monday morning. Are you married, *chica?*"

The man oozed more testosterone than the entire NRA. Amused, she said, "No."

Beneath the Pancho Villa moustache, his grin broadened. "Involved in a deep and meaningful relationship?"

"No," she said, taking a sip of coffee. Folding her arms, she added, "And what business of yours might it be?"

"A man wants to know a woman's not already spoken for, *chica,* before he asks her to have his babies."

She nearly spit out the mouthful of coffee she'd just taken. "Thank you, Ray," she said weakly, "but I think the telephone will be enough for this morning."

He shrugged good-naturedly. "You can't blame a guy for trying." And went back to tinkering.

Ten minutes later, he was gone, and she had a shiny new telephone sitting on her desk. She picked it up, listened to the dial tone, and replaced it in its cradle. When she looked up again, Lorna Abrams was leaning on her office door frame.

"Who's the major eye candy hanging all over Isabel?" Lorna said.

"I can't say for sure without checking," Caro said, "but I suspect it would be one Ray Ortiz of the telephone company."

"Ortiz, is it?" Lorna said. "What a hot tamale."

"I thought you were a married woman."

"I am," Lorna said. "That doesn't stop me from looking."

"You're welcome to him," Carolyn said. "I prefer my men with a little less machismo and a little more subtlety. Señor Ortiz has the subtlety of a sledgehammer."

"Screw subtlety," Lorna said. "Did you see those biceps?"

Carolyn grinned. "He's all yours. You can name your firstborn after me."

"Of course," Lorna said, coming into the office and sitting in the hard wooden chair that Isabel had barely managed to squeeze into the room alongside the desk, "maybe you're failing to appreciate the finer qualities of Señor Ortiz because you're interested in somebody else. Say...somebody with a little less machismo and a little more subtlety."

Carolyn eyed her steadily. "Would you care to clarify that?"

"You and Rafferty. Every time you're in the same room with him, the air's charged with so much electricity it makes the hair on my arms stand up."

Her mouth fell open. "Rafferty and me?" She shook her head and snapped open the locks on her briefcase. "No," she said firmly. "Absolutely not."

"You should have seen him when he found out you were coming here to work the case."

Caro flipped open the briefcase and began rummaging around inside it. Conor Rafferty was no concern of hers. It wasn't at all pertinent that every time he walked into the room, her insides bubbled like molten lava. She was here to do a job, and when that job was done, she was going to get into her little red car and drive back to Virginia as fast as I-95 would get her there. Her relationship with Rafferty was history, and she wasn't foolish enough to let history repeat itself.

She spent another moment or two rummaging before she gave in to the inevitable. Sighing, she looked at Lorna and said, "What do you mean?"

"For two days after he heard you were coming, he ran around here with a face that could have been carved from New Hampshire granite. On the rare occasions when he deigned to speak to any of us, his words came out like hard little chunks of ice. All because of you."

"No," Carolyn said, her heart beating too rapidly. "That's not possible."

"Oh, believe me, it's possible. I saw it with my own eyes. I've known Conor since our first week at the academy. We were partners for six years. He's godfather to both of my kids. I remember what he was like when you were together, and I've watched him go through women since then like other men go through socks. I've never seen him like this before."

"It's the case. He's under a tremendous amount of pressure."

"We all are. This is different. This is personal."

The telephone on her desk rang. "How is this possible?" Carolyn said, staring balefully at it. "Ten minutes ago, I didn't even have a phone number and now it's ringing."

"Better answer it. It could be Ed McMahon, calling to tell you that you just won a million bucks." With a grin, Lorna unfolded her long legs from the chair and was gone.

Carolyn answered the phone warily. A lively male voice at the other end said cheerfully, "Carolyn Monahan."

She leaned back in her swivel chair until it bumped

against the wall. She'd never have to worry about falling over backward in it. There was no room to fall. "Tommy Malone," she said. "How the hell did you get my number? I've only had it for ten minutes."

"I called the main number, and the lady with the dulcet tones and the charming Spanish accent gave me your extension."

"That would be Isabel," she said, and crossed one leg over the other. "So, how goes the pulp rag business?"

"You tell me. Did you read my front-page story this morning?"

"I wouldn't have missed it for the world. You paint such exquisite word pictures with the gory details. Something I can do for you this morning, Malone?"

"I'm still looking for that exclusive. And before you turn me down, remember that Bradford's ready to sell his left nut for publicity. I have him all figured out. The way he sees it, the more media coverage, the better chance there is that somebody out there will know something about your killer. Ergo, here I am, to provide you with the media coverage you need."

"You should have been a cop, Malone. You think like one."

"I don't have the stomach for it. I'd rather sit on the sidelines and write about those gory details than have to deal with them up close and personal. So what do you say to an interview, Special Agent Monahan? We can keep Bradford ecstatic by highlighting your involvement in this case."

She'd done similar interviews in the past, but she had a suspicion that in this particular case, Rafferty would blow a gasket. On the other hand, Bradford had made the Department's position abundantly clear. "Let me get back to you," she said.

She found Rafferty on the phone, his mouth set in a thin line and his eyebrows scrunched close together. "Uh-huh," he said into the phone, and waved her into his office. "I know it's outrageous. Look, I have to go now, somebody just came in." He listened, rolled his eyes. "Yes," he said, "I promise. I'll talk to you later."

He hung up the phone and raked his fingers through his hair. "My mother," he said.

"She still bugging you about taking time off?"

"Yes. But that's not why she called. She called to complain about the vet."

Carolyn raised a single eyebrow. "The vet?"

"She took the cat to have his rabies shot this morning. While he was there, the vet said the cat ought to have his teeth cleaned. Seems he has bad breath. So she made an appointment to bring him back. It's going to cost her eighty bucks."

"Ouch."

"I told her—" he leaned back in his chair and clasped his hands behind his neck "—that as long as she didn't plan to kiss the cat, she shouldn't have to worry about his breath, and she could save the eighty bucks."

Thinking of Fiona Rafferty, Carolyn broke into a grin. "I bet that went over well."

"Like the proverbial lead balloon." Those green eyes studied her with frank warmth. "You needed something?"

"I have a policy question for you. Not Department policy. Rafferty policy. Tommy Malone is hounding the hell out of me for an interview. He wants to write about my experiences, what I do, how I help cops catch bad guys, and so on and so forth. Using this case as the cornerstone of his article, of course. I thought if I said yes, it would get him off my back, but I know how you feel about it.

I also remember Bradford's position, which is that we should be generating as much publicity as possible. So I thought I'd run it by you before I gave him an answer.''

He lowered his arms. ''You're asking for my permission, Monahan? That doesn't sound like you at all.''

''I'm not asking for permission. I'm trying to stay off your shit list.''

The corner of his mouth turned up. ''I'm flattered that you care.''

''Don't get a swollen head, Rafferty. It's just that you're easier to work with when you're speaking to me.''

''Ah, hell,'' he said in disgust, ''you might as well go ahead and talk to him. I don't like it, but once again, I've been outranked. Sometimes I wonder who's really running this investigation. Did you see all those goddamn telephones out there?''

''How could I miss them? They're all ringing at once.''

''Before, we only had a few nutcases calling us. Now, they're all calling. Do you have any idea how many fruitcakes there are in the greater Boston area?''

''Quite a few?'' she guessed.

''Quite a few is right. And just to be helpful, they sent us three detectives from Narcotics and three from Vice. As long as our perp starts selling drugs or making book, they should do a bang-up job.''

She went back to her office and called Malone. ''So,'' he said when he heard her voice, ''did Himself give his blessing?''

''Himself did, albeit reluctantly. And just how did you know I was running it past Rafferty?''

''You're very transparent, Agent Monahan. And you like to play by the rules. It must be all that government training.''

She met him at twelve-thirty at the Union Oyster

House, where the hostess directed her up the steep staircase to a table near the window with a clear view of the Holocaust Memorial, a grouping of slender glass cubicles that represented the crematorium chimneys at infamous places with names like Auschwitz and Treblinka. She found Malone staring out the window and nursing a glass of white wine. He stood when she arrived. "Can I order you a drink?" he said, once they'd settled down.

"Coffee will be fine. I have to work this afternoon, and I'd like to keep a clear head."

"They serve a great chowder," Malone said as she perused the menu.

She skipped the chowder, ordered broiled sole instead. Malone ordered a bowl of the chowder, and she tried to avoid the lure of the corn bread the waitress brought as an appetizer. "Go ahead," Malone said. "Live dangerously."

Carolyn took a thin slice of corn bread and ate it without butter. It was crumbly, and kept disintegrating before she could get it into her mouth. "I bet the task force is hopping," Malone said.

She picked up a crumb with a damp fingertip and ate it. "The place is a zoo. Rafferty's tearing his hair out."

"Rafferty's in over his head," he said flatly. "I don't know why they put him in charge of a case this big, a lieutenant with only ten years on the force."

"He's a good cop," she said. "Levelheaded, cautious, and thorough."

Malone unfolded his napkin. "You're quick to defend him."

"I'd trust him with my life."

"Well. That's quite a recommendation. I hope he doesn't disappoint you."

Instead of taking the bait, she said, "How do you want to do this thing, Malone?"

"Actually—" he pulled out a small pocket recorder "—if you don't mind, I thought I'd turn this on, set it on the table, and we'd just talk. Later, I can pull it all together into some kind of coherent whole."

So while they ate, he asked questions and she answered. She talked about her training, about her years with the Bureau, recounted anecdotes about cases she'd worked in the past. He listened carefully to everything she said, asked intelligent and incisive questions, and her opinion of him rose a grudging notch or two. "You're a good journalist," she told him. "What are you doing at a rag like the *Trib*?"

"I like it there," he said, signaling the waitress for another white wine. "I'm a free spirit, and their editorial policy allows me a great deal of latitude. The *Globe*, even the *Herald*, wouldn't give me the freedom I get at the *Trib*. So there I stay."

"I suppose there's a certain logic to that."

The waitress brought his wine and refilled her coffee, and he leaned back on his tailbone. "You do realize," he said, "that ever since *Silence of the Lambs*, the public has been fascinated by what you people do. In the public perception, there's a certain mystique to it, a sense that you're practicing some kind of witchcraft."

She grimaced. "It's not just the general public," she said. "I've heard the word *witchcraft* coming from the mouths of more than one cop who ought to know better." Including Conor Rafferty, but she didn't say it out loud. "There's nothing mystical about it. It's simple behavioral psychology."

Malone leaned his chin on his palm. "So tell me about profiling in general. How does it work?"

"In a nutshell, behavior reflects personality. After years of researching and interviewing convicted sexual killers, we've seen behavioral patterns emerge. Patterns that are repeated over and over again, in case after case. Instead of looking at the individual personality and then predicting behavior, we turn it around the other way. We look at the behavior, and from that, we determine personality. It's surprisingly accurate."

His nod was slow and thoughtful. "What kind of patterns might you see?"

She took a sip of coffee. "One in particular that comes to mind is what we call the homicidal triad. When we look at the backgrounds of convicted serial killers, more often than not we see a pattern of telltale childhood behaviors—cruelty to animals, bedwetting, and fire-starting. These killers started out young on some twisted path and never deviated from it."

"So is it nature or nurture? Biology or environment that creates a serial killer?"

"If I knew the answer to that," she said wryly, "I'd be a rich woman."

"Fair enough. What are you looking for in this particular case? You've profiled this killer. Who is he, behaviorally speaking?"

She finished her last bite of sole and thought about his question. "Unfortunately," she said, "because it's an ongoing investigation, there's not much specific information I can give you. Except for the obvious, which is that, considering how easily he seems to have plucked five women off the street without a struggle, without even being noticed, he probably appears as normal as you or I. This is what makes finding these people so difficult. If they all looked like Quasimodo, my job would be a lot easier."

He smiled. "One last question," he said. "Sane or insane? What's your opinion?"

She glanced out the window at the Holocaust Memorial, where fascinated tourists were snapping photos and walking in and out of the open glass structures. "What about the Nazis," she said, "who committed so many atrocities at the death camps? They killed millions of people. Were they insane?"

He followed her glance, pausing before returning his attention to her. "I think it's generally accepted these days that Hitler was crazy."

"But charismatic," she pointed out. "Able to lead supposedly sane men to commit unspeakable acts against their fellow man. Yet nobody calls them insane. Monsters, perhaps, but not insane."

"So you're saying that your basic serial killer is some kind of monster? A sane monster, but a monster nevertheless?"

"By a legal definition," she said, "most of them—at least the ones we call organized killers, which is what we're talking about in this case—are not insane. Even Jeffrey Dahmer, who committed some of the worst atrocities on record, was judged to be sane. But nobody would argue that he wasn't a monster. Looking at it from a wholly personal perspective, I'm not sure what drives them. Is it insanity, or is it simply evil in its purest form? For each of these killers like Dahmer, and Bundy, and Gacy, at some point along the way, at a young age, their budding sexuality took a bizarre and dangerous turn. Insane or not, it's certainly not normal to equate sex, the creator of life, with death, which ends it. So I guess there really isn't any correct answer to your question. Each of us has to come up with our own definition of what constitutes evil versus insanity."

Malone turned off the tape player and tucked it into his pocket. "Thanks," he said. "Thanks for the interview, and thanks for your time. I know how busy you are. I think we have some really good material here. Would you like to take a look at the finished article before it goes to print?"

She raised an eyebrow. "Is that a privilege you generally offer your interviewees?"

There was something feral about his grin. "Only the ones I like," he said, and she wondered if he was flirting with her.

"Yes," she said. "I'd appreciate a look before it goes to print."

"Great. I'll give you a call sometime tomorrow. I should have it ready by then." He hesitated. "Tell me, what do you do when you're not on duty?"

So she'd been right about the flirting. It was a shame, she thought, as she studied his face. He was intelligent, attractive, pleasant of demeanor. And she had absolutely no interest in him. Gathering up her purse, she said with a smile she hoped would soften her words, "I'm a Federal agent, Malone. I'm always on duty. Thanks for the lunch."

Because the day was so beautiful, she took the long way back to City Hall, around the Memorial, up Sudbury Street past the police station, and around the unimaginative gray box that was the John F. Kennedy Federal Building. If City Hall was Boston's ugliest building, the Federal Building had to run a close second. A pair of tourists stood arm in arm in front of the hideous sculpture outside the entrance, smiling for the camera lens while a third tourist snapped their picture. City Hall Plaza was open and inviting in spite of the winos who hovered around the subway entrance in hopes of a handout. A couple of prepubescent boys were skateboarding down one of the flights of stairs that connected the various levels of the Plaza. And on a length of polished brick bench, long legs stretched out, eyes closed and face up to the warm summer sun, lay Conor Rafferty. He wore a blue-and-white pinstriped shirt, his necktie was crooked, and he had one hand wrapped around a paper cup with a straw sticking through its lid.

Somewhere nearby, a boom box was tuned to an oldies station. Martha Reeves and the Vandellas singing *Heat Wave.* Carolyn discreetly tucked a finger inside the neck of her silk blouse and pulled it away from skin that was suddenly damp with sweat. *Stay away from him,* she told herself, remembering what Lorna had said earlier. *The man is nothing but T-R-O-U-B-L-E.* She stood rooted to the spot as one of the kids skated past her, so close that she felt the wind on her face.

She didn't remember crossing the space between them, but she must have, because somehow, she found herself standing next to him. With that radar that all cops seemed to have, Rafferty sensed her presence and opened his eyes. Christ, he was gorgeous. There was no other word for him. He didn't say anything, just looked at her with those damnable green eyes, and she felt their heat all the way to the marrow in her bones. He looked her up and down, from her eyes down to her Manolo Blahniks and back, but still he didn't say anything.

"You look so comfortable, Lieutenant," she said, "I'm tempted to hang a sign around your neck that says, Your Tax Dollars at Work."

Martha and the Vandellas finished their song, and Smokey Robinson began crooning in that distinctive sweet tremolo that always gave her goose bumps. *Ooh, baby, baby.* Rafferty held out his paper cup, rattled the ice in it. Lazily, he said, "Did you and Malone have a cozy lunch?"

"Very. We got along marvelously. It seems that the two of you have a mutual admiration society going, Rafferty. In the course of one short hour, he managed to get in four or five digs about you."

As Smokey crooned softly in the background, those green eyes continued to regard her with avid interest. "I trust that you defended my honor."

"Of course. He seems to think you're not qualified to head this investigation."

His eyes narrowed. "That little pissant."

"Don't worry. I made sure he knew you were righteous and steadfast. Not to mention thrifty, clean and reverent."

"Good thing." Rafferty sat upright and swung his feet to the ground, and they began walking side by side toward the entrance. "Did anything else of significance transpire during this interview?"

"Other than the fact that he hit on me, not really."

He stopped dead, caught her by the arm and swung her around to face him. "He hit on you?"

"Sort of," she said in surprise, trying unsuccessfully to disengage her arm from his grip. "It was just harmless flirting. He asked me what I do when I'm not on duty."

Tersely, he said, "What did you tell him?"

"I told him that I'm always on duty. Damn it, Rafferty, do you think you could let go of my arm?"

"I don't want you going out with him."

Floored by his incredible audacity, she stared at him. "Since when," she said, "do I have to answer to you?"

"I don't trust him, Monahan. I don't trust the little asshole as far as I can throw him."

"This might surprise you, Rafferty, but I actually happen to find him charming."

"Then you're showing pisspoor judgment."

"Why? Because he doesn't like you? Life isn't a popularity contest, Conor."

"No," he said irritably. "It has nothing to do with that. You're showing pisspoor judgment because he's sniffing around you for just one reason, the newspaper article that'll move him one step higher on the career ladder. Don't make the mistake of thinking he gives a damn about you, because he doesn't. Malone's a user, and he doesn't give a damn about anything except getting the story ahead of everybody else."

Her mouth fell open. "You are so goddamn insulting, I can't believe it. And if you don't let go of my arm in the next three seconds, I swear to Christ I'll drop you right here."

Those green eyes widened. "You'll *what?*"

"You heard me, Rafferty. I have a black belt in karate, courtesy of our benevolent Uncle Sam. You want to take me on, it's your funeral. Just remember, there are some particularly nasty penalties they reserve for any idiot who's stupid enough to assault a Federal agent."

His expression went from surprise to anger to amusement, and then he was grinning, and she wanted to use her fist to wipe that smugness from his face. He studied her inch by inch, took in her entire five foot four and 107 pounds. "Think you're big enough to do it?"

Her blood pressure shot sky-high. "You egotistical son of a bitch," she said, wrenching her arm free of his grip. "Go to hell." And she turned and strode furiously in the direction of the building.

"Jesus Christ," he said. "Damn it, Carolyn, come back here."

Ignoring him, she stormed through the front door and strode across the lobby, heedless of the raised eyebrows

and the curious glances. She passed the elevators, continued on to the stairs at the back of the building. Behind
her he said, "Goddamn it, Caro—" as she took the first
turn, effectively cutting off his words midsentence.

She clattered up the stairs, her footsteps echoing like
gunshots in the stairwell. Half a flight below her, his muffled tread followed. She reached the fourth floor and
strode down the hall and into the office suite, swept past
the reception desk, sidestepped Isabel and kept going. Isabel's mouth fell open, and half a dozen heads looked up
in avid curiosity. Rafferty stormed in behind her and
heaved his soda cup into a nearby wastebasket. It landed
with a hollow thud. Isabel took a step backward, and suddenly everybody was exceedingly busy again.

Carolyn slammed her purse down on top of her desk
and turned to confront him. He was standing in the doorway, his shoulders nearly blocking the opening. "Get
out," she said.

"You're making a goddamn scene over nothing. Nothing!"

"What the hell is it today?" she said. "Is it something
in the air? Something in the water?" She turned away
from him and began shuffling through the mail that was
sitting on her desk. "Every goddamn man I've run into
today is suffering from testosterone poisoning." She
chose a small manila envelope from the stack and tore
into it. "Neanderthals!" she said. "Every last one of them
a—"

She stopped midsentence to stare at the photo that had
dropped out into her hand. At first her mind refused to
register what she was seeing. Then it hit her like a hard
fist to the abdomen. Her body turned to ice, and her lungs
ceased to function. Through a red haze of disbelief, she

stared at the dead woman in the photograph and let out a tiny whimper.

"Caro?" he said, and took a step into the office.

"Jesus. Oh, Jesus." She struggled for breath, but a red-hot fist had clamped itself over her lungs, and she couldn't seem to take in any oxygen. "Conor—" she squeaked.

"What the hell is it?" As she began to sway, he crossed the tiny room in a single step and grabbed the photograph from her hand. "What is it?" he repeated.

With the last particle of oxygen left to her, she whispered, "Meg. Oh, God, Conor, it's Meg."

8

At first, he didn't believe what he was seeing. But his eyes had never lied to him, and they weren't lying now. He'd seen the crime scene photos, back when he was just a rookie cop, and it all came back to him with sickening familiarity.

Belatedly, he became aware that beside him, Carolyn was swaying drunkenly. He dropped the photo and grabbed her by the arms to steady her. She was trembling violently, and through the material of the expensive dove-gray jacket, her body was like ice. Her chest rose and fell too rapidly, and her lips had developed a bluish tint. Her terrified eyes pleaded with him as she gasped. "Can't…breathe," she said.

He looked around frantically for the chair that had been here this morning, but some idiot had moved it. When he found out who, heads would roll. "Sit," he ordered, and guided her to the floor. Limp as a rag doll, she was surprisingly heavy for such a small woman. Trying to hide his panic, he bellowed for Isabel and knelt helplessly on the floor beside her. Knees pressed together beneath her chin, her ridiculously tiny little skirt riding up her thighs, Carolyn sat there gasping, her fingers clutching at his, tightening around them hard enough to hurt.

Isabel paused in the doorway. "*Dios,*" she breathed, and stood there frozen, like a plant that had taken root.

"She's hyperventilating," he snapped. "Jesus Christ, don't just stand there! Do something!"

Behind Isabel, Lorna said crisply, "Get a paper bag." She poked Isabel hard in the shoulder, and the young woman finally came to life. She went running, came back a moment later with a crumpled paper bag left over from somebody's lunch. Lorna took it from her, shook it open with a crisp snap, and knelt beside him in the crowded space between the desk and the wall.

"Breathe into this, sweetie," she said. "Don't be scared. It'll be okay."

His heart thudding in terror, he held Carolyn's shoulders while she continued to gasp into the paper bag that Lorna had crammed tight against her face. "Good," Lorna said, and smoothed her hair back from her face. "Keep it up."

Eventually, the gasping stopped and her breathing slowed. "Okay?" Lorna said, and Carolyn nodded. Lorna removed the bag, and Caro closed her eyes and let her head fall back limply. She was still trembling, or maybe he was the one shaking like a wet dog. She moistened her lips with the tip of her tongue. "Oh, God," she said. "I'm going to be sick."

With his hand on the back of her neck, he gently bent her forward. "Put your head between your knees," he ordered, shoving her skirt nearly to her waist as he made room for her head between her bowed legs.

"Jesus, Rafferty," she said weakly, swiping his arm away, "allow me a little modesty, will you?"

"Goddamn it, Caro," he snapped, "I'm not trying to look up your dress. I don't get that big a thrill out of victimizing helpless women."

She raised her head to retort, and he shoved it back between her knees. He turned to Lorna and Isabel, caught them exchanging a glance. "What the hell are you staring at?" he said.

"Nothing," Lorna said. "Nothing at all."

He glared at her, then turned his attention back to Carolyn. She tightened her fingers on his hand. Gently, he said, "Better?" and she nodded. She raised her head, and he awkwardly drew her skirt back down to adequately cover her. "Is the nausea gone?" he said.

"Yes," she said thickly. "I need to go wash my face."

"Can you stand up now?"

"I'm fine. I just need some cold water."

"Isabel," he said, "go with her. Make sure she doesn't pass out in the john."

Still on his knees, he watched them go. Then, with a shudder, he fell back on his heels and closed his eyes.

"The big, tough Homicide cop," Lorna said with affection. "Jesus Christ, Conor, you're as white as my mother-in-law's bed linens. Are you all right?"

"Give me a couple minutes to dislodge my testicles from my Adam's apple, and then ask me again." He forced his breathing and his heart rate to slow. Eyes still closed, he said, "Where'd you learn the paper bag routine?"

"Lamaze class. It's one of the emergency supplies you keep in your Lamaze bag, along with baby lotion, warm socks and a tomato soup can."

"I don't even want to know what the soup can's for. Take a look at the picture on the desk."

While he stood unsteadily on legs that felt as if they were made from fresh Play-Doh, Lorna leaned over the desk and lifted the photo by its edges. "This one's different," she said. "It's not a Polaroid. Who the hell developed this?"

Rafferty ran his hands over his face. "It gets better," he said. "It's her sister."

Lorna looked at him in openmouthed amazement. For a long moment, they gazed at each other in silence. "Does this mean what I think it does?"

"Forensics will have to confirm it," he said, "but this isn't a police photo. I don't think there's any way this could have been doctored up. This was taken with one of those little el cheapo point-and-click cameras, the kind you can buy at any department store for about six bucks. He must have his own darkroom tucked away somewhere. Or at least he did."

"Ten years ago."

He rubbed his temple wearily. "It certainly looks that way."

"Then where the hell's he been for the last nine-and-a-half years?"

"That's what you and I have to find out."

It was a subdued group that convened a half hour later in the conference room. He'd spent most of that half hour on the phone with his superiors, informing them of this new development, arguing over policy, groveling for unnecessary permissions so he wouldn't step on any toes. He'd also held a brief conversation with Richard Armitage in Washington about Carolyn's continued involvement in the case. Now, perching on one end of the long conference table, he looked out wearily at the faces of his people: Abrams, Rizzoli, Lassiter. Mendez and Smith. Hailstock. All good people. All good detectives. At the other end of the table, by herself, sat Carolyn, white of face but otherwise showing no outward indication of what she'd just been through.

"In case you could possibly have missed hearing," he

said to them, "we just came into possession of evidence that links this case to a ten-year-old unsolved homicide."

"Just how solid is this link?" Greg Lassiter asked, his pen poised over the steno pad he'd brought with him.

"Solid enough that we're acting as if it's real while we wait for a confirmation from Forensics."

"Do you think this means he's been killing all along?" Mendez asked.

"Killers like this," he said, "don't just stop killing. Agent Monahan?" He looked to Carolyn for confirmation.

She cleared her throat. "That's right. Assuming the link is verified and these homicides are connected to the earlier one, this means he's almost certainly been either incarcerated during the interim, or killing in another location."

"Shit," somebody muttered.

Greg leaned forward and said in a cool and sensible voice, "What does this mean for us?"

"It means that we go back," Rafferty said, "and start over again at square one. I've already asked for the file on the Monahan case. We start with that, and we sit down with Agent Monahan's profile, along with everything we have on all the other victims, and we go through it all over again. And we keep going through it until we find something."

"Jesus Christ, Conor," Rizzoli said.

He eyed Rizzoli coolly. "You have a problem with that?"

"Damn right, I have a problem with it. We're all dying here. Nobody's getting any sleep. I haven't had a day off in three weeks. How much more can we be expected to do? We're not superhuman, you know."

"I already told you, if you want off the task force, just say so." He looked around from face to face. "That goes for all of you. Anybody who wants out had better say so now. Otherwise, don't come whining to me later.''

Nobody broke the heavy silence that had descended upon the room. ''Good,'' he said after a moment. ''Starting immediately, every one of you is ordered to take off at least one day a week. There are enough of us so we can stagger days off. If you're rested, you'll be thinking more clearly, and I need clearheaded cops.''

''What about you?'' Lorna said. ''I don't see you taking any time off.''

''Don't worry about me.''

''Somebody has to if you're not smart enough to worry about yourself.''

One of these days, he and Lorna were going to have a little chat about things like rank and insubordination. But right now, he had more important things on his mind. Ignoring her, he folded his arms across his chest and said, ''The seven of us—plus Agent Monahan, for as much as she can help us—are the nucleus of this task force. The new people can continue manning the phones. Personally, I don't expect anything to come of it, but it's busywork to keep them occupied and Bradford happy, and it frees us to do more important work. The Monahan file should be on its way over right now. Give me tonight to go over it. We'll all meet here tomorrow morning at eight-thirty. Bring your files, your notes, anything and everything you have on the case. I'll see you all then.''

As they began to stir, Aubrey Hailstock spoke from the back of the room. ''About this ten-year-old homicide—''

Rafferty looked at him. ''Yes?''

''You said the name was Monahan.'' He cast a quick glance at Carolyn. ''I was just wondering—''

''She was my sister,'' Caro said flatly, and picked up her briefcase and walked out of the room.

When he went looking for her a few minutes later, her office was empty. "She left," Isabel said. "She told me she'd be back in the morning." The young woman's dark eyes widened. "Should I try to track her down?"

"No. No, she's had a rough day. It's all right, Isabel. Look…" He paused, not sure how to frame his apology. "I know I've been a little rough on you lately. It's this damn case, and—"

"I know," she said, and patted his arm. "It's all right."

"I just wanted you to know I appreciate everything you do. I'd be lost without you."

"Now that's the truth," she said, and handed him a fat manila envelope. "This came in while you were in your meeting."

The file was a good three inches thick. "I'm going to take this home to read it," he said. It was the only place he could get uninterrupted quiet. "If Agent Monahan happens to call—"

Isabel waited. "Yes?"

"Never mind. I'll see you in the morning."

His apartment was cool and quiet. He heard Nero's toenails clicking against the wooden floor as the dog hopped down off the bed and came to greet him. Nero sat on the kitchen floor, tail wagging, looking at him through mismatched eyes in that crazy lopsided face that was half black and half white. Rafferty set down the file on the kitchen table and bent to ruffle the dog's fur. "Hey, guy," he said. "You haven't had much attention lately, have you?"

Nero thumped his tail against the floor. Ever since he'd been working this case, Rafferty had been paying the fifteen-year-old kid who lived upstairs to walk Nero twice a day and to make sure he had food and water. But it wasn't enough. The dog deserved something better than an owner who was away more than he was at home. He'd thought about getting rid of the animal, giving him away to somebody with kids, somebody who could give the dog the attention he deserved. But they'd been together for a long time, and he just couldn't bring himself to part with the mutt.

Instead, he changed into a T-shirt and athletic shorts, and they went jogging together, down seven blocks to the church, then over four blocks, returning the long way around. When they got back, Nero flopped on the rug inside the front door, ready for a snooze, and Rafferty hit the shower. Then, refreshed and energized, he settled down to read the Monahan file.

It was slow going. The damn thing was a mess. Whoever had worked the case had suffered from a severe lack of organizational skills. Papers were out of order, somebody had spilled coffee all over the autopsy report, and it took him ten minutes to locate the crime scene photos, stuck in the middle of a typed transcript of an interrogation session with Clancy Donovan that had gone on for three hours. He read through a few pages of the transcript, wondering why the detective in charge had concentrated on Clancy to the exclusion of all other suspects. Considering that they had not a shred of evidence to connect Clancy to Meg Monahan's murder, it seemed pisspoor police work to ignore the possibility that somebody else might have committed the crime.

With a sigh, he set the file aside, glanced at the clock and saw that it was nearly six-thirty and he'd been wrapped up in Meg's murder for the past three hours. Stretching, he stood and crossed the room, pulled the phone book from the drawer and looked up the number of the Boylston House.

When Carolyn answered, he said, "Hi. It's me."

There was the merest suggestion of a pause before she said, "Hi."

"You took off so fast this afternoon, I just wanted to make sure you were really all right."

"I had one of my killer headaches, so I came back here and took something. Then I went to bed for a while."

Cradling the phone between his ear and his shoulder, he opened the refrigerator and took out a bottle of Coke. He unscrewed the cap and said, "Is your headache gone now?"

"It's gone now." Again, she paused. "I'm so sorry," she said, "for what happened this afternoon. I can't believe I was that unprofessional."

He took a swig of Coke. "You don't have anything to apologize for. You had one hell of a shock."

"But all my years of training just went out the window."

"She was your sister, Carolyn. You reacted like any normal person would have."

"You know," she said, "from the beginning, this case has felt different from any of the other cases I've worked. Now I understand why. It's turned personal, Conor."

"I know."

"I'm not letting him get away with it. You do understand that? No matter what happens, I intend to see to it that this son of a bitch is caught."

"We'll get him," he said. "Have you eaten?"

"No. Why?"

"I've been sitting here at my kitchen table for the past three hours, going over the file on Meg's murder. I thought if you were up to it, we could get together, toss some ideas around. Order in a pizza—"

"Yes," she said. "I want to see the file."

Thinking of the crime scene photos, the autopsy pictures, he said, "There are some things in it that you'd be better off not seeing."

"It's what I do, Rafferty. I've seen that kind of thing before."

"Jesus Christ, Carolyn, this is different. She was your sister."

"Don't you understand? I have to see them. It's the only way I'm going to be able to put it behind me."

He wanted to argue, but he couldn't, because he knew she was right. "My place or yours?" he said.

"Yours. We'll have more room to spread out."

"I'll call and order pizza. Does a half hour sound okay?"

"A half hour's fine. And, Rafferty—"

He swallowed the mouthful of Coke he'd just taken. "Yes?"

"I like pepperoni and olives on my pizza. Be sure you get it right."

Carolyn paged through the photos silently, stoically, willing herself to be objective, to view this as just another case, just another victim in a long line of victims. Beside her, the pepperoni and olive pizza had gone cold, and the fizz had long since dissipated from the Diet Coke that Rafferty had served to her in a chipped jelly glass that matched all the other chipped jelly glasses in his cupboard. She'd read the autopsy report, read the initial report from the cop who'd been first on-scene, skimmed sections of the voluminous transcript of Clancy's interrogation by the police.

She closed the file. "So there was no evidence whatsoever," she said, "to connect Clancy to the murder?"

Across the table, Rafferty looked up. "No witnesses, no physical evidence, nothing."

"Why did the cops focus so hard on him?"

"It's the same question I've been asking myself, and I keep coming up with the same dumb answer. He and Meg were sleeping together, and he didn't have an alibi for that night. It's enough to make him a suspect. But not enough to make him the sole suspect, not without evidence. If you want my professional opinion, it looks like sloppy police work."

She looked back at the closed file in front of her. "I'm not a cop," she said. "I've never run a homicide investigation. But I've worked a lot of them, and it certainly sounds as though you're right. Who was in charge of the investigation?"

He leaned back on his tailbone and stretched out his long legs. "Detective by the name of Frawley. Bob Frawley. I never knew him. He retired a couple of years before I landed in Homicide. That was one of the first things I checked on this afternoon. I wanted to talk to him, see if he could remember anything about the case that might not be in the file. But right now, he's backpacking somewhere in Tibet, and his wife said she doesn't expect to hear from him for at least a couple of weeks."

She raised an eyebrow. "Tibet?"

"My sentiments exactly." Rafferty shrugged, and those green eyes warmed appreciably.

"So who inherited the case?"

"Francis Kelley. He's a good cop. But he already had a full caseload, and since this case was at a dead end, it just sat, gathering dust, while he worked on the ones where he could make a difference."

"While the trail went cold," she said with a trace of bitterness she couldn't hide.

"I know it's no excuse," he said. "But there's not a cop on the force who isn't overworked. When you factor in escalating crime statistics, budget restraints and politics, it doesn't paint a pretty picture. It's not just here in Boston. You'll find the same thing in every big-city police department across the country. We're all understaffed and overworked.''

"I realize that." She leaned her head back, drew the hair back from her face and let it fall. "I've worked with a number of them. Things are tough all over. It's just that when the victim is a member of your own family, you tend to look at it differently."

"Of course you do. And I wish I could say that solving a case like Meg's is easy. But you know the reality as well as I do. After ten years, the chances of solving a case are about a million to one. Witnesses move away or they die, memories fade, cops retire. The people who may have cared passionately at one time have either moved along to some other place in their lives, or that passion has faded with the years."

Leaning forward in her chair, she said vehemently, "My passion hasn't faded."

"Neither has mine. And we have a much better chance than usual of solving a ten-year-old case. If Forensics confirms that the photo is genuine—and I expect they will—then we know that the perp is still killing, and we have solid evidence that will close Meg's case for good once we've nailed the guy. And there's one thing I'll promise you—we are going to nail him." He paused to study her with those green eyes of his. "I want your opinion on something. Your professional opinion. Understanding that this is strictly hypothesizing, do you think that Meg knew her attacker, or was it a random slaying?"

She considered his question carefully. "I've thought about it so many times over the years. I suspect he knew her, even if she didn't know him. It seems such an unlikely place for a random killing. It's much more likely that he was waiting for her, and when she came out of the bar alone, he pounced. Unless he knew she worked there, knew I hadn't shown up to walk her home, why would he have been waiting outside that particular bar on that particular night?'' She grimaced as a dull pain struck beneath her skull, just above the base of her neck.

"Coincidence?"

"You're a cop," she said, rubbing languidly at her neck. "Do you believe in coincidence?"

"Not particularly."

"Neither do I."

He leaned his chair back on two legs. "There is one other important question we need to answer. Was Meg his first, or was he killing somewhere else before that?"

Carolyn reopened the file folder, took the crime scene photos back out, studied them as she considered her answer. "Based on the information I have in front of me, I'd have to say she was probably his first. This killing was much less sophisticated than the others. There was no posing of the body, no fancy little touches like the scarf. As far as we can tell, he didn't take any trophies. Except, of course, the photo, which implies premeditation. But he hadn't yet polished his style. The scene looks sloppy and hurried, as though he panicked once he realized he'd actually followed through with something he may have been fantasizing about for a long time."

He dropped the chair back to the floor. "Intriguing," he said slowly, "the idea that he may have been watching her, thinking about her, for some time."

"It's not uncommon. And she worked with the public. She came into contact with dozens of people every day. There was the usual crowd that hung around Rafferty's, but there were also strangers who came and went. Hell, for that matter, he could have been a cop. The place was always swarming with them.''

"That seems a little far-fetched.''

"What's the matter, Lieutenant? Can't believe that a member of your sainted blue brotherhood could possibly be a killer? You'd better think that one through carefully before you give me an answer.''

"I'm not that naive,'' he said dryly. "But the idea doesn't sit well with me. We're sworn to protect. If I ever found out it was a cop, I'm not sure he'd survive long enough to stand trial.''

She closed her eyes and exhaled a hard breath in an effort to ward off the pain that was building beneath her skull.

"The headache's back, isn't it?'' he said.

"I'll be fine.''

"You seem to get these headaches pretty often. I don't suppose you've seen a doctor?''

"As a matter of fact, I have. The esteemed Dr. Farris of Georgetown University Hospital.''

He stood up and walked around the table. From somewhere behind her, he said, "And what did the esteemed doctor have to say?''

Eyes still closed, she said, "Stress. Can you imagine that? And in my line of work. According to my good friend Dr. Farris, my job is slowly killing me.''

Softly, he said, "What did he recommend? Or was it she?''

"She. In lieu of quitting my job, which was her first recommendation, she suggested a number of things. Meditation. A stress management class. Long, hot bubble baths, relaxation exercises. Joining a health club. She even recommended taking a nip every so often. And if that doesn't work, there's always the psychiatrist's couch.''

Near her ear, he said, "That seems a bit drastic," and lifted the long hair off the back of her neck.

At his touch, she jerked as though she'd been licked by fire. Goose bumps broke out on her skin, and her eyes flew open. In a panic, she said, "What the hell do you think you're doing, Rafferty?"

"Shut up and relax." He gently twisted the fall of hair and tucked it over her shoulder. With his thumbs, he prodded the vertebrae at the base of her neck.

"Damn it," she said. "That hurts."

"It's the source of your problem," he said, still prodding. "Give me ten minutes, and I can make your headache go away."

Her heart began to beat too quickly. "Is that a proposition, or did you earn a chiropractic degree in your spare time?"

"I used to date a massage therapist. She taught me all about this kind of thing. Where does it hurt?"

"I just bet she did. What else did she teach you?"

"Shut up, Monahan, and get your mind out of the gutter. She was a licensed physical therapist, and she worked in the rehab department at Mass General." His thumbs prodded some more, digging mercilessly into the muscles of her shoulders. "It's no wonder you have a headache. Your muscles are strung tighter than catgut on a fiddle. You need to relax."

"I've tried, but the last couple of days, it doesn't seem to be working."

"Start by relaxing your fingers and toes. Make them go limp. Then let it work its way up your arms and legs, and let the rest of your body follow."

She wanted to argue, but there was something hypnotic about his voice. And his hands, those wonderful hands that she'd dreamed about for years, were doing incredible things to her, kneading and squeezing, each fingertip a tiny volcanic point against her collarbone as his thumbs massaged the knotted muscles of her neck and shoulders until she wanted to cry out in pain, except that the pain was somehow connected to pleasure, and the heat that was spreading throughout her body was honey-warm and lethargic.

Beneath the fabric of her silk blouse, squeezed tight against her lacy brassiere, her nipples went rock hard. She bit down on her lip to keep from moaning in pleasure. This was better than sex. Or at least as good. She hadn't realized that the neck and shoulders were a cluster of erogenous zones. His hands left her shoulders, glided up either side of her neck and began rotating her head, slowly and gently. "Relax," he said. "Just let yourself go limp."

Eyes closed, she gave in and let him work his magic while her body remembered another time and place when those hands had worked a similar magic on her. Seduced by his touch and by the yearning she'd never been able to extinguish, she made a muddled attempt to remember precisely why it was that she'd left him.

His hands stilled on her shoulders and he cleared his throat. "How's the headache?" he said.

It took her a moment to come back. Then reality came rushing in, and she remembered who she was and who he was and all the reasons why a relationship between them could never work out. It didn't matter that he still possessed the power to thrill her with his touch. They didn't want the same things in life. He wanted nothing more than to live out the rest of his days in South Boston. She wanted the world. The gap between them was too wide to bridge.

"The headache's gone," she said. "Thank you."

He removed his hands and she stood, leaning against

the edge of the kitchen table long enough to steady her shaky legs. "I have to go now," she said.

He didn't argue. "Give me a minute, and I'll walk you to your car. I have to take Nero out anyway."

The walk downstairs was silent, fraught with a tension that hadn't been there earlier. When they reached the street, she climbed silently into the Mitsubishi, started the engine, and rolled down the window. While Nero danced nearby on his leash, impatient to move on with things, Rafferty crouched beside her open window, elbows resting atop the opening. In the darkness, they studied each other, green eyes to blue, until finally he broke the silence. "Rough day," he said softly.

"Yes. Rough day."

Still leaning against the car, he lifted two fingers and touched her shoulder, then straightened. "I'll see you tomorrow," he said, and tapped the roof of the car.

"Sure," she said. "Good night."

She put the car in gear and pulled away from the curb, wondering why she felt so much like crying, wondering why, after all these years, it was so difficult to leave him. When she reached the corner, she finally trusted herself to look in the rearview mirror. Haloed in the light from the streetlamp overhead, Nero dancing about his feet and tangling the leash around his legs, Rafferty was still standing in the street, watching her drive away.

She was in the office at eight the next morning, grainy-eyed and hungover from a sleepless night spent alternately waking and dreaming. Around 4:00 a.m. she'd finally given up, turned on the light and spent the next two hours reading the newest Sidney Sheldon novel.

Tommy Malone's article was sitting on her desk with a sticky note attached: "Here it is. Sorry I missed you. If there's anything that needs clarification or change, call me. I still have a few hours before deadline. T.''

Carolyn set down her coffee cup, peeled off the sticky note, and read the article while she poured coffee down her throat in an effort to restore herself to a condition that bordered on human. He'd done a good job with it, had made an effort to show the reality of her job as a profiler instead of the myth. He'd presented her in a positive light without making her look superhuman, and not once had he misquoted her or taken something she said out of context to alter its meaning. He'd used the current case as a building block, then had expanded to concentrate on her, on her background, her history, the things she'd accomplished in seven years with the Bureau. Tommy Malone was something she'd seldom seen in her years with the agency: a talented journalist who preferred to tell the real story instead of embellishing it with manufactured details in order to sell newspapers.

A noise at the door caught her attention. She glanced up to see a gaunt, twentyish man hovering in her doorway, an expensive camera hanging from a strap around his neck. ''Agent Monahan?'' he said.

She set down Tommy's article. ''Yes,'' she said.

''I'm Rick Jonah from the *Trib*. Malone sent me over to get a picture of you to run with his article.''

Caro eyed him warily and reached for the phone. ''Wait,'' she said, and dialed Malone's number.

He was effervescent as usual. ''What did you think of the article?'' he said, an eager pup desperate for her praise.

''It was excellent. All your stories are excellent, Malone. You're wasting your talent at that rag you work for.''

''So you're giving me the green light to print it as is?''

"Yes, but that's not why I'm calling. There's a man standing in my doorway with a camera who says you sent him over. I just want to make sure he's legitimate."

"That would be Rick Jonah. The kid's legit. I always run a photo to go along with any profile I write. Susie Reader likes to have a picture in her mind to go along with my written description. You know the old saying, one picture's worth a thousand words."

If it was possible to judge by the impact of the photos she'd seen of her sister, she had to agree. "Thanks," she said, and hung up.

She hated having her picture taken. Rick Jonah suggested a couple of poses, put some props in front of her, and she sat there stiffly behind the desk, trying to look somber and bureaucratic while she endured his attentions. When it was over, she snatched up her papers and files and headed for the conference room, where she settled herself as far away from the front as she could manage.

Rafferty was already there, sitting on the corner of a small desk he'd dragged in from somewhere, engrossed in conversation with Greg Lassiter. He glanced up, and his eyes met hers. During the couple of seconds while their gazes held, all her bodily systems ceased to function. Then he looked back at Lassiter, and her heart began pumping blood again.

Shit. This was not good news. Somehow, the man had managed to burrow under her skin, and now she couldn't dislodge him. The case was complicated enough already without this. Her whole goddamn life was complicated enough already without this. She didn't need the memory of a man's hands on her body distracting her from her job, interfering with her thought processes, getting in the way of her handling of the case. Then there was the Bureau to consider. Washington didn't have a sense of humor. The brass would yank her in a heartbeat if they ever found out that she had a major case of the hots for the lieutenant in charge of the case.

Ted Rizzoli came in looking like the undead, dropped his files on the table, and plopped into a chair near hers. She wasn't sure what the detective's problem was, but he had the social graces of a baboon. Every interaction she'd ever had with him had been bizarre, ranging from a snarled greeting as they passed in the hallway to outright avoidance if he saw her coming far enough in advance to escape a face-to-face confrontation. She wondered if he treated all women this way, or if it was only her. Did he hold some personal or professional grudge against her, or did he just naturally have the personality of a pit bull?

She didn't have time to pursue the line of thought. Rafferty closed the door to the conference room and sat back down on the corner of the desk. "I just got word in from Forensics," he said, crossing his arms. "It's their opinion that the photo we received yesterday is the real McCoy. This means a couple of things. First, that our killer has been at this for a long time. Ten years or more. Second, it means that the scope of our investigation just widened dramatically. We have to go back at least twelve years and turn over every rock we find."

"What's our game plan," Lassiter said, furiously scratching in the ubiquitous notebook, "for turning over rocks?"

"Good question. First, we go over what we know, and what we think we know. Then we look at Agent Monahan's profile, point by point, until we all have it memorized. After that, we're going to work in pairs to dig deeper."

Lassiter raised his head. "Doing what?" he said.

"There are three areas I want to explore in depth.

Abrams and Rizzoli will be going over the Meg Monahan case file—I have Isabel copying it right now—and each of our current case files, looking for anything, no matter how small, that might connect any of them to any of the others. Lassiter, you and Smith are going to pull a list of sex offenders from the past twelve years, concentrating on anybody who was incarcerated at some point after the Monahan homicide and released at some point in the past eighteen months. Mendez and Hailstock, I want you to go back over the records of everyone we've interviewed, find out where they were at the time of the Monahan homicide. See if anything jumps out at you."

There was murmured assent, nodding of heads. "I'm going to start querying other police departments," he said, "to see if they have any similar unsolved homicides. It's the only way to cover all the bases. If our boy wasn't incarcerated in the nine years between the Monahan and Magnusson homicides, he was somewhere else, and we're going to find him. Agent Monahan and I will be available at any time to any of you for consultation. Questions, concerns, theories, hits—bring them to us."

"I have a problem with that," Ted Rizzoli said. "Agent Monahan isn't a trained homicide investigator. I don't think she's qualified to be offering me advice on a case I'm working."

Rafferty studied him coolly. "Do you have some kind of personal problem with Agent Monahan?"

"She's not a goddamn cop! And her sister was one of the victims. With all due respect, Lieutenant—" he met Rafferty's cold stare, but didn't back off "—we're treading dangerous ground here, a fine line between proper procedure and conflict of interest. If the D.A. smells even a hint of anything funky in this case, it'll be tossed out on its ear, and our perp will be walking free."

"Point taken," Rafferty said rigidly, "and duly noted. For your information, yesterday afternoon, immediately after we received the photograph, I discussed with my superiors and with Agent Monahan's the advisability of replacing her with another agent. All parties were in full agreement that Agent Monahan's involvement is not a threat to this investigation and that her continued presence, given the perpetrator's apparent fixation on her, is essential to the successful resolution of the case." He paused for breath. "It was further felt by all parties concerned that given Agent Monahan's flawless service record, she's enough of a professional to remove herself from the case if at any point in time she should feel that her presence is in danger of compromising the investigation. Does that satisfy you, Ted?"

Rizzoli shot Carolyn a hostile look. "I still don't think she should be on the case," he muttered.

"As far as I remember, Rizzoli, I'm still in charge of this case. And I say she stays. Is that clear?"

"Crystal," Rizzoli said caustically. "Sir."

"Good. As soon as we're done here this morning, you're to take the rest of the day off. As for the rest of you, I should have a schedule posted by the end of the day. If you don't see it on the bulletin board before you leave, check with Isabel." And he smoothly segued into his next topic of discussion, leaving Carolyn stewing over the fact that he'd spoken to Richard about whether or not to dump her from the case.

She knew he'd been following procedure. Covering his ass. But it hurt that he hadn't at least informed her before he announced it to the world at large. Worse still was the knowledge that it shouldn't have hurt. This was a homicide case they were involved in, not a Saturday night date.

But she'd let it become personal, and that was something a good agent never did.

As a group, they went over the details of her profile. The detectives asked questions and she answered them. The session dragged on endlessly, and they were all glassy-eyed by the time Rafferty finally dismissed them. Rizzoli brushed past her rudely, and when she got a whiff of his breath, her eyebrows nearly went up in flames. The man smelled like a brewery.

She gathered up her files and headed for the door. "Agent Monahan?" Rafferty said casually as she passed.

Caro froze, closed her eyes for a fraction of a second. "Yes?"

"Do you have a few minutes?" He was busy scribbling something on a sheet of paper, and didn't bother to look up. "I'd like to talk to you in my office."

"Of course." She escaped down the hall, dropped the case files on her desk, and headed for his office. Arms folded, she paced the room while she waited for him, wondering what he wanted to talk to her about. Was it professional or personal? Going to his apartment last night had been a huge mistake. By being alone together, they'd opened Pandora's box and unleashed all manner of disastrous consequences upon an unsuspecting world.

Rafferty came in, and she swung around to face him. "Thanks for waiting," he said, closing the door behind him. "Sit down. Please."

Still standing, she said, "What are you going to do about Rizzoli? I smelled his breath this morning. It had to be at least one hundred proof."

He looked tired, and she wondered if his night had been as restless as hers. "I'll have another talk with him. I'm sorry he's been so rude to you."

"You're not the one who owes me an apology."

"I'm his commanding officer. Look, I'm not trying to make excuses for him, but he's not always like this. Rizzoli's a good cop. He's going through a rough time right now. His wife just left him, and the guy's in pieces."

"Then maybe he should take those pieces elsewhere until he gets them glued back together."

"I already suggested that. He told me he has to keep working or he'll go off the deep end."

"Look, Rafferty, I feel for the guy. But he's making things miserable for everybody."

Perching on a corner of his desk, Rafferty sighed. "I'll talk to him again. In the meantime, I wanted to talk to you about Eric Dudley."

So the discussion wasn't going to be personal. Relief and disappointment washed over her, both of them vying for top billing. "What about him?" she said.

"This new development—the connection between this case and Meg's—seems to put him out of the running as a suspect. I just wanted to make sure we're on the same page here."

"He's twenty-four years old," she said. "Unless he was some kind of child prodigy who started killing at the age of fourteen—and that's not unheard of—I think we're safe in removing him from the list."

"The problem is that Dudley *is* our list."

"Nothing worthwhile from the phones?"

"Busywork. Pure and simple busywork. Just like I knew it would be."

"So where do you go from here? And what can I do to help?"

"I have an appointment at ten o'clock to talk to Deborah Stavros. She worked with Lavoie at the Golden Pussycat. I want to know what happened on Lavoie's last night. Maybe Stavros knows something that can help us.

If we don't get a break in this case pretty soon, I'll be back in Southie, in a uniform, walking a beat.''

"Come now, Lieutenant, it can't be that bad."

His smile was lopsided, and it shot a shaft of pure longing straight to her heart. "Want to come along for the ride?" he said. "Stavros may be more willing to talk to a woman. I'd take Lorna, but she's pretty well tied up."

"Since you asked so prettily, Rafferty, how can I turn you down?"

"By the way, I forgot to tell you last night. Armitage wants you to call him. He said he's left a couple of messages, but you haven't returned his calls."

And Hell would probably freeze over before she did, but she didn't tell him that. "Thanks," she said. "I'll take care of it."

"Well," he said, and glanced at his watch. Then he fell silent, and for a time, they just looked at each other.

There was a knock at the door, and she cleared her throat. "I guess I should go call Richard."

"Right," he said crisply.

At the door, she came face-to-face with Ted Rizzoli. He stiffened, then he nodded and stepped aside so she could exit the room. Behind her, she heard the door closing a little more firmly than was necessary. She squared her shoulders, strode down the hall to her own little cubicle, and picked up the phone.

In Quantico, Penny answered on the second ring. Caro leaned back in her chair and said, "It's me. Who's kicking around the place this morning?"

"Hey, girl! How are things in Boston?"

"Moving right along. Is Richard there?"

"I think he may be down the hall, talking to Lou. Want me to check?"

"No! I don't want to talk to him. Who else is in?"

"Trudy's here."

She grimaced. "Trudy has the biggest mouth outside the Beltway. I don't think so. Who else?"

"Jackson's in."

"Uh-uh."

"Steinberg."

Carolyn rolled her eyes. "You can't do any better than that?"

"Geez, you're picky. How about Sully?"

"Yes! That's more like it. Let me talk to him."

A moment later, there was a click, and a gravelly male voice said, "Agent Sullivan."

"Sully, it's Caro."

"Ah, the black sheep returns to the fold."

"Very funny. Listen, do you have any idea why Richard's been trying to reach me? He keeps leaving messages, but I really don't have any burning desire to talk to him."

"I couldn't begin to guess, Monahan. I don't suppose you've considered asking him? I know it's a radical approach, but you might want to try it. You'd be amazed at how well it works."

"Jesus, Sully, you're just a barrel of laughs."

"I aim to please."

With her fountain pen, she began doodling on the notepad in front of her. "He hasn't made any noises about pulling me off this case, has he?"

"In actuality, he's been exceedingly closemouthed of late. Rumor has it that a certain young lady of questionable reputation may have found a replacement for him."

Unable to hide her glee, she said, "Brandy dumped him already?"

"Of course," Sully drawled, "I don't generally listen to rumor."

"Of course not. Thanks, babe. You just brightened my day considerably."

"Glad I could be of assistance. Shall I convey your regards to our fearless leader?"

"Sully, darling, if you were to convey the full extent of my regards, you'd have to spend the next six months in confession. Top of the morning to you."

Deborah Stavros lived in a bright and airy fourth-floor walk-up in a remodeled brownstone on outer Commonwealth. She greeted them at the door and offered them iced tea. They both declined, and she led them into a sitting room that held a butter-soft leather sofa in a warm shade of cream. A svelte seal point Siamese cat lay in a patch of sunlight on the hardwood floor. There was an antique rolltop desk in one corner of the room, beside a wall that held floor-to-ceiling bookshelves filled with books of every shape and size. Rafferty exchanged a glance with Carolyn as she seated herself beside him on the sofa. Stavros sat in the overstuffed armchair across from them and crossed her spectacular legs.

"Thanks for talking to us," he said. "I hope we're not upsetting your schedule."

"Hardly. I want this guy caught just as much as you do. This whole thing is just a little too creepy. I'll do whatever I can to help." She caught Carolyn studying the spines of the eclectic collection of books that lined the white wooden shelves. "In case you're wondering," she said, "I'm a graduate student at B.U. Economics of Underdeveloped Nations."

Carolyn raised an eyebrow. "And you're working as a stripper?"

Stavros tucked a strand of dark hair behind her ear and gave them a pixie grin. "Exotic dancer," she said. "It pays a hell of a lot better than working as a salesclerk at Filene's.''

Rafferty stroked the leather couch. "It certainly looks that way."

"I have other means of support," she said. "I have a number of...gentleman friends, who contribute generous amounts of money in exchange for certain of my talents."

"You're a call girl," he said.

"In a manner of speaking. I only have a few clients, all of them wealthy, all of them regulars. That and the Golden Pussycat are paying my way through college." Again, she smiled. "My parents, back in Ohio, think I'm working as an executive secretary. I don't see any reason to disabuse them of that notion."

"Well," Carolyn said. "That certainly gives a whole new definition to the term *student financial aid*."

"That it does," Stavros said pleasantly, and turned her attention back to him. "So what can I tell you, Lieutenant?"

"How long have you known Tonia Lavoie?"

"About eight months. I think she started working at the Golden Pussycat right before Christmas."

"How well did you know her?"

The Siamese stood and stretched, then sauntered over to Rafferty. He bent and absently scratched the cat behind one ear, and it purred and rubbed against his legs. Stavros leaned back in her chair and shrugged. "How well do you know anybody? We worked together, saw each other every day. Talked a little about our personal lives, the way women do when they're thrown together in a work situation. We didn't see each other outside of work." Her smile was a little wry. "We didn't exactly have all that much in common."

Rubbing the cat under the chin, he said, "You told me

on the phone that Eric didn't like her working there. What else can you tell me about their relationship?"

She snorted. "Eric is a turd. He beat her. Quite often, and quite thoroughly. The neighbors would call the cops and they'd haul Eric off to jail. Tonia would never press charges. I wanted to tell her what I thought, but I didn't think she'd welcome the advice. We weren't that close."

"What about other men?" he said. "Did she ever mention anyone else?"

"Nobody specific, but there were plenty of them. I'm pretty sure that Tonia traded sexual favors for drugs. I think she'd spent time in rehab or some such thing. Her past was a little murky. But that's the way it is when you work in a place like that. Nobody talks much about their past. In most cases, it's just as well."

"What happened the night she died?"

"It was a typical night. We each dance a forty-minute set, then take a break. Tonia came off stage about nine-thirty, came into the dressing room, and changed into her street clothes. Said she'd run into an old friend and was headed out for a drink with him. She seemed quite subdued, but she didn't elaborate and I didn't ask. Around that place, you don't blab, and you don't ask questions. I figured she needed to score, and he was one of her suppliers. She left about quarter to ten, and she never came back."

Rafferty and Carolyn exchanged glances. "And nobody questioned her whereabouts?" he said.

Stavros shrugged. "It wasn't uncommon for Tonia to disappear, especially once she'd scored a high. Neal—he's the manager—would ream her out about it every so often, but he didn't fire her because she was one of the club favorites. That face—God, I should have been born with a face like that! And she had a body to match. All of it real. Nothing plastic. She drove the men crazy.''

"What did she say about this friend?"

Stavros closed her eyes as if trying to conjure up a picture in her mind. "She said he was an old friend who'd helped her out of a bind a while back. She hadn't seen him in a while." Opening her eyes, she added, "They were headed out for drinks, but she didn't say where, or when she'd be back."

Rafferty ran a hand along the cat's back. "And you never saw him?"

"Unfortunately, no."

"What about the other girls who were working that night? Do you suppose any of them got a look at this guy?"

"I suppose it's possible. Let's see, Darcy and Adrienne had the night off, but Tanesha was working that night. She might know something."

"How do I get in touch with her?"

"Neal would know. Hang on a minute, I have his number on my Rolodex."

Neal Horton was somewhere in his fifties, with a greasy ponytail and furtive eyes that never quite made contact with theirs. He danced all around their questions until, in exasperation, Rafferty said, "Look, Horton, we're not Vice. We're not interested in shutting down your little operation. A woman's been murdered, and all we want is to find the guy who did it. We'd appreciate a little co-operation."

Horton leaned back in his chair and visibly relaxed. "I don't know anything about how she died," he said. "I didn't see her leave. I was in here—" he indicated the shabby office they sat in "—going over liquor invoices.

When I found out she was gone, I was pissed off. I intended to have it out with her the next day.'' His expression turned morose. ''Tonia was a nice kid. But she was a junkie. I kept her on because she brought in customers, and customers bring in money. Bottom line. And she wasn't exactly hard on the eyes.''

Rafferty looked around the windowless room, at the stained walls, the empty foam coffee cups and piles of dusty papers on Horton's desk. ''Were you involved with her?''

Horton flushed. ''Are you kidding, man? Have you seen that boyfriend of hers? Built like a fucking gorilla.''

''What about Tanesha?'' Carolyn said. ''Deborah Stavros told us she was working that night. How can we get in touch with her?''

''You can't. She's on her honeymoon. She won't be back until next week.''

Rafferty pulled a card from his pocket and handed it to Horton. ''When she gets back, tell her I'd like to talk to her.''

When they returned to City Hall, Lorna was waiting in his office. ''I have to talk to you,'' she said tersely. Eyeing Carolyn, she said, ''You'd better hear this, too.'' She closed the door behind her and leaned on it. ''Something's come up. I've found a connection between three of our six cases.''

He gave her a long, level glance. ''Tell me why you don't look happier about it.''

''You know me too damn well, Conor. You're not going to like this.'' Lorna looked at them both, took a breath. ''I was going over the files on Lavoie and Magnusson. I can't believe we missed this before. Except that we didn't know the Monahan case was connected, and sometimes it's so easy to overlook something if you're not expecting it.''

Rafferty folded his arms. "Go on."

"Lavoie and Magnusson," she said. "They were both prostitutes. I was going through Lavoie's file, and there was a previous address on her arrest record. It just jumped out at me. I knew I'd seen it before. I went back to Magnusson's file and there it was. She'd lived at the same address for a while."

"And?" he said tersely.

"It was the Erin J. Donovan House." She took another deep breath. "Clancy Donovan knew all three of them. Monahan, Magnusson and Lavoie."

9

"That's preposterous," Carolyn said. "Completely and totally asinine!" She looked to Rafferty for confirmation, absently registering the stricken look on his face. "It's not possible," she continued. "The man's a priest, for God's sake. He's no killer!"

Rafferty didn't look at her. His gaze still locked with Lorna's, he said hoarsely, "Does he fit the profile?"

"No," Carolyn said without hesitation. "Of course not. It's ridiculous to even suggest such a thing!"

He finally looked at her, and she saw in his eyes the same stunned disbelief she was feeling. "Goddamn it, Monahan," he said quietly, "does he or does he not fit the fucking profile?"

She went through her profile mentally, point by point. *White male. Early thirties. Highly personable, with the gift of gab. Works in a profession where he meets a number of people on a daily basis. Average-looking, nothing about his appearance to make him stand out. Drives a late-model sedan, possibly blue. Lives by himself, has no significant relationship with a member of the opposite sex.*

Oh, God.

But those were superficial similarities. A thousand men could match that description. There were others that were more important. Frantic now, her heart beating a mile a minute, she continued her mental inventory. *Father absent from the home. Parental discipline inconsistent. Mother who exhibited sexually inappropriate behavior: a string of live-in boyfriends, Saturday-night pickups, perhaps even prostitution—*

"Shit," she whispered. "Oh, shit."

She never saw a single muscle move, but somehow Rafferty's face hardened. "Go pick him up," he said tersely to Lorna. "Bring him in for questioning."

Lorna nodded briskly and left the room, quietly closing the door behind her. Caro sank onto a chair. "You can't seriously believe—" She wet her lips. "You can't— Oh, Jesus. This is not happening."

He stood and began pacing. "I never even considered him. Not for a fucking minute did I ever consider him. What kind of fool does that make me?"

She sat there in the chair, trembling, trying to take in all the implications. They were staggering. "Conor," she said.

He paused, wheeled around. "What?"

"You have to remove yourself from the case. You can't do this."

"Why? What can't I do? You don't think I'm capable of being unbiased? You don't think I'm capable of running this investigation anymore?"

"The man is a friend of yours. You're dangerously close to a breach of professional ethics."

"Let me tell you something," he said. "I'm a goddamn cop. It's not just what I do, it's who I am. It's inside me, in here." He jammed his thumb into his breastbone. "I don't give a damn if he's my friend. I don't give a damn if he's a priest, or if he's the fucking Pope, or if he's Jesus Christ Almighty." He narrowed his eyes. "If he did this, then, by God, I am going to take him down."

"Are you crazy? Do you think they'll let you keep the

case? They'll yank you faster than you can say Jack Shit. Christ, Conor, they could take your badge over something like this.''

She saw the defiance in his eyes fade as the truth of her words sank in. ''Fuck,'' he said, and sat down at his desk, running his fingers through his hair.

Caro got up from the chair, crossed the room, and sat on the corner of the desk, near his elbow. ''Look,'' she said, ''I understand how you feel. But you have to think about how it looks to the world.''

He gazed at her through tired eyes. ''You don't have a goddamn clue how I feel.''

''Fine. Suppose you tell me.''

''Betrayed,'' he snapped. ''Is that word clear enough?''

''I can understand that. He's your friend. But you can't set yourself up as judge and jury. That's not your responsibility.''

''You don't get it,'' he said wearily. ''It's not about him. It's about me. I'm a cop. I learned a long time ago not to have high expectations of people, because it's human nature to disappoint. Clancy didn't betray me. It's my own goddamn gut that betrayed me, the gut that didn't believe he did it ten years ago, and still refuses to believe it now.''

She rested a hand on his shoulder, squeezed ineffectually.

''I don't care how many years you spend at the police academy,'' he continued. ''I don't care how many college degrees you have, or how many trainings you've been to. There's just one thing of value that a cop has, and that's his gut instinct. Every officer who's ever worked the street knows what I'm talking about. It's what makes you a cop, what keeps you alive on the street, day after day. It's the one thing that stands between you and them. But once it's gone—'' He ran his hands through his hair again. ''Once you lose your gut, you might as well just kiss it all good-bye and go flip burgers for a living. Because you're not a cop anymore.''

She didn't know what to say. Because there was nothing she could say, she squeezed his shoulder.

''Maybe I can go to work selling bedroom suites for my brother Frank,'' he said bitterly. ''The Mattress King of the North Shore.''

If it hadn't been so awful, she might have laughed. ''I'm sorry,'' she said instead.

''Yeah. That makes two of us.''

Her hand still on his shoulder, she said, ''So what are you going to do?''

Grimly, he said, ''He's coming in for questioning. I'm going to question him.''

She swore softly under her breath. ''Are you trying to deep-six this whole investigation, Rafferty?''

''I'm trying to get at the goddamn truth.''

''You want the truth? Right now, the truth is that you're standing on the gallows with your neck in the noose, and you're about to step off the platform.''

He looked at the hand that rested on his shoulder, followed the curve of her arm, up to her face. His green eyes intent on hers, he said softly, ''And are you going to be the one who shoves me over the edge?''

She felt the jolt all the way to the pit of her stomach. It wasn't fair that he should ask something like this of her. Not fair for him to ask her to keep a vital piece of information secret, not fair for him to ask her to choose between what she'd been taught was right and what she felt in her heart. ''Christ, Conor,'' she said, folding her arms and turning away from him, toward the window.

''Sometimes,'' he said quietly, ''there are more important things than so-called professional ethics.'' He got up from his chair and stood behind her. ''Like truth.'' He closed his hands over her upper arms. ''Like getting a killer off the street.''

Across the street, at Faneuil Hall Marketplace, she watched the tourists in brightly colored clothes wander in and out of the shops. Her heart was beating double-time, and his breath, warm on the back of her neck, raised goose bumps on her flesh. ''You're asking me to lie for you.''

''No,'' he said near her ear. ''I'd never ask you to lie for me. I'm asking you to help me catch a killer. I'm asking you to help me catch the man who killed your sister. Damn it, Caro, I'm asking you to trust me.''

What was it she'd told Tommy Malone yesterday at lunch, a million years ago? *I'd trust him with my life.* She hadn't expected to be put to the test so quickly. Turning from the window, she squared her shoulders and faced him head-on. ''And what if we don't take him down?'' she said. ''What if we go down instead?''

''We'll know that we went down fighting for what was right.''

''That'll be a big comfort while I'm doing five to ten in San Quentin.''

He touched a strand of her hair, rubbed it between his fingers. ''It's in your hands,'' he said. ''You're either with me, or you're against me. But I can't do this without you.''

''What about Lorna?''

''She'd go to the wall for me. She'll give me the time I need to find out the truth. Look, I'm a good cop, Carolyn. I've never broken the rules. I've followed procedure, gone by the book, since my first day on the force. But we have one hell of a mess here, and following the rules doesn't seem to be working. My gut tells me Clancy's not guilty, but I know I could be wrong. I'll promise you one thing, though. If I uncover any evidence—any evidence at all—that convinces me my gut's wrong, I'll step aside and let somebody else take the case.''

She felt herself weakening. "How much time are you asking for?"

"A few days. A week at the most. If I can't find the evidence I need in that amount of time, I'll remove myself from the case. I'll take full responsibility for screwing up. I won't let you or Lorna take any of the heat for it. I'm the man in charge, and I'll carry it all on my shoulders. If they take my badge, fine. Let them take it. But if I go down, I'll go down alone. I won't drag you with me.''

A few days. He was asking her to keep her mouth shut for just a few days. "Oh, hell," she said, knowing she was about to go against every ounce of training that Uncle Sam had drilled into her head.

He squeezed her arms and released them. "Trust me," he said again. "I'll talk to Lorna."

Dressed all in black, with his dark hair hanging in loose waves that touched the starched clerical collar, Father Clancy Donovan looked more like an emissary of Satan than an agent of God. He sat in the hot seat at one end of the conference room table, his face guarded, his eyes shuttered.

"I'm assuming," he said, "that this isn't a social occasion."

Rafferty perched on the corner of the gleaming wooden table and said, "We want to ask you some questions regarding the homicides of Tonia Lavoie and Anna Magnusson."

Carolyn leaned against the ugly brown paneling and shoved her fists into the pockets of her jacket. "I see," the priest said, stretching out his long legs in front of him. "Does this mean that I'm a suspect?"

Rafferty was fiddling with a mini-cassette recorder. Instead of answering, he said, "If you have no objections, I'm going to tape the interview."

Clancy leaned back on his tailbone and folded his arms. "And if I do have objections?"

Rafferty met his eyes. "I'm going to tape the interview."

Clancy sat a little straighter. "Fine," he said amiably. "Run your tape recorder. I have nothing to hide."

"Before we get started," Lorna said briskly, "can I get you something, Father? Coffee, tea? A soda?"

"I don't suppose you have a lawyer in your back pocket?"

"You don't need a lawyer," Rafferty snapped. "You have nothing to hide, remember?"

Carolyn winced and closed her eyes. When she opened them again, Rafferty was speaking into the microphone, reciting the particulars of the interview he was about to conduct. He shoved the tape recorder into the center of the table and faced the priest.

"It's my understanding," he said, "that you were acquainted with both Tonia Lavoie and Anna Magnusson. As well as Meg Monahan. Is that correct?"

Clancy crossed his long legs and adjusted the material of his trousers. "I knew them. I know Monsignor Fiorelli and the girl who works the counter at the dry cleaner's, too. Is there anything you'd like to ask me about them while we're at it?"

A muscle twitched in Rafferty's cheek. "Stop dicking me around," he said, "and just answer the question."

The priest eyed him coolly. "Yes," he said. "I knew them."

"All three of them?"

"Yes."

"Just how do you account for that, Father Donovan? Just how do you account for this amazing coincidence that we have here? What do you suppose the chances are that you'd know three of our six murder victims? Ten to one? A hundred to one? A billion to one?"

Tightly, the priest said, "I couldn't say, but I'm sure you'd be happy to clarify those odds for me, Lieutenant."

"Do you believe in coincidence, Father Donovan?"

"Considering the circumstances, I suppose I should say yes. Any other answer would brand me a fool." Clancy boldly returned the heated gaze of his persecutor. "Or a murderer."

"Nobody's calling you a murderer," Lorna said smoothly. "These are routine questions, Father. We have to ask them."

Rafferty stared at her balefully. "When I need a translator, Detective, I'll be sure to let you know."

Lorna's cheeks flushed pink, and she stepped back against the wall beside Carolyn. Under her breath, she muttered a cussword too softly for her lieutenant to hear.

Intently, Rafferty said, "Were you acquainted with any of the other victims? Becky Shields, Lindsay Helms, or Katie Ann Perry?"

"No."

"You never met any of them?"

"No."

"But you did know Lavoie and Magnusson. What was your relationship with them?"

"They were both prostitutes. They both spent time at the Donovan House. I'm the chief administrator there. I know all the girls."

"Spent time as in lived there?"

"Yes."

"When? During what time period?"

"I couldn't say for sure. Not without consulting my records. Sometime in the past year."

"In the past six months?"

"Possibly. As I said, I'd have to check my records."

"Were they both living there at the same time?"

Clancy furrowed his brow and considered the question. "No," he said at last. "I don't think so. Tonia was there first. Anna came along after she left. Tonia wasn't one of my success stories. I lost track of her after she left."

"What was the nature of your relationship with Meg Monahan?"

Clancy straightened in his chair. "I've already been down this road, ten years ago. Is there some really good reason why we're digging it all back up? Because if there isn't a good reason for you to be asking, I'd prefer to let the dead stay buried."

Rafferty took a deep breath. "Answer the goddamn question."

He was losing his cool, and Carolyn had to struggle to keep from stepping forward and laying a warning hand on his shoulder. Clancy met her eyes, stared at her without expression, then turned his gaze back on Rafferty. "We were lovers," he said.

Tersely, Rafferty said, "Did you kill her?"

"My answer hasn't changed since I gave it to the police ten years ago."

"Goddamn it, I asked you a question. Did you kill her?"

"No."

"Have you ever killed anyone, Father Donovan?"

Something flickered in the priest's eyes, so briefly that, had she blinked, Carolyn would have missed it. "I'm a priest," he said. "In case you've forgotten, there's a line in the Bible that forbids killing."

Rafferty leaned forward and spoke so softly that anybody who didn't know him wouldn't have recognized the danger in his voice. "That's not an answer, Father."

Clancy hunched over the table and rested both elbows on the gleaming wood. "I don't believe," he said, "that the answer has any pertinence to the situation at hand."

"Answer the fucking question, Donovan. Have you or have you not ever killed anyone?"

For a long, frozen moment, the two men locked gazes while Carolyn's heart beat too rapidly in her chest. "Yes," the priest said, "but it has nothing to do with this."

The silence in the room was so absolute that Carolyn could hear the ticking of the clock on the wall. "Tell us about it," Rafferty said in a voice like cool, smooth steel.

"After high school," Clancy said, "I drifted for a while. There was nothing much to keep me here. A rattrap of an apartment and a mother who was blind drunk all the time. I was young, I was lost, I was looking for something. I thought I'd found it when I stumbled across this paramilitary group in Hong Kong. Mercenaries. These men came from all over the world, yet there was a cohesiveness to the group that spoke to that empty spot inside me. They offered me something I'd never had before. A sense of belonging. Of family. For a while, I was content with them. But the killing that went along with the job made me sick to my stomach. It wasn't long before I realized that I wasn't cut out to be a soldier. I believed in God's laws then, and I still do. 'Thou shalt not kill' meant more to me than just words printed on a piece of paper. So I came home, put my past behind me, and became a priest. End of story."

"Not precisely," Rafferty said. "Before you became a priest, you started an affair with Meg Monahan, and six months later, she was dead."

"I didn't kill her," Clancy said, with so much anguish in his voice that it nearly broke Carolyn's heart. "I loved her. I wanted to marry her."

Rafferty tapped his fingertips on the table top. In the tense silence of the room, the tapping echoed like gunshots. "Do you own a camera?" he said.

Carolyn held her breath and waited for the answer. "A camera?" Clancy said. "Yes. Why?"

"I'm asking the questions here. What kind of camera?"

"I own a couple. I have a Polaroid that I use for christenings. Quick and easy, and the parents can tote the pictures home with them right then and there. I also have a Minolta 35 millimeter with a zoom lens. I use it for birdwatching."

"Who develops your 35 millimeter film? What photo lab do you use?"

In her pockets, Carolyn's fists were clenched so hard that her nails bit into her palms. "I don't use a photo lab," Clancy said. "I develop them myself. Why?"

She felt the nausea rise from her stomach into the back of her throat, and thought she would lose her breakfast. "That's just ducky," Rafferty muttered.

There was a moment of charged silence before Lorna stepped in. "Father Donovan," she said briskly, "where were you last Friday night between nine and eleven?"

"Friday night?" His eyes narrowed, and for the first time, he hesitated. "I was out driving around. Cruising the streets."

Lorna raised an eyebrow. "Cruising the streets? Cruising the streets for what?"

But it wasn't the priest who answered. It was Rafferty.

"Prostitutes," he said dully, sounding drained and defeated. "He was cruising for prostitutes."

Carolyn and Lorna exchanged glances. "Prostitutes?" Lorna said.

"It's how I work," Clancy explained. "I go out at night, looking for young working girls, and I talk them into leaving the streets. I bring them to the Donovan House and give them a second chance at life."

Lorna blew out a breath. "Oh, boy," she said.

Rafferty leaned over the table and turned off the tape player, and he and the priest stared at each other in a charged silence. Bracing his palms against the edge of the table, he leaned closer. "Do you have any idea," he said quietly, "any fucking idea at all, how much trouble you're in?"

"I didn't kill anyone."

"You knew I was working this case. You've known it for months. Yet it never occurred to you to mention to me the insignificant little fact that you knew Magnusson and Lavoie? Didn't you realize that it would come out, sooner or later?"

The priest rested both elbows on the table and leaned forward. Heatedly, he said, "And how many other people do you suppose knew them both? I didn't tell you because I knew you'd react this way. I wasn't hiding anything. I don't have anything to hide. And in case you've forgotten, Tonia died just a few days ago. I couldn't exactly tell you in advance that I knew her, could I? I'm not psychic." He paused for breath. "And I'm not a killer."

"Goddamn it," Rafferty shouted, "you could have told me about Magnusson!"

It was the first time Carolyn had ever seen him lose his cool. Even when he was angry, he always maintained a facade of calmness.

Lorna stepped forward and laid a hand on his arm. "Conor," she said firmly, "this is getting us nowhere."

He shook off her hand. "Christ," he muttered, sitting down hard in the nearest chair, burying his fingers in his hair.

"We'll need to know where you were," Lorna said to the priest, "and what you were doing on the nights the murders occurred."

"You expect me to remember where I was on a given night five or six months ago?"

Crisply, she said, "You must keep an appointment book."

"Yes. I do." He nodded slowly. "I hadn't thought of that. It might help me to remember."

"We'll need to see it. Conor?" She swung around. "Are we done here?"

He raised his head. "We're done," he said, and eyed the priest balefully. "For now."

"Thank you for cooperating, Father," she said briskly. "If you'll wait for me outside, I'll be right with you."

On his way to the door, Clancy met Carolyn's eyes. His expression hardened, and he looked away without acknowledging her. To her horror, she felt the prick of tears behind her eyelids. She blinked them back, not certain precisely who they were for. Herself? Clancy? Her dead sister? Lorna closed the conference room door behind the priest and turned to Rafferty.

"You," she said hotly, "are out of here. As of this instant, you're off duty, and I don't want to see you back here before Thursday. Is that understood?"

"I happen to be your commanding officer," he said. "I could have you hauled in for insubordination."

"And I could have you hauled in," she snapped, "for conflict of interest."

Rafferty glared at her, and she glared right back. "I don't want to see you back here," she said, "until you get your head on straight. I'll deal with this Father Donovan mess." She glanced at Caro, and the corners of her mouth took a downward turn. "I can sure as hell be more objective about it than either of you can." Hand on the door knob, she paused. "I'm leaving now, to give our suspect a ride home, and to get a look at that appointment book. When I get back, you'd better be gone."

She shut the door firmly, leaving silence behind her. Rafferty cleared his throat. "Well," he said.

Carolyn's hands were trembling. She needed to touch him, but she wasn't sure which need was more urgent: the need to give comfort, or to receive it. She moved slowly across the floor and stopped behind his chair. Resting her hands on his shoulders, she said hoarsely, "She's right, you know."

"Sure," he said wearily. "That makes it all better. So do you still think he's innocent?"

With a fingertip, she traced the line of his collar before toying with the hair at the nape of his neck. "I want him to be innocent," she said. "It's not the same thing."

Rafferty leaned his head back and sighed. "I was too hard on him, wasn't I?"

"You were doing your job." She returned her hands to the relative safety of his shoulders. "Did you know?" she said. "About the mercenary thing?"

"It was a stab in the dark. I suspected he'd done something illegal, because he never talked about it. I knew he'd been in the Orient for a couple of years, but he didn't volunteer any information about what he did there. I always figured if he wanted me to know, he would have told me."

"Does it really matter?" she said. "It's all circumstantial. There's absolutely nothing concrete to link him to this case.''

"Coincidence, Caro. You know as well as I do how slight the chances are.''

She thought about Clancy Donovan's time as a mercenary, thought about the cameras and the darkroom and the nightly trolling he did for prostitutes, and her stomach clenched into a tight ball. "It doesn't look good, does it?'' she said, removing her hands from Rafferty's shoulders.

"It looks pisspoor.'' He got up from the chair. "I'm out of here. I've been given my walking papers.''

"Where are you going?''

"Home,'' he said sourly. "Maybe if I get lucky, I can drink myself into oblivion.''

After he was gone, Carolyn walked to the window and stood there staring out at a gray, dismal city. Fat clouds loomed on the horizon, dark and heavy, promising rain and perfectly matching her mood. Was it possible that a man she'd trusted, a man she'd grown up with, a man she'd loved as a brother, could be a killer? She thought about Clancy's hands, long and angular, and tried to picture them around her sister's neck, squeezing the breath out of Meg until there was no more breath left. But the image was too painful, and she was terrified that the truth, when it finally came out, would be unbearable.

And then there was Conor, who presented a whole different set of problems. She exhaled a ragged breath. What on God's green earth was she going to do about Conor? The man might as well have been wearing flashing amber lights that screamed Warning! Warning! Warning! And she might as well have been wearing blinders, for all the good the warning had done her. Just a few days back in Boston, and already she was in danger. But Thomas Wolfe was right; you couldn't go home again. You couldn't go backward. There was only one direction a person could go, and that was forward. Conor Rafferty was part of her past, not her future, and no amount of yearning could change that.

She wandered back to her cubicle, but it was impossible to work, and after a few minutes, she gave up, packed her briefcase, and walked back to her hotel. She stripped and showered and dressed in a plain white T-shirt and jeans. Maybe she couldn't go backward, she thought as she pulled on her sneakers and grabbed a gray hooded fleece jacket, but there was something else she needed to do.

The cemetery sat on a hill not far from the shore in Southie, and as she walked the five blocks from the bus stop, it began to rain, fat drops that bounced when they hit the pavement. Meg's grave was at the eastern end, overlooking the water, marked by a simple granite stone that read Margaret Monahan. Near the headstone, somebody had planted pansies—a riot of purple and pink and yellow. Her mother? Somehow, she couldn't picture the monochromatic Roberta Monahan planting anything so vibrant and beautiful. But who else could possibly have put them here? Meg would have loved them, for she, too, had been beautiful and vibrant and full of life.

Caro shoved back the hood of her jacket and knelt in the wet grass. Raggedly, she said, "I need your help, Meggie. It's all such a mess. You and Clancy. Conor and me. Tell me what to do, Meg. I can't do this without you."

The soft patter of the rain against the flowers was soothing. A raindrop trickled down her cheek to the corner of her mouth. She licked it with her tongue, tasted salt, and realized it hadn't been a raindrop at all. "I trusted Clancy," she told her sister. "I never questioned his innocence when you died, and I never questioned it this time around, either. Now, I don't know what to think. I don't want to believe he could have done this to you. But I'm so confused, Meg. You hold the key to all of this. You're the only one who knows the truth." She swiped a wet strand of hair away from her face. "You have to help me," she said. "Give me something. Anything! Help us stop him before he kills someone else."

Meg didn't answer. Across the harbor at Logan, a jet engine whined, preparing for takeoff, drowning out the birdsong and the patter of the rain. There were people who would call her crazy for sitting here in a cemetery, in the rain, talking to a dead woman. But Meg would understand, would see the humor in it. And even if she couldn't answer, Meg could listen.

"And then," Caro confided to her sister, "there's Rafferty. Hell, Meggie, I thought I was over him years ago. But every time he walks into the room, it turns me inside out." She lifted her head, looked out across the harbor, watched a jet lift off from the runway and climb until it disappeared into the clouds. In spite of the fleece jacket she wore, she shivered in the dampness. "I'd be lying if I told you I didn't want him."

At the center of her jumbled emotions, that one piece of knowledge shone suddenly, painfully clear. "Oh, shit," she said. "I'm in trouble, aren't I?"

Meg remained silent as the rain fell steadily. It was twelve blocks to M Street. Twelve blocks in the pouring rain, with no guarantee that he'd even let her in the door when she got there. Twelve blocks to a relationship with no future, no hope of anything beyond the touching, the tasting, the feeding of a hunger that wouldn't leave her alone. Twelve blocks that could lead her to heaven, or leave her cold and shivering in purgatory.

If she hurried, she could make it in fifteen minutes.

10

When Rafferty opened the door, she could hear music playing, slow and sultry and funky, a zydeco love ballad that seemed to fit with the rain pattering softly outside the open windows of his apartment. He was wearing dark-blue sweats and holding a cordless phone to his ear, and his eyes widened when he saw her.

"I'll have to call you back," he said into the phone, and hung it up. "Caro," he said.

She swallowed and tried to smile. "May I come in?"

"Of course." He set down the phone, opened the door wider and ushered her inside. Closing it behind her, he said, "You look like something the cat dragged in, Monahan. Are you all right?"

The music swirled around her head, its bluesy rhythm syncopating with the beating of her heart. "Are you kidding, Rafferty?" she said, hating the catch she heard in her own voice. "I'm a Fed. We're tough as nails. It comes with the job."

He moved closer, gently lowered the hood of her soggy fleece jacket. "Is that so?"

Her hair was hanging in sodden strings, her makeup was gone, and she knew she looked like the bride of Frankenstein. "We chew ground glass for breakfast," she said, misery lending an edge to her words. "Bullets bounce off us."

He unzipped the wet jacket and peeled it off her. Dropped it to the floor. With something that sounded suspiciously like tenderness, he said, "I hear you can leap tall buildings in a single bound, too."

Damning tears burned her eyelids, and she was acutely aware of the goose bumps that dotted her flesh, acutely aware of her hard nipples beneath the wet T-shirt that was the only thing covering them. Rafferty moved closer, so close she could feel the heat from his body, and rested a hand on the door above her shoulder. "You're drenched to the bone. What have you been doing, Monahan? Rolling around in mud puddles?"

"I've been to the cemetery. To talk to Meg."

"Ah. I see." With one finger, he traced the line of her jaw, all the way from her chin to her ear, setting her entire body atremble. "What did Meg have to say to you?"

She looked into his eyes, just inches from hers. "She told me that if I knew what was good for me, I'd stay away from a certain handsome, green-eyed Homicide cop."

He toyed with a strand of soggy hair. "And are you planning to listen to her?"

She touched his arm with a fingertip, ran it up to his shoulder, watched his eyes go from green to a soft gray. "I never was any good," she said, raising her hand to his cheek, "at paying attention to what was in my best interests." She ran her fingertips across coarse razor stubble. Breathlessly, she added, "It seems I have to learn everything the hard way."

"Good," he said. "Because I'm going to kiss you now, Monahan, and I'd really hate to compromise your principles."

He tasted the same. *Oh, God.* After all these years, he still tasted the same. She could have resisted him if only he'd been a stranger, foreign, unfamiliar. But he still tasted of hot sex and wild emotion and a young girl's dreams. She opened to him: arms, legs, mouth, heart, as he pinned her to the door, and like two people who'd been starving for eons they took vast, lingering draughts of each other. He tangled his fists in her wet hair while her hands slipped beneath his sweatshirt and found the smooth expanse of his chest. Beneath her palms, his heart beat wildly, a perfect match for hers.

He broke away, pressed his forehead to the door, his cheek to hers, warm and rough against her soft skin. Breathing hard, one hand still tangled in her hair, he whispered, "Caro. My sweet Caro."

She ran her hands up over his shoulders, rubbed the back of his neck, so warm and somehow so vulnerable. His mouth touched the sensitive spot behind her ear, toyed with it as her breathing grew harsh and her fingers tightened on his shoulders. "If this isn't what you want," he said against her skin, "tell me now." His breath tickled the hairs at the back of her neck. "Because once we get started—" he touched the tip of his tongue to the underside of her jaw, and she gasped "—we won't be stopping any time soon."

Her heart thundering, she drew her hands back down his chest, skimming the flat nipples that beaded up at her touch, exploring the hills and valleys that marked his rib cage. When she caught the hem of his sweatshirt in her hands, she heard his sharp intake of breath. He helped her peel the shirt off over his head, and she dropped it to the floor.

He was as beautiful as she remembered. Even more so, for time had honed his body, sculpting the boy she'd known into a man in his prime. Caro touched whisper-soft lips to his skin and felt him shudder. His shoulders were sleek and satin-smooth, and her hands lingered there a moment before she wound them into his hair and drew his mouth down to hers.

The kiss was hot and wet. He pressed her hard against the door, kissing her cheek, her neck, feasting upon her, his mouth worrying the soft flesh of her throat. She let out a whimper, then gasped as he lowered his head and sank his teeth into the swell of her breast.

Beneath the wet T-shirt, her nipples were rock hard. He cupped her breast in his hand, lifted it, and closed his mouth over it. Through damp cotton, he drew deeply on her. She opened her mouth to breathe, heard a shuddering sob, took a moment to recognize that the sound had come from her.

He tugged her T-shirt from her waistband and lifted it. While she clung to him for support, he kissed his way down her body, buried his face in her midriff, explored her navel with the tip of his tongue. His mouth moved lower, and through thick denim she felt his heat as he pressed his face to the hollow at the juncture of her thighs.

Hoarsely, he said, ''Wrap your legs around me.'' And he stood and lifted her off her feet.

She wrapped herself around him, clung tight as he crossed the room and paused at the bedroom door. Nero was sleeping on the bed. Rafferty spoke a single, harsh syllable, and with a sigh, the dog hopped down and slunk from the room.

He shut the door, and she braced her hands against his shoulders as he leaned forward to kiss her. His mouth intent on hers, he fumbled behind his back for her sneaker, pulled it off and dropped it to the floor. Removed the other one and dropped it, then carried her to the bed and knelt on the edge. She loosened her legs and went limp, and slid down his body until her knees reached the mattress.

He peeled off her T-shirt and dropped it. Outside the open window, rain pattered softly. A breeze billowed the lace curtain and then let it fall. The light that filtered through was dim and gauzy, like the curtain. Her breath coming in short, hard gusts, she watched Rafferty's eyes as he slid the fingers of both hands beneath her waistband. His warm knuckles brushed against her skin, shooting a thrill through her. His thumbs toyed with the brass button. Eyes still on hers, he released it, unlocked the zipper with his thumb, and yanked hard with both hands.

Caro gasped, closing her eyes as he pulled down her damp jeans, her delicate, lacy panties. He raised first her left knee and then her right, pulled the clothing past her ankles and tossed it on the floor. Naked, she knelt before him, unembarrassed as his eyes took in every curve, every line of her body. She ran a hand down his bare chest, past the thickening of hair around his navel. He peeled off the sweatpants and discarded them. Then they were lying on the bed in the dim light, with the rain still pattering softly, and he ran his hands up her forearms to her wrists, threaded his fingers with hers. "Caro," he said softly.

"What?" she whispered.

"Nothing," he said. "Just Caro."

And he buried himself inside her.

She let out a shocked cry, raised her hips, locked herself around him. She would have thought it impossible after ten years, but her body remembered him, remembered his shape and his size and his feel. He pinned her hands to the mattress on either side of her head and drove her, hard and fast. She gasped, tried to catch her breath, rolled with him, cried out his name as her body shattered in a billion pieces.

He slowed, released her hands, buried his fingers in her

tangled hair. Raggedly, he said, ''Your hair's like silk. Just the way I remember it.''

Still trembling from the aftershocks, she was unable to respond. Freed, her hands found his shoulders, satin-sleek and damp. Worked their way down smooth flesh to his biceps. With the ball of her thumb, she traced the ridge of a vein.

''Don't you think,'' he said hoarsely, ''that there's a certain…inevitability…to this?''

''Don't ask me to think,'' she said. ''I don't want to think right now. I only want to—*oh*. Oh, God.''

He touched his tongue to the pulse point at the base of her throat. ''You liked it fast,'' he said. ''Do you like it slow?''

Her fingers tightened on him. ''Oh, Jesus, Conor.''

''Mmm. I think you do. Caro?''

Weakly, she said, ''What?''

''Look at me.''

She opened her eyes and looked into his. Passion had turned them a sultry, grayish-green. ''Hi,'' he said.

Breathlessly, she said, ''Hi.''

''You're still so goddamn beautiful.''

''So are you.'' Her hands left his biceps, found his face, that magnificent face she'd never been able to get over.

Outside, a car passed, tires hissing on the wet pavement. She drew his mouth to hers and for a time there was no more talk as they danced the dance, sweet and hot and agonizingly slow, the bedding beneath them growing sticky and damp as the outside world ceased to exist. Nothing existed but the feel of him, hot and slick inside her, his warm breath on her face, his body, hard and sleek and smooth, rolling with hers in exquisite harmony.

This time, when she toppled off the edge of the world, she took him with her. Depleted, they lay in a ragged tangle, muscles lax and hearts thundering, while she tried to remember all the reasons this was a mistake. There had to be at least a dozen reasons she shouldn't be here, but she couldn't think of a single one. Not now. Not yet, while she was lying in his arms, his skin sticky-sweet against hers.

He drew her head down to his shoulder. With a sigh of contentment, she snuggled against him and allowed herself to drift as the cool air from the open window dried the sweat from her body.

Later, she told herself as she absorbed his body heat. She'd sort it all out later.

He hadn't used protection.

It was his first thought once the blood returned to his brain, although while he'd been buried deep inside Special Agent Carolyn Monahan, making love to her with exacting thoroughness, the thought hadn't even crossed his mind. The crime was unforgivable on both their parts. They were both intelligent, educated adults, both of them recently sexually active with other partners, yet neither of them had given even a passing thought to using protection.

He knew it was a lousy excuse, but all he'd thought of—if he'd thought at all—had been the drive to couple, the blinding need to be inside her as quickly as possible, for when Caro touched him, every civilized thought left his head. She possessed some kind of powerful allure that drove him mad, something that, if he could only bottle and sell it, would make him a wealthy man.

"Three billion women," he murmured against her neck.

She shifted position, adjusted her hands on his back. "What did you say?"

"I said that there are roughly three billion women on this planet, give or take a few, but there's just one—" he gently drew a lengthy strand of blond hair away from the corner of his mouth "—that I can't stay away from. Why do you suppose that is?"

"I don't know," she said. "I can't think right now. My brain's turned to mush."

He buried his nose in her hair. She smelled so goddamn wonderful. "I screwed up," he said. "I'm sorry."

Her hands, those smooth, cool hands, traced a pattern up and down his back with ten soft little fingertips. "I must have missed that part," she said lazily. "I only remember the part where you took me to paradise."

"I forgot to use protection."

"Oh," she said. And then, more somberly, "Oh."

"I've never done that before. I can't believe I forgot. I always use protection. Always."

"So do I. So the chances are minute that either one of us is carrying anything."

What she was saying made sense. But it didn't tell the whole story. "There is one other little aspect to the situation," he said.

"Don't worry about that. I have it covered. I'm not planning on any little surprises."

He relaxed a little, wondering why the image of her with a rounded belly, with his baby inside, seemed so appealing. He hadn't been able to imagine making babies with Gwen, but he could see himself making them with Caro, and he tried not think about what that might mean. He drew her close, molded her warm backside against him, and she laid her head on his shoulder. "Why'd you leave me?" he said into her hair. "All those years ago?"

She stiffened in his arms, and for a few seconds, as the rain pattered softly outside the window, he thought she wasn't going to answer him. Then she took his hand in hers and threaded their fingers together. "I was twenty-two years old," she said. "You do stupid things at twenty-two. It had nothing to do with you, and everything to do with me."

"Because of Meg?"

She stroked his palm with her thumb. "My sister died because I was too busy dallying with you to remember her. The guilt was so crushing that I could barely stand to look at you. Not because I blamed you, but because I blamed myself. I had absolutely no restraint where you were concerned, and Meggie paid the price for what I lacked."

"And here you are, ten years later, still struggling with the guilt."

"And right back where I started." She ran a fingertip down his arm. "But the guilt was only part of it. I felt so stifled in South Boston. So closed in. It was a matter of survival. I took the only route I could see. Escape." She turned in his arms and her eyes met his, frank and warm, without apology. "But it was never you I wanted to escape from. Only what you represented."

"Which was what?"

"A way of life I was desperate to get away from. I was terrified of turning into my mother. Brittle, resentful, disappointed by life."

"You're nothing like your mother. You're warm where she's cold, strong where she's weak. You care about people. You hurt for them. The way you talked to Katie Perry's mother—you can't fake that kind of compassion."

"But I'm afraid," she said. "I'm afraid all the time."

He gently brushed his knuckles against her cheek. "Afraid of what?"

"Afraid of failure. Afraid of drowning in a sea of mediocrity. Afraid that someday the world will look past the facade I've created and see who I really am and where I come from.'' She paused. ''I'm not a very nice person, Conor. I want too many things I'm not sure I'm entitled to.''

''That's the way you see it,'' he said. ''Now let me tell you what I see. I see an intelligent, vibrant woman who's not willing to settle for less than she deserves. And you don't have a mediocre bone in your body.''

She let out a tiny sigh. ''We're in trouble, aren't we?''

''Why?''

''It's all so mixed-up. You and me. Meg and Clancy. This case. It's all intertwined to the point where I can't tell what's what anymore.''

''Right now,'' he said, ''there isn't any case. There's just you—'' he kissed her knuckles ''—and me.''

Her breath was warm and sweet against his face. ''And Nero,'' she said. ''We can't forget Nero.''

''He'll have to find his own girl. This one's already taken.''

When she smiled, something happened to his insides, something elemental and intoxicating and terrifying.

''You always did have a way with words, Lieutenant,'' she said.

Hours later, he rolled over and said, ''When was the last time you ate something?''

She raised an arm and brushed the long hair back from her face. ''I don't know. Breakfast, I guess.''

''It's six o'clock at night, Monahan. Were you thinking of eating sometime before tomorrow?''

A gentle breeze blew through the window, cooling her skin. ''I haven't exactly been concentrating on my stomach.''

He kissed her hard on the lips and rolled away from her and out of bed. She watched in admiration as he bent and picked up his sweats from the floor. He tugged them on, then walked to the closet and began rummaging around. He pulled out a faded blue shirt and tossed it at her. "Here," he said. "This ought to do it."

She caught it in midair. "Classy," she said.

He bent again and picked up her jeans and panties. Held up the damp scrap of scarlet lace and said, "Victoria's Secret?"

She sat, the sheet tucked beneath her chin while she cradled the wrinkled shirt to her breasts. "How did you know?"

Instead of answering, he said, "You're one of those high-maintenance women, aren't you, Monahan?"

"And damn proud of it. You have a problem with that, Rafferty?"

"Why should I? I'll just run these through the dryer while I'm making supper."

He disappeared through the doorway, and she heard the dryer door open and close. "You cook?" she said, shrugging into the shirt and buttoning it.

The dryer began humming. "I'm a single man," he said from somewhere outside the bedroom. "I live alone. A man has to eat."

She pulled her hair free from the shirt collar and let it fall, then padded barefoot to find him. He was in the kitchen, rummaging through the cupboards. "I just thought," she said, "with your mother living downstairs, you wouldn't have much need for domesticity."

"I'm thirty-four years old. I had to cut the apron strings sometime." He closed the cupboard door, grabbed a sweatshirt from the back of a chair and pulled it on over his head. "What about you?" he said, tugging it down over his chest. "Do you cook?"

"Not unless you count frozen microwave dinners. I can nuke a Lean Cuisine with the best of them."

"That's sacrilege," he said. "If you'll give me ten minutes to run to the store for milk, I'll cook you pancakes so good you'll think you died and went to heaven."

Even as she was preparing to argue, her stomach growled. "See?" he said. "You're starving. Ten minutes. Make yourself at home. Talk to Nero while I'm gone." At the sound of his name, the dog raised his head and wagged his tail. "He loves attention," Rafferty added.

Alone, she wandered around his apartment. It was tidy and unpretentious, the furniture old but functional, the woodwork a warm honey color, the hardwood floors recently refinished. In the bay window that overlooked the street, a half-dozen African violets grew in clay pots. The apartment had a homey feel that was a world away from her condo in Alexandria, where every item had been chosen with utmost care from stores like Crate and Barrel, Williams-Sonoma, and Pier One. Rafferty fit in here, with the mismatched dishes and the six-year-old Taurus and the dog who actually slept on his bed. While she, with her sports car and her designer suits and her five-hundred-dollar shoes, was an interloper, an imposter.

"It's just sex," she told the dog irritably. "That's all it is."

It was a lie, of course. It had never been just sex between her and Rafferty. Tied up somewhere in that heated tangle of arms and legs and bodies were two hearts bursting with emotions they couldn't seem to figure out what to do with.

Wagging his tail tentatively, Nero looked at her with his mismatched eyes, one blue and one brown. She didn't know anything about dogs. Although she and Mike had begged repeatedly, their mother had never allowed them to have one. "They're dirty," Roberta had said. "They leave hair everywhere, and you have to walk them. I'm the one who'll end up taking care of it." At the time, Carolyn had thought her mother was grossly unfair. Now, looking back, she realized that Roberta was right. Once the newness wore off, she would undoubtedly have ended up being the animal's primary caretaker.

She and the shaggy black dog eyed each other guardedly. "I think he wants us to be friends," she said, wondering just how to make small talk to a dog. *Read any good books lately?* somehow didn't seem to cut it. She knelt and reached out a hand. The dog sniffed it delicately. Carolyn touched one of his ears and was delighted by the silky feel of it. She scratched behind it, and Nero closed his eyes in satisfaction and rubbed his head against her hand. "Aha!" she said. "I think I've found the secret."

There was a knock on the door. Caro glanced down at herself, clad only in Rafferty's shirt. "I'm not expecting company," she said to the dog. "Are you?"

Nero remained silent, and the knock came again. "Hellfire and damnation," she muttered. If Rafferty had forgotten his key, he wouldn't appreciate standing outside, waiting to be let in, while she cowered in the kitchen with his dog.

With a feeling of impending doom, she crossed the room. "Yes?" she said at the closed door. "Who is it?"

"It's Mrs. Rafferty. Open the door, please."

Mrs. Rafferty? Carolyn blinked twice before comprehension dawned. She quickly undid the locks and flung the door open. "Fiona!" she said.

Fiona's stern expression changed to amazement and then delight. "Carolyn!" she said. "Caro, sweetheart!"

She swept into the room, her flowered purple caftan swirling around her, held out her arms, and took Carolyn in a hard embrace. "I can't believe you're here!"

And I can't believe you're here, Carolyn thought. Painfully aware of her state of undress, she said, "Conor's not home right now."

"I know that, darling. I saw him leave. I came up here to find out just who this hussy was that he'd brought home to amuse himself with, under his own mother's roof, right in broad daylight. I had no idea it was you." Fiona laid a hand on her arm. Her fingernails were painted cherry-red, a perfect complement to her bottle-auburn hair. "Not that you're a hussy, sweetheart. Your mother told me you were in town, but I had no idea that you and Conor were—" she paused delicately "—seeing each other again."

Mortified, Carolyn wanted to say, "It's not what it looks like," except that, of course, it was. Squirming, she said lamely, "My clothes are in the dryer. I went to the cemetery in the rain and I got drenched—"

"Don't waste your breath, sweetheart. You might want to tell my son that the next time he decides to entertain a young lady, he should close the bedroom window first."

As the meaning of Fiona's words became clear, she flushed crimson from the soles of her feet to the roots of her hair. "Oh, God," she said.

"It's all right, darling. You can't know how relieved I am. I've been so worried ever since Josie told me he was thinking about marrying that Gwen person. Thank God he's come to his senses."

Carolyn closed her eyes and counted to ten. "Look, Fiona," she said, "please don't read more into this than there is."

Fiona moved toward her, took Carolyn's face between her hands. "The two of you were meant to be together," she said. "Conor knows it, and so do you. Stop fighting it. The road to true love is always riddled with potholes. You have to drive around them and keep on going. The destination is worth the journey."

When Rafferty returned from the store, Carolyn was sitting at the kitchen table with a cup of tea. She watched him set down the grocery bag and begin unpacking it. Taking a sip of tea, she said casually, "Who's Gwen?"

He froze, a quart of milk in his hand, then set it down carefully and cleared his throat. "Why do you ask?"

"While you were gone, your mother stopped by for a little visit. Who's Gwen?"

Rafferty turned, his eyes deliberately blank. "She's just a woman I've been dating."

Her stomach plunged like a roller coaster. "Exclusively?"

"No, of course not. Nothing like that. We're just…you know…" He trailed off, clamped his mouth shut, and went back to unpacking groceries.

"That's interesting," she said to his back, "because your mother seemed to be under the impression that you're planning to marry her."

His shoulders stiffened. "Goddamn that Josie," he said irritably. "I'm going to wring her neck."

Raising an eyebrow, Carolyn said, "Considering our present circumstances, I'm going to pretend you didn't say that."

He unpacked groceries with renewed vigor, and she watched a flush climb the back of his neck. "I don't give a damn what Josie told my mother," he said, "I'm not getting married. That's why I don't tell them anything, because they twist it all around and turn it into something it isn't. All I told her was that Gwen had brought up the subject of marriage. I didn't say I was planning to marry her. Josie made that part up."

She marveled at the colossal stupidity of any creature with a Y chromosome. "Considering your reputation, Rafferty, I'd expect you to know more about women than you do."

He looked at her in bewilderment. "What reputation?"

"According to my mother, you've dated, and broken the hearts of every woman on the East Coast between the ages of eight and eighty."

"See what I mean? They twist everything around until it's not recognizable anymore."

"That's not the point, Conor. If Gwen's brought up the subject of marriage, it means she's confident that she's one step away from having a ring on her finger."

Rafferty silently folded the grocery bag, opened a drawer and tucked the bag inside. Then he closed the drawer and crossed the room. Kneeling on the floor in front of her, he said, "Caro."

Her heart began to hammer. "What?"

He caught her by the hips and slid her to the edge of the chair, inched his own body closer, until her thighs were wrapped around his waist and she couldn't have inserted a sheet of tissue paper between them. Softly, he said, "Do you see anybody named Gwen anywhere in this kitchen?"

While a troupe of flamenco dancers tapped their way around her stomach, she whispered, "No."

With slow deliberation, he worked open the top button of her shirt. The second one. He dipped his head and tasted her, and of their own volition, her arms went around him, cradling his head to her breast. "Then I'd suggest," he said pleasantly, "that you shut the fuck up."

* * *

"Have you ever killed anyone?" she said. "In the line of duty?"

Their empty plates sat between them, sticky with maple syrup and melted butter. She couldn't remember the last time she'd eaten this much food. Rafferty set his knife and fork neatly across his plate. "Once," he said. "My third year on the force."

She reached across the table and laid her hand on the underside of his wrist, smoothed her palm over his. "What happened?"

His fingers linked with hers. "Liquor store robbery. Lorna and I were the first officers to respond to the call. Two suspects, both of them high on crack. They'd shot the old guy behind the counter and emptied the cash register. Killed him for a lousy two hundred bucks. They were just coming out of the store when we got there, and one of them left the scene on foot. Lorna took off in pursuit. The other suspect turned his gun on me. I told him to drop his weapon, but he was too wasted. He was waving it around, and there was a crowd of onlookers standing there. Women and kids. I told him a second time to drop the weapon, and he started shooting into the crowd. I had to take him down."

"Was it terrible?"

"I felt empty afterward. I knew I didn't have a choice. I did what I had to do. But he was only nineteen years old, and it was a while before I stopped seeing his face in my sleep every night. I got a few days off, had a visit with the Department shrink. Standard procedure. But it took some time for me to come to terms with the fact that I'd taken a human life."

"I've been lucky," she said softly. "I carry a gun every day of my life, and I'm a top-notch marksman. But target shooting isn't the same as shooting another person. Sometimes I wonder what I'd do. Would I freeze at the last minute and not be able to go through with it?''

"You'd go through with it," he said. "When you're in a situation like that, your training takes over, and you do what you have to do.''

"I'm just glad I haven't been forced to find out." She got up from the table and began clearing away plates and silverware. Setting them in the sink, she said, "Whatever will you do with yourself until Thursday?''

"I have a sailboat," he said, precariously balancing a small mountain of coffee cups and milk glasses in the crook of his elbow. "On the Cape. The family's been hounding me to take some time off and take her out on the water." He set his load on the sideboard without incident and wiped his hands on a dish towel. "I'll probably take a drive down there.''

Carolyn fit the plug into the drain, squirted a stream of dish detergent into the sink, and turned on the hot water. As the suds began to rise, Rafferty said, "Why don't you come with me?''

Hands buried in soap suds, she looked at him in surprise. "To the Cape?''

"Frank has a great house there. We could go sailing, walk the beach, and act like normal people for a few hours. I've been working this case for so long, I don't remember what it feels like to be a civilian.''

It would be a mistake. She was already in danger of becoming too involved. She should end this now, while she could still escape relatively unscathed. "I shouldn't take the time off," she said, briskly scrubbing a plate and rinsing it. "One of us should stay here." She handed him the plate.

"What's the matter, Monahan?" He held the plate over the sink to let the remaining water drip off it. "You're not allowed days off? You've been here for a week, and there hasn't been a single day I haven't seen you with your nose buried in that damn case file." He picked up a towel and wiped the plate dry.

It was best, she decided, for him to believe it was the case that made her hesitate. "I'm a workaholic," she said.

"Tell me about it. It takes one to know one. It's a lousy excuse."

She felt herself waver.

"If we drive down tonight," he said, "we'll have all day tomorrow to be beach bums. We can come back Thursday morning. You'll only be gone for thirty-six hours. We'll give Lorna your cell phone number if you're worried. That way, she can reach us if she needs to."

She'd known all along that she would cave. It was inevitable. "All right," she said. "But there's one thing I have to do first. I want to stop by my mother's place and go through Meg's room. I keep thinking I might find something that would help us."

"I'll come with you," he said. "Unless you'd rather I stayed as far away from Roberta as possible."

She pulled the plug, and water gurgled down the drain. "You might as well come. I imagine my mother already knows we're sleeping together. Fiona's known it for just under two hours. My mother probably heard about it before you got back with the milk."

Judging by the look on Roberta's face when she answered the door, it was entirely possible that Carolyn had gravely misjudged Fiona. Her mother gaped at them in openmouthed wonder, as though seeing them in the same place at the same time defied some immutable law of physics. Her eyes zeroed in on Carolyn in a mildly accusing way, and a matched set of tiny vertical lines appeared at the corners of her mouth. Caro squirmed, wondering if it really was written all over her in Day-Glo-orange, where and how she'd spent the last few hours, or if it only felt that way. It was as infuriating as it was absurd; in her seven-year career with the Bureau, she'd faced countless killers without flinching. But her own mother never failed to intimidate her.

Roberta turned her gaze on Rafferty, and pleasure softened her features, erasing years from her face. "Conor!" she said in the first show of enthusiasm Carolyn had seen from her in ten years. "Come in." She swiped nervously at an invisible strand of hair and tucked it behind her ear. "I haven't seen you in months."

"Mrs. Monahan," Rafferty said politely. "I hope we're not bothering you."

Her cheeks turned a florid pink. "Of course you're not bothering me. Come in, come in."

Carolyn gaped at the sight of her characteristically lackluster mother transformed into a simpering Betty Boop, complete with heightened coloring and fluttering hands. Caro clamped her jaw shut, and when she regained her voice, she said, "Hi, Mom."

"Carolyn," her mother acknowledged, with just enough of an edge to her voice to let her daughter know she'd committed yet another transgression. "Why didn't you tell me you were bringing company? I would have made something special. All I have is a store-bought coffee cake."

A mortal sin, serving a store-bought dessert to a guest. Carolyn suspected she'd be the one paying penance.

"That's not necessary," Rafferty said. "We can't stay long."

"I insist," Roberta said. "Sit down and tell me how

your mother's been.'' She perched on the arm of a chair, across from them, and beamed invitingly.

They sat. Caro wasn't sure who her mother was trying to bamboozle, but she'd be willing to bet it hadn't been more than twelve hours since Roberta had last seen Fiona Rafferty alive and kicking. ''Mom,'' she said gravely, ''we're here because I need to ask a favor. I need to go through Meg's room.''

Roberta froze, glanced carefully from her daughter to Rafferty and back. ''Meg?'' she said. ''What does Meg have to do with anything?''

She wasn't ready yet to tell her mother all of it. ''I'm looking for something that might help us with the case we're working on.''

Her mother's face went suddenly, inexplicably hard. ''I won't have you tarnishing your sister's memory just so you can play Nancy Drew,'' she said. ''Let the dead stay buried.''

It was uncanny, the way Roberta had unknowingly echoed Clancy Donovan's words. Caro leaned forward, her hands on her thighs, her fingers digging into the soft flesh above her knees. ''Mother,'' she said firmly, ''this is important. It might help us to find out who killed Meg.''

Warring emotions crossed her mother's face. Anger and resentment. Grief and guilt. Roberta looked to Rafferty for confirmation. He nodded, and like a blown-up beach toy pierced by a shard of broken glass, she deflated. ''Fine,'' she said with resignation. ''You'll find everything just the way she left it.''

Meg's room faced southwest. The rain had finally stopped, and a watery sunset was painting the walls with a rosy glow. Although there wasn't a speck of dust to mar the room's perfection, Carolyn could smell an overriding odor of must and disuse. She closed the door behind her,

muffling the conversation from the living room. A life-
size poster of Jon Bon Jovi with big hair hung on the wall
over the bed, his black leather jacket at odds with the
innocence of that boyish grin. Atop the bureau, the ce-
ramic ballerina that Roberta had bought at Woolworth's
for Meg's ninth birthday stood frozen in a graceful pir-
ouette. A pair of concert ticket stubs was tucked into the
wooden frame around the mirror, beside a snapshot of
Meg and Clancy at somebody's backyard barbecue. At the
sight of her sister's pink ruffled bathrobe, girlish and un-
sophisticated, hanging from a hook on the back of the
door, an overwhelming mixture of love and grief hit her
like a hard slap to the face. It had been years since she'd
been in here, and time had altered her perspective. For
the first time, she realized just how young and innocent
Meg had been.

And how truly culpable she was.

Intellectually, of course, she knew that responsibility
for her sister's death lay squarely on the shoulders of the
man whose hands had wrapped themselves around Meg's
neck and choked the life out of her. But no amount of
rationalizing could erase the ingrained belief that she had
killed her sister as surely as if it had been her own hands
around Meg's neck. If not for her, Meg would be a married woman today, an overworked lawyer with three kids,
a husband who adored her, and a bad case of the super-
woman syndrome. Clancy would be a husband, and somebody else would be conducting Sunday morning Mass at
Saint Bart's. With the seemingly inconsequential act of
forgetting her sister on that steamy summer night ten years
ago, it was she who had set all this in motion, and there
was only one way she could make atonement: by finding
Meg's killer and putting him away until fifty years past
the time when hell froze rock solid.

She cleared her throat, wet her lips, and tried to get past the ick factor. She'd been trained well in Room Tossing 101; she could search a room this size in ten minutes, and when she was done, not even a trained investigator could tell that anything had been touched. But this was different. This was her sister's room, and rifling through it was tantamount to sacrilege.

She started with the closet, worked her way quickly and efficiently through tie-dyed T-shirts and oxford button-downs and simple polyester-and-cotton slacks. A picture formed in her mind, a picture of Meg on a hot summer day at Revere Beach, wearing a white cotton eyelet sundress threaded with white satin ribbon, crossing her eyes and laughing as she held her straw hat clamped hard against her head to prevent a gust of wind from stealing it.

Caro bit her lip and forced herself to continue. In the pocket of an oversize, moth-eaten coat sweater, she found a sales receipt from Barnes & Noble and a petrified stick of Doublemint gum. She returned them both to the pocket. Finished with the closet, she walked to the dresser and removed the two concert tickets, turned them over to read the back side, then tucked them back into the mirror frame. Ditto for the photo of Meg and Clancy. The reverse side held no secret messages, no fortuitous clues to the identity of Meg's killer.

There was a soft rap at the door, and it creaked open. Gerald Monahan stood in the doorway, broad-shouldered and barrel-chested, a strand of thinning white hair combed over his bald spot. He looked around the room, and his shoulders slumped. "She should get rid of all this stuff," he said wearily. "But she won't. She says it's all she has left. It's not healthy. She wasn't always like this, you know."

"No?"

"She was such a pretty little thing, your mother. Always laughing, like Meggie. We'd go out dancing on Saturday nights, and she was always the belle of the ball. The men used to line up to dance with her. After you kids came along, she changed. She stopped laughing, stopped going out with me. She said it was because we couldn't afford a baby-sitter, but that was just an excuse. I think life just hardened her. She hated my job, hated the worrying, hated me having to work holidays and birthdays. She said she felt like she was raising you kids alone. And then, of course, when Meggie died, it was like something inside her died, too."

"Oh, Daddy," she said, "I'm so sorry."

"Nothing for you to be sorry about," he said. "You haven't done anything wrong."

"It was my fault," she said. "I'll never be able to forgive myself for that."

"Christ Jesus, Carolyn Eileen, is that what you believe? Your mother and I never blamed you. Never! Nobody blames you."

"I do," she said flatly. "Isn't that enough?"

He turned and closed the door quietly. "It was just rotten bad luck. That's all."

"I have to find him, Dad."

"That's what this is all about, then?"

She closed her eyes, nodded. Opening them, she said, "We have evidence that leads us to believe our killer is the same man who murdered Meg."

The cop in him spent a moment taking it in. "What evidence?" he said at last.

"The killer's been sending me pictures of dead women. One of them was Meg."

She watched his inner struggle, the struggle between

the street cop who'd seen it all and the bereaved father who still couldn't accept, even after ten years, that violent death had happened to his own daughter. He took a deep, shuddering breath, and nodded. "You do whatever you have to do. I'll keep your mother out of your way."

He shut the door firmly behind him and she resumed her search, opening drawer after drawer, methodically and distastefully pawing through her sister's serviceable white cotton panties and bras. "Come on, Meggie," she muttered, shoving a strand of hair away from her face. "Help me here."

She knelt beside the bed, lifted the spread, and burrowed her hand between the spring and mattress. When her fingers bumped into a hard object, she leaned into the mattress and burrowed deeper. She caught the object, snagged it and pried it loose. Still kneeling, she pulled it out and sat back on her heels, staring at the familiar gilt-edged pages of her sister's journal.

"I'll be damned," she said.

11

June 12, 1992

Clancy's been pressuring me, and I don't know what to do. He wants to get married now, but I have four years of college ahead of me, and law school after that. I tried to tell him, and he said it shouldn't make a difference, that UMass is full of married women. But I'm only eighteen years old. How can I be really, really sure that he's the one? Because it has to be absolutely right. I won't walk down that aisle until I know it's going to be forever. When I told Clancy that, he just laughed and said he's known since I was fourteen years old that I was the one. He was just waiting for me to grow up. Sometimes, when he says things like that, it scares me. He's so sure of himself. Maybe it's because he's older, and he's done so much living. I don't know. I just know there's a whole lot of living I still want to do before I tie myself down to a husband. But what if I say no, and he gets tired of waiting? I don't want to lose him.

"You keep that up, you'll ruin your eyes."

Carolyn glanced over at Rafferty. With a sigh, she clicked off the penlight she'd been reading by and flipped her sister's journal shut. She leaned back against the seat and let the hum of the engine lull her as the car slipped silently through the velvet summer night. The high beams picked out a cluster of roadside marsh grass. "It almost sounds," she said, "as though Meg was afraid of him."

"You should've left the damn journal in Boston. You're supposed to be off duty."

"I'm never off duty."

"I've noticed."

"What if Clancy's guilty? What if he does turn out to be the killer?"

Rafferty's hands rested calm and steady at ten and two on the wheel. "Then we'll put him away for the next two hundred years."

They drove for a while in silence before she said, "I suppose that should comfort me. So why doesn't it?"

Instead of answering, he clicked on his blinker and turned off the main highway, onto a secondary road that wound through acres of scrub pine and salt marsh. After a while, he turned again, this time onto an unpaved road carved between rows of grasses that danced in the sea breeze. A single red reflector marked the driveway. "Here we are," he said, making a sharp right past a sign that read Private Property. Trespassers Will Be Eaten.

"Cute," Caro said. "Twisted, but cute."

"Frankie's idea of humor."

The winding driveway ended abruptly in a clearing. The house sat on stilts, nestled amongst the beach grass and the dunes above the high-tide line. When Rafferty shut off the car, she heard the muffled roar of the breakers. She got out, stood by the open door and stretched. Nero bounded out of the back seat, paused to sniff the ground, then disappeared around the corner of the house. Rafferty popped the trunk and took out their luggage. Caro hoisted

her overnight bag over her shoulder and followed him up
the back steps and into the kitchen.

While he returned for the groceries they'd picked up at
Star Market, she explored the single-story bungalow. It
was tidy and uncluttered, charming in its simplicity. The
rattan furniture sported cushions covered in a flowered
chintz that matched the café curtains at the windows and
achieved just the right balance between casual and tasteful. There was a TV and VCR, an inexpensive stereo system, a small bookcase stuffed with paperbacks.

She set her overnight bag and her sister's journal on
the couch. Rafferty clattered back up the steps with the
groceries. While he unpacked them, Carolyn wandered to
the sliding glass doors that overlooked the beach. Behind
her, the refrigerator door opened and shut. She unlocked
the sliders, kicked off her shoes, and stepped out onto the
deck.

The moon rode full and high in the sky, washing the
sea in a cool blue light. Nero stood at the water's edge,
sniffing intently at a dark clump of seaweed. Back in Boston, it had been a warm evening, but here, the sea breeze
raised the surf to a moderate chop, and as she leaned on
the railing, she shivered and folded her arms.

Behind her, she heard Rafferty rattling around the
kitchen. She hoped he was a better cook than she was, or
else they'd starve. Inside the house, the stereo came on.
Soft, relaxing music dominated by a bluesy saxophone.
Quiet footsteps approached, and he touched her shoulder.

"Here," he said, handing her a sweater. "Sometimes
it gets cold out here at night."

"Thanks." She pulled it on over her head. The sleeves
were too long, and she rolled up the cuffs. Rafferty set
two wineglasses on the railing, uncapped a bottle of wine
and filled them. He replaced the cap and handed her one
of the glasses.

She took it without comment. He picked up his own glass and, in amicable silence, they leaned side by side against the railing, watching the moon-drenched sea. "Tomorrow should be a good day for sailing," he said.

Caro gazed out over the swirling water. "How can you tell?"

"It's breezy and clear. Not a cloud in the sky. Perfect sailing weather."

She took a sip of wine and leaned her hip against the railing. "How long have you been sailing?"

"Five years. Two with this boat. But I've only had her out once this year. If I had her berthed in Boston, I could take her out in the evenings, sail the harbor, the river. But the Cape's too far away for that, and I just don't have the time to get down here as often as I'd like. As it is, I'm standing here thinking about all the things I should be doing back home."

"Who's the workaholic now, Lieutenant?"

In the distance, the surf beat relentlessly against the shore. He raised his wineglass and took a sip. "I've never been very good at compartmentalizing."

"I think it comes with the job."

"It does something to you." He twirled his wineglass by its stem. "Dealing with violent death all the time, day after day. You reach a point where it loses its impact. At first, it bothers you. But after a while, you get hardened. You have to, or you couldn't survive. Then one day, you're working a double homicide, and right in the middle of wading through the blood and the guts and the bodies, you realize that you've been trying to remember if you were supposed to pick up toilet paper on your way home. That's when you start to wonder if you're losing your mind."

She looped her arm through his. He felt warm and solid. "I think it takes a very special kind of person to do what you do, going out there and putting yourself on the line, day after day."

Darkly, he said, "I'm no hero. Just a cop, doing my job."

The breeze blew a lock of hair across her face, and she brushed it away with the hand that held the glass. "That's the same thing my dad used to say."

"What about you? Your job's not exactly a picnic."

"It's not the same thing at all. You're out there in the trenches. I spend most of my time sitting at a desk, analyzing data. The biggest hazard I face is the potential to develop a lard ass."

His smile took her breath away. "I'm a lieutenant," he pointed out. "They tell me that's a desk job."

"Right," she said. "When we get back, remind me to introduce you to your desk." Wineglass still in hand, she turned into his arms, and he buried his face in her hair. Beneath her cheek, his heart beat strong and steady, while in the background, Barbra Streisand crooned wistfully, "What are you doing the rest of your life?"

"You smell wonderful," he said.

She twined her arms around his neck and they swayed to the rhythm of the music. He'd always been a graceful dancer, and she followed his steps with ease, their movements so smooth that the liquid in her glass never even sloshed. Caro raised her face and saw in his eyes the same jumble of emotions she felt. As they moved together in perfect synchronicity, she wondered how she had ended up here, on a Cape Cod beach, dancing barefoot in the moonlight with the one man she'd never been able to forget. In his arms, she didn't care that this was madness, didn't care that the instant this case was over, she'd be gone, back to Virginia, back to her world and away from his. In his arms, there was no case, no geography, no reason. There was only a man and a woman struggling to understand their own hearts.

"Remember those Sunday nights?" he said. "Remember what we used to do?"

While her heart thudded erratically, she said with forced lightness, "You mean the hot jungle sex in your friend's apartment while he worked graveyard shift? What was his name?"

Humor flickered in his eyes, but his mouth remained serious. "O'Halloran," he said. "Dennis O'Halloran. And I wasn't thinking so much about the hot jungle sex as I was about what came before it."

It came back to her then, in a riot of color and sound and scents. "The dance hall in Revere. I haven't thought of that in years."

He lowered his head, pressed his cheek against hers and said softly, "We'd spend three or four hours every Sunday night slow dancing, getting all hot and horny and primed, waiting for O'Halloran to leave for work so we could go to his apartment and screw our brains out."

She squeezed her eyes shut at the intensity of the emotions that crushed her chest so tight, she could barely breathe. "It was the only place we could be alone."

"Caro," he said softly.

"What?" she whispered.

"We're alone right now."

She opened her eyes and met his gaze. Setting her wineglass on the railing, she took his face between her hands and kissed him. "So we are," she said.

He whistled for the dog, and Nero raced across the sand and scrambled up the stairs and into the house. Caro picked up their glasses and Rafferty grabbed the wine bottle by the neck. He locked the sliders behind them, turned out the lights, and hand in hand, they walked to the bedroom.

It was the middle of the night when the dog woke her.

She stirred beneath the covers, disoriented by the unfamiliar room, the unfamiliar bed, the hard male body tangled with hers. Then Rafferty wrapped an arm around her and pulled her close, and she remembered where she was. "Conor," she said, "the dog's barking."

"Mmph," he said, and exhaled a soft snore. Conor Rafferty was not the kind of man to do things halfway. He worked hard and he loved hard, and when he finally allowed himself to slow down, he slept hard.

Caro raised herself on her elbow and studied him in the moonlight, the blue-black shadow of whisker stubble on his cheek, the rise and fall of his chest. He slept the way he did everything: simple and clean and straightforward. On his side of the bed, the blankets were barely mussed, while her side looked as though a wrestling match had taken place there while she slept.

He was the only man she'd ever known who possessed the ability to wear down her edge, to totally disarm her. She was used to being in control of her emotions, but Conor Rafferty simply climbed over the wall she'd erected and plowed straight through to her heart.

They'd never spent a night together. As twenty-somethings, they had both lived at home with their parents, so sleeping together hadn't been an option. After each romantic encounter in Dennis O'Halloran's tiny third-floor apartment, they had dressed and gone home to sleep alone in their separate bedrooms. She was struck by the intimacy involved in sharing a bed, by the level of trust that somehow made sleeping together far more intimate than any sexual act that two people could perform.

It was relatively easy to keep sex casual, but sleeping together implied a disquieting level of commitment that she wasn't ready for.

In the living room, Nero continued to bark. Carolyn peeled herself away from Rafferty and crawled out of bed, pulled on her panties and Conor's sweatshirt. It smelled of him, musky and male, instantly transporting her back to last night's heated mingling of bodies and the creative uses they'd found for the rest of that bottle of wine.

Nero was at the back door, yapping and scratching furiously. Caro peered out into the darkness, but she saw nothing. While Nero whimpered and danced at her feet, she flicked on the outside light. There was no movement except for the gentle swaying of the beach grass. She unlocked the door and opened it, and Nero shot through it. Nose to the ground, he circled the clearing, then disappeared into the woods behind the house.

"Damn it," she muttered, and stepped outside.

The wind blew her hair around her face, and even in Rafferty's sweatshirt, she could feel goose bumps popping up on her bare legs. "Nero!" she called softly. "Here, boy."

There was no response except for the rattle of dry grass. Caro crossed her arms over her breasts, tucked her hands inside the cuffs of the sweatshirt, and tried to rub some warmth back into her wrists. She'd forgotten how chilly summer nights could get in New England, especially here on the coast. In Virginia, even into the fall, the surf was tepid as bath water.

"Nero!" she called again. "Come back here!"

But the dog had disappeared, swallowed up by the darkness. She stood at the foot of the stairs, her bare feet buried in fine, cool sand, and wondered what she should do. She wasn't about to go after him. There were unspeak-

able things out there. Bats and snakes and spiders, and—
for all she knew—lions and tigers and bears. Carolyn
Monahan was a city girl, and pigs would fly before she'd
venture into those woods after dark.

She tried to ward off the eerie sensation that she was
being watched. Paranoia, she told herself. It was nothing
more than paranoia. Nobody was skulking out there in the
dark, watching her run around in her underwear.

"Fetching ensemble, Agent Monahan."

She nearly jumped out of her skin. "Mother of Mary,"
she said, holding a hand to her heart. "You scared the
bejesus out of me."

Framed in the doorway, wearing just a pair of jeans,
his black hair tinged bluish by the moonlight, Rafferty
looked dark and dangerous. "Care to tell me what you're
doing?" he said.

"Nero was barking. I tried to wake you up, but you
were out for the count. I let him out, and now he's taken
off."

"Get back in the house before you freeze to death.
He'll come back."

She climbed the stairs, brushed past that broad expanse
of bare chest and into the house. "I think something was
out there," she said, "but I couldn't see anything."

"Probably a raccoon. They like to stop by at night to
dine al fresco from Frankie's garbage cans." He stuck two
fingers into his mouth and let out a shrill whistle that
could have stopped a freight train. A moment later, the
dog bounded out of the woods and up the steps, wagging
a happy greeting, as if it were high noon instead of three
o'clock in the morning.

"Very effective technique," Carolyn said. "You'll
have to teach me how to do it."

"And ruin your elegant feminine manner? I think not."

He paused to take a long, searching look around the yard before he closed the door. "Nothing there," he announced, locking the dead bolt. "Party's over. Let's go back to bed."

It was a glorious day for sailing. Carolyn leaned back in the bow of the boat, eyes closed, her face turned up to the sun, loving the scent of salt air, the tang of sea spray on her skin, the caress of the wind in her hair as the boat sliced like an arrow through the water. "I'll give you this, Rafferty," she said. "You know how to show a lady a good time."

Perched in the stern of the boat, doing something incomprehensible with the sails, he looked up and smiled. Bronzed by the sun, his hair tousled by the wind, he looked like some kind of pagan god, and she wondered how he'd managed to get that incredible tan when he'd spent his entire summer working indoors. "Are you?" he said. "Having a good time?"

"The best."

He studied her for a moment, warmth radiating from those green eyes, and then he turned his attention back to the sails. She hadn't thought he knew how to relax, but the transformation she'd witnessed had been amazing. The instant he stepped aboard the *Painted Lady,* the driven Homicide cop had vanished, leaving in his place a barefoot, laid-back weekend sailor without a care in the world.

And what a world it was, gliding in a peculiar state of isolation even while surrounded by fishing vessels and pleasure craft of every imaginable variety. They sailed around rocky islands dotted with spiky evergreens, breezed in and out of picturesque coves where sandpipers raced along the beaches. Herons stood sentinel in the marshes, gulls and cormorants bobbed in the surf, and a family of seals lay sunning themselves on a rocky shoal.

When starvation finally forced their hand, they nosed the *Lady* into a shallow cove, dropped anchor, and waded ashore with Nero splashing merrily beside them. On a rocky promontory, they ate homemade hoagies and fresh strawberries, washing them down with warm bottles of Evian water. While Nero explored the shore, they stretched out in a field of nodding wildflowers, Carolyn's head on Rafferty's shoulder, lazing in the sun like a pair of well-fed felines.

Nearby, insects buzzed from flower to flower, and above them, the sky was a heartbreaking shade of blue. It was difficult to believe that this idyllic world existed just a few hours away from Boston. Harder still to believe, in the midst of this pristine paradise, that Boston, with its grim realities and awesome responsibilities, was anything more than a particularly vivid nightmare.

"The sky's so blue," she said. "And so big."

"That's what it looks like when you get out from under the smog and the skyscrapers."

She turned, settled herself more comfortably against him. "So tell me, Lieutenant, why is it that you've never married?"

"I'm married to my career. It's hard to split your focus when so much of your energy's expended on the job. You don't have enough to go around. Inevitably, it's the family that suffers."

"Ah, yes. That compartmentalizing that you have such a hard time with."

"We all do. You know that. It's why cops have such a high divorce rate. We're not there when the people we love need us the most. It's why Rizzoli's marriage is falling apart. Even when he was home with Jeannie and the kids, he wasn't really there.''

She raised herself on an elbow and plucked a daisy. Twirling it, she said, ''And I thought it was his scintillating personality.''

His smile was wry. ''That, too. What about you?''

''Me?'' She tickled the end of his nose with the daisy, and he swatted it away good-naturedly.

''Yes,'' he said. ''You. Why are you still single?''

''You sound just like my mother. Still single. You do realize that a generation ago, I would have been called a spinster?''

Those green eyes warmed, and a smile played about the corners of his mouth. ''Some spinster,'' he said, lifting a strand of blond hair and tucking it behind her ear. ''More like Clint Eastwood in drag.''

''I shouldn't have told you about that. You're never going to let me live it down.''

''I don't like any of this. It scares the hell out of me, the way this guy's obsessing over you.''

''I'm a big girl, Rafferty. I can take care of myself. And he's not obsessing.''

''Call it what you will,'' he said. ''But I happen to care about you. Probably more than I should, considering our history.''

For an instant, as his remark hovered in the air between them, time seemed to stand still. ''I know,'' she said. ''I care about you, too.''

He was the first to recover. Clearing his throat, he said, ''So tell me, *Just Plain Monahan,* why haven't you married some nice guy and started making babies?''

She rolled away from him and sat up. ''I suppose, at least in part, for the same reasons as you. I've been so focused on the job. I spend two hundred days a year on the road. It's hard to achieve the right balance.'' She paused to watch a freighter chug along the horizon. ''I lived with a guy for a couple of years. He wanted to get married, but I didn't. So he found somebody who was willing, and I sent a Crock-Pot. After that, I was alone for a while, until I drifted into the relationship with Richard.''

''Your boss.''

''My boss. I'm not really sure how or why it happened. I don't make a habit of sleeping with married men, and I'm not usually gullible. There just seemed to be this empty spot inside me, and I thought he could fill it. I was wrong. He wasn't at all the right kind of man for me.''

''What is the right kind of man for you?''

''For starters, one who doesn't lie.''

''That's a good place to start.''

''What about you, Rafferty?'' She drew up her knees and wrapped her arms around them. ''What kind of woman are you looking for?''

He balled up his T-shirt and tucked it behind his head. ''I'm not looking.''

''But if you were?''

''If I were—'' he gazed out to sea, toward the *Painted Lady,* bobbing gently at anchor ''—she'd probably be a lot like my mother.''

Caro raised an eyebrow. ''Your mother? God in heaven, Conor, you'll be looking for the rest of your life. Fiona's one of a kind. There *is* nobody like her.''

His grin was slow and lazy. ''My point exactly.''

The afternoon shadows were long on the sand when they sailed back into home port and she helped him drag the *Lady* up onto the beach. Inside the house, it was so still she could hear the ticking of the kitchen clock. Nero flopped in exhaustion onto the rug in front of the couch, and Rafferty said, "It's still warm. Let's take a swim before supper."

In the bedroom, Carolyn changed into the bikini she'd packed, then checked her reflection in the full-length mirror on the back of the door. Her thighs were still firm instead of crepey but, at thirty-two, it was only a matter of time. She wrapped the orange flowered sarong around her hips and assessed the damage. Her hair looked like straw, and her skin was red and scaly from the sun and the wind. If she didn't use moisturizer tonight, by tomorrow she'd look like she'd aged ten years overnight.

Caught by something unexpected in her reflection, she leaned closer to the mirror. In her eyes lay something she hadn't seen in so long, she barely recognized it: contentment. This day had been as near to perfect as any day she could remember, and she tried not to think about the significance of that perfection.

Rafferty waited for her at the water's edge, his khakis rolled up, hands in his pockets, water washing around his ankles. He stood with his back to the sea, a slight breeze lifting strands of his dark hair, and watched as she crossed the beach toward him. The breeze blew her hair into her face, and she raised an arm to brush it back. "Hi," she said.

He lifted a hand, touched her bare shoulder with a fingertip, slipped it beneath the strap of her bikini top. "Nice color," he said, sliding his finger along her skin. "What do you call it?"

"Tangerine."

"And this pink-and-orange flowered thing." His knuckles brushed her bare belly. "Knotted at the hip, and slit—" his hand slid along her inner thigh and she let out a soft gasp "—up to here. What do you call this thing, Monahan?"

"It's called a sarong," she said breathlessly. "You know, Rafferty, you really need to get out of Southie a little more often."

"I get around."

"So I've heard."

The corner of his mouth turned up, and he drew her hard against him. "You can't believe everything you hear," he said, and kissed her.

She braced a hand against his bare shoulder, ran the other hand up his neck and wound it into his hair. His skin was gritty with sand, and he tasted of fresh air and salt water and that heady, unmistakable taste that was Conor. His hands roamed her back, beneath her hair, and his fingers toyed with the knot at the nape of her neck.

"What are you doing?" she murmured.

"It seems to me," he said near her ear, "that there's a little inequity going on here. But I think I have it covered." The straps tied behind her neck fell, and with a swift flick of the wrist, he released the back clasp of her bikini top. Tossing it a good twelve feet away, he said, "There. I just leveled the playing field."

"Christ, Conor!" She glanced up and down the beach. "It's broad daylight here, in case you hadn't noticed."

"It's a private beach. There's no one around for miles."

She narrowed her eyes. "How private?"

He nodded over her left shoulder. "Over there's the game preserve, and Frank owns everything for a couple of miles in the other direction...I'd say the nearest human is probably at least two miles away."

Her mouth fell open. "You're telling me that your brother owns two miles of pristine Cape Cod beach-front?"

"It boggles the imagination, doesn't it?" He lowered

his head and ran his tongue along the tendon that ran from her jaw to her shoulder, and she closed her eyes and melted against him. "What can I say?" he added. "Frankie married well."

Weakly, she murmured, "I should say so."

"Beacon Hill." He kissed her throat. Her collarbone. "Old money. Sheila was an only child." Nibbling at her shoulder, he said, "When Daddy died, she got it all. Including this place." He paused in his nibbling to cup her breast, his fingers stroking, shaping, teasing. "Frankie didn't get to be the Mattress King of the North Shore on his good looks. Sheila's father bankrolled him."

The surf lapped and tickled at their feet. Carolyn opened her eyes. Lazily, she said, "I thought we were going swimming, Lieutenant."

"Later. Right now, I have other things in mind."

"You should come with a warning label, Rafferty."

"If you have any complaints, put them in writing. In triplicate." He knelt in the sand, and his tongue traversed the valley between her breasts, continuing in a straight line to her navel. "If it's on my desk first thing tomorrow morning, I'll take it under consideration."

The laughter wasn't intentional. It simply bubbled up from inside her, a sudden burst of happiness that she was helpless to stop. She clapped a hand over her mouth, and Rafferty raised his head and lifted a dark eyebrow. "Was that a giggle I heard?" he said. "Coming from the hard-assed and cynical Agent Monahan?"

"I'm sorry," she said primly. "I can't imagine what could have come over me. I'll try not to do it again."

On his knees in the swirling surf, he held out a hand to her. "Come on in," he said. "The water's fine."

She took his hand and he yanked her off her feet. They fell to the sand, the surf curling and licking around them as they kissed, belly to belly, thigh to thigh, legs tangled and hearts pumping wildly. Beneath her palms, the wet sand kept washing away, and when she opened her eyes again, his had gone a rich, smoky gray, and the playfulness was gone. "Jesus, Caro," he said raggedly.

The two of you were meant to be together, she heard Fiona's voice saying. *Stop fighting it.* Then she opened her arms to him and he rolled her over in the sand, and she didn't think about anything for a very long time.

She couldn't remember the last time she'd eaten a hot dog, but her best guess was circa 1992.

They weren't really even meat, just chemicals, filler, and meat by-products. She didn't even want to think about what meat by-products meant. Probably hoof, tail, and snout of bovine, with a little *eau de piggy* tossed in for good measure. She hadn't eaten one of the damned things in years, and she couldn't recall ever eating one that tasted as good as the hot dog Lieutenant Conor Rafferty had served her fresh from the backyard grill, a little overdone, its blackened skin swimming in golden mustard and sweet relish and fried onions. As a matter of fact, it had tasted so good, she'd eaten a second one.

Now, her belly disgracefully full, she sprawled on a lounge chair next to Rafferty, replete, lethargic, so relaxed her bones might have been made of rubber. It was a combination of the food, the sun and the salt air, and the rough-and-tumble sex with the man stretched out in the chair next to hers that had turned her into a spineless slug. For the first time in years, she'd lost the compulsion to work. She had less than zero interest in reading any more of her sister's journal, had absolutely no desire to jump back on the merry-go-round. All she wanted was to lie here beside Rafferty like an old married couple, lulled by the rhythm of the surf, as the sun sank low on the western horizon and the sole of his bare foot slid idly up and down her calf.

She was in trouble, on the cusp of tumbling ass over teakettle, as Roberta would put it, for a man she couldn't have. It didn't matter that he could make her laugh when she hadn't laughed in so long, didn't matter that when he touched her, she went up in flames. Didn't matter that she respected him tremendously because he hadn't let the job harden him. None of that mattered because there was no place for their relationship to go. There was no future in it. She couldn't give him what he wanted, and he couldn't give her what she needed. He had a life in Boston, a successful career, a loveable but smothering extended family that adored him. A dog, for Christ's sake.

A girlfriend named Gwen.

While she had a life in Virginia that included the mortgage from hell, a small but carefully chosen circle of friends, a doctoral program at Georgetown U that was waiting on her dissertation, and a job search to begin when she got home.

Rafferty was a hometown boy who belonged in South Boston, while she'd felt like an alien there, even as a girl growing up on K Street.

Besides, he wasn't looking. He'd already said so.

And, damn it, neither was she. She'd just left one disastrous relationship. She wasn't about to jump from the frying pan into the fire.

She pondered that empty spot inside her, the one she'd thought Richard could fill, the one that was shaped suspiciously like Conor Rafferty, and felt like a hypocrite. She couldn't have him. Period. It was a simple matter of one plus one not equaling one. Her life plus his life didn't tally up to a sum that either of them could live with.

But she could have one more night with him before reason took over and forced both of them to take a hard, analytical look at reality. Tomorrow would be soon enough for logic and reason. Tomorrow morning, her coach would turn back into a pumpkin, and she and Conor would morph back into Lieutenant Rafferty and Special Agent Monahan. But tonight, they were still just Carolyn and Conor. Tonight, she would fall asleep in his arms, lulled by the cry of the gulls and the whisper of the surf.

Beside her, he slapped at a mosquito. "The bugs are starting to get thick," he said. "You might want to change into something that covers up a little more skin, or they'll eat you alive."

Inside the house, a cell phone rang. Her gaze met Rafferty's, and she saw it in his eyes, the same resentment she felt at the intrusion of the real world into this Shangri-la they'd created.

He sighed. "Yours or mine?"

"Yours. Mine's set for a double ring."

He got up and went through the sliding glass doors. After a moment, she followed him. He was hunched over the kitchen counter, one hand buried in his hair, his shoulders rigid. The knuckles of the hand that held the phone against his ear were as white as the bleached bones of a corpse. And she knew. "We're on our way," he said, and hung up.

When he turned, his eyes were shuttered, impenetrable. The mask he wore was one she recognized because she'd worn it so many times herself. "Conor?" she said.

His voice was flat. "We have another one. This time, he left a note with the body. A personal message, addressed to you."

Her stomach lurched. "I'll get dressed."

"There's more."

She paused, seeing something in his eyes, hearing something in his voice, that she wanted to run away from. But she couldn't. She was a sworn U.S. government agent, and this was her job. She wasn't allowed to run away.

"This one wasn't strangled," he said, "and the murder didn't take place in Boston."

Her heart plummeted. She knew what he was going to say, knew even before he said it, but she had to ask anyway. "Where?" she demanded. "Where did it happen?"

"In Manhasset," he said. "That's about five miles from where you're standing right now. He's here, Monahan. He followed us here."

12

It was identical to every small-town crime scene she'd ever worked. The chaos, the jurisdictional squabbles, the wide-eyed locals who'd stomped all over the scene, contaminating and destroying what little evidence might have been left behind. Manhasset, Massachusetts, was too small to have its own police department. There was just the town constable, who right now was locked in heated dispute with a sheriff's deputy, both of them looking as though they'd like to end the altercation with a well-placed right hook.

Nearby stood a third man in a navy suitcoat and neatly creased pants. Arms crossed and feet braced rigidly apart, he looked ready to step in should it become necessary, and Caro pegged him immediately as a state police detective. She and Rafferty were about to further complicate the mix. Technically, they were off duty. Technically, neither of them had jurisdiction. But the UNSUB had sent her an invitation to the ball, so here she was, with her dancing shoes on.

She stepped out of the car and took a breath of salt air. It carried a trace of something else, something sickly-sweet and pungent and familiar. Death. So much death. She wondered if it would ever end.

She and Rafferty showed their IDs to the deputy who was securing the scene and then crossed the beach to where the three men stood, illuminated by moonlight. The altercation came to a halt as all three lifted their heads, like dogs sniffing a scent on the ocean breeze, and watched them approach.

Caro held up her shield. "Monahan, FBI," she said. "This is Lieutenant Rafferty, Boston P.D. I understand you have something for me."

The group of men gawked at her, three pairs of eyes gaping as though she were some kind of space alien who'd just landed in their midst. Uncomfortably aware of her attire, of the Nikes, the wrinkled jeans, the oversize sweatshirt she'd borrowed from Rafferty, she said, "Gentlemen, please excuse my appearance. It's my day off."

The man in blue recovered first, stepping forward to shake her hand, then Rafferty's. "Nichols," he said. "State Police Homicide Unit."

With his sandy hair and lantern jaw, Detective Nichols bore a striking resemblance to Dudley Do-Right. But he oozed a commanding presence that established definitively that he recognized the difference between his ass and his elbow. She couldn't have said the same for either of the other two men.

"What do you have?" Rafferty asked him.

"Twenty-one-year-old girl, worked at Pilcher's Tavern. It's a local watering hole. We're pretty familiar with it, as is the Sheriff's Department. She left work at twelve-thirty last night. As far as we know, nobody saw her after that. This is a private beach, so there's no tourist traffic, and the body was hidden in the tall grass. Looks like she was here all day before anybody found her."

Carolyn's throat constricted. "Who found her?"

"Couple of teenagers, out for a little beach blanket bingo in the moonlight. Cooled their ardor pretty quickly."

She met Rafferty's eyes. He lifted a single eyebrow, and she cleared her throat. "Where's the note?"

It was written on plain loose-leaf paper, wide ruled, the kind you could buy in any department store on the planet. The handwriting was bold and confident, the message as straightforward as the medium.

Consider this one a gift, just for you, Carolyn, a little reminder of my high regard for you. I'll be seeing you soon. Sweet dreams, Agent Monahan.

Reading over her shoulder, Rafferty swore softly.

Nichols cleared his throat. "I think you're going to want to take a look at the body."

The girl lay hidden in the waving beach grass. As they approached the body, the stench of death grew stronger. Caro braced her shoulders, felt Rafferty's hand, feather-light against the small of her back, as they stood over the dead girl.

She was naked. There was a small tattoo of a butterfly on her right shoulder, and on the outside of her thigh, clearly delineated, was a human bite mark. The back of her head was misshapen, her skull cleverly redesigned by some blunt object. There wasn't much blood. She hadn't been killed here, just dumped here like a rotting sack of potatoes.

A coroner's attendant stood by, body bag in hand, ready to wrap and roll. "Flip her," Nichols said, and the attendant obliged. The girl's head lolled as though her neck were made of jelly, and Caro got a good look at her face.

"Son of a bitch," Rafferty whispered.

Everything inside her stilled as she stared down at a mirror image of her own face. She finally understood why they'd all looked at her so oddly. Feature for feature, the dead girl looked enough like her to have been her twin.

July 7, 1992

Johnny says that Clancy's selfish, and doesn't care about my feelings. He thinks I should do what feels right for me, instead of letting Clancy push me into anything. Johnny is the most levelheaded man I've ever met, and he really cares about what I think. He doesn't tell me what to do. He listens to what I have to say. He cares about my feelings and values me as a person. That's something Clancy doesn't get. He only sees me in terms of how I relate to him. In Clancy's eyes, I'm not a separate person, I'm not Meg, I'm just his girlfriend. An extension of him. But he has a big surprise coming, because I'm not going through life as his shadow.

Carolyn clicked off the penlight and tucked it into Meg's journal to mark the spot where she'd left off, then stared out into the darkness that surrounded the car. Who in the bloody hell was Johnny? She couldn't recall her sister ever mentioning him. He must have been one of Meg's countless admirers. Meggie'd had legions of friends, both male and female. She'd drawn people the way honey draws bees.

Caro tilted her head forward, rotated her shoulders, her neck, to try to dispel the tension. It didn't work. She raised both hands and rubbed the back of her neck. "He was out there, wasn't he? Last night, at the beach house. That's why Nero was barking."

Rafferty didn't answer her question. She glanced over at him, recognized the tension in the line of his jaw, knew how exhausted he must be. "I know you don't want to hear this," he said, leaning back in the driver's seat, "but maybe you should withdraw from the case. Pack your bags and go back to Virginia. Lay low until it's over."

"Are you crazy? We're so damn close to getting him, Rafferty. This murder wasn't like the others. It was more brutal. Less controlled. More angry."

"It was a fucking dress rehearsal, Monahan. But you don't seem to be getting the point."

"I don't think so. I think he's starting to fall apart. I've seen it before. It's the same thing Bundy did, and it was his downfall. He started getting sloppy. He went from strangling to bludgeoning, and that's when he got caught."

"After he pulled a blitzkrieg attack on a sorority house. I know more about this than you think. If this guy's really falling apart like you say he is, nobody is safe. Nobody's daughter, nobody's sister, nobody's wife. I'd like to keep you off the list of potential victims."

"You're forgetting one thing, Rafferty. I'm not some naive young sorority girl. I'm a professional who's dealt with killers like this for years. I know what the hell I'm doing."

"And just how many *killers like this* have targeted you specifically?"

She opened her mouth to answer, realized she had no response.

"That's what I thought," he said. "Look, this guy is watching every goddamn move you make. He followed us here. I don't think this is about Meg. Maybe it was never about Meg. Maybe it's your background we should be prying into, instead of hers."

Above the treetops, the eastern sky had begun to lighten. They drove in silence while she turned it over and over in her mind, analyzing the situation from every possible angle, looking for a crack in the surface, a glitch, something they'd missed. But she couldn't see anything. The pieces were too scattered to fit together in any way that made sense.

"I've already thought about that," she admitted. "I've helped to put away so many killers over the years. But it doesn't make sense. There's no way he could have known that I'd be assigned to the case. And the picture of Meg was real. This isn't about me. It's about him. It's a game he's playing and, for some reason, he's decided I'm the only opponent worthy of his attention."

"Big of him."

She lapsed into silence again, closed her eyes, let the exhaustion take her. After a while, she said quietly, "Sometimes, I think I should feel more compassion."

"For the victims?"

"Not for the victims. For the killers."

"They don't deserve compassion. They're monsters."

She opened her eyes again. "But not monsters of their own making. They're driven by something they can't control."

"We're all responsible for our actions, Caro."

"In a legal sense, yes. As long as we possess the ability to discriminate between right and wrong, we're held accountable for our actions. Even in an ethical sense, I agree with you. But in a psychological sense, I'm not so sure. What drives a man to kill, over and over again? What compulsion is it that builds up in him until it's bigger than he is and he has no choice but to obey it? I'm not sure we'll ever find the answer."

"The law's still the law. Dead is still dead."

"Spoken like a true cop," she said. "But I'm not just

a cop. I'm also a social scientist. I don't necessarily look at it the same way you do.''

''I see. You're one of those left-wing bleeding-heart liberals who think we should rehabilitate all our prisoners and turn them back out onto the street.''

In spite of her exhaustion, she grinned. ''You're missing the other piece of my personality, Rafferty, the right-wing vigilante who walks around wearing a psychological bumper sticker that says Charlton Heston Is My President.''

''I'm glad we've clarified that.''

''I met Ed Kemper once,'' she said into the darkness, ''when I was a rookie with the Behavioral Sciences Unit. I was in California with a couple of seasoned agents, working a case. When it was over, they decided to drop by Vacaville and pay Ed a visit, and they let me tag along. He was one of the biggest men I'd ever seen. Terrifying in size alone. But he was intelligent, insightful, congenial. He had a wonderful sense of humor. I liked him, Rafferty. Do you know about Ed Kemper?''

''The name's familiar, but I don't remember the details.''

''When he was a teenager, he shot his grandparents dead, just to see what it felt like. He spent time in a juvenile facility, where the doctors recommended that he not be returned to his mother. But the all-knowing, all-seeing California authorities declared him rehabilitated, and when he came of age, they shipped him right back to live with mom. Over the next year or two, he raped and strangled a half-dozen coeds. Carried the head of one of them around in his car for a while. And then he bludgeoned his mother to death and killed her best friend before calling the cops and turning himself in.'' She paused. ''Helluva nice guy, old Ed. A model prisoner. But even he recognizes the monster that's inside him. Even he knows that if anybody was fool enough to put him back on the street, he'd go right back to killing. It's the nature of the beast.''

The sky was rosy with dawn when they pulled up in front of the Boylston House. Julio, the night doorman, stood stiffly in his maroon uniform, discreetly pretending not to notice that she was being dropped off at five-thirty in the morning by a sinfully handsome man. They were so discreet here at the Boylston that she could have marched through the lobby carrying a warthog under her arm, and nobody would have looked twice.

Rafferty parked at the curb and turned to look at her, his arm trailing along the back of her seat, his hand dangling near her shoulder. His fingers were long and lean, the back of his hand dusted with fine black hairs. Carolyn had *The Speech* all prepared. It had been a long drive from the Cape; she'd had plenty of time to rehearse it. ''Thank you,'' she said. ''In spite of recent events, I had a lovely time.''

''Is that a 'but' I'm hearing at the end of that sentence?''

''But,'' she said carefully. ''There's no place for this to go. You have your life, and I have mine. There's too much potential for hurt on either side.'' She lost herself for a moment in those incredible green eyes before she was able to pull free of the current and swim back to shore. ''And we have to work together,'' she added. ''It could get messy. Neither one of us can afford to be distracted while we're working this case. Which is why I think we should end this right now, before it goes any further.''

''I agree,'' he said. ''You're absolutely right.''

Taken aback, she blinked. Opened her mouth. She

hadn't expected him to be so readily agreeable. She'd been prepared for argument, not placid acceptance. "Well," she said, casting about frantically for something to say that wouldn't make her look even more like a fool.

"We tried it once, Caro, a long time ago. It didn't work out. There's no shame in that."

"No," she said. "I suppose there isn't."

"So I'll see you later," he said, reaching past her and opening her door. "Try to get some sleep."

She'd been dismissed. Just like that, she'd been dismissed from his car, from his life. She'd planned to dump him. Instead, he'd dumped her, unceremoniously and with such devious cleverness that she hadn't realized what was happening until it was over. Feeling as though she'd been sucker-punched, Carolyn shouldered her overnight bag, scooped up Meg's journal, and stepped out of the car. He pulled the door shut and for an endless moment, they gazed at each other through the window.

Then he put the car into gear and drove away.

Rafferty hung up the phone and leaned back in his chair. Idly clicking his Paper Mate with his thumb, he stared out his office window. Four stories below him, morning traffic idled at its usual standstill. Dark clouds, heavy with rain, hung low on the horizon, imbuing the day with an ominous quality that perfectly complemented his mood. He swiveled around to study the photos pinned to the bulletin board. Six of them now. Seven, including the girl in Manhasset. Seven dead women who were probably a preview of coming attractions if Conor Rafferty didn't find the perp, and find him soon. Were their expressions faintly accusatory, or was it an overactive imagination, colored by guilt, that made them appear that way?

Working this case was like chasing rabbits down a hole.

He was beginning to feel like Alice in freaking Wonderland. Every time he thought he was getting close to something, it disappeared. Rafferty set down the pen, braced his elbows on the desktop, and raked his fingers through his hair. If he didn't get a break soon, some kind of solid lead, some piece of evidence that was more concrete than circumstantial, the entire case was going to crash and burn. When it did, his career would plummet and lie smoldering in the ruins along with it.

Carolyn wasn't going to like what he'd just done. Sometimes, she reminded him of his aunt Freda's six-pound Pomeranian: all heart and fierce courage, ready to chase off the biggest, baddest interloper, yet totally oblivious to her own size and limitations. She was fond of citing her FBI credentials as proof of her invincibility, but this perp wasn't impressed by credentials. He'd already killed at least seven women, probably more. His intentions were clear: he wanted Carolyn. And if he wanted her, he wouldn't stop until he got her. Relationship or no relationship, Rafferty couldn't just leave her out there, open and unprotected. This morning, he'd made a couple of quick phone calls, called in a couple of favors, and arranged for police protection. She would undoubtedly pitch a fit, but he wouldn't be swayed. Until the case was over, he intended to keep a man on her at all times.

He didn't even want to think about their non-relationship. When Conor Rafferty set out to screw up his life, he screwed it up big-time. He'd known since Day One that sooner or later, he'd end up in her bed. Or she in his. There was a fatal attraction between them that had nothing to do with logic or reason, nothing to do with their history or the roles they were expected to play in this case. It was simply there, had been there since that night ten years ago when he'd walked into his father's bar and found Josie's childhood friend serving beer and Irish stew and a small slice of heaven with every smile.

There was no way he could get involved with her. They both had lives, and those lives didn't run on parallel tracks. It wouldn't work. It couldn't. They'd done the right thing, nipping it in the bud, putting an end to it right at the start. That had been the only reasonable option.

So why the hell was he so pissed off?

He raised his cup of coffee, glared at its murky contents. "Fuck," he said eloquently.

"Good morning to you, too," Lorna said from the doorway. "Enjoy your day off?"

He eyed her lanky body, leaning against his door frame, and narrowed his eyes. "I was enjoying it immensely, until you called and ruined it for me."

She grinned. "Glad I could be of assistance." Crossing her arms and lowering her eyelids modestly, she said, "I won the pool, by the way."

"What pool?"

"The office pool." She looked up at him through lowered lids. "We've all been laying bets on just how long it would take you to get the lovely Agent Monahan into bed. I won."

Jesus Christ. He picked up his coffee cup and took a sip. The coffee was cold, and it tasted like sewer sludge. Stonily, he said, "It's not like that."

"Oh, come on, Conor. Don't try to tell me you didn't sleep with her."

He stiffened and repeated, "It's not like that."

Lorna's eyebrows went sky-high. "I see," she said, the words buried in layers of meaning.

He set down the coffee and said irritably, "There's nothing to see. Are you going to loiter in my doorway all day, or can I expect a report sometime before noon?"

"Touchy today, aren't we?"

"What did you find out from Clancy's date book?"

She shoved a pile of papers away from the corner of his desk, plunked her bony posterior down in the cleared space, and made herself at home. "Zilch. Nothing to give him an alibi for any of the murder dates."

"What about Tuesday night? I want you to check on his whereabouts, find out if he was anywhere near Manhasset. I want witnesses, verification."

"I already checked. I called him first thing this morning. It seems that the good Father was home alone Tuesday night. He watched *Jeopardy,* and then he went to bed. No witnesses, no verification, no alibi. Church secretary says he was at work yesterday morning at his usual time."

"Wonderful. Anything else?"

"I thought you'd find this interesting." She opened up the folder in her lap and handed him a sheaf of papers. "These came in yesterday. Responses to the feelers you sent out to other jurisdictions."

He took them from her, scanned the first page. Paused, raised his eyes to hers.

"Three unsolved homicides," she confirmed. "Daytona Beach. Milwaukee. Chapel Hill. All of them virtually identical to ours. It could just be that our boy has done a bit of moving around."

He leafed quickly through the pages. "Did you check the dates?"

"They all happened after the Monahan homicide and before our first one. This could be our guy, Conor."

Thinking out loud, he said, "So why would he start killing in Boston, move around the country for nine years, then come back to Boston? Job transfers?"

"Could be. If it's the same guy, there's a high degree

of mobility. What kind of jobs involve that level of mobility?''

''He could be a career military man. Or a salesman.''

''Truck driver,'' Lorna said.

''Midlevel executive, transferred every two years.''

''Carnie.''

''Airline pilot. Flight attendant. Bus driver. Shit.'' He shuffled the papers, straightened them into a neat stack. ''I'd give my left testicle for a solid scrap of DNA evidence. But this guy's sharp. Whatever he takes in, he carries out. No blood, no hair, no semen, not even so much as a drop of spit. He must wear a wetsuit while he rapes and pillages.''

''Boston's probably home,'' Lorna mused. ''He most likely grew up here. Maybe he came back to take care of an elderly parent.''

''Closure.''

''Closure?''

''He's come full circle. Maybe there's some kind of symbolic meaning to it. Maybe, in order to achieve closure, he needs to end where he started.''

''Christ, Conor, don't tell me that after only two nights with our illustrious profiler, you're going all touchy-feely on me.''

''I'm not going all touchy-feely. But there's no way of telling what's driving this guy. Serial homicide is complex. These killers aren't driven by your usual motives of jealousy-slash-greed-slash-revenge. They run on motives that make no sense to anybody else on the planet.'' He tapped his fingers against the desktop. ''I put a plain-clothes tag on Monahan. She won't like it.''

Lorna's gaze was steady. ''You think he's after her.''

''He followed us to the Cape. He killed a girl who looked enough like her to be her sister, and then he left a personal note, addressed to her, on the corpse. Yes, I think he's after her, and I'm not leaving her vulnerable until we get him.''

He called the team together in his office for a quick meeting from which Carolyn Monahan was noticeably absent. ''The report on Katie Perry's car came back this morning from Forensics,'' he told them. ''There were a number of latents on the dash, the door handles, even the fenders, but no matches with anything NCIC has on file. Perry was eighteen years old. She probably carted dozens of teenagers around in her car, but apparently nobody who's ever been arrested. She lifted the hood herself. Her prints were all over it. We didn't really expect to find anything. Our boy's too smart to leave latents on a victim's car.''

''Nice try,'' Greg Lassiter said.

''Not nice enough. Meantime, we have something that might prove to be a real break in the case.'' He filled them in on the reports he'd received from Chapel Hill, Milwaukee and Daytona. ''I've asked for the full police reports from each of those jurisdictions. Once they get here, I intend to go over them personally, word for word.'' From his perch on the corner of his desk, he picked up his glass paperweight and tossed it from hand to hand. ''Any progress on the Monahan case?''

Hailstock sighed and rubbed his temple. ''It's slow going. Mendez and I have spent two days working our way through the records of people we've interviewed since April. So far, we've been able to disqualify some of them because they weren't living here at the time Monahan was killed. Some of them were incarcerated, and couldn't have done it. But it's going to take us some time to wade through all of it and track everybody back ten years. Mendez has today off, so I'm working alone. That slows things down, too.''

"Fair enough. Abrams, Rizzoli?''

"We've both gone through the Monahan file,'' Ted said. "Nothing yet, so we're going through it a second time.''

"Good. Lassiter and Smith?''

"We're almost to the end of the list,'' Smith said. "It's been slow going, but we should have something for you this afternoon.''

"All right, people, you've done some good, solid work. We'll meet again tomorrow morning. If anything breaks in the meantime, you know where to find me.''

13

August 11, 1992

I told Clancy tonight that we were through. To say
he didn't take it well would be a gross understatement. I've never seen him this way before. He was
half out of his head, talking crazy, telling me I was
throwing my life away, swearing that I'd be back
once I realized what a mistake I'd made. He terrifies
me, the way he runs hot and cold. Johnny is so different. He makes me feel good about myself in a
way that Clancy never has. I think I'm really in love.
I can't wait to tell him that it's over with Clancy
and now I'm free to be with him.

Caro had been reading nonstop for two hours, and she
had to backtrack and read her sister's final journal entry
a second time before its significance sank in. She sat upright, forgetting the headache that seemed to have taken
up permanent residence at the base of her skull. Meg had
broken her engagement less than a week before she died.
There had to be a connection. Caro didn't believe in coincidence. Meg's death had to be related somehow to the
split with Clancy, a split that she hadn't bothered to share
with her family.

She'd been so certain of Clancy's innocence, but now

that certainty had been shaken. Seeing him through Meg's eyes had colored her perception of the man she'd thought she knew. Was it possible he'd killed her sister in a jealous rage? Caro tried to pull up a clear memory of Clancy Donovan at twenty-four, but the passage of time had blurred her memory, and the best she could conjure was an indistinct image of an impetuous young man with a volatile temper.

And just who was the elusive Johnny? He'd played her sister like a finely tuned fiddle, cleverly and systematically driving a wedge between her and Clancy. Had he loved her, or had he simply used her for his own purposes? If his intentions had been honorable, why hadn't he come forward when she was murdered to demand that her killer be found? Why hadn't he spilled out his grief at her funeral, as the rest of them had? Why hadn't he knocked on her mother's door and introduced himself to the family?

So many questions. Somebody, somewhere, had the answers. Somebody, somewhere, knew what had happened to her sister, and he was standing in the shadows, chortling with glee as he watched them fall all over their own feet like Keystone Kops. He was clever, she'd give him that. Clever, devious, and crafty to have eluded capture for so long. But he wasn't as smart as he thought. He wasn't smarter than the combined brainpower of the Boston Police Department and the Federal Bureau of Investigation. Sooner or later, he would make a fatal error, and then they would nail his hide to the wall.

She had to tell Conor what she'd learned. It could be important to the case. As a professional, she couldn't allow personal feelings to get in the way. That was the reason she'd chosen to back away from him in the first place, wasn't it? She'd learned her lesson the hard way with Richard: the workplace was no place for romantic entanglements.

It wasn't supposed to hurt this much, damn it. She wasn't some innocent young girl, mired in the depths of her first love affair. She was thirty-two years old. There'd been men in her life. Not a steady parade of them, but she'd never lacked male companionship. What made Conor Rafferty different? Why was he the only man who could tear out her heart and leave her bleeding?

With a nasty oath, Caro snatched up the telephone receiver and punched a series of numbers she hadn't realized she knew by heart. She didn't have time to be a sniveling fool. That could come later, when the case was over and Conor Rafferty was safely relegated to the dim reaches of memory. Right now, she had a job to do.

"Rafferty."

He sounded distracted, and his voice sent an unwelcome tingle shooting down her spine. She hunched her shoulders. "There's something you need to know," she told him. "Meg broke her engagement."

A moment of silence passed before he said, "What are you talking about?"

"About a week before she died, Meg broke up with Clancy. Called off the engagement. She dumped him for this Johnny person she kept gushing about. I don't like the smell of it. The timing seems a little too convenient for coincidence."

"Shit. This thickens the plot, doesn't it?"

"It gets better. Apparently, Clancy didn't take it well."

"Wonderful."

She let out a hard breath. "So you didn't know about it, either?"

"No. Clancy never breathed a word of it to me."

"We have to find out who this Johnny was. I have a

feeling he holds the key to the case. Somebody has to know about him. Meg must have confided in someone.''

''What about your mother?''

''I can't believe she would've told Mom. She would have been too afraid of being browbeaten into taking Clancy back.''

''Maybe she talked to Mike. Or one of her girlfriends.''

She tried to picture Meg confiding in their older brother, but it was difficult to imagine. Not impossible, but difficult. Meg had always shared her confidences with Carolyn. But that summer, Caro had been too wrapped up in her own life, her own love affair, to have time for her sister. Guilt wrapped itself around her heart and squeezed tight. She supposed it was conceivable that Meg might have turned to Mike as a substitute. Certainly she would have confided in Mike before she would have talked to their mother. He'd always doted on his baby sister.

''I'll talk to Mike,'' she said. ''As for girlfriends, Meggie had dozens of them, but only one that she was really close to, the kind of close where you share confidences. Louise Doherty. But I have no idea where she is now. I haven't seen her since Meg's funeral.''

''I know where she is. She's married to Bobby Moriarty and still living in Southie. Maybe it's time for me to renew old acquaintances. Caro—'' He paused, and she waited out the silence, her heart thumping too rapidly. ''There's something you need to know, too. This morning, I ordered police protection for you.''

She gripped the phone so hard her fingers hurt. ''You did what?''

''There's a plainclothes detective stationed outside your door. His name's Policzki. He's been ordered to stay with you at all times. Don't make it hard for him, he's just doing his job.''

Heat rushed in a prickling wave up her torso to her scalp. "Damn it, Conor, I'm not a civilian. I don't need a baby-sitter."

"Humor me. Just go about your business and pretend he's not there."

"Does staying with me at all times mean he gets to sleep on the spare bed in my room? Does he get to follow me into the bathroom? You just never know who might be hiding behind the shower curtain."

"I'm sure he'll practice discretion. He'll check behind the curtain, and then he'll leave you alone."

"Conor!"

"I was kidding, Carolyn. You've lost your sense of humor. Look, most of the time, you won't even know he's there. I'm doing this for your own safety."

Phone in hand, she strode to the door of her room and looked out through the peephole. A young man in a charcoal suit and a red power tie stood across the hall. His posture appeared casual, but even from her distorted viewpoint, the buzz cut and the alert watchfulness in his eyes screamed cop. "Christ, Conor," she said, "he's a fifteen-year-old Twinkie. My mother looks tougher than he does."

"He's a decorated officer who just made detective. And he's twenty-five years old. Be gentle with him. You're his first Special Agent."

She said something decidedly unladylike, and at the other end of the phone, he let out a short burst of laughter. "What?" she demanded, still steaming.

"Some things never change. Check in with me later." And she was left holding a dead phone.

When she opened the door, the young man leaning casually against the wall snapped to attention. "Detective Policzki, I presume," she said.

"Agent Monahan."

"Identification, please."

Policzki reached into his pocket, pulled out his badge, and held it up. She studied it closely, looked him up and down, and nodded.

"Lieutenant Rafferty requested protection for you," Policzki said, "because he has reason to believe your life may be in danger."

"I'm aware of the lieutenant's reasoning. I'm also aware that he could be right. But I resent being treated like some helpless civilian. I'm no Barbie doll. Stay out of my hair, Policzki, and we'll get along just fine. Understood?"

He folded his arms. "Understood. Now, I'd like you to understand something. I don't take orders from you. You have no authority over me. I take my orders from Lieutenant Rafferty, and nobody else. As long as you don't try to ditch me or tell me what to do, we'll get along fine. Understood?"

She had to admire the kid; he had balls. "I'd say we understand each other quite clearly," she said.

They'd cordoned off a section of the street and barricaded it with chain-link fence. Behind the wire mesh, two burly construction workers were pulverizing the pavement with jackhammers that rattled loud enough to make her teeth ache. Dust rose from the rubble, coating everything in a thick layer of dull brown. A cement truck parked at the curb spewed its contents down a chute into a concrete form set below street level. A crane lifted a steel girder high in the air above her head, accompanied by the rapid-fire cacophony of a half-dozen rivet guns.

On an upper floor of the skeletal structure, the foreman approached a husky riveter in a yellow hard hat and shouted into his ear. The rivet gun fell abruptly silent, and the man in the yellow hat turned and stared in her direction. Caro raised a hand in greeting. The two men conferred briefly, then her brother set down the gun and headed for the elevator.

She watched him approach, expertly dodging wheelbarrows and stepping over hoses. Mike was the only one of the three siblings who had inherited Gerald Monahan's reddish hair and ruddy complexion, his barrel chest and bandy-legged walk. Six years had passed since she'd seen her brother, and the years had not been kind to him. Barely thirty-five, he could have easily passed for fifty. Too many years in the sun, combined with a two-pack-a-day cigarette habit, had left Mike's face a spiderweb of lines and wrinkles. His cheeks were puffy, and his gut spilled over his belt. He looked like a heart attack waiting to happen.

"Carolyn," he said.

"Mike." She hesitated, not sure how to greet him. A hug seemed too intimate, so she settled for grasping his hand and squeezing his fingers. She waited for him to squeeze back, but it didn't happen. Withdrawing her hand, she said breezily, "That's some building you're putting up." She raised her head to study the high-rise. "What's it going to be?"

"A luxury hotel. A place for rich tourists—" he paused meaningfully, eyed her suit, her shoes, the silk print scarf knotted loosely around her neck "—to blow all that money they don't know what to do with."

Determined to ignore his dig, she said, "How have you been? How are Mandy and the kids?"

His blue eyes, so like their father's, held steady on hers. "Fine. Is there something you wanted? I'm a little busy here."

She forced the hurt back down. "I'd like to talk to you. Is there someplace nearby where I can buy you a cup of coffee?"

"I'm working."

She felt a flicker of irritation. "Your foreman told me you were due for a break. Come on, Mike, I'm only asking for ten minutes out of your life. Then you can go back to pretending I don't exist."

He led her to a grimy hole-in-the-wall on the next block that sold phone cards and film, lottery tickets and Skoal in little green tins. Just inside the door, a plastic trash can held an assortment of three-dollar umbrellas that the proprietor probably made a killing on whenever it rained. The coffee was scalding, and came in a politically incorrect foam cup. Policzki waited outside, eyes hidden behind opaque Ray●Bans, hands loosely tucked into his pockets as he feigned interest in the Bruce Lee movie poster Scotch-taped to the smudged plate glass window.

They walked for a while in silence, Policzki following at a leisurely pace. Farther down the block, next to a jammed parking lot, Mike stopped and lowered himself onto a dusty guardrail. "What do you want to talk about?"

Caro wiped clean a spot on the guardrail and sat down beside him. Balancing her cup on the discolored aluminum, she said, "I need to talk to you about Meg."

"Meg's dead. There's nothing to say."

"Look, Mike, I found out something today. Before she died, Meg broke up with Clancy. She ditched him for some guy she'd been seeing, somebody she called Johnny. I was hoping you might know something about him. Like who he was, and where he is now."

He took his time peeling back the plastic tab on his cup

lid and they both watched the steam rise. "Why? Why do you want to know?"

Caro leaned forward, trying to ignore the hardness in his voice. "The police have reopened the case. We're convinced that the man we're looking for, the one who's killed all those young girls, is the same man who killed Meg."

He took a sip of coffee. "Been ten years," he said. "Hard to believe it's the same guy."

"Our evidence is pretty damn convincing."

"I can't help you."

"Can't, or won't?"

A muscle twitched in his cheek. "I don't want you stirring it all up again. What's done is done. Let it be."

"Damn it, Mike, I can't let it be. Women are dying. We have to stop it."

"When Meg died, it almost killed Mom and Dad. You bring it back up, it'll be like losing her all over again. I won't let you put them through that again. You breathe a word of this to them, I swear to Christ I'll break your frigging neck."

"Dad already knows some of it."

His face reddened. "Goddamn it, Caro, do you have to go around stirring up turds? Is this some mission you're on? Can't you just leave us the hell alone?"

She leaned forward. "This is important, Michael. I'm asking for your help here. Don't you give a damn?"

His eyes hardened. "Not if it puts Mom and Dad through hell again. You don't know. You weren't here to see it. You weren't the one that had to try and put the pieces back together again." He took a sip of coffee. "You just did your damage, and then you got the hell out of Dodge. I was the one left holding the bag."

"Christ, Mike, it's been ten years. Are you ever going to stop blaming me?"

His eyes were like ice cubes, hard and cold and brittle. "No."

"That's not fair!"

"Yeah? Well, it wasn't fair what happened to Meg, either." He shifted position on the guardrail. "See, the thing about you, Caro, is you always thought you were better than the rest of us. You with your fancy degrees and your fancy clothes and your fancy job." Balancing his cup between meaty thighs, he held out both hands, palms up. They were a working man's hands, hard with calluses, dirt under the nails, cuticles torn, knuckles bruised and scarred. "See these hands? This is my Ph.D. I didn't get a fancy college education. Every penny I earn comes from a strong back and these hands. And I'm proud of it. I'm not ashamed of where I come from. I'm not trying to run away from who I am."

"Damn it, I know who I am! And I'm not running away!"

"Is that so? Tell me, do you have any intention of staying here once this case is over? Or are you just gonna walk out of our lives again, the way you always do?"

She opened her mouth, discovered there were no words, and closed it.

"You've been running since the day you were born, Caro. You're still running. When you split, I was the one left behind. The one who stayed here and did his duty."

"Because you made the choice to stay, Michael! We all make choices in life. It's called free will. You didn't have to stay here and play the martyr. That was your own decision. Just like it was my decision to leave. I had a right to my own life."

"Bullshit! What choice did I have?" He stood abruptly

and flung his coffee cup into a nearby trash receptacle. "Somebody had to take care of them!"

"Give them a little credit. They're grown adults, they don't need a keeper. They haven't exactly reached doddering old age yet. They're barely sixty, for Christ's sake!"

"Go back," he said, fists clenched. "Go back where you came from, Carolyn. Everybody will be better off." And he turned and walked away.

"Damn you!" she shouted at his retreating back, no longer caring who heard what should have been a private conversation. "If you know something and you're not telling me, it's on your shoulders! If more girls die because of what you held back, you're the one who has to live with it!"

He kept on walking, and she ditched her coffee and followed him. "We're not the only ones," she said, moving rapidly, trying to catch up. "We're not the only ones hurting. Young girls are dying, Mike." She hated the sound of pleading that she heard in her own voice. "Young girls like Meg, with their whole lives ahead of them, and the only crime they've committed was being in the wrong place at the wrong time. They all have people they've left behind. Mothers, fathers, sisters, brothers. Those people are all hurting, just like you and I. If you know something that can help us, you have to tell me. Otherwise, God help you, I hope you can look at yourself in the mirror every morning for the rest of your life."

He paused, didn't turn, but waited to hear the rest of what she had to say. "If you don't care about them," she said, "think of Meg. This might be our only chance to catch the bastard who killed her."

He finally turned around. Beneath the brim of the hard

hat, his eyes were dark and mournful. "I don't know who he was," he said. "Except—"

"Except what?"

"He was married. That's all I know."

"Married," she said. "Meg was involved with a married man? You knew this, and you didn't tell the police?"

His voice was bitter. "It wasn't going to bring Meggie back, now, was it?" Without another word, he turned and trudged back to the construction site.

Behind her, Policzki's voice, surprisingly gentle, said, "You okay?"

Hellfire and damnation. She'd forgotten he was there. "Yeah," she said, trying to ease the thickness out of her voice. "I'm okay."

"He was pretty hard on you."

"You think that was hard, Policzki? That was practically a lovefest. At least he spoke to me. It's the first time in almost ten years."

"Your brother hasn't spoken to you in ten years?"

Her laughter was brittle. "Welcome to my world. Come on, Detective, let's get out of here. There's somebody I have to talk to."

"Terry Finnegan," Detective Greg Lassiter said, handing Rafferty a mug shot that showed a sullen, dark-haired young man with deep-set eyes and a perpetual scowl. "And Marvin Williamson. They're our best bets. Both convicted sex offenders, incarcerated after the Monahan homicide and released at some point in the eighteen months prior to Magnusson."

Rafferty shuffled the photos. Williamson's face was slender and bony, like a ferret. "Both white," Detective Kayla Smith added, "both in their midthirties, both still residing in the Boston area."

"Finnegan's got a sheet as long as his arm," Lassiter said. "Unlawful sexual contact, gross sexual misconduct, aggravated sexual assault. Etcetera, etcetera, etcetera."

"And a pretty face to go along with it. What's he doing back on the street?"

"Good behavior. Model prisoner. Need I say more?"

Rafferty sighed. "Never mind. Stupid question. All right, people, good work." He dropped the photos. "Now go out and round them up. Let's lean on them and see what happens. Maybe we'll get lucky."

The two detectives stood, Greg stretching lanky limbs and adjusting his raspberry-colored tie. With a grin, he said, "Always happy to oblige, Lieutenant."

Alone again, Rafferty studied the photos spread out on the desk in front of him. It was probably a long shot. Neither of these guys had a previous murder rap. But the type of offender he was seeking often received an elementary education in minor sex offenses, earned his postsecondary degree in rape, then did graduate work in homicide. He couldn't discount the possibility that one of them could be Mr. X.

Beside his elbow, the phone rang. Still studying the ferret-faced Williamson, he picked up the receiver, brought it to his ear and muttered, "Rafferty."

"I must say, Lieutenant, you're a difficult man to catch."

He dropped the mug shots, leaned back in his chair, and attempted to shift gears. Had it really been just a few days since he'd last spoken to her, a lifetime ago? "Gwen," he said, running a hand through his hair. "How's the Heffernan case coming along?"

"Better if you don't ask, darling. How about your case?"

"Better if you don't ask."

"I just called to remind you that tomorrow's the third Friday of the month."

Christ. He'd forgotten. The timing couldn't have been worse. He'd just taken a day off, and this case had him up to his ass in alligators. He didn't have time for an evening with Gwen that would start with dinner and end up in bed. He wasn't even sure he wanted it. But the third Friday was a long-standing tradition, and if he backed out, she would smell a rat. Gwen might have the soul of a barracuda, but she had the nose of a bloodhound.

He cleared his throat. "Pick you up at six?"

"Six is perfect. And, Conor?" Her voice turned silken. "Plan to stay over."

He clicked the button to break the connection, glanced at the clock, and sighed. Not yet eleven, and already the day was headed south. He dialed Lorna's extension.

"Yo," she said. "What's shaking?"

"You free for lunch? I'm buying."

"Holy shit, Conor, you win the lottery or something?"

"Something."

"That's what I was afraid of. Payback's always a bitch. The last time I let you buy me lunch, I wound up assisting you with an arrest. I was real fond of that shirt, too."

"Just think of it as material for your memoirs. *Lorna Abrams, Girl Detective.*"

"That's what I love most about you, Conor, your impressive sensitivity to the plight of women. Good thing you're on the other end of the phone. Otherwise, I'd have to grab you by the throat and choke you as an example to male chauvinist pigs everywhere."

"If you're real nice to me, I'll spring for dessert."

"Be still, my beating heart. What do I have to do to qualify for the Conor Rafferty Welfare Fund?"

"No big, fat, hairy deal. I just need you to come with me to question somebody."

"Oh, goody. Drug runner, murder suspect, pimp?"

"Nope," he said. "Housewife." And hung up the phone.

Blood of the Lamb.

Caro stepped into the church foyer, her eyes drawn inescapably to the plaster crucifix that hung on the wall behind the altar. Jesus looked down on her with mild reproach through eyes that seemed surprised by the amount of blood that dripped from his palms. His face, contorted with pain, spoke of sacrifice, and Carolyn shuddered and averted her gaze, unable to look any longer. When she was a child, she'd been terrified of Him, in much the same way she'd been terrified of Freddy Kruger. Now that she was grown, He simply made her uncomfortable, as if she'd committed some unpardonable sin and He was sorely disappointed in her.

Little had changed in the ten years since she'd last been inside Saint Bart's. The hard oak pews, the kneelers padded in maroon velvet, the ornate candelabra, were all the same. A bloodred carpet still hushed the footsteps of the holy and the not-so-holy as they stood in line to receive communion. The vaulted ceiling that always sent the most minute sounds bouncing back, magnified in the stillness, filled her with the same hushed sense of infinity that had brought goose bumps to her flesh when she was a girl and still believed that God lived somewhere in the midst of all this stained-glass splendor.

Behind her, Policzki cleared his throat, and she left that lost little girl behind. "This way," she said softly, and led him down a darkened corridor and into the parish office in the north wing of the church. Behind a massive mahogany desk, a slender young woman cradled the telephone between ear and shoulder while her fingers raced over the computer keyboard. "That's Saturday, November 12," she said into the phone, her fingers pausing on the keyboard. "Noon to five. You're good to go, Mrs. Finley. See you on Sunday."

She hung up the phone and turned her gaze on them. Her gray eyes, huge behind owlish glasses, shone with intelligence. "Good morning," she said. "Can I help you?"

"Is Father Donovan in? I'd like to speak with him."

"I'm afraid he's tied up at the moment. He's working on tomorrow night's Rotary Club speech." The woman's smile reeked of goodwill. "If you'd like to make an appointment, I'm sure he can see you sometime tomorrow afternoon."

Caro glanced at the woman's name plate. Pulling out her FBI shield and holding it up, she said, "I need to speak with him now, Melissa. Tell him Caro's here. He'll see me."

The secretary eyed Caro's ID, and some of the goodwill left her face. "Just a minute," she said, and shoved back her chair.

On a shelf near the desk, a twenty-gallon fish tank gurgled. Brightly colored travel posters decorated the walls. Father O'Rourke would never have allowed such frivolities. And she'd bet dollars to doughnuts that if he were still here, sweet young Melissa would be typing on the ancient Olivetti that Gertrude Hollister had used for thirty years, instead of a spanking-new Gateway. Caro wandered to the window. Outside, a negligible patch of dried grass edged up to a cracked sidewalk that should have been replaced years ago. A dusty blue Chevy, fifteen years past its prime, sat at the curb.

"Caro?"

She turned. The priest was framed in the doorway, shoulders nearly brushing the wood on both sides. He was wearing a wine-colored turtleneck and faded jeans. His hair was mussed, and dark circles ringed his eyes. She suspected that his last few days hadn't been conducive to restorative sleep. Beside him, the devoted Melissa stood guard like a bulldog, and Caro wondered if he had any idea that his secretary had a crush on him. "Father," she said. "Can I have a few minutes of your time?"

Without speaking, he stepped aside so she could enter his sanctum. "Wait here," she told Policzki. "Keep Melissa company."

Clancy swung the door shut behind them. The walls of his office were lined with books, most of them dealing with various aspects of theology. "Have you read all these?" she asked.

"Some of them. Most of them were already here when I took over. My legacy from Father O'Rourke. What is it you want, Caro? It seems I can't get through a day without at least one visitation from the authorities."

"I'm not here in a professional capacity. This is personal. I need to talk to you, not priest to profiler, but Clancy to Caro. That's why I left Policzki outside, because what we say here today will never go beyond that door." She paced across the small room, glanced out the window at the parking lot. Wheeling around, she said, "I know the truth."

The priest folded his arms and leaned one hip against the wall. "What truth might that be?"

"I've been reading Meg's journal. I know about the breakup."

His face remained motionless. "And?"

"She died just a few days later. Doesn't the timing strike you as a little odd?"

"I see. She broke up with me, therefore I must have killed her."

"You know as well as I do that most murders are committed by somebody close to the victim."

"Do I?"

"Damn it, Clancy—" She glanced toward the ceiling, belatedly aware that she stood in this holiest of holy places. "I want to know the truth, do you hear me? The plain, unvarnished truth. There's nobody else here, nobody to hear it but you, me and God." She took a deep breath. "Did you kill my sister?"

He stepped away from the wall and leaned over her, his bulk blocking what little light managed to come through the window. "No," he said.

Without warning, all the starch went out of her. Wearily, she said, "I want to believe you. I want so much to believe you."

"Let me tell you something." He ran a hand through unruly dark hair. "Before Meg came into my life, I was lost. Floundering, with no direction, no focus, no meaning to my life. Your sister changed all that. She saved me, Caro. When she died, I needed to blame somebody. Since there wasn't any convenient target, I blamed God. I raged at Him, demanded to know how a supposedly benevolent God could let something like this happen to Meg, to me. I started drinking, because it was the only way I could deal with the pain and the rage. But then a funny thing happened. God started talking back. And one morning, I found myself, bleary-eyed and hungover, standing on the sidewalk in front of Saint Bart's. Somehow, I found the courage to walk up those steps and into the church. I turned the pain and the rage over to God. He's been taking care of me ever since."

Caro swallowed the hard lump that had lodged in her

throat and struggled to find a discreet way of wording what she had to say, but there was none. "Did Meg tell you why she was calling off the engagement?"

"She didn't have to tell me. She was an eighteen-year-old girl. Too young to get married, but it was a long time before I understood that. I pushed too hard. She wasn't ready."

"No," she said. "That may be what she wanted you to think. But that wasn't the real reason." She closely observed his eyes as she plunged in headfirst. "There was another man."

Those amber eyes narrowed in disbelief too raw, too pained, to be anything but genuine. Clancy Donovan might be a priest, but beneath the rosary there still beat the heart of a man. Her missile had made a direct hit, and Caro deeply regretted having been the one to launch it.

"Another man," he said. "Who?"

"That's what I'm trying to find out. Did she ever mention anyone named Johnny? Does the name mean anything to you?"

"It was all such a long time ago. I—no." He turned to stare out the window. "I'm sorry."

"I'm the one who should apologize. I couldn't be sure until I confronted you with it."

He swung back around to face her. "Sure of what?"

Her eyes held steady on his. "That you didn't kill her."

Muddled emotions flitted over his face. Anger. Grief. Gratitude. "Do you think—" he cleared his throat "—that he..." For probably the first time in his life, Clancy Donovan fell speechless.

"Killed her?" she said. "Let me put it this way, Father. If you didn't, then chances are damn good that he did."

"Caro?" His voice was raw with emotion. "Get him."

14

Louise Moriarty bounced a baby on her hip while a toddler of indeterminate gender tugged at her Levi's. Her strawberry-blond hair hung loose, slightly mussed, and he couldn't be certain, since he'd never had the pleasure of experiencing it personally, but he thought he recognized spit-up on her shirt. In spite of being housebound with two small children, Louise still wore the same buoyant air she'd always possessed, the same engaging grin, the one she poured over him right now.

"Conor Rafferty," she said. "What a surprise! What on earth are you doing here?"

Although Louise was five or six years younger than he was, they'd known each other forever. For all its urban sprawl, South Boston was in many ways a small town. If you grew up here, you regularly ran into the same people at church, at the dry cleaner's, the pool hall, the corner pizza joint. "Can we come in?" he said. "We'd like to ask you a few questions about Meg Monahan."

Her smile faltered. "Meg," she said. "Good God, I haven't thought of her in ages. Have you reopened the case?"

"Yes," he said, without going into detail.

"Well, come on in. Make yourselves at home. I'll get these heathens settled in front of *Sesame Street,* and we'll talk. Can I get you anything? Coffee, tea, Kool-Aid?"

"No, thanks. We just ate." The souvlaki he'd let Lorna talk him into eating for lunch was coming back to haunt him, and he wondered if this was how it started: indigestion, and then a slow slide into senility. He sat on the couch, encountered something hard and painful, and unearthed a plastic wrestling figure from under his backside. He set it on the coffee table and settled gingerly into the couch cushion. Looking up, he met Lorna's eye. The gleam there put a scowl on his face.

"Stop it," he said. "I hate it when you look at me that way."

"I'm just trying to picture you with a half-dozen little Raffertys running around your feet. I can't wait for the day."

"It's a day that's never coming, so forget it."

"Really? Gee, I hope you remembered to mention that to Agent Monahan."

He was saved from having to respond by the reappearance of Louise Moriarty, minus the two rug rats. She'd run a comb through her hair and changed into a soft blue sweater that draped attractively over breasts that were firm and full. Like Carolyn's. She plopped into an easy chair, tossed her hair back from her face. "So," she said. "What can I help you with?"

He banished Carolyn Monahan from his mind, concentrated instead on the reason he'd come here. "Before she died, Meg became involved with a man named Johnny. Tell me what you know about their relationship."

Louise's eyebrows shot sky-high. "Wow," she said. "You go right for the jugular, don't you?" She paused to think, then said, "You have to understand that we were kids. At eighteen, we were invincible, and life was a grand adventure." Her smile was wry. "Meg was chafing under the restrictions placed on her at home. She didn't talk about it much, but I know it bothered her. If Roberta had been my mother I would have run away by the time I was twelve. She was on Meg every waking minute.'' Louise grimaced, glanced apologetically at Lorna. ''You know Roberta,'' she told Conor. ''Always criticizing, always complaining. Always full of impossible expectations.''

He nodded. ''Go on.''

''Unfortunately, Clancy was putting pressure on her, too. He was older—twenty-four—and ready to settle down. Meg wanted to sow a few wild oats. She liked to have a good time.'' Louise leaned forward. ''Don't get me wrong. Meg was a good girl. She had her head screwed on straight. Until this guy came along, anyway. Meg fell for him like a ton of bricks.''

Excitement built in his already churning stomach. ''Who was he, Louise?''

''I wish I could tell you, but I can't.'' Louise's smile was rueful. ''I knew something was up, but for the longest time, she wouldn't tell me anything. I think she was afraid that it would get back to Clancy, and she wasn't ready to burn any bridges. From what I could gather, this Johnny courted her with flowers and candy. He got her where he wanted her, and then he just reeled her in. She was in pretty deep before she told me, and even then, she kept his identity a secret. All she ever divulged was his first name. I don't even know where she met him. It could have been anywhere. She interacted with dozens of people every day at the pub, and she was socking away money for college expenses, so she was baby-sitting on the side. And she had so many friends. Anybody could have introduced them.''

His excitement fizzled and took a nosedive. Lorna leaned forward. ''Could you give us a list of names? Everybody you can think of who knew her?''

"Sure, if you can give me a little time. I may have to go back through my high school yearbook. It's been ten years."

"Is there anything else you can think of?" he said. "Anything that might help us?"

Louise shook her head. "Not offhand. But I'll call you if I remember anything."

He left Louise Moriarty with his card, and he and Lorna walked silently back to the Taurus. Rafferty slid his keys into the ignition, then paused with his hand still clutching the key ring. "You want to know what frustrates me the most about this? We're working on the assumption that whoever killed Meg Monahan knew her. But we don't know for sure, and it's driving me crazy. Just because the perp knows who Carolyn is, knows that Meg was her sister, doesn't mean he knew Meg. It could just as easily have been a stranger killing."

"What about Smith and Lassiter?" Lorna said. "They come up with anything yet?"

"They've narrowed it down to a couple of pretty faces who've been in and out of the Walpole Hilton like they had a revolving door on the place. I sent Lassiter and Smith to pick them up. Christ, it's like target shooting in the dark."

She gave his shoulder a motherly pat. "Don't let it get to you," she said. "You're one of the best shots I know. Even in the dark."

"Yeah?" He cranked the ignition and threw the car into gear. "Then how come I keep missing?"

The minute he walked through the door of the office, Isabel accosted him, a sheaf of pink message slips in her hand and murder in her eyes. *"Dios,"* she spat, "if things get any crazier around here, I'm going to take a nice, boring job as a file clerk at the DMV.''

''Bad day?''

''Don't even ask.'' She shadowed him down the hall, shuffling through pink slips as she went. ''You have messages from three newspapers, two TV stations, and one radio station. They all want statements.''

''Round file 'em.''

''Your mother called. Her toilet is broken, and she wants to know if you can fix it tonight because she's tired of flushing with a bucket of water.''

''She has two other kids, for Christ's sake. Why doesn't she call Frankie?''

''That's what I said. I told her she might want to call Frank because the lieutenant's a very busy man right now.''

''I bet that went over well.''

''*Sí.* Some detective from the State Police—name of Nichols—called to talk about the dead girl on the Cape.'' She turned doe eyes up to his in silent accusation. ''You didn't tell me about that one.''

''I haven't seen you. What else?''

''The mayor's office called yesterday afternoon to invite you over for tea and your head on a silver platter—''

''Shit.''

''—but I told them you had urgent business out of town and wouldn't be back until today. And Jeannie Rizzoli wants you to give her a call at her sister's house in California.'' The Spanish word rolled off her tongue with a musical lilt. ''The number's on the slip.'' She shoved the sheaf of messages into his hand. ''The rest of them can wait.''

''Isabel,'' he said, ''what would I do without you?''

"You'd be in deep shit," she said, so somberly that he had to laugh.

"Call my mother," he said. "Tell her I'll be over tonight to fix the toilet. I'll take care of the rest of these."

Before he could return any of his calls, the phone rang. "Lieutenant," boomed a hearty voice at the other end. "This is Pete Reardon."

He sat up straighter, mentally combed his hair and straightened his tie. "Mayor Reardon," he said.

"Have you seen today's *Globe,* Lieutenant?"

The man must be joking. He barely had time to go to the bathroom, let alone read the newspaper. "Sorry, I haven't. Why?"

"There's an editorial calling for your replacement as head of the task force. Wilt O'Malley's questioning your competency to run the investigation."

"Wilt O'Malley is a withered-up old windbag."

"But he sells a lot of newspapers. Look, Lieutenant." Reardon's voice grew more intimate, more mellow. Just a couple of old buddies having a casual conversation. "You wouldn't be heading this investigation if your commanding officers hadn't believed you were capable of the job."

Rafferty squared his shoulders. "But?"

"There is no but. I have every confidence that you can successfully resolve this matter within a reasonable time frame."

Like yesterday, Rafferty thought, but he didn't say it out loud. "Thank you, sir," he said instead.

"I am concerned, though. It's been six days since Tonia Lavoie was killed, and you don't seem to be getting any closer to finding her killer. This is really starting to get out of hand. We need to move quickly and decisively."

"We're sifting through a great deal of information right

now, Mayor. We're being as quick and decisive as it's possible to be, given the circumstances. Our perpetrator isn't leaving us any forensic evidence to go on. I'm sure the term *needle in a haystack* is something you're familiar with.''

Reardon cleared his throat. ''Well,'' he said heartily, ''I'm sure you'll continue to perform to a standard of which the City of Boston and the Boston Police Department can be proud. Maybe I'll give old Wilt O'Malley a call. Talk to him personally, ask if he'll print a retraction. Tell him you're close to making an arrest.''

He felt a nagging headache beginning just behind his right temple. ''You do whatever you feel is appropriate, sir, and I'll do the same.''

There was silence at the other end of the phone, and then Reardon chuckled. ''I'll be in touch, Lieutenant.''

Rafferty broke the connection. ''I'm sure you will,'' he muttered. He clicked the button once, waited for a dial tone, then began punching buttons.

He called Nichols first, exchanged information, scheduled a time to get together to discuss the case in more detail, then he picked up Jeannie Rizzoli's message and examined it. He'd met Ted's wife a few times, but he didn't know her well, and he wondered what possible reason she could have for calling him.

Her voice, at the other end of the phone, was wary. ''Jeannie,'' he said, ''it's Conor Rafferty.''

''Oh!'' she said. ''Thank you for calling back. I know you're busy. I wasn't even sure I should call you. I feel stupid, bothering you with personal business, but I decided that since you're Ted's supervisor, you should know what's going on. I'm so worried about him. I'm sure you must have noticed that his behavior's been a little erratic lately.''

There was a knock on his door. He glanced up, saw Greg Lassiter standing in the opening. He held up one finger, and Greg nodded. "I've noticed that he hasn't been himself," he told her. "I assumed it was, ah—marital difficulties—and I've tried not to push him too hard."

"It's not just that. I mean, yes, we're having problems. If we weren't, I wouldn't be here. I'd be in Boston, with my husband. But a lot of the difficulties resulted from Ted's behavior, not the other way around."

"Oh?"

"He's obsessed with this case, Conor. Obsessed to the point where I'm not sure I even know him anymore."

"We're all a little obsessed, Jeannie. The pressure, the responsibility, are tremendous."

"I understand that. I've been a cop's wife for fifteen years. But this case is different. It's like he takes it personally. It's all he talks about, all he thinks about. It's taken over his life. He gets furious if I try to talk to him about it, says the problem is with me, not him. He's short-tempered and irritable, he hardly ever sleeps anymore. When he's not working, he's drinking."

She hesitated. "Booze makes him mean, and that's the real reason I took the girls and left. I know Ted worships the ground those two girls walk on, and he'd never deliberately do anything to hurt them. But when he drinks...well, he becomes a different person."

He'd seen this kind of thing before. Homicide was a vicious mistress, and she'd burned out more than one good cop. The hours, the stress, the pressure of dealing, day after day, with the results of what supposedly sane people could do to one another, had shoved more than one cop over the edge. "How can I help?" he said.

"I thought you might talk to him. Maybe he needs to be pulled off the case. Have a few meetings with the Department shrink. Whatever it takes.'' She paused. ''Yesterday was Kim's birthday. She waited all day for her dad to call, but he never did. I was so angry, I tried calling him last night. I was going to give him a big piece of my mind. But the phone just rang and rang. He never picked up.''

''I'll talk to him. See what I can do.''

He hung up the phone and rubbed his eyes with the heels of his hands. Lassiter was still loitering in the doorway. He eyed the detective with irritation. ''Have you seen Rizzoli?''

''He called in sick today,'' Lassiter told him. ''Said he had a bad case of the flu.''

''Wonderful. I guess that means our little chat will have to wait. Did you manage to bring in Williamson and Finnegan?''

''Well, boss man, I got good news and I got bad news. The good news is, Finnegan's cooling his heels in the conference room. The bad news is that Williamson didn't show up yesterday for his weekly appointment with his parole officer.''

''I knew I wasn't going to like the bad news.''

Lassiter grinned. ''When he didn't show, P and P sent somebody over to check his apartment. It's cleaned out. Looks like our buddy skipped town and forgot to leave a forwarding address. Downtown put an APB on his vehicle, but until we locate him, Finnegan's our boy.''

Rafferty sighed. ''I should have stayed in bed this morning. Is Monahan in?'' He spoke her name with breezy casualness, but he wasn't fooling anybody, least of all himself.

''Yeah. I saw her sitting at her desk when I walked by.''

"Go get her, then." He stood and stretched his aching muscles. "I want her to sit in on this."

She should have guessed a day that started out as lousy as this one had nowhere to go but downhill. Caro dropped her purse on her desk, leaned over the phone and activated her voice mail. A tinny recording of Richard's voice, dripping irritation, floated from the speaker. "Carolyn," he said, in his most somber lecture tone, "there's no sense in you trying to avoid me. We're both adults. This is ridiculous. I need to talk to you. Call me."

"Adult, my ass," she muttered as she picked up the receiver. "And when are you ever in the damn office anyway?" She glanced up at Policzki, hovering in her doorway because there was no place for him to sit in her airless cubicle. "For Christ's sake," she said, "don't you ever take a break? Go get a cup of coffee or something."

"I'm not supposed to leave you unattended."

"Look, Policzki, I admire your allegiance to duty, but let's be realistic. I'm surrounded by cops here. Every one of them is carrying a loaded gun, and every one of them would come running to save me the minute I started screaming for help. Go get a Hershey's bar or something. Better yet—" She realized belatedly that she'd missed lunch, and her stomach was screaming at her. She opened her purse, tore through the clutter inside—perfume, lip gloss, nail polish, .38-caliber handgun—and tossed him a five-dollar bill. "Go get me a sandwich. Turkey on rye, all white meat, lettuce and tomato, hold the mayo. And an iced tea, unsweetened."

He stood there bouncing from one foot to the other, uncertainty written on his face. "Go," she said. "Shoo. I have to make a phone call."

When his footsteps had receded down the hall, she dialed the office in Quantico. Penny answered, in her customary effervescent state. "If you're looking for Richard," she bubbled, "he's in New Haven."

"New Haven? What the hell is he doing in New Haven?"

"Conference. He's not very happy with you right now, missy. He keeps leaving messages, but you don't call back."

"I've called back," Caro said. "I'm calling back right now. It's not my fault he's never there."

"According to what I hear, you're never there, either."

"I'm working a case. There's a lot of legwork. And I took yesterday off."

"Wait a minute. Hold the presses. You took a day off? In the middle of a case?"

"Don't hyperventilate. It's not that big a deal."

"Oh, yes, it is. There has to be a man involved. Nothing else would drag you away in the middle of a case."

"I plead the Fifth. Listen, kiddo, my other line is ringing. I'll talk to you later." She disconnected, picked up the ringing line. "Monahan."

"So sweet, the way you bark your name into the phone. It makes me tingle all over."

Caro leaned back against her chair with a sigh. "Thomas," she said. "If you're calling to squeeze me for information, I'm fresh out."

"I'm calling to hear the sweet sound of your voice."

"And I'm the Pope's daughter. What is it you want, Malone?"

"I have a pair of tickets to a lecture on Asian art tomorrow night at the Museum of Fine Arts. My date backed out on me. I thought you might like to go."

She rubbed at an ink spot on her desktop. "I don't know, Tommy. I don't think it's a good idea."

"So don't think about it. Just say yes."

"Asian art," she said skeptically.

"Complete with slides. Don't try to tell me you're not interested in fourteenth-century Ming vases, because I know better."

"I have nothing but the highest regard for Ming vases. But I'm working a case. It's impossible to make a commitment that far in advance."

"Twenty-four hours? Come on, Carolyn, you need to get out of your rut. Look at something besides blood spatters. Experience a little culture."

He was right, of course. She couldn't spend all her time wrapped up in murder and mayhem. Tommy was sweet and harmless, and she wouldn't have to worry about making small talk. He'd talk enough for both of them. Besides, an evening spent in his company would be an evening she didn't spend thinking about Conor Rafferty. "I'm probably going to regret this," she said, "but yes, I'll come with you."

"Great. I'll pick you up at six. That'll give us time to catch a bite to eat first. The Boylston House, right?"

"How'd you know I was staying at the Boylston House?"

"I don't know. I guess you must have mentioned it at some point. See you then."

When she looked up again, Greg Lassiter was standing in her doorway. "Lieutenant's getting ready to interrogate a suspect," he said. "He'd like you to sit in."

She glanced at her watch and thought longingly of her empty stomach and the sandwich she'd sent Policzki to fetch. "Right now?"

"Right now."

It probably didn't matter. The prospect of seeing Conor again so soon had her stomach tied up in knots so tight she wouldn't be able to eat anyway. She pushed her chair back. "All right, Lassiter," she said, "fill me in."

They passed Policzki in the hallway outside her office. He was sitting in a straight chair, arms crossed, eyes closed, his features carefully arranged in that solemn expression he always wore. One foot tapped an awkward rhythm against the leg of his chair.

"Policzki?" she said. "Where's my sandwich?"

His eyes flew open and he sat up straighter. "I sent Isabel for it."

So he hadn't deserted his post after all. She wasn't sure whether to kick him or congratulate him. "When it gets here," she said, "put it in the refrigerator in the break room. Think you can keep the vultures away from it for an hour or two?"

"I'll guard it with my life."

In the conference room, Terry Finnegan slouched in his chair, sullen and uncooperative, wearing the unmistakable look of a man who'd done hard time. Ten years ago, he might have been handsome, but life had eroded his looks and given his eyes the flinty and soulless expression of a predator. "I want a lawyer," he said.

Carolyn perched on the HVAC unit just inside the door, and Greg closed the door behind them. Rafferty pulled out a chair, turned it around backward, and straddled it. "Come on, Terry," he said, unbuttoning his cuff and rolling up his shirtsleeve, "cut us some slack." He took his time rolling up the other sleeve. "We haven't even started asking questions yet."

The room was unspeakably hot. Rafferty must have turned off the air conditioner. It was an old trick. Make the suspect as uncomfortable as possible during interrogation. It was amazing how easily some people could be broken down.

Finnegan squared his jaw. "You got the wrong guy. I don't know nothing." His gaze darted around the room, landed on Carolyn. "Who's she?"

"That's Agent Monahan from the FBI. I asked her to sit in."

"Yeah?" Finnegan sounded more intrigued than unnerved. "I never met no FBI agent before."

Rafferty laid a stack of photographs on the table in front of Finnegan and fanned them out. "Forget her," he said. "Any of these women look familiar to you, Terry?"

Finnegan narrowed his eyes and studied the pictures, one by one. "Nope. Never seen any of 'em before."

"How long you been out this time?"

"Six months. And I've kept my nose clean."

"Yeah, I just bet you have. I bet you've been a real upstanding citizen."

"Hey, man, you don't believe me, just ask my parole officer. Pete Boudreau. He'll tell you."

Rafferty nodded toward the photos. "Take a second look, Terry. A long one. And think real hard this time before you give me an answer."

Finnegan glared at him, then he snatched up the pictures and thumbed through them. "I told you," he said, tossing them back onto the table, "I don't know none of these women."

Rafferty gathered up the photos, straightened them like a deck of cards, rapped the stack a couple of times against the tabletop to align it. Setting it aside, he said, "Let's talk about something else, Terry. What were you in for this last time?"

"Rape," Finnegan said. "Aggravated assault."

"And how many times you been in before?"

Finnegan stared at him without blinking. "Twice."

"Assault," Rafferty said. "Rape. Unlawful sexual contact." He shook his head mournfully. "Bad news, Terry."

"Shit, man, how the fuck was I supposed to know she was underage?"

"Tell me about the assault charge."

"Fucking bitch deserved it. She was always talking back. She opened her big yap one too many times and got what she deserved."

Carolyn's stomach rumbled, and a trickle of sweat ran down her back. She didn't know how it was working on Finnegan, but the broken air conditioner trick was certainly working on her. Rafferty leaned back in his chair, raised his arms, and clasped his hands behind his head. Casually, he said, "You ever kill anybody, Terry?"

For the first time, Finnegan's composure slipped. "Shit, no, man. You gotta be kidding. I ain't never killed nobody. Man, that's just wrong."

Behind his head, Rafferty tapped his thumbs together. "Let me be sure I have this right. You rape your women and you beat them, but you always leave them alive. You're a prince among men, Terry."

Finnegan squared his jaw. "I can't say it any plainer. I ain't no killer, and I don't know none of these women."

While Caro's stomach gurgled and wispy curls formed in the damp hair at her temples, the two men went around and around in circles, tempers growing short as the room grew hotter and the questioning got them nowhere. By the time Rafferty finally called a halt to the proceedings and cut Finnegan loose, she was limp and sticky and lethargic. While Lassiter escorted the suspect out, Caro stretched her muscles and lifted her damp hair off the nape of her neck.

"Turn the AC back on before we all pass out," Rafferty told Lorna. Turning to Caro, he said, "What do you think about Finnegan?"

Blessed cool air began to pour out of the unit behind her. It felt wonderful on the back of her neck. "I think he's a true asset to the human race," she said.

"And?"

"Do I think he's our killer?" She dropped the fall of hair, and it tumbled back into place. "No. He didn't blink when you introduced me, and I watched while he looked at the photos. Nothing in his eyes to indicate recognition."

"Shit. I was hoping you might have seen something I missed."

"Not to mention that I don't think he's smart enough to have pulled this off. Certainly not smart enough to have written that note. He would've stumbled over all the big words. I think Finnegan is just your garden-variety scumbag. The scumbag we're looking for is a tad more sophisticated."

Lorna sat on the edge of the tabletop. "Where does that leave us?"

"We keep close watch on Clancy Donovan," Rafferty said, "and start working our way through the list of names Louise Moriarty gave us."

"Clancy didn't do it," Carolyn said.

They both looked at her. "And you know this because?" Rafferty said.

"I talked to him this morning. I told him about Johnny. I wanted to see his reaction. If he'd known, I would have seen it in his eyes. He had no idea Meg was seeing anybody else. Clancy's innocent."

"Because you saw it in his eyes."

She crossed her arms. "Because I asked him straight out if he killed my sister, and he told me he didn't."

"Oh, well, that makes a difference. Killers never lie."

"You can believe me or not. It's your choice. But if

you keep concentrating your efforts on Clancy, you'll never find your killer.''

"I can't dismiss him as a suspect. He's still the only lead I have that's more substantial than a Kleenex."

"Maybe. Maybe not. I also talked to Mike today, and he seems to believe that the man Meg was involved with was married."

Lorna lifted an eyebrow. "Married?" Rafferty said. "Are you sure?"

"He didn't bother to elaborate, but he seemed quite sure of it."

Rafferty nodded slowly. "It could explain a few things, like why she kept the relationship a secret."

"And it could open a whole slew of possibilities we haven't even considered. I have a feeling about this, Conor. I think that when we find this Johnny, we've found our killer."

There was a moment of silence as they all deliberated. Then Lorna said quietly, "Baby-sitting."

"Baby-sitting?" Rafferty said.

"Remember Louise told us that Meg was baby-sitting to make extra money for college? If Johnny was married, maybe she was his baby-sitter."

"It's one more angle to follow. Caro? Do you know who she baby-sat for? Did she have regulars?"

"I imagine she did, but I have no clue who they might have been. My mother might."

"You'll talk to her?"

"I'll talk to her. In the morning, after I've eaten my Wheaties. I need fortification before I face Roberta Monahan again."

Rafferty glanced at his watch, grimaced. "All right, people, let's call it a day. There's someplace I have to be."

Carolyn's stomach clenched. She bent and rubbed a smudge from the toe of her shoe. With deliberate casualness, she said, "Hot date?"

Silence. She glanced up, saw something inexplicable in his eyes before they went hard. "Yes," he said. "Something like that."

She tried not to let the disappointment crush her. It had taken him less than twelve hours to move on. So much for the significance of their brief reunion. "Let me know what you find out," he said, and left them.

"Goddamn men," Lorna said cheerfully, as his footsteps echoed down the corridor. "You look like you just got kicked in the gut with a steel-toed boot. I know a place where the beer is cheap and plentiful, and nobody will try to hit on you. What do you say we lift a few and drown our sorrows?"

Caro closed her eyes. Swallowed. "I'll be all right. Besides, I thought you had a husband and kids to get home to."

"Occupational hazard. You marry a cop, you put up with their hours."

She tried a smile, but it felt stiff and unnatural. "Even if said cop is helping a friend drown her sorrows?"

"Especially then." Lorna slid off the table and shoved Conor's chair back into place. "Come on. I guarantee you'll feel better afterward."

Caro weakened, yielded. "If they serve food in any form, I'm with you. I haven't eaten all day. But we'll have to take my extra appendage along."

"Policzki? I forgot about him. You can't ditch him?"

"Are you kidding? The kid sticks closer to me than a skin graft. It's annoying as hell."

"Then I hope he has a strong stomach, because I have

a feeling he's about to witness some heavy-duty male bashing.''

"The thing about Conor," Lorna said, "is that he's been walking around with this reputation for so long, he's begun to believe that what they're saying about him is true." She picked up her long-necked bottle of Miller and pointed it in Caro's direction. "And the reputation's really undeserved. He's been painted as a heartless womanizer because he's dated so many women. But Conor's not some macho, sexist jerk. Sure, he's tough when he has to be. He's a cop. It comes with the job. But when he's off duty, he's the kind of guy who grows flowers and bounces babies on his knee. I know this firsthand, because some of the babies he's bounced were mine."

"It's not his fault," Caro said mournfully. "I knew it was a mistake, getting involved with him again, but I couldn't help myself." She picked up an onion ring from the greasy stack in the center of the table and bit into it. "I'm addicted to self-destructive behavior."

"Who could blame you? If you could bottle the man and sell him, you'd have women lined up from here to Morocco just to get a whiff."

Caro narrowed her eyes and studied the other woman closely. "And would you be standing in line?"

Lorna leaned back against the red leather booth. "I'm a happily married woman. That doesn't mean I'm dead. I can appreciate a gorgeous man as well as the next female. But it's not like that between us. Conor's my best friend, and one damn good cop. We partnered together for years, and partners develop a bond that's not like any other. I know he'd take a bullet for me without question. I'd do the same for him. And there's nothing I'd like better than to see him happy. I'm telling you, Monahan, he's ready to settle down. He's ripe for the plucking. All you have to do is pluck."

"I'm not sure I want to pluck."

Lorna snorted. "Should I hold a mirror up in front of your face and show you a picture of a woman who's smitten?"

"It's not that simple. We're both carrying too much baggage. There's my family, and his. We lead separate lives in separate cities, hundreds of miles apart. We've both built solid careers, important careers, and we're both upwardly mobile. We have responsibilities. We don't want the same things out of life. We have a history, damn it, and it isn't a pretty one."

"Excuses. All excuses. You're building barriers and using them as an excuse to run away because you're scared. For just one minute, I want you to forget all of that. Pretend none of it exists. There's just the two of you, with nothing to keep you from being together. What would you do?"

"That's not a fair question."

"No, it's not. But it's an honest one. Now give me an honest answer."

The booze had loosened her emotions, her tongue. "I'd lap him up," she said, "like a cat with a bowl of warm cream."

"Well, there you have it. Stop making excuses, and go after what you want."

Caro busied herself arranging their empty beer bottles into a neat row. "It takes two to tango. He doesn't want me."

"Lady, there's where you're wrong. He wants you. He may not know it yet, but he wants you. He's just scared, the same as you are. It's up to you to show him there's nothing to be scared of."

Policzki cleared his throat, and both women turned to look at him. He'd been so quiet while they talked that Caro had forgotten he was there. "If you want my opinion," he said, "and I mean this in the most respectful way, the man would have to be a fool to not want you."

"Aw, geez," Lorna said, propping her chin on her palm. "Is that sweet, or what? This kid's all right, Monahan."

Caro picked up his glass of Pepsi and sniffed it. "Are you sure you're not tippling under the table, Policzki?"

"I have three sisters," he said. "I've had twenty-five years of training in how to be a New Age Sensitive Man." He plucked an onion ring from the stack, crammed it into his mouth, brushed the crumbs from his hands and made a beeline for the corner jukebox.

"So help me God," Lorna said, "if what comes out of that thing bears any resemblance to rap, I'm going to shoot him dead right on the spot. There's not a court in the land that would convict me."

Policzki leaned intently over the jukebox to scan its offerings, and his suitcoat rode up his back.

"Nice ass," Lorna observed.

Caro pretended to be scandalized. "Shame on you. You're old enough to be his mother."

"I'm broadening my horizons."

Policzki dropped in a fistful of change and began pushing buttons. Loud enough to wake the dead, the music poured out, the rollicking, unmistakable opening bars of the Beatles' "Twist and Shout."

The two women looked at each other. "Oh, man," Lorna said, "I like this kid. I like this kid a lot."

It was past eleven when they left the bar, Policzki the only one in a state of total sobriety. At the Government

Center T stop, Lorna caught her train for home, and Policzki and Caro headed off on foot to the Boylston House. Even this late on a summer evening, it was close to ninety degrees, and Tremont Street was choked with the pungent aroma of automobile exhaust. They passed the Granary Burying Ground, final resting place of such varied luminaries as Paul Revere and Mother Goose, and Policzki took her elbow and steered her around a section of broken pavement.

She studied him from the corner of her eye. "Tell me, Policzki, do you have a wife or a girlfriend somewhere waiting for you to come home?"

"Nope. I live at home with my mother. When Dad died last year, I moved back in to keep her company."

"My, my. Not only a gentleman, but a dutiful son. I have great admiration for dutiful sons. My brother happens to be one of them. I, on the other hand, am the prodigal daughter. Does your mother have a prodigal daughter, Policzki?"

"No. We're just one big, happy family."

"Lucky you."

At the Boylston House, Julio, in his usual spot on the sidewalk, tipped his hat as he held the door for them. "Evening, ma'am. Sir." If he found it odd that she was coming in at eleven-thirty at night with a different man than the one who'd dropped her off at five this morning, he kept his thoughts to himself.

In the corridor outside her room, a uniformed cop sat on a hard-backed chair, pencil in hand, working the *New York Times* crossword puzzle. Caro came to an abrupt halt. "Who's that?"

"My replacement," Policzki said. "My shift was up two hours ago."

"You're deserting me? Shit. And just when we were starting to like each other."

"Only until morning. I'll be back tomorrow."

"Promise?" She suddenly felt like a little girl left alone at summer camp, bereft of all that was familiar.

"I promise. This is Officer Stuart."

She held out a hand to the uniform. "Carolyn Monahan."

Stuart abandoned his crossword puzzle and shook her hand. Policzki fixed him with a steely glare. "Take good care of her," he said, "or I'll break your ass."

Before he left, he made a thorough check of her room. "Don't open your door for anyone except Officer Stuart or me. Understood?"

"I'm familiar with the drill, Detective."

"Look," he said, "I know how hard this is for you. I just wanted you to know that I thought you did great today."

"You did great today, too, Policzki. I'll see you tomorrow."

Caro double-locked the door behind him, peeled off her clothes, and wrapped her silk robe around her. She shouldn't have had so much to drink; it always made her woozy and emotional. She tied the belt to her robe, flicked off the light switch, and stood in the dark at the open window, breathing in the city's ambiance. On the street below, traffic still moved steadily despite the late hour. A siren wailed in the distance. Lighted windows dotted the downtown high-rise office buildings, and Caro folded her arms over her breasts and wondered just who was working so late. Janitorial crews? Or perhaps driven executives, workaholics with no lives. People like her.

She swiped furiously at a tear. Was Mike right? Had she deliberately forgotten who she was? Was she running away because she was ashamed of where and what she'd come from? Or maybe it was something more than that: the bitter taste of guilt in its various forms. Culpability, because if she'd been where she was supposed to be that night ten years ago, Meg would be alive now. Survivor guilt because, no matter how she looked at it, Meg had been the better person, and she would have to spend the rest of her life remembering that.

It should have been me.

The knowledge was a hard pain in her chest, and that pain was a dark thing that drove her. But as a driving force, it was wasted effort. As Mike had so eloquently pointed out, no matter how many killers she put behind bars, no matter how many lives she saved, she couldn't undo what had been done. She couldn't make atonement for her sins. Nothing she could do would bring Meggie back.

She rubbed languidly at the back of her neck, remembered Conor's hands on her shoulders, her body. Maybe she had given up on him too easily. Maybe she should have given their relationship more of a chance. But it was too late. He'd already moved on without her, and she had nobody to blame but herself. Conor Rafferty was simply one more regret she would have to put behind her.

The booze had made her maudlin, and the headache was already taking hold. Drugs and sleep were the only things that would help her now. She left the window, fumbled in her purse for aspirin, swallowed two with a cup of tepid tap water. If she was fortunate, they wouldn't interact with the booze and kill her. She stripped off the robe, burrowed beneath the bedsheets, and pulled the pillow over her head.

And slept, hard and deep and dreamless, until the ringing phone bored into her consciousness. It took her a while to come fully awake. She fumbled, her fingers clumsy in the darkness of the unfamiliar hotel room. "Monahan," she mumbled into the receiver.

"Hi."

The world stopped revolving, and sensation coiled inside her, pooling like a river of chocolate in that warm place between her thighs. The headache, or maybe it was the booze, had left her cotton-mouthed, and she wet her lips once, twice. "Hi."

"I just wanted you to know—" Conor paused, and she could hear his breathing "—that my hot date tonight was with Fiona's plumbing."

She tried to wrap her brain around his words, but she was too groggy, his words too alien. The silence stretched, heavy with meaning, as she searched for a response.

"That's all I wanted to say," he told her. "I'm sorry I woke you. Go back to sleep."

She opened her mouth to respond, but he was already gone.

15

A cup of Starbucks high-test went a long way toward curing a hangover, but even a strong dose of caffeine couldn't cure humiliation. As far as she could remember, she hadn't done anything excessively embarrassing last night, with the possible exception of keeping Policzki out a couple of hours past his curfew. Even though she wasn't exactly Miss Congeniality, the kid had gone out of his way for her. When all this was over, she'd have to repay him somehow. Dinner at a nice restaurant, maybe a pair of Red Sox tickets. Something to show her gratitude.

She dodged the cluster of media people outside City Hall and took the stairs to the fourth floor. Ted Rizzoli was back at his desk this morning, his skin the color of putty, a bloody nick in his chin where he'd clipped himself with his razor. His hand, wrapped around a cup of coffee, trembled visibly as he perused the sports section of the *Globe*. Must have been one hell of a case of the flu. In spite of everything, Carolyn couldn't help feeling sorry for the man. "Good morning, Rizzoli," she said briskly as she passed his desk.

He looked up, studied her for a moment as though trying to gauge her sincerity. His glance moved to Policzki and then back to her. "Morning," he mumbled, and returned to his newspaper.

Carolyn felt an almost childish glee because she'd managed to elicit some kind of civilized behavior from him. She was riding high on her victory when Isabel shot her down. "The lieutenant wants to talk to you," she said, and Caro's mood took a nosedive.

She dropped her briefcase on her desk, tossed her purse at the chair. Smoothed nonexistent wrinkles from her skirt. Taking a deep breath, she told Policzki, "Wait here." Heart thudding, she headed for Rafferty's office.

Her palms were sweating. She'd never had sweaty palms in her life. Maybe she'd caught Rizzoli's flu. Maybe she'd get lucky and it would flatten her before she reached that open door.

But luck wasn't with her. When had it ever been? She paused in the doorway, disgustingly healthy, and watched him sign his name to a stack of authorization forms while she remembered what she'd told Lorna last night. *I'd lap him up like a cat with a bowl of warm cream.* She felt color rising in her face. It had been the booze talking. Nothing more than that.

He sensed her presence, glanced up, and their eyes caught and held. He looked tired this morning, as though he hadn't slept much last night, and she struggled with an overwhelming urge to run her hands through his dark hair and cradle his head to her bosom. Christ, what in hell was wrong with her? The next thing she knew, she'd be baking cookies.

Somehow, she found her voice. "You wanted to see me?"

"Yes. Come in. Sit down."

Like a trained poodle, she sat while he finished signing authorizations. He set the stack of papers aside and clicked his Paper Mate, and the sound was so loud in the stillness that she jumped. He set down the pen, picked up an oversize paper clip and began torturing it. "I'm sorry about last night. The phone call.'' His eyes met hers, and her heart stopped. ''I had no business calling you that late.'' He twisted the paper clip so hard it snapped. ''It was stupid.''

He swept up the broken pieces of metal and tossed them into the wastebasket, where they landed with a muffled metallic chink.

''It's all right,'' she said, her words possessing all the grace of those twisted pieces of aluminum hitting the bottom of the trash can.

''I, ah—'' He cleared his throat, picked up the Paper Mate and began clicking it. ''Fiona's toilet wasn't working.'' Click, click. ''Ballcock malfunctioned. I had to replace it.''

''Of course. How is your mother?'' She was acting like a twelve-year-old ninny. She'd seen Fiona just three days ago. How much could the status quo have changed since then?

''Fine. Same as always.'' He glanced up, past her shoulder, and straightened in his chair. ''Yes?'' he said gruffly.

''I need to talk to you.'' Ted Rizzoli stood in the doorway, hands braced against the frame on either side of him.

''We're busy right now. Can't it wait?''

Caro let out the breath she'd been holding and rose from the chair. ''It's all right. I was just leaving.''

''No,'' Rizzoli said. ''Stay. I need to talk to both of you.''

All she wanted was to escape, but once again, the gods were plotting against her. She sat back down, and Conor beckoned Rizzoli into his office. Ted closed the door and sat in the empty chair beside her. ''What's up?'' Conor said.

Rizzoli laced slender fingers together in his lap. ''I

don't have the flu,'' he said. "I quit drinking three days ago. Cold turkey. It's been hell.''

Conor clicked his Paper Mate. "I see.''

"Things at home were going sour, and then I got wrapped up in this case, and it just mushroomed. That's why Jeannie left. She didn't say so, but she didn't have to.''

The silence in the room was so absolute that Carolyn could hear her own heartbeat. "When I started having blackouts,'' Rizzoli continued, "it scared the hell out of me. Big chunks of my life were just missing. Gone. I felt like everything in my life was falling apart. I was a failure as a husband, as a father, as a cop, as a human being. I was drinking all the time, on and off the job. So a couple of weeks ago, I made the decision to quit the force.''

Caro cleared her throat. "Maybe I should leave. This sounds a little too—''

"No,'' Rizzoli said. "Stay. You need to hear what I have to say, because this involves you.'' He turned back to Conor. "A week ago, I made the decision to quit the force. A couple of nights later, I drove to your house to turn in my gun and my badge. I was parked across the street with a bottle of vodka, trying to work up the courage to knock on your door, when this red Mitsubishi sports car came down the street, moving too slow. It stopped for a while, just sat there, and then it took off like a bat out of hell. All my cop instincts kicked in, so I pulled out and followed it.''

"Holy Christ,'' Caro said. "That was you?''

"It was me.''

"I don't get it. When I stopped and pulled my weapon on you, you turned and ran. Why the hell didn't you identify yourself?''

"I was wearing a badge and carrying a gun, and I had

half a pint of vodka in me. If I'd come clean, the Department would've yanked my badge. When I pulled out and went after you, I realized that no matter what else I might be, I was a cop, and I wasn't ready to give that up. So I ran. That's why I've treated you so rotten. I resented you at the beginning because you were a Fed, and I didn't think you belonged here. After that night, I resented you because every time I saw your face, it reminded me of what a fool I'd made of myself."

"I can still yank your badge," Conor said. "I *should* still yank your badge."

"Look," Rizzoli said, "I'm a cop. It's all I know how to do. I'm trying to put the pieces back together. I've joined AA, and I'm determined to stay sober. I talked to Jeannie, and she said that if I'm willing to go to marriage counseling, she'll come home and give me another chance. I miss my little girls, Conor. I need things to go back to normal. And I need my job. If you take that away, I'll have nothing."

Conor drummed his fingers on the desktop. "I can't just ignore this."

"I could have kept my mouth shut, and you never would've known the difference."

"True. But this is a serious infraction, Rizzoli. Drinking on duty. You're asking me to just sweep it under the rug."

"I'm asking you to give me a second chance."

"I'll need some time to think about this. And I'll need to talk to your AA sponsor. Furthermore, it goes without saying, but I'll say it anyway— If I catch you drinking on duty again, I'll take your gun and your badge on the spot."

"You're a fair man," Rizzoli said, "and I just laid my entire future in your hands." He stood, paused with his hand on the doorknob. "I'm trusting you to do the right thing with it."

For a full ten seconds after he left, there was silence. Then Conor said, "I don't believe this. What in hell am I supposed to do about him?"

"You're smart." She stood, tugged needlessly at the hem of her jacket. Edging toward the door, she added, "I'm sure you'll figure something out."

"Not so fast, Monahan. Where do you think you're going?"

She froze, her heart thudding at a terrifying rate. "In case you've forgotten, Rafferty, we're in the middle of a homicide investigation. I have work to do."

Those green eyes studied her with bemusement. "You told me somebody tailed you around Southie. You never told me where he picked you up."

She could crumble, or she could brazen it out. There was a reason she'd earned a reputation for having brass balls. "You never asked."

"What were you doing outside my apartment?"

"Idle curiosity!" she snapped. "Don't try to make anything more out of it."

She strode down the hallway, swept past Policzki, who hovered outside her office. "If you let anybody through this door," she told him, "I swear to Christ I'll have you shot." And she slammed the door behind her.

Claustrophobic was too kind a word to describe the office space the Boston P.D. had so generously allotted her. She couldn't even pace the six-by-six room; she had to walk sideways just to get behind the desk. Instead, she slumped on the chair and buried her face in her hands.

Relax your muscles. Breathe in, breathe out.

It didn't work. Her blood simmering, she was primed for combat. Since she couldn't squelch it, she might as well roll with it. Still trembling, she picked up the phone and dialed her mother's number.

"Mother," she said when Roberta picked up the phone, "I need to know the names of the people Meg baby-sat for."

"Why, that was ten years ago. I can't—" Roberta came to an abrupt halt. "Why would you want to know that?"

Ten years was long enough to walk on eggshells. If Mike didn't like it, tough. "Because unless I miss my guess," she said, "one of them killed her."

"*What?* What are you talking about?"

"I'm talking about an eighteen-year-old girl who was having an affair with a married man. I don't know who he was, and I don't know what happened between them. I just know that my sister didn't deserve to die, and if it's the last thing I do in this life, I'm going to fry the son of a bitch who killed her." She was on a roll now, unstoppable, spewing ten years of pain and rage and guilt. "I know I've been a big disappointment as a daughter. I've never been able to live up to your expectations, and everybody would have been better off if I'd been the one who died. But I wasn't, and I can't do anything to change that."

Her voice cracked, and she hunched over the desk, rested her forehead against her palm. "But you know what, Mother? I loved her, too. I loved her so damn much, and she died because of me. There hasn't been a day since then that I haven't wondered why. Why her, and not me? You never loved me the way you loved her, and you stopped being my mother the day she died. But I'm still your daughter. And here I am, thirty-two frigging years old, still trying to make you love me. Damn it." She paused to rummage in her purse for a tissue, swiped furiously at her runny nose. "Goddamn it, Mom, I need you, too."

The silence at the other end of the phone was deafening. Then her mother said, "In the name of God, Carolyn, you can't believe I'd trade your life for Meg's."

"Why not? She was the good daughter. I'm the evil one."

"You're talking crazy. You really think it would've been easier if it'd been you?"

"I killed her, Mom. I killed her with my own self-centeredness."

"That's ridiculous. Nobody's ever blamed you for your sister's death."

"You blame me. Mike blames me." She swiped at her nose again with the crumpled tissue. "I blame me."

"I don't blame you. And Mike's wrong. So are you. I never loved Meg more than you. Maybe it looked that way sometimes because she was who she was, and you're who you are. It wasn't that I didn't want to be your mother. I didn't know how. I never knew how to be your mother."

Caro sniffed, dabbed at the corner of her eye. "What do you mean?"

"You weren't exactly an easy child. I knew by the time you were four years old that South Boston wouldn't be big enough to hold you. You had this curiosity about the world that Mike and Meggie didn't have. We'd go out walking, and you had to turn over every rock you came across, just to see what was under it, no matter how slimy and ugly it was. I couldn't keep up with you. You were too smart for your own good."

"I wasn't the only smart one! Meg was just as smart as I was! She was going to be a lawyer, for Christ's sake!"

"Meg was a homebody. A mama's girl. She would've become a lawyer, but she wouldn't have left Southie. Not for long. She didn't give a hoot about what was out there, only what was here. But you wanted the whole world. No matter what I gave you, it was never enough. You always wanted more." Roberta's voice went soft. "Remember when I used to read Dr. Seuss to you kids at bedtime? Meggie loved it. She'd beg me to read *Hop on Pop* over and over again. But sooner or later, you'd get bored and wander off. I'd find you sitting in the kitchen with your father, all bug-eyed over one of his cop stories."

She smiled through her tears. "Dad always told the greatest stories."

"I used to get so mad at him. I thought they'd give you nightmares."

"They never did."

"Of course not," Roberta said bitterly. "You're Gerald Monahan's daughter."

"You never wanted me to be a cop."

"No, I didn't. It's no kind of life. Putting your life on the line every time you walk out the door. Seeing the awful things that people do to each other. Missing birthdays and holidays and family gatherings because the job always has to come first. And don't bother to tell me it's different because you're FBI. A cop's a cop. I should know. I've been married to one for thirty-six years. It doesn't matter that he's retired, because once it's in your blood, it never goes away. A cop's a cop until he dies. I wanted more than that for you."

"What about what I wanted, Mom?"

"I don't know, Caro. I guess you'll have to answer that. Do you have what you want?"

She thought about Conor Rafferty and decided it wasn't a question she was ready to answer. Her fingers tightened on the telephone receiver. "Why've you been so damn hard on me all these years?"

"Maybe some of it was resentment."

"Resentment? Why?"

"You were absolutely fearless in the way you faced the world. You left me feeling useless. You didn't need me, Caro. The only thing I knew how to do was be a mother and, with you, I couldn't even get that right."

"But that's not true. I did need you. You've just never been there for me."

"You wouldn't let me be there! No matter what I said about anything, you always said the opposite. If I said the sky was blue, you said it was black. No matter what I tried to do for you, you always had to tear it apart and analyze it, instead of just accepting it." A tremor shook her voice. "Sometimes I felt like you were acting as unlovable as possible, and daring me to love you."

"Oh, Mom." An overwhelming sadness swept through her, settling like a dark cloak around her heart. "Don't you realize that all you've ever done is nag and prod and criticize?"

"I do it because I care! I do it because I want you to have a life that's something more than chasing down criminals! I want you to have a husband and babies, so you won't look back on your life someday and wish you'd made different choices!"

"Isn't that up to me to decide?"

"I don't claim to be a perfect mother. But if I prodded and nagged and criticized, I did it for you, because I wanted you to be happy. I don't want you to go through life alone."

Caro closed her eyes, rubbed her forehead. "Who are you to talk? Your marriage certainly hasn't been a match made in heaven."

There was a pause as her arrow hit its target. "Maybe not," her mother said with quiet dignity. "But when I get into bed at night, your father's there, hogging the blankets and snoring loud enough to wake the dead. If we're still together after all these years, we must be doing something right. That's what I want for you. That's why I was so happy when I saw you with Conor the other night. I was hoping it meant you were getting back together."

"I don't get it, Mom. He's a cop. What makes him any different? If the lifestyle's so terrible, how come he's acceptable to you?"

"Acceptable to *me?*" Her mother's voice was awash with astonishment. "It's got nothing to do with me, Carolyn. It's you. When he walks into a room, you light up like Filene's the week before Christmas."

She nearly canceled the date with Malone. After the emotionally draining confrontation with her mother, she wasn't sure she was up to dealing with Tommy's irrepressible enthusiasm. She spent the rest of the day avoiding Conor and tracking down the handful of baby-sitting clients whose names Roberta had managed to recall. In spite of her mother's disapproval, she was good at this, good at digging until she got the information she needed, good at analyzing it and putting the puzzle pieces together into some kind of coherent whole. She liked digging under rocks. Was that really such a terrible thing? In spite of the stress and the pressure, she enjoyed her job. Maybe it was time to rethink her resignation. After the last few days, the idea of continuing to work with Richard had lost its abhorrence. Richard Armitage no longer possessed the power to move her in any way, and she realized that their relationship had been over long before she'd sounded its death knell.

She left work early, indulged herself in a long, hot bath that eased her tensions and left her mellow and more hopeful than she'd felt in months. She and Roberta might not have made much progress, but perhaps the dialogue she'd opened up with her mother would be a first step toward healing their broken relationship. They'd both acknowledged hurt, both acknowledged their need for each other. It was a start.

She'd brought only one dress with her from Virginia. It was a fire-engine-red silk sheath, and she rigorously scrutinized her reflection in the mirror, assessing the amount of flesh it left uncovered before deciding it was acceptable to wear to dinner and a lecture at the MFA. She fluffed her hair and applied red lipstick, then spritzed herself with Obsession, determined to treat this evening as though it were a real date, and not an attempt to redirect her attention away from a certain green-eyed Homicide lieutenant.

Tommy showed up precisely at six, looked her up and down, and nodded his approval. "Who's the guy in the hall?" he said. "He practically strip-searched me before he let me through, and just in case I didn't get the hint, he made sure I got a really good look at his gun."

"That's my shadow. Name's Policzki." She shouldered her purse, tucked her key card inside. "And if he thinks he's coming with us tonight, he has another think coming."

Tommy's eyes narrowed. "He's a bodyguard?"

"He's not a bodyguard," she said irritably. "He's police protection."

"Also known as a bodyguard. Has somebody threatened you?"

"Not overtly. Rafferty's just being overprotective because he knows how much it annoys me."

"I can't believe I'm saying this, but for once, I'm with him." He held the door for her, pressed himself against the door frame to let her pass, and closed it tight behind her.

Policzki stood when they entered the corridor. "I won't be needing your services tonight," she told him.

"It doesn't work that way, Agent Monahan," he said with infuriating patience. "You know better."

She braced herself for battle. Enunciating each syllable, she said, "You are not coming with us."

"Yes," Tommy said, tugging at her elbow, "he is."

Caro yanked her arm away from him. "For Christ's sake, Malone, nobody's coming after me while I'm with you. This guy targets women who are alone. You're all the protection I need."

"I'm a reporter, not a cop. At the first sign of gunfire, I'm under the table. If Rafferty thinks you need protection, then Officer Policzki's coming with us."

"Detective," she said through clenched teeth. "Detective Policzki."

"Whatever. Just be philosophical about it. As long as we have a chaperon, you don't have to worry about me making any moves on you."

"You make any moves on me, Malone, you're going to find yourself missing a few crucial body parts."

They ate dinner at a cozy Italian place in the North End, where candles flickered on the tables and soft music played from speakers tucked away inside the ceiling. The atmosphere was wonderfully romantic, or would have been if she'd been here with the right man, under the right circumstances. Instead, she sat across the table from the effervescent Tommy Malone, while three discreet tables away, Policzki delicately sipped minestrone from a silver soupspoon.

"So what happened after you got divorced?" she said, trying to focus on Malone and keep up her end of the conversation.

He broke off a piece of crusty bread and picked up his butter knife. "I left Boston," he said, leaning back in his chair and liberally spreading butter on his bread. "I moved around a lot, worked at small papers up and down the East Coast, but I never settled any place for long. Boston has a long reach, and she kept calling me home. My kid's here, and I got tired of seeing him for two weeks every summer. Three years ago, the *Trib* offered me a position, so I came home."

"I still think you're too good a reporter to work for that rag."

He bit off a piece of bread, chewed and swallowed. "That's me," he said. "The classic underachiever. So what's the story with you and Rafferty?"

She took a sip of wine. "There is no story."

"That's not what I hear. My sources tell me that the two of you used to be hot and heavy."

"Jesus Christ, Malone, where do you get this stuff?"

"This is the information age. I'm a reporter. I deal in information."

"Well, for your information, Rafferty and I are history. You can mark that down in your notebook."

"Does that mean—" he wound linguini around the tines of his fork "—that you're available?"

"I thought we agreed that you weren't going to make any moves on me tonight."

"You agreed." He flashed her a boyish grin. "I never agreed to anything."

"I carry a gun, Thomas. Tread carefully."

"That just makes you more attractive. I like dangerous women." He set down his fork, held both wrists in the air. "Get out your cuffs, Agent Monahan. Take me in. I'm all yours."

In spite of herself, she snickered. "You are one sick puppy, Malone."

"That I am, but I made you laugh. You should do it more often." He rested his chin on his palm. "You know, you look so much like your sister, but you're really nothing like she was."

She paused with her fork halfway to her mouth. "You knew Meg?"

"I told you, I went to high school with you." He reached out two fingers, hovered over her plate, then plucked a mushroom from her marinara sauce. "Meg and I used to hang out sometimes." He popped the mushroom into his mouth.

"All right, Malone, I'll bite. How are we different?"

"Meg was sweet. Sunshine and goodness. Lots of laughter in that girl. Life hadn't yet had a chance to disappoint her. You, on the other hand, have a dark side, one that's mysterious and alluring. I bet you have men falling all over you."

"None of the right ones," she said tartly, and he grinned.

"See what I mean? You have an edge like a Ginsu knife."

The lecture hall at the MFA was packed, and Caro scanned the crowd in amazement. She would never have guessed that Boston held this many people with an interest in Asian art. The speaker, an expert on Chinese antiquities, managed to convey his passion and enthusiasm to the audience. The slides he presented were clean and crisp, and Caro pulled an old electric bill from her purse and scribbled notes on the envelope. Never in this lifetime would she be able to afford an original, but there was an empty corner in her condo where a reproduction of a seventh-century Tang dynasty vase would look smashing.

At ten o'clock, they joined the throng headed toward the exit. With Policzki trailing a few paces behind and Tommy's arm joined loosely with hers, they wound their way to the lobby, where the crowd had thinned out. Museum patrons stood in small clusters, chatting enthusiastically about the lecture they'd just attended. A display case housing a small collection of African tribal art caught Caro's attention. "Excuse me a moment," she said, and escaped from Malone's grip.

An attractive woman dressed in black joined her at the display case. "Intriguing, isn't it?" she said. "Such a vivid mixture of passion and naiveté. Do you collect?"

"Only on a limited basis, I'm afraid," Caro said. "And only reproductions."

The woman turned and spoke to her escort, who was engrossed in conversation a few feet away. "Conor, darling, you really should see this."

The man swung around, and Carolyn found herself face-to-face with Conor Rafferty.

16

The impact was like slamming face first into a brick wall. Her lungs ceased to function, and for several endless, torturous moments they gazed at each other in mute agony. He wore a custom-tailored black suit and a black tie with a crisp, snowy shirt that rendered him achingly handsome. Her chest afire from the need to breathe, Caro turned her attention to the woman. She was exquisite, fine-boned and elegant, with pale, almost translucent skin that gave her the delicate look of porcelain. The woman stared back at her, then glanced at Conor's face. Something she saw there made her clutch his arm in an unmistakable act of possession.

"Darling?" she said. "Do you two know each other?"

Still, they remained mute, both of them seemingly struck dumb. Carolyn knew precisely what he felt like buried deep inside her, was intimately familiar with the words he uttered in the depths of passion, could recall in vivid detail the exact color of his eyes at the moment of release. She knew the feel and the taste of his skin, knew the appendectomy scar that lay low on his belly, knew the look of him as he lay sleeping beside her. Knew how it felt to dance barefoot in the moonlight with him to the ocean's muffled roar, and she wasn't sure how she would get past the knowledge. It was unbearable, the anguish of wondering if the woman standing in front of her also knew these things.

The woman looked at Conor again, rapidly assessed the situation, and took charge. Stepping between them, she held out her hand. "Gwen Sloane," she said. "And you are…?"

Caro recovered her senses, drew in a sharp breath of oxygen. "Carolyn Monahan," she said, and woodenly shook Gwen Sloane's hand.

"Of course," Gwen said dryly. "The FBI agent. Conor's mentioned you."

"Yes. He's mentioned you, too."

Tommy eased up beside her and looped his arm casually through hers. "Rafferty," he said heartily. "Small world, isn't it?"

Conor's expression didn't change. "Malone."

None of them quite sure what to say next, they stood stiffly, like a modern art tableau, a museum exhibit, frozen in time and space. *Man with Two Lovers,* it would be called. Or perhaps *Ménage à Trois.* Nausea rose in Caro's throat. "Excuse me," she said. "I'm not feeling well."

She turned and fled, almost mowing down Policzki in her rush to escape, not caring if she looked like a fool. Let Conor explain to his ladylove why the FBI agent had run away as though the hounds of hell were nipping at her heels. She didn't give a damn.

Bursting through the doors and out into the heat of the evening, she sucked in breath after breath in an attempt to replenish the oxygen that the sight of Conor with Gwen Sloane had sucked from her lungs. She heard footsteps behind her, then a hand touched her arm. "Go away, Tommy," she said. "Just give me a minute to—" She glanced up, realized it wasn't Tommy, but Policzki who stood beside her.

"You okay?" he asked softly.

She bit her lip, then shook her head as tears welled up in her eyes. "Where's Malone?"

"I told him I'd see you home."

In astonishment, she said, "And he let you get away with that?"

His eyes were brown, a deep, rich chocolate. She'd never noticed before. "I carry a gun," he said, and the corner of his mouth twitched. "He doesn't." Policzki held out his arm. "Come on. We'll catch the T."

At this time of night, the green line train was half-empty, populated primarily by museum patrons and students from Northeastern. Caro sat silently beside Policzki, a tiny, huddled ball of misery, as the train rattled and screeched its way downtown. They got off at Arlington, walked in silence to her hotel. Julio wasn't yet on duty, and she nodded mutely to the stranger in a gold-piped maroon uniform who held open the door for them.

In the hallway upstairs, Stuart was reading a paperback with a lurid cover. "Evening," he said in his broad Boston accent.

She cleared her throat, opened her mouth, closed it again, and Policzki frowned and gave Stuart a sharp shake of his head. Caro slid her key card into the lock and the door popped open.

"Wait here," Policzki said, and stepped inside the room to repeat last night's routine. When he was certain the room was secure, he beckoned her inside. "Will you be okay alone? I can stay for a little while if—"

"Thank you, Policzki. For everything. But I'd rather be alone."

"If you need anything, Officer Stuart's right outside."

Then he was gone, and she was alone. She locked the door behind him, pressed her face against its smooth coolness. "Idiot," she whispered. "Idiot, idiot, idiot!" She should have turned around and driven back to Virginia the instant she discovered that Conor Rafferty was in charge of the case. Instead, she'd stayed and played with fire. It was her own fault she'd been burned. It was her own fault she'd fallen ass over elbow in love with a man she couldn't have.

She walked into the bathroom and flicked the light switch. The harsh fluorescent lighting highlighted every line and wrinkle in her face. Mascara tracks marred her cheeks. She wet a washcloth, tore open a bar of hotel soap, and attempted to scrub Conor Rafferty out of her system.

It didn't work. Her face looked marginally better, but the misery still lodged against her heart like the cool, steel blade of a knife. If she moved too quickly, let down her guard for an instant, it would nick her heart and she wouldn't be able to stanch the bleeding. Caro picked up her hairbrush and dragged it through her hair with vicious strokes while pictures played in her head, pictures of various violent methods by which Gwen Sloane might meet an early demise.

When a knock sounded on her door, she froze, met her own startled gaze in the mirror. Policzki, perhaps, coming back to check on her? Or, God forbid, Tommy, come to offer whatever comfort she'd be willing to accept? Surely it wasn't Conor, here to torment her further. She might be strong, but there were limits to what she could take. Hands trembling, she dropped the hairbrush and walked to the door.

The man who stood on the other side of the peephole wore a dark green Armani suit and an impatient expression on his handsome face. His sandy hair had been recently styled by Philippe, proprietor of D.C.'s most chic unisex salon. She knew that if she could see his feet, his shoes would be polished to a high gloss. Her heart sank, and she briefly considered going back into the bathroom, locking the door, and hiding there until he went away. But she would only be postponing the inevitable; she knew him well enough to know he would station himself outside her door until she was forced to talk to him.

Knowing that the worst day of her life was about to take another nosedive, she unlocked the door and flung it open.

"Richard," she said wearily, "what in hell are you doing here?"

Conor stared out the living room window of Gwen's condo, his shoulders squared, his hands crammed into his pockets. Outside the window, sodium-arc lights cast surreal shadows over the parking lot. In the kitchen, Gwen rattled cups and saucers while her cappuccino machine whined and growled. He was already wired so high that any more caffeine would probably launch him into outer space.

He'd always known that sooner or later, it would come down to this. He'd have to make a choice. But he'd supposed that when it happened, it would be polite and reserved and civilized. He couldn't have predicted that the sight of Carolyn Monahan in that heart-stopping red dress, her arm linked through Tommy Malone's, would hit him with all the force of an eighty-pound cannonball slamming into his gut. There was nothing civilized, nothing easy about his feelings for Caro. There never had been. He should have been smart enough to figure that out before tonight.

Gwen slipped her arms around him from behind. "You

haven't said a word," she purred, "since we left the museum."

He opened his mouth to speak, but the words that came out weren't the ones he'd planned to say. "Do you love me?" he said.

Her embrace stiffened, and the whir of the cappuccino machine, grinding away in the kitchen, seemed extraordinarily loud. "Excuse me?"

He wriggled away from her, turned to study her stricken face. "You heard the question, Gwen. But just for the hell of it, I'll ask it again. Do you love me?"

"I—" Her mouth opened wide. She wet her lips. "You're handsome, intelligent, a scintillating companion, a spectacular lover. I'm not sure I understand the question."

"It's not all that difficult, prosecutor. Pretend you're in a courtroom, in the witness box, being cross-examined by a particularly aggressive attorney. One like you. You've just been asked the sixty-five-thousand-dollar question: Do you love Conor Rafferty? How do you answer?"

Her eyes searched his face, perhaps seeking an answer she couldn't find anywhere else. She looked more than a little like a trapped animal. "You're tremendously attractive, Conor. I respect you, and more than that, I like you. I think we could make a good marriage. No, I *know* we could make a good one. But quite honestly, I never considered love to be part of the deal."

"I'm relieved to hear that," he said, "because to tell you the truth, I don't love you, either." It felt good to finally say the words out loud, to acknowledge what his heart had known all along.

"But it doesn't matter," she said quickly. "Love isn't necessary for a successful marriage. Love doesn't last, Conor. Ask any divorce lawyer out there. They'll all tell you the same thing. It's the love matches that end up in divorce court.''

"I'm not sure," he said, "but I suspect that divorce lawyers aren't the most reliable experts on successful marriage.''

"If you're worried about me taking advantage of you, we can do a prenup. I have a friend who—"

"Gwen," he said softly.

She paused in her babbling, and he saw the glint of a tear in her eye. "What?"

"Why are you so desperate to marry a man who's just admitted he doesn't love you?"

"I told you, Conor. It doesn't matter to me."

"But it does to me."

"It's her, isn't it? That FBI agent? You're in love with her, aren't you?"

"Of course not." He shoved his hands into his pockets and began to pace. Thought about it for a while. "I don't know," he conceded, "maybe." Still pacing, he thought about it some more, and sighed. "Probably."

"How long has she been here? A week? Ten days? You don't even know her."

He leaned against the windowsill and crossed his arms. Stabbing at the carpet with the toe of his shoe, he said, "I've known her most of my life. We have a history." He leveled a glance at her. "Maybe that's why I've found it so hard to commit to anybody. Maybe I've never stopped loving her."

"So it's over." Her voice was flat, emotionless. "Just like that."

"It's over. Gwen, I'm sorry. You must know that I didn't expect this to happen."

"Don't look so crestfallen, Conor. It's not the end of the world. We had a good six-month run. I should consider myself honored. Judging by what I hear, that's some kind of a record with you. You know what they call you behind your back? Love 'em and leave 'em Rafferty.''

He winced. "Christ, Gwen."

"She's very attractive," she said waspishly. "You'll make beautiful babies together."

He gaped at her, and her laughter was brittle. "I wish I had a camera handy," she said. "The look on your face is priceless. I don't suppose you still want that cappuccino?"

"Not if I want to sleep tonight." He ran a hand over his face. "Hell, I probably won't sleep tonight anyway."

"Then I'd suggest you gather up whatever belongs to you and leave as quietly as possible. I can do my crying after you're gone."

"Don't you ever return your phone calls?" Richard said, barging into her hotel room as though it were his name on the register instead of hers. "I've been calling and calling, and—"

"This is a really bad time, Richard. Can't it wait until tomorrow?"

"No, it can't. Shut the door. Sit down. I have to talk to you."

"I'd rather stand."

"Fine, then. I'll sit." He eyed the bed, apparently thought better of it, circled it gingerly, and parked himself on the air-conditioning unit beneath the window.

"I thought you were in New Haven."

"I was. I gave up trying to reach you by phone, so I rented a car and drove up. I thought the traffic in D.C. was bad. Jesus."

She folded her arms and smiled with saccharine insincerity. "Welcome to Boston. Look, Richard, do you think you could make this quick? It's late, and I think I'm coming down with the flu.'' It was a lie, but knowing how fastidious he was, she hoped it would be enough to frighten him off.

''I'm leaving the agency, Caro. They offered me a job at the State Department, and I've accepted it.''

He'd managed to snag her attention after all. ''You're leaving?'' she said, incredulous. ''When?''

''Next week. That's why I've been calling. Caro, the brass want you to have my job.''

Adrenaline raced through her body. This was the moment she'd spent years waiting for, preparing for. ''But that's not possible,'' she said. ''I've already turned in my resignation.''

Richard crossed his legs and adjusted the crease in his trousers. ''It's still sitting on my desk.''

''You never passed it on?''

His smile was too smooth, his chin too weak. He reminded her of a used car salesman. How could she ever have thought she loved this man? ''You resigned for personal reasons,'' he said. ''Because of what happened between us.'' He grew somber. ''I knew when you had time to cool off and think it through, you'd regret what you'd done. I wanted to give you time to rethink it. And I figured that once I was gone, there'd be no reason for you to leave.''

''Wait a minute,'' she said. ''Would you repeat that part?''

He blinked twice in rapid succession. ''I thought that once I was gone, there'd be no reason—''

''That's it,'' she said. ''That's the part I wanted to hear again. Just how long have you known about this, Richard?''

For the first time, his smarmy smile faltered. "Three weeks," he said.

"Three weeks? Three fucking weeks, and you didn't bother to tell me? You let me turn in my resignation, knowing damn well that you were leaving the Bureau and the job I'd waited four years for was about to open up?"

"I couldn't tell anybody until it was confirmed."

"Bullshit. You wanted to save your trump card until you were ready to play it. You're the most manipulative excuse for a human being that I've ever met."

His mouth thinned. "Now that we're done with the pleasantries, I'm here to offer you the job, Caro. A big promotion, and a hefty raise to go with it. Are you going to accept it?"

"Why me?" she demanded. "Why do the brass want me so badly?" She began pacing with long, brisk strides. Wheeling on him, she said, "Why not Sully, or Lou? They're both damn good agents. They've both been there longer than I have. Christ, Sully's been there for fifteen years. He's the one who deserves the job, not me."

"I advocated for you. I thought it was what you wanted." Now Richard looked like a little boy, wounded and sulking on Christmas morning because he'd just learned there was no Santa Claus. "You're one of the best agents I've ever worked with, Carolyn. I spent years training you, molding you. I taught you everything you know."

"No, Richard," she said, "you used me to boost your own ego. It made you feel so self-important, playing Pygmalion. You took an ignorant little girl from the wrong side of the tracks and turned her into what you wanted her to be. You taught me how walk, how to dress, what kind of wine to order. You introduced me to the finer things in life, taught me to have an appetite for them. I'm a full-fledged graduate of the Richard Armitage Finishing School. None of those things had anything to do with my job. They were just the icing on the cake.''

"You're wrong, Carolyn. In some ways, you're still incredibly naive. If you intend to climb the career ladder, you have to know all those things. Regardless of how you feel about them, polite society still finds them important.''

"Screw polite society!''

"That's my little Caro,'' he said dryly. "Always looking out for her own best interests.''

"I'm not your little Caro. I haven't been for a long time. That was the one thing you didn't expect—that I'd turn out smarter than you. Well, guess what? I've got your number, Richard. I know just where your vulnerabilities lie, and don't think I wouldn't use that knowledge if it became necessary.''

He paled, or perhaps it was a trick of the lighting. "Look,'' he said, "do you want this job, or not? Washington's pressuring me for an answer.''

"I need some time to think it over.''

"I don't have any time. If you turn it down, I only have a week to find somebody else.''

"And you were so certain of me, weren't you, Richard?'' She saw the truth on his face, and it was infuriating. "Twenty-four hours,'' she told him. "I'll give you an answer in twenty-four hours. It's as good as you're going to get.''

There was a knock at the door. "Now what?'' she said. "It's eleven o'clock at night. Who else would pick this ridiculous hour to come calling?''

From his perch on the air conditioner, Richard crossed his arms and looked at her curiously. "Aren't you going to answer it?''

Reluctantly, she crossed the room and looked through

the peephole. Conor was standing in the hallway outside her hotel room, his back to her, hands in his pockets as he studied the watercolor of a Newbury Street sidewalk café that hung on the opposite wall. She undid the locks, her heart beating much too rapidly. He heard her open the door, and swung around to face her. He was still wearing the clothes he'd worn to the MFA. With his dark hair and that gorgeous face, in the black suit and the snowy-white shirt, he looked stunning. And, to his credit, as miserable as she felt.

"Hi," he said tentatively.

She leaned her head against the door. Why did she always have to fall for the good-looking ones? "Hi."

He jingled a fistful of change in his pocket. "We need to talk."

"Yes," she said. "I suppose we do."

"So." He jingled the change again. "Do you think I could come in?"

She'd heard that there were women in existence somewhere who actually learned from their mistakes. Obviously, she would never be one of them. "Why not?" she said, stepping back so he could enter the room. "You might as well join the party."

He stepped through the door and stopped short when he saw Richard. "I didn't realize you had company."

She shut the door behind her. "Richard Armitage," she said wearily, "meet Lieutenant Conor Rafferty."

Conor's back stiffened, but Richard moved away from the window with elegant grace. "Rafferty," he said affably, thrusting out his hand. "I was hoping I'd get a chance to talk to you in person about the case while I'm here. I've been having trouble getting Carolyn to return my phone calls."

The case. Was there still a case going on? Somehow,

over the last couple of days, her personal life had totally eclipsed it.

The two men exchanged a brief handshake. "Give me a call tomorrow," Conor said stiffly, "and I'll bring you up to date on the investigation."

Carolyn crossed her arms and gave Richard a pointed look. He glanced from her to Conor and back again and raised an eyebrow. "Well," he said, rubbing his hands together, "I have to be going. Nice to meet you, Rafferty. I'll talk to you tomorrow," he said to Carolyn as he brushed past her.

The scent of his expensive cologne lingered after he'd gone. She double-locked the door and stood there with her hands pressed against it while she tried to get her galloping heart back under control.

"What the hell is he doing here?"

She took a deep breath and turned away from the door. Conor had removed his tie and dropped it on the bed, and was yanking loose the collar of his shirt.

"Business," she said flatly. "A better question would be what you're doing here."

"Damn it, Caro," he said, "stop looking at me that way."

"How the hell am I looking at you?"

"You're looking at me as though I'm something you'd like to scrape off your shoe."

"You know what they say. If the cliché fits—"

"Stop it! Did I ever once make any promises to you? Did we ever once lay any private claims on each other? Was I the one who decided we didn't stand a snowball's chance in hell of making it together?"

She opened her mouth. Closed it. "No," she said miserably.

"Then why the hell are you so pissed off at me?"

"I'm not pissed off at you." Oh, shit. She was going to cry. It was an unforgivable sin.

"Damn it," he muttered. He turned away from her, walked to the window and looked out. "This wasn't supposed to happen. It's all wrong." He wheeled around and began pacing back and forth in front of the bed. "Wrong time, wrong place, wrong person." In bewilderment, he said, "I don't let women get to me. Ever. Old love 'em and leave 'em Rafferty. That's what Gwen called me tonight." He stopped pacing, finally met her eyes. "I broke things off with her tonight."

It was the last thing she'd expected him to say. Her heart began thudding like a jackhammer. "Why?" she said.

"Jesus Christ, Monahan, that's what I've been trying to tell you. Aren't you listening?"

"I'm listening, but I might understand better if you tried speaking English."

"I won't lie and say I'm happy about it," he said, more to himself than to her. "But here it is, and I have to deal with it."

"Conor," she said, "what the hell are you talking about?"

"Us," he said, sounding surprised, as if she should have known without asking. "You and me. Damn it, Caro, I broke up with Gwen because I'm in love with you."

She didn't know whether to laugh or cry. "Oh, God," she said, and crossed her arms over her chest. She took a deep breath and thought about what to say. "Okay, Rafferty, here's the way it lays out. Your timing sucks. Richard came here tonight to tell me he's leaving the agency. They've offered me his job."

She watched his face as the meaning of her words sank in. "In Quantico," he said.

"In Quantico." Now it was her turn to pace. "Richard's been grooming me to be his replacement since the day I went to work for him. For four years, I've wanted this job so bad I could taste it." Arms crossed, she studied him. "And you," she accused. "You're everything I've spent the last ten years running away from. Jesus, Conor, my mother actually likes you. Do you have any idea what a lousy recommendation that is?"

Looking wretched, he said, "Can I help it if I'm loaded with charm?"

His attempt at humor crashed and burned like the Hindenburg. "There's no way this can possibly work out," she said. "Talk about wrong time, wrong place, wrong person."

"So exactly what are you saying?"

She swiped furiously at a tear. "Are you really this dense? I'm telling you that I love you, too!"

He crossed the room in two steps, swept her into his arms, and she closed her eyes and pressed her cheek to his lapel. Beneath it, his heartbeat was strong, and as rapid as hers. He buried his nose in her hair and said hoarsely, "What did you tell Richard?"

She laid a hand on his chest, ran it up and down the smooth material of his lapel. "I told him I needed twenty-four hours to think it over."

"You'd be a goddamn fool to turn it down."

"I know."

"Do you think you could turn off the waterworks, Monahan? You're getting mascara all over my shirt."

"Oh, shut up. I'll buy you a new one."

He fingered the red silk material that barely covered

her shoulder. Sounding wounded, he said, "You dressed like this for Malone?"

"I dressed like this," she said, "for you."

He caught her chin in his hand and raised it until their eyes met. "For me?"

"I was thumbing my nose at you. Do you have any idea how pissed off I was when you dumped me like that?"

"It was self-preservation. You were about to dump me. My red-blooded American male ego wouldn't allow it. I had to do something."

"I can't make you any promises. If I take this job, I'll be tied up most of the time. Washington's a long way from Boston."

"Not that far. Planes fly back and forth all the time." He stroked her cheek with his thumb. "And I hear there's this newfangled invention called a telephone."

She caught his hand in hers and stilled his wandering fingers. "A long-distance relationship. How thrilling. I can leave messages with Isabel, and you can leave messages with Penny. Better yet, we can e-mail back and forth. Find out if cybersex is really all it's cracked up to be."

"Look, for what it's worth—" he paused, his fingers playing in her hair "—I never slept with Gwen after you got here."

"Damn it, Rafferty, how is it you do that? Every time I try to be a hard-ass, you have this way of defusing me."

"It's a rare talent. Caro, I want you to pack your bags. You're checking out of this place. Tonight."

"Checking out? Where am I going?"

"Home with me," he said. "Where you belong."

He cleared out half his bureau drawers and made space in his closet, and while he walked Nero, she unpacked.

Even as a temporary arrangement, this was a terrifying step. Her cosmetics took up too much space atop the dresser, and when she hung her toothbrush in the medicine cabinet next to his, she felt as though she'd permanently sealed her fate. It all fit together so neatly. Her Mitsubishi, pulled up snug against the curb, left just enough room to fit his Taurus into the opening behind it. She was thirty-two years old, too old for playing house, yet that was exactly how she felt. It hadn't been this way on the Cape; their trip had been a short jaunt with no pretense of permanence. But this—this involved unpacking all her luggage and finding places to tuck away everything she'd brought with her from Virginia. This smacked of commitment.

She heard Nero loping up the stairs, heard his dog tags rattling, and then the door opened and both of them, man and dog, filled the kitchen with sound and motion. Conor released Nero from his leash and tossed it on top of the refrigerator. "You weren't gone long," she said.

He turned those incredible green eyes on her. "I stayed within sight of the house. Tonight, I'm the one guarding your body."

"This gives a whole new meaning to the term *police protection*. Isn't there something in the policy book, Lieutenant, that forbids you to sleep with someone you're supposed to be protecting?"

"Probably." His deliberate, measured steps as he crossed the room accelerated her pulse rate. "What do you propose we do about it?"

She slipped both hands beneath his T-shirt, found the sleek muscled flesh of his chest. "I might have to arrest you."

He rested a hand on the door frame above her head.

Leaning close, he said, "Tell me, Special Agent Monahan, do you have jurisdiction?"

She ran a single fingernail delicately down the center of his chest. Breathlessly, she said, "Only if you've committed a Federal offense."

His breath was warm in her ear. "And if I haven't?"

Toying with the button to his Levi's, she said, "I carry a big gun."

"Is that so?" His mouth hovered bare inches away from hers. "Mine's bigger," he said, right before he kissed her senseless.

As a morning stimulant, sex had coffee beat all to hell. She was surprised that it wasn't recommended by doctors everywhere. No calories, no caffeine hangover, just a great aerobic workout, followed by a smile for the rest of the day. Afterward, while Conor shaved, she made a pathetic attempt to find something in his kitchen that resembled breakfast. A bagel, perhaps, or even a box of instant oatmeal. But the search was futile.

"I usually just grab an Egg McMuffin," he explained, his face still covered with lather as he stood in front of the bathroom mirror. "I don't have time in the morning to do breakfast."

Caro winced, imagining the condition of his arteries, and made a mental note to hit the grocery store on the way home.

They drove to work together. Ignoring the raised eyebrows that marked their mutual arrival, Caro strode briskly to her tiny cubicle. She passed Isabel's desk, where the distinct Latin rhythm of a Gloria Estefan song poured from the radio. "Good morning, Isabel," she said.

Isabel glanced at Carolyn, then at Conor, gauged their

expressions, and grinned. "Good morning," she said, her lyrical accent giving the words untold shades of meaning.

Policzki was parked at his customary station outside her office, flipping through the pages of a magazine. "Good morning, Policzki," she said. "Beautiful day, isn't it?" She rounded her desk, tossed her purse and her briefcase onto the desktop, and plopped into the swivel chair. She was leaning back against the wall, staring at the ceiling and grinning like a fool, when Isabel dropped the morning mail onto her desk.

"Sleep well?" Isabel said sweetly.

"Oh, yes." She might not have slept long, but she'd slept well.

"Maybe now the lieutenant will act a little less like a grizzly," Isabel said, two deep dimples appearing in her cheeks. "As a matter of fact, I think this would be the perfect time to ask him for a raise." She scooted back out the door, and Caro turned her attention to the mail.

The bulging white envelope bore a government seal, and she set it aside to open later. Penny had been faithfully forwarding her mail from Quantico—every piece of it—and she didn't have the stomach this morning to wade through countless come-ons and sales flyers. They could wait until tonight.

Her buoyant mood went splat the instant she saw the manila envelope. Smudged and dog-eared, it looked as though it had weathered a hurricane. Labels had been peeled off and then crookedly reapplied, her name and address printed in neat block letters. She gingerly stood the envelope on end, sliced it open with her letter opener, and spilled its contents onto her desk.

Half a dozen color photographs lay fanned out before her. Caro picked up the first one and recognized herself immediately. She lay back in the *Painted Lady,* eyes closed, face tilted toward the sun, one arm falling loosely over the bow, fingers trailing in the water. Whoever had shot it knew his stuff. The picture had been taken from a distance with a powerful zoom lens, and despite the velocity of the sailboat, the image was as crisp and clean as a still life.

Her hands began to tremble. She dropped the first photo, picked up the second, her stomach contracting at the sight of herself on the beach with Conor, his hand resting intimately on her shoulder. Swallowing the dread that choked her, she moved on to the third. Mr. X had zoomed in even closer for this shot of her naked to the waist, Conor kneeling in the sand, his face pressed to her belly.

She shuffled through the rest of them numbly, her stomach growing sicker as the images turned progressively more intimate. In the sixth and final photo, the artist's pièce de résistance, she and Conor were both naked, her knees buried in the sand as she straddled his hips. Her back was arched, her head thrown back, her hair falling in a silken veil behind her. Her breasts were etched in vivid relief against a sunset sky, and the photographer, whoever he was, had eloquently captured the rapture that permeated her features.

Nausea rose in her throat, nausea and rage because somebody had intruded on her most intimate moments and turned them into porn. The UNSUB had taken something beautiful, something meaningful, and cheapened it. Caro took a deep breath to still her trembling, picked up the phone and dialed Conor's extension. "Come here," she said, her throat feeling like sandpaper. "Right now."

He was there within seconds, filling her doorway, his face taut with concern, and it took all her strength to keep from throwing herself into his arms. But this was a homicide investigation, and she had to maintain profession-alism.

"Caro?" he said. "What's wrong?"

She closed her eyes, willing the nausea to recede. "Shut the door," she said weakly. "I don't want anybody else to see this."

Her face burning with embarrassment, she watched as he worked his way through the photos, watched his expression shift from concern to grimness and then to the same rage she felt.

"Son of a bitch," he growled when he reached number six. "When I catch this sorry bastard, he won't have to worry about a fair trial, because I'm going to kill him with my bare hands." He paged through the photos again with harsh, staccato motions. "I want you off the case. Immediately. I want you off the case and in protective custody, hidden away someplace where you're safe until this is over."

"No!"

"The last time I checked, Monahan, I was still in charge of this investigation."

"You have no authority over me, Rafferty, and I intend to see this case through to the end!"

"Goddamn it, Caro, we don't have any idea who this guy is. He could be anybody. I can't take that chance with you. I won't." Conor picked up the envelope, squeezed it open so he could return the offending photos to the place she wished she'd never taken them from. He paused, then said, "What's this?" He reached into the envelope and pulled out a scrap of paper. He stared at it, and his face went hard.

"What?" she said. "What is it?"

He tossed it down onto the desk in front of her. "I think we just got the answer we've been looking for."

It was a dry cleaning receipt, and Caro's eyes were instantly drawn to the name computer-printed at the top.

T. Malone.

17

Malone wasn't at work, and the city editor at the *Trib* didn't have a clue as to his whereabouts. "Tommy's a free spirit," she told Carolyn. "He does his own thing, and I pretty much give him free rein. He knows his job, and he does it well, so I don't quibble when he disappears for a few hours. He always comes back with something wonderful."

Caro hung up the phone and faced the grim cluster of cops gathered in Rafferty's office. "He's MIA right now," she said, "but I managed to get his home address out of her. And the address of his ex-wife in Brookline."

"All right," Conor said quietly. "We'll work with what we have. Lorna, take Lassiter and see if you can track him down at home. Smith, Mendez, you take the *Trib*. Hang around and see if he shows up. Rizzoli, you and—" He looked around. "Where the hell is Hailstock?"

"Day off," Lorna said.

"Rizzoli, scare up somebody and go out to Brookline, talk to the ex-wife, see what you can pull out of her."

"I'll go," Caro said. "I'll go with Rizzoli."

Those green eyes darkened with displeasure. "I don't like it," he said.

"I'm as involved in this investigation as any of you.

Maybe more so, and if you think I'm sitting on my hands while you take him down, Rafferty, you're full of shit.''

Their eyes telegraphed silent messages back and forth. ''Fine,'' he said brusquely, and she knew how difficult the concession was for him. He didn't say the rest of the sentence: *Be careful.* But she heard it anyway. ''Let's try to be as discreet as possible,'' he said. ''We don't want to scare him off before we close the net around him. If he runs, we'll lose him.''

''Rizzoli?'' Caro said. ''Are you with me?''

Ted's color had improved since yesterday, and the shakiness was gone. ''I'm with you,'' he said. ''Let's roll.''

Policzki stood when they approached, and Rizzoli shot him a look of disdain. ''We don't need you riding shot-gun, Junior,'' he said. ''If all three of us show up, the ex-Mrs. Malone will think it's a fucking cop convention, and we won't get anything out of her.''

''He's right,'' Caro said, shouldering her purse. ''I'd say we're pretty well covered for now, Policzki. If any-body comes after me, Rizzoli will shoot them. You're off the hook for a couple of hours. Go outside, sit in the sunshine, and watch the pretty girls. Lots of secretaries taking coffee breaks in the plaza.''

Policzki opened his mouth to argue, glanced down at Rizzoli's gun gleaming in its shoulder holster, and clamped his mouth shut. ''Take care of her,'' he snapped, and stalked off in the direction of Conor's office.

As Rizzoli wound his way through heavy weekday traf-fic, Caro pushed the button to lower her window. ''I should have figured it out,'' she said. ''I could kick my-self. He was too damn interested in the investigation. He wanted to know everything.''

Rizzoli stopped for a red light, and she watched a ragged old woman with a shopping cart panhandling on the Common. "He knew Meg," she said. "That should have set my radar off right away. But everybody knew Meg. She was so damn popular." The car started moving again. "He knew I was staying at the Boylston, although I never told him that. He tried to say I'd mentioned it when we were talking, but I know damn well I didn't. Hell, he even knew that Conor and I used to date. I should have put all this stuff together and figured it out. I just attributed it to reportorial zeal."

"You've worked your ass off on this case," Ted said. "Don't be so hard on yourself. Nobody put the pieces together."

"Maybe not, but—"

"But what?" They passed through Copley Square and picked up Huntington Avenue.

But I was supposed to be the one. The thought came out of nowhere. "I think," she said in surprise, "that I may have some control issues I need to deal with."

Rizzoli laughed and said, "Show me a cop who doesn't."

"Zilch," Lorna reported. "We knocked on the door, but nobody answered. Landlady says he left this morning at his usual time. Made sure we knew what an admirable fellow he is. If you go by what she says, he's next in line for canonization."

"And Lucifer was God's most beautiful angel," Conor said into the phone. "Hang around for a while, but try not to look too conspicuous."

"House next door's empty. Got a For Sale sign out front."

Conor leaned back in his chair. "Go peek in the windows. Get chummy with Lassiter. Act like you're thinking about square footage and dry rot.''

Lorna snickered. "Ten-four. Oh, Conor? Greg says if things get sticky, you can explain the situation to my other half.''

He hung up the phone, ambled down the hall to Isabel's desk. "Run me a computer search on Tommy Malone. Anything you can come up with in the past ten years. Employment history, prior addresses, credit rating. See if you can come up with any priors. Where's Policzki?''

"He left. I thought you told him to.''

"I didn't tell him anything. He came whining to me about Rizzoli usurping his position, and I blew him off. I had too much going on.'' Conor checked his watch. "Kid disappears in the middle of a crisis. This won't look good on his record.''

He glanced up, found himself looking directly into the eyes of a lean, dark-haired man who stood on the other side of Isabel's desk. Father Clancy Donovan appeared gaunt and drained. Thirty years of friendship, seasoned by betrayal, shimmered in the air between them on waves so vibrant they were nearly visible. "I was looking for Caro,'' Clancy said stiffly.

"She's not here right now. Look, Clance—''

"I was worried about her. She was so upset the last time I saw her. I'll catch her another time.''

Rafferty glanced at Isabel, who was taking in this little exchange with lively curiosity. "Can you step into my office for a minute?''

"I really have to be going. I have an appointment—''

"Damn it, Donovan, I need to talk to you in private.''

Clancy's amber gaze stared at him, blank and emotionless. Without speaking, the priest turned and strode down the hall. Rafferty closed the door behind them. "We've had a break in the case," he said.

"How fortunate," Clancy said. "For all of us."

"I can't go into any details yet, but we've uncovered physical evidence that may lead us directly to the killer."

"And your point is?"

"Jesus H. Christ." He ran a hand through his hair. "Look, I'm trying to find a way to apologize without making too much of an ass out of myself."

Clancy shoved his hands into his pockets. The gold crucifix around his neck gleamed in the sunlight pouring through the window. "I can't wait to hear this. Go ahead. Apologize."

"I'm sorry. I'm sorry for what I put you through, and I'm sorry if this has ruined our friendship. But I did what I had to do, Clance, and I'd do it over again if I had to. It's my job. Sometimes my job really reeks. But I still have to do it."

Some of the tension left Clancy's shoulders. "I understand," he said. "Sometimes my job really reeks, too." He turned to leave. "Tell Caro I was asking about her."

Rafferty let out a hard sigh. "Donovan."

The priest paused, his hand on the doorknob, and turned slowly. "Give me a little time. I have to work through this on my own. Call me in a couple of weeks. Maybe by then, I'll be in the mood to take you for a game of racquetball. The Donovan House is running short on funding again."

The door shut behind him, quietly, decisively. With a sigh, Rafferty sat down in his swivel chair, rolled it over to the window, and stared out at the summer sky. He thought about thirty years of friendship, thought about the scrawny kid he'd dragged home to Fiona's table for supper, night after night, because he needed fattening up and his own mother's definition of a balanced meal was an Old Milwaukee and a pack of Camels.

They'd get through this. Over the course of thirty years, they'd gotten through worse. One way or another, they would get through this.

Ten minutes later, Isabel produced the paperwork on Tommy Malone, and he sat down to look it over. Malone had never had so much as a traffic ticket. His employment records matched his various changes of address over the past ten years. None of it was very exciting. He'd worked at small dailies in Bangor, Maine and Laurel, Maryland. He'd spent six months at the *Miami Herald,* but that was two years after the Daytona homicide. Three years ago, he'd left Miami and returned to Boston to take his current position at the *Trib.* Since then, he'd been living on the second floor of a frame duplex in Southie. There was nothing here to link Malone to any of the homicides.

He was going over the record for the third time when Isabel buzzed him. "Yes?" he said impatiently.

"There's a lady here to see you. She says it's about the murders."

"I'm busy. Isn't there somebody else she can talk to?"

"I told her you were a busy man. But she showed me your card and said you wanted to talk to her."

He tried to remember who he'd left his card with. "Who is she?"

"Her name's Tanesha Livingston. She works at the Golden Pussycat."

It came back to him then. Neal Horton. Shabby office in a dark corner behind the stage. He'd left his card with Horton, asked him to give it to the girl who'd been away on her honeymoon.

He went to greet her in person. Tanesha Livingston was a lanky black woman with exotic, almond-shaped eyes.

She had to stand at least six foot one in her stocking feet; in her heels, she towered over his six-foot frame. Her handshake was firm and warm. "Neal told me you wanted to talk about the night Tonia died," she said.

"Yes. Thanks for coming down." He led her to his office, settled her in a chair, and perched on the corner of his desk. Playing with a rubber band, he said, "I'm not sure how much you can help us, but I'd appreciate knowing whatever you can remember."

"I remember a lot. I saw the man she left with that night."

His hands, worrying the rubber band, stilled. If they had a witness, they could put Malone away for seven life sentences. "You saw him? Could you identify him if you saw him again?"

"I think so. I got a pretty good look when they were going out the door. I was curious about him, because she'd mentioned him before. She said he took care of her, and she took care of him."

"What did she mean by that?"

"She gave him for free what she was selling on the street, and he kept her ass out of the slammer."

He tried to piece it together, but it wasn't making sense yet. "I don't understand," he said. "How could he do that?"

Livingston leaned back in her chair and crossed endless, elegant legs. "The same way you could, I imagine. He was a cop."

Her words hit him deep and hard in the gut. "A cop?" he said intently. "Are you sure?"

"She said he was a Vice cop with a yen for blondes. But she was scared of him. He'd been getting weirder and weirder over the last few months, was into some real kinky stuff. Bondage. S and M. Wanted her to play dead while he pretended to choke her. The last time she was with him, he left bruises on her neck. I saw them with my own eyes. The night she died, she told me she was going to break it off with him. He was scaring her, and he couldn't protect her anymore.''

The sick feeling in his stomach told him he wasn't going to like what she said next. ''Why not?''

''He doesn't work Vice anymore. A few months ago, he transferred to Homicide.''

''Drop everything,'' he told Lorna, ''and get back here. Right now. While you're on the way, call Jeannie Rizzoli and ask her if the name Meg Monahan means anything to her.''

''Conor?''

''Just do it!'' He disconnected, dialed Isabel. ''Do you know how to pull up personnel records on the computer?''

''*Sí.* Of course. You think I'm a dummy, or what?''

''Pull up Rizzoli's record. I'll be right there.'' To Livingston, he said, ''I'll be back. Get yourself a cup of coffee or something.''

He appropriated Isabel's chair and squinted at the screen. Rizzoli's photo was at the top of the page, and the name beside it leaped out at him instantly, the full name he hadn't known about until now: John Theodore Rizzoli.

Johnny.

''Shit,'' he said.

The sick feeling in his stomach worsened as he scrolled through Ted's record. Rizzoli had worked for the B.P.D. for fifteen years. He'd been a solid employee, but he'd done nothing to distinguish himself. The Department had paid to send him to a half-dozen conferences over the years, conferences that took place in cities like Milwaukee, Chapel Hill, Daytona Beach. The dates matched up. Every damn one of them matched up. They'd been looking at this thing all wrong, looking for a man who'd moved around a lot. But Ted had been smarter than all of them, hiding right in front of their eyes. Keeping his two lives, his two personalities, separate. In Boston, he'd been a husband, a father, a good cop. It was only when he felt safe, in some random city hundreds of miles from home, that he unleashed the monster.

Until six months ago, when the monster had taken control.

He looked up into Isabel's soft brown eyes, saw the concern there. "Can you print me a copy of his picture?"

"*Sí.*"

They traded places and she performed some mysterious computer magic that was beyond his understanding. A moment later, the printer hummed and spit out a colored likeness of John Theodore Rizzoli. He snatched it up and marched back to his office, where Livingston waited.

He thrust the photo at her. "Do you recognize this man?"

She took the sheet of paper, glanced at it, nodded. "Oh, yeah," she said. "That's him, all right."

He heard footsteps in the corridor, and Lorna sprinted through his door, followed closely by Greg Lassiter. "Conor?" she said. "What the hell is going on?"

He took a hard, sharp breath. "Did you talk to Jeannie Rizzoli?"

She studied his eyes. After all these years, they didn't need many words, he and Lorna. "Oh, fuck," she said.

"She used to baby-sit for them, didn't she?"

"Yes. Goddamn it."

"It's Ted," he said. "Ted's the killer."

"That was a waste of time," Caro said as Rizzoli pulled his Oldsmobile away from the curb. "She laughed at us. She actually laughed at us."

When they'd identified themselves and explained why they were there, Barbara Malone Kingsbury had thrown back her elegantly coiffed blond head and laughed out loud. "Tommy?" she'd said. "Mixed up in a homicide? Oh, that's precious."

Caro bristled. "I don't suppose you'd mind if I ask why you're laughing?"

"I'm sorry." Mrs. Kingsbury wiped a tear from the corner of her eye. "But you're way out in left field if you think Tommy could've had anything to do with a murder. His interest in all that stuff is strictly academic. He's fascinated by people's motivations. He minored in psychology at Columbia. Not many people know that. But Tommy would never get involved in anything like that. He simply wouldn't have the stomach for it."

"What do you mean?"

"When we went to have our blood tests to get married, Tommy passed out at the sight of his own blood."

She'd still been chortling when she ushered them out the door.

As the car passed block after block of residential streets, Caro stared out the window and sighed. "Now what?"

"Now, we wait," Rizzoli said. "Sooner or later, he'll show up somewhere, and we'll nab him."

"It's not much," she said. "A dry cleaning ticket. Will it be enough to give us probable cause?"

In the distance, the Prudential tower rose above the city, dwarfing the buildings that surrounded it. "It should be enough to justify a search warrant," Ted said. "Once we collect more evidence, we can get an indictment."

Her cell phone rang, and she pulled it out of her purse to answer it. "Monahan."

"I want you to put on your best cop face," Conor said with quiet urgency, "and listen carefully to what I'm saying. Keep your responses neutral and low-key. Everything's fine, we're just having a casual conversation. Understand?"

Every muscle in her body went on red alert. "Yes."

"Are you carrying?"

Her Glock, in its shoulder holster, was a familiar weight against her rib cage. "Of course."

"Ted Rizzoli's full name is John Theodore Rizzoli. Ten years ago, your sister baby-sat for Ted and Jeannie. According to Jeannie, Ted always insisted on driving her home."

Her throat tightened. "I see."

"Over the past ten years, Ted's attended conferences in six different cities. In at least three of those cities, a young girl died while he was there. Lorna's checking on the others right now. I'm willing to bet we're going to find three more. Are you with me?"

Her stomach knotted as it hit her, the full significance of what he was telling her. "Yes," she said.

"We also have a witness who identified Ted as the man she saw leaving the Golden Pussycat with Tonia Lavoie the night she died. Caro, I have an APB out on Ted's car. I know you're somewhere between Brookline and downtown. I called Barbara Kingsbury and she told me you'd already left. We'll find you. I don't give a damn about Rizzoli. I only care about getting you back in one piece. Nothing else matters, do you understand?"

She closed her eyes, exhaled. "Conor?"

"Yes?"

Precious seconds reeled out between them, a lifetime of unspoken words in their silence. At the other end of the phone, she could hear him breathing. "I love you," she said.

"I love you, too," he said. And then he was gone.

She switched off the phone and took a hard, bracing breath, realized belatedly that Rizzoli had pulled the car over to the curb. At some point, while she wasn't paying attention, they'd left Huntington Avenue. Now they were parked along the Back Bay Fens, Frederick Law Olmsted's grand vision, an oasis of green in the midst of concrete and stone. "That was touching," Ted said. "Now give me the phone."

She turned to look at him. In all her years with the Bureau, she'd never before faced the business end of a loaded gun. It was a surreal experience, one that left her feeling oddly calm.

"Oh, Rizzoli," she said, "I'm so disappointed in you."

"Give me the phone, please. Slowly."

She handed it to him and he tossed it out the open window and into the street. It hit the pavement and bounced. "Now," he said, "the gun. Arms over your head."

She did what he said. He removed the Glock from her shoulder holster. His own weapon still trained on her, he leaned to tuck the Glock under the driver's seat. "We're going to get out of the car now," he said, "and we're going to take a little walk."

Caro raised her chin and gripped the shoulder strap to her purse. "And if I refuse to go with you?"

"Then I'll kill you right here. Quite simple, Agent Monahan. Even a Fed should be able to understand."

It was a glorious summer day in the Fens, the private gardens awash with bloom, birds darting in and out of the trees that overhung the river as it meandered lazily through Olmsted's fantasy. On the rare occasions when she'd thought about dying, she'd never pictured it happening on a day like this, with the sun so bright and the sky so blue it hurt to look at it. With the gun pressed tight against her ribs beneath her jacket and her purse strap clutched in her hand, they walked together in a stilted two-step, away from the road and deeper into the park, away from the mothers walking babies in strollers, away from the blue-haired society matrons tending their gardens, away from the young couples necking on blankets on the riverbank.

"That was a clever trick with the dry cleaning slip," she said. "How'd you pull that one off?" Maybe if she could keep him talking, she'd have a chance. By this time, every cop in Boston had to be looking for her. It maddened her to realize that despite all those years of self-defense training, she was helpless as a newborn kitten. Even a black belt in karate was no defense against a loaded gun.

"I have a friend who works at the *Trib*. I stopped by to visit him the other day. Malone's desk looks like the wreck of the *Titanic*. It was sitting right on top of the pile."

Bitterly, she said, "You killed my sister."

"Meg," he said. "Sweet Meggie. She was my first."

"Why?" she demanded. "How could you do that to her? She loved you!"

"Meg was an accident," he said. "I didn't mean to kill her. But I had these pictures in my head that wouldn't go away. Things I wanted to do. Things I needed to do. I was driven, do you understand? And it just…happened. I was so scared. So excited. I'd been thinking about it for so long."

She fought back the nausea that rose in her throat.

"You took pictures of her," she accused. "How can you call it an accident when you had a camera with you?"

His eyes softened with something that looked very much like pleasure. "That was part of the fantasy. I needed the pictures so I could look at them later and remember what it felt like. When I realized Meg was dead, I remembered Jeannie's camera, in the glove compartment." His smile was ghoulish. "It was the start of a whole new hobby."

"Christ, Rizzoli, you're deranged."

He laughed, and a shiver danced down her spine. "Sometimes," he agreed.

They neared the eastern perimeter of the park, and he steered her toward the reeds that grew in a thick forest along the riverbank. With stems bigger around than a man's thumb, these exotic rushes sprouted in a shimmering curtain that rivaled the nearby trees in height. The ground inside this thicket was crisscrossed with dozens of paths worn by human feet, for its lush cover made this an ideal spot for drug deals and homosexual trysts. And, occasionally, murder.

"I didn't want you to know," he said, his voice laced with regret. "Not until I was ready for you. The cat-and-mouse game was going so well. I wanted to draw it out, build up the anticipation, until I was ready to make you mine. There was such poetic justice to it. Meg, the innocent victim. You, the avenger. Once I had both sisters, the circle would be complete." His voice darkened. "But it wasn't supposed to happen like this, in a city park, in the middle of the day. There's no time. No privacy. No ambiance." He pressed the gun harder against her side, and she winced and bit her lip. "I didn't want to have to kill you this way."

He shoved her down a path and the thicket swallowed

her up. Inside, she quickly lost her bearings, for all she could see was blue sky and yellowed grass. The ground was littered with refuse: a broken beer bottle, a used condom. Inexplicably, a baby's diaper. For the first time, she felt real fear. This wasn't a game. Ted Rizzoli truly meant to kill her.

Above their heads, a passing breeze rattled the rushes. Ted paused at the center of a small clearing, removed the gun from her ribs, and she took a deep breath. Slowly, she turned to look at him. Madness glittered in his eyes. "I don't understand," she said. "Why do you have to kill me at all?"

"Salvation, of course," he said in a tone that implied she already knew the answer.

"Salvation?"

"Don't you see? It's the only way. I have to close the circle. Then—" He paused, and she saw regret in his eyes. Regret, and resignation. With his free hand, he stroked the barrel of his gun, lovingly, as though he were caressing a woman. "Then," he said, "I can destroy the monster that's living inside me."

"Look, Ted, you don't have to do this. We can get you help. With a good psychiatrist on your side, you can plead insanity. You won't even have to do time."

"There isn't any help. Don't you understand that? It's over, Carolyn. Everything's over." He sounded bewildered, as though he couldn't quite figure out how it had come to this. "I couldn't help it, you know. You can't imagine how it feels. How it builds up and builds up inside you, until it's all you can think about. Voices, screaming in your head, until you have to do something about it or go crazy. And then, for a while, the voices go quiet."

Softly, she said, ''But not for as long as they used to, do they, Ted?''

''It's funny. I used to be able to go a year or more between kills. I'd barely think about it until the voices started up again. But now, I only get a few days before I have to go hunting again.''

Behind his back, the rushes parted silently, and Policzki stepped into the clearing, gun drawn. Gone was the fresh-faced youth who'd escorted her home from the museum. His expression was grim, and one hundred percent cop. His eyes met hers, and she clutched her purse more tightly. ''How did you know?'' she said. ''The phone call? How did you know what Conor had told me?''

Rizzoli smiled his serpent's smile. ''You gave yourself away when you told him you loved him. It was very unprofessional, not like you at all. That was when I knew. It was your way of saying goodbye.''

Behind him, Policzki said, ''Rizzoli.''

Ted spun around and fired his gun wildly. Policzki staggered and fell, and Caro dropped to the ground, yanked her .38 from her purse and fired.

The bullet caught Rizzoli as he turned, and she saw the surprise on his face. ''This is for Meg,'' she said, ''you son of a bitch.'' And she emptied the gun into him.

His body danced, limp like a rag doll, and fell to the ground. Caro lay there for a moment, gasping, numbness settling in as her fingers continued to clutch the gun and she realized she'd just killed someone.

Slowly, she drew herself to a sitting position. Her panty hose were destroyed, and her suit probably was, too. But she was alive. She dropped the gun and crawled through the dirt, past Ted's body, to Policzki. ''If you die on me, Policzki,'' she said, ''I swear to Christ I'll never speak to you again. How bad are you hurt?''

His face was ashen, but he was conscious. "Leg," he rasped. "Think it's broken."

The bullet had gone clean through, and she suspected he was right, that the femur was shattered. But the bleeding wasn't as bad as she'd feared. "You have a first name, Policzki?" she said, stripping off her jacket and wrapping it around his thigh.

He winced, and his face went a couple of shades paler. "Doug," he whispered.

She knotted the arms of the jacket and pulled them tight, into a makeshift tourniquet. His wound had to be hurting like hell, but he never made a sound. "Well, Doug," she said, "since you just saved my life, I think it would be appropriate for you to call me Caro."

In spite of his pallor, he came close to smiling, and it was the most beautiful thing she'd ever seen. "Caro?" he said.

"What?"

"You're a royal pain in the ass."

For a moment, she thought she was going to cry. "I love you, too, Policzki. How the hell did you find me out here?"

"I followed you. He pissed me off."

"Thank God you have a temper. Where's your cell phone, Douglas?"

"Inside breast pocket."

She pulled it out, dialed 911. "This is FBI Special Agent Carolyn Monahan," she told the operator. "I need a rescue unit ASAP. I have an officer down, and he needs immediate medical attention. We're in the Back Bay Fens, eastern end, in the reeds. I just killed the gunman. I'd appreciate police backup. While you're at it—" She swiped her forearm across her temple. It came away bloody. "—call Lieutenant Conor Rafferty, Boston P.D.

Tell him his presence at the scene would be greatly appreciated."

When he arrived, there were three black-and-whites parked at odd angles, red-and-blue lights flashing, a couple of rescue vehicles standing by, and uniformed cops crawling all over the scene. Heart hammering, he climbed out of the Taurus and moved across the grass, following the curve of the river toward the opening in the reeds. Thirty feet inside the thicket, Rizzoli's body lay on the ground, sightless eyes staring heavenward. Conor crouched beside the body and counted the half-dozen holes drilled in Rizzoli's chest.

"Lieutenant Rafferty?"

Still crouching, he looked up at the uniformed rookie who stood over him. "Yes," he said.

"I'm Giberson, sir. I was first on the scene. We haven't called anybody yet. I was waiting to see what you wanted to do."

Without answering, he stood and walked back out into the summer afternoon. "Where's his car?"

"Parked over by the museum, sir."

"Seal it off for Forensics," he ordered. "Don't let anybody touch it."

"Yes, sir."

"Who killed him?"

"Agent Monahan, sir. When I got here, she—"

"Where is she?" he said brusquely.

"Over there, in the ambulance. Shouldn't we be calling—"

The rookie kept on talking, but he didn't hear any of it. He turned slowly, his eyes scanning the scene, past the police cars, finally landing on the open back door of the ambulance where Carolyn sat, legs dangling, feet not quite reaching the ground.

His bowels turned to spaghetti, and for a second or two, his legs refused to function. She had a blanket wrapped around her shoulders and a Dunkin' Donuts cup in her hand, and she winced as a paramedic applied something to a cut on her cheek. But her eyes were on him. Their gazes locked, and he somehow found the strength to put one foot in front of the other and move toward her.

"Lieutenant?" Giberson called from behind him. "What about the M.E.? What about Forensics?"

"Take care of it," he said, and kept walking.

Carolyn brushed aside the paramedic and slid out of the ambulance. The young man followed her gaze, took in Rafferty's face, and suddenly remembered something important he had to do elsewhere. The blanket still around her shoulders, she held aloft the Dunkin' Donuts cup. "Cops," she said, her voice shaky. "They always seem to know the best places to get coffee."

Then her fingers loosened on the cup and it fell to the ground, and he took another step and folded her trembling body into his arms. "I killed him," she said, burrowing against his chest. "Oh, Christ, Conor, I killed him."

Beyond words, beyond caring who saw or what they thought, he held her hard against him and tried not to think about how close he'd come to losing her. "You did what you had to do," he said. "It's over now."

Over, but not forgotten. He knew, from firsthand experience, that it would be a while before she'd sleep without being haunted by Ted Rizzoli's face. "What about Policzki?" he said. "What's his condition?"

"They took him to Brigham and Women's. He took a bullet to the leg. He may need surgery, but he'll survive. It was a brave thing he did, Conor." She raised her face to his. Muddy and tear-splattered, in ruined Donna Karan, she was still the most beautiful woman in the world. "I think you should give him a promotion."

The corner of his mouth twitched. "I'll take it under consideration."

"I've been thinking," she said tremulously, "that a long, cold winter in South Boston would be the perfect time and place to write a dissertation. What do you think?"

His heart kicked into overdrive. "I think you'd better be sure. Because if you stay, I won't be letting you go again."

She threaded slender fingers through his much larger ones. "The only place I'm going is home with you. Where I belong."

He buried his face in her hair. She smelled of antiseptic, with just the faintest hint of Obsession. "Not just yet, you're not," he said with regret. "I have one cop in the hospital and another one headed for the morgue. It'll be a few hours before I can tie this up and break free."

She turned her face up to his, and he brushed a speck of dirt from her cheek. "I've waited this long for you, Rafferty," she said, "I can wait a little longer. I'm in no hurry. After all—" she smiled, and he saw his future in those blue eyes "—I have the rest of my life."

"*Home Before Dark* is a beautiful novel, tender and wise. Susan Wiggs writes with bright assurance, humor and compassion about sisters, children and the sweet and heartbreaking trials of life—about how much better it is to go through them together."

—Luanne Rice

SUSAN WIGGS

Though she's seen the world through her camera lens, Jessie Ryder has never traveled far enough to escape the painful moment she gave her baby daughter away. Now, sixteen years later, she's decided to seek out Lila, even if it means she has to upset the world of Lila's adoptive mother… her very own sister, Luz.

As Jessie and Luz examine the true meaning of love, loyalty and family, they are drawn into an emotional tug-of-war filled with moments of unexpected humor, surprising sweetness and unbearable sadness. But as the pain, regrets and mistakes of the past slowly rise to the surface, a new picture emerges—a picture filled with hope and promise and the redeeming power of the human heart.

HOME BEFORE DARK

"With its lively prose, well-developed conflict and passionate characters, this enjoyable, poignant tale is certain to enchant."
—*Publishers Weekly* on *Halfway to Heaven* (starred review)

On sale April 2003 wherever hardcovers are sold!

MIRA®

She looked like an angel, acted like a vixen
and sang like an alley cat.

NAUGHTY MARIETTA

Marietta Stone had a glorious future ahead. But it did not include
being kidnapped by Cole Heflin, a ruthless, conniving scoundrel
who'd been paid to bring her back to the one place she'd vowed
never to set foot again—home.

Cole had never met a woman he didn't like, nor one he wasn't happy
to love. Until Marietta. But even with her benefactor's hired gunmen
on their trail and a dangerous frontier ahead, the trip home was not
nearly as dangerous as the temptation naughty Marietta inspired....

NAN RYAN

MIRA®

*On sale April 2003
wherever paperbacks are sold!*

Visit us at www.mirabooks.com

MNR676